THE KEEPERS' CHRONICLES

THE STORYSPINNER

THE KEEPERS' CHRONICLES

THE STOR

Also by Becky Wallace

The Skylighter

SPINNER

BECKY WALLACE

MARGARET K. McELDERRY BOOKS
NEW YORK LONDON TORONTO SYDNEY NEW DELHI

MARGARET K. McELDERRY BOOKS
An imprint of Simon & Schuster Children's Publishing Division
1230 Avenue of the Americas, New York, New York 10020

Also available in a Margaret K. McElderry Books hardcover edition
The text for this book is set in Kepler Std.
Manufactured in the United States of America
First Margaret K. McElderry Books paperback edition March 2016
2 4 6 8 10 9 7 5 3 1
The Library of Congress has cataloged the hardcover edition as follows:
Wallace, Becky.
The storyspinner / Becky Wallace.—1st edition.
p. cm.—(The Keepers' chronicles)
Summary: The Keepers, a race of people with magical abilities, are seeking a supposedly dead princess to place her on the throne and end political turmoil but girls who look like the princess are being murdered and Johanna Von Arlo, forced to work for Lord Rafael DeSilva after her father's suspicious death, is a dead ringer.
ISBN 978-1-4814-0565-2 (hc)
ISBN 978-1-4814-0566-9 (pbk)
ISBN 978-1-4814-0567-6 (eBook)
[1. Fantasy. 2. Magic—Fiction. 3. Identity—Fiction.
4. Princesses—Fiction. 5. Murder—Fiction.] I. Title.
PZ7.W15472Sto 2015
[Fic]—dc23 2014015912

For Jamie

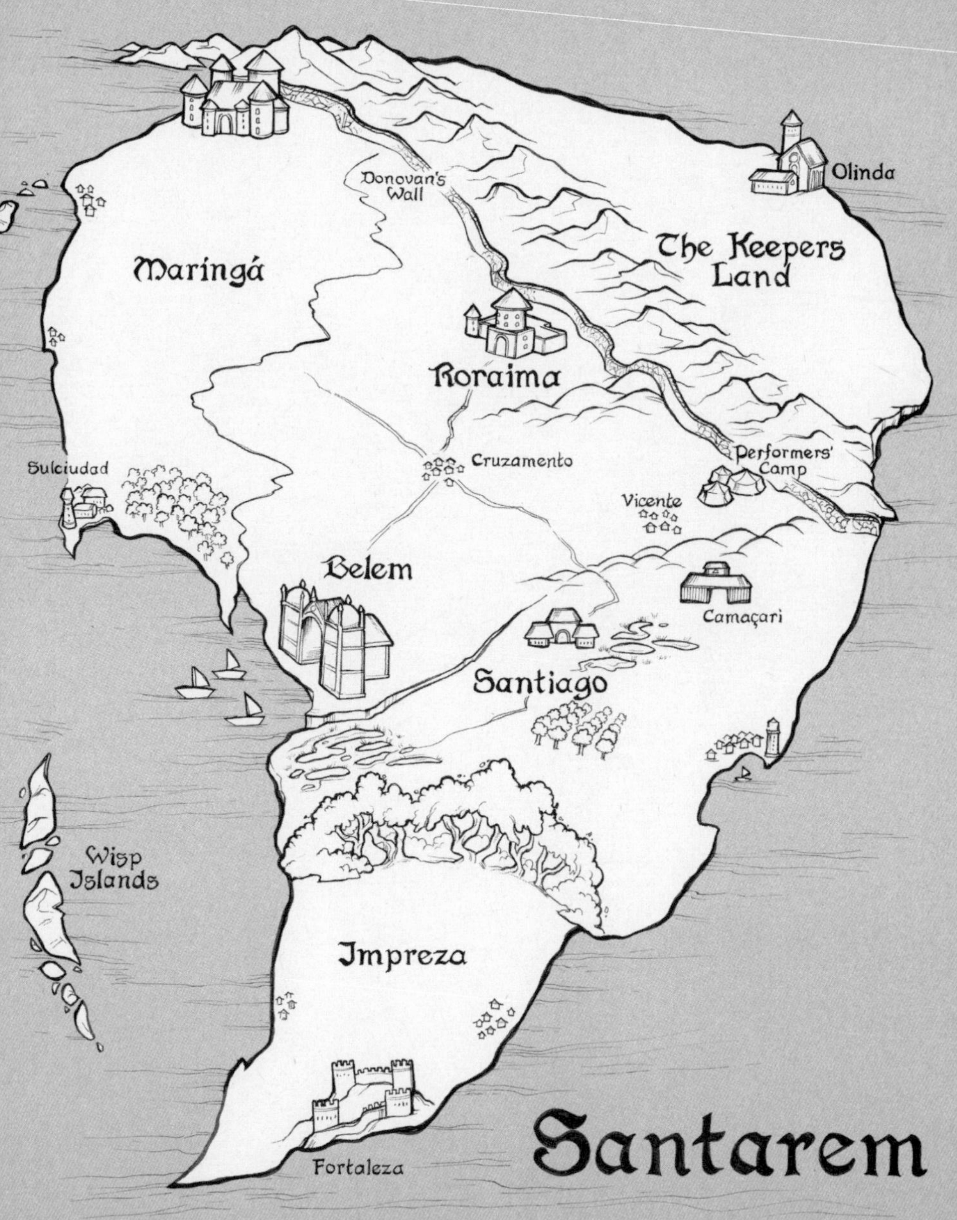
Donovan's Wall
Olinda
Maringá
The Keepers Land
Roraima
Sulciudad
Cruzamento
Performers' Camp
Vicente
Belem
Camaçari
Santiago
Wisp Islands
Impreza
Fortaleza
Santarem

Chapter 1

Johanna

Johanna could feel it. The fear, the haste, the pebbles sliding under her feet, the hiss of arrows as they sliced through the air.

She could see the dark clouds kissing the gray stone of the Citadel, hear the clash of steel and the cries of the dying. Blood and desperation hung thick in the air.

Every word her father murmured—his voice pitched low to match the intensity of the tale—rang with images, sounds, and pictures. Some people told stories, but her father played every audience on taut strings, strumming their senses and plucking at their emotions. People would travel for days to hear one of his specially created works of art, to be entranced by his voice and the not-quite-magical powders he employed to illustrate each tale.

The story of "The Thief and the Great Tree" was his personal specialty, but he didn't tell it often.

Johanna leaned forward, memorizing every pitch and cadence, waiting for the moment when he'd reach into one of the hidden pockets of his cloak for the handful of powder stored there. Even knowing it was coming, even watching carefully, she missed the trick.

A cloud of fine brown dust filled the air between them, seeming to appear out of nowhere. His hands danced in the smoke, shaping the ephemeral mist into a great tree.

"Fool," a voice like a rockslide thundered from above. Twigs cracked as they spread wide, weaving and twining to form a cage that trapped the Thief from neck to knees. "Who are you to break the pact?"

Her father's hands twirled across the dust. A gnarled face materialized in the tree's trunk.

Its eyes reflected and magnified the scattered starlight, glaring pure malevolence at its captive, he said, and Johanna mouthed along.

The Tree's breath, icy as the last days of autumn, brushed the Thief's skin and made him tremble.

"P-please," the Thief stuttered. "I only ventured onto the sacred mount to save the—"

Footfalls sliding on the shale and loose gravel drew the Tree's attention. "More oathbreakers!"

"Let me go!" begged the Thief as he struggled against the Tree's wooden embrace. "I only crossed onto the mountain to save King Wilhelm's greatest treasure."

There was a moment of stillness, of awful silence, when the Thief knew the Tree weighed the truth of the words. The Thief held his breath, waiting to be crushed in the Tree's grip. He heard nothing save the clank of armor as his pursuers drew nearer.

Then the Great Tree's topmost branches bent parallel to the ground, as if a sudden gale had forced them forward. The Thief realized it was a nod.

"Take the treasure and run." The cage disappeared, re-forming into a second hand, which lifted the Thief to his feet. "Run!" the Tree shouted.

The Thief sprinted away, only looking back to see if the mountain was tumbling down behind him. It wasn't. The Tree drew its roots out of the ground, pulverizing stone as it yanked tentacles out of the rock. They wound together, becoming giant legs that straddled the path. The Tree snatched the nearest soldier, and with a wet twist, the man became two halves.

The Tree roared—

"Arlo!" The tent snapped open as Johanna's mother stepped into the enclosed space, the train of her emerald gown dragging behind her. "You have to be on the high wire in less than ten minutes."

Johanna rocked back on her heels, her heart still pounding from the power of her father's tale.

"Marin, my love." He offered his wife the grin that endeared him to every audience. "I was just giving our daughter a few tips that will improve her Storyspinning."

"Not now, Arlo!" She hurried to her husband's side, whisking the Storyspinner's cloak from his shoulders to reveal the tight-fitting acrobat's costume beneath. "Stories can wait for tomorrow. Paying crowds wait for nothing!"

Marin's words sounded sharp, but Johanna knew they were said with love. Her parents hissed at each other like mad cats before every show, but it was all preperformance anxiety.

A good audience had the heady effect of strong champagne, making the Performers drunk on applause and accord. Once their routines were over and they received their ovation, her parents couldn't remember what they had argued over.

"She needed a refresher on some of the finer details—"

"Oh please!" Johanna rolled her eyes. "I'd steal your listeners now if you'd let me take the stage."

Marin couldn't restrain a grin in her daughter's direction. They always stood together as a team to tease Arlo or cajole him to their way of thinking.

"I'm afraid she's right, my dear," Marin said with a click of her tongue. "Johanna's learned every bit of your trade and has a much prettier face."

Arlo spluttered with mock affront, and was ignored as his wife stripped off the outer layer of her gown and turned it inside out.

A voice bellowed from outside their red-and-white dressing tent, calling Marin to her next position—a vocal performance on one of the smaller stages. She pulled a clip out of her hair. Her ash-blond curls fell free and completed the transformation for her next act.

"Don't let him be late!" she cautioned Johanna with a quick hug. "And check on your brothers. They were watching the acrobats warm up."

"Of course, Mama." Johanna pecked her mother's powdered cheek. "Sing the birds out of the trees."

"Always." Marin disappeared through the tent flaps and didn't look back.

Johanna turned, expecting some witty remark or quick joke at her mother's expense, but a troubled look marred her father's face.

"Papa," she asked, instantly concerned. "What's wrong? Is your back bothering you? I can get the jar of liniment. . . ." Her voice trailed off when she realized that he couldn't hear her. He'd disappeared into a memory; and, from the slump of his shoulders, it wasn't a pleasant one.

"Papa?"

Arlo shook himself out of his daze and straightened his spine, but the ghostly thoughts traced hard lines about his mouth.

"Johanna, you remember the rest of the story, don't you?" His voice was deep and husky, his eyes intense.

"Of course. The Thief travels along the mountains till finally crossing back into Santarem, carrying King Wilhelm's treasure the entire way. He promises to guard it for the rest of his life, never using it for his own gain."

Her father nodded along, his face still serious. "Good. It's an important story. One you should take to heart."

"I know, I know. It teaches bravery and honor—"

"It's more than that, *cara.*" He called her by her pet name. "It's a true story."

Johanna put her hands on her hips and adopted the glare her mother wore when her father was being ridiculous. With brown hair instead of blond and gray eyes instead of blue, Johanna didn't resemble her mother, but she could imitate Marin perfectly. "You believe someone survived the massacre? That's impossible. The troops killed everyone and burned everything."

Their travels from Performers' Camp took them past the ruins of Roraima several times every year. She remembered the tumble-down walls of the former capital. The charred skeletons of homes and businesses reached through the ground, bones rising from the graveyard Roraima had become. Above it all was the Citadel, the once-proud castle of their deceased king, cowering like some terrified animal at the foot of the Keepers' Mountains.

Few people ventured into the ruins, claiming that evil things lurked in the shadow of the Citadel's walls, and that the stench of death lingered—even fifteen years after the city's destruction.

"And yet, someone did survive," her father insisted. "How else would we have the story?"

Johanna opened her mouth to counter, but a Performer shouted for Arlo to get to his position. The grim seriousness dropped away from her father's countenance in less time than it took his cloak to hit the floor.

"We'll talk about it more later." He brushed her cheek with a quick kiss and bounded out of the tent with his typical grace. "Don't go into the crowd alone and don't let the boys get into mischief!"

"Then you should wish *me* luck!" she yelled as the flap fell, and heard her father laugh in response.

Her younger brothers, Joshua and Michael, weren't typically naughty, but a Performers' tent city was rife with opportunities for pranks and practical jokes—swapping the lids of the makeup containers or switching the pennants that flew over the performing area with several pairs of bloomers.

As she left the tent, she scanned the sky for purple underthings flapping in the wind. Her younger siblings hadn't replaced the flags. Yet.

Performers costumed in a riot of colors, bangles, and patterns hurried through the temporary canvas town. Others warmed up soon-to-be-used voices, stretched well-trained muscles, or painted their lips red and outlined their eyes with dramatic black lines.

Johanna smiled at the familiarity of it all. These people, seemingly crazy and loud, were her family. Not all of them were blood relatives, though she had a handful of cousins and an uncle in the troupe, but they cared for each other like kin.

The acrobats were stacked three high, balancing on hands and shoulders. As she approached, her eldest brother, Thomas, climbed to the top of the teetering tower.

"Have you seen the boys?" she yelled as he placed his palms on another acrobat's head. Thomas shifted his weight and pushed himself into a handstand.

"They were near the wagons," he responded, pointing his toes to the sky.

The man on the bottom row shifted his feet. "When you coming back, Jo?"

Johanna ached to be back in the show, to hear the applause and her name shouted with adoration. An unfortunate incident with a flaming firesword had left her with a hideously short haircut and a nasty wound on her forearm. The injury didn't bother her anymore, though the skin was tight and puckered.

"I'd come back today, if the Council would let me." She threw a series of back handsprings to demonstrate how well she'd recovered.

"Good," grunted the base of the tower. "You don't fidget as much as Thomas!"

"Hey! I'm doing my best," her brother muttered.

"Still . . ."

Their bickering and laughter was drowned out by a small explosion. Red sparks shot into the air, cartwheeling over the camp.

"Joshua! Michael!" the troupe's Skylighter growled. The man was protective—and rightly so—of the volatile powders he used to paint the night sky with colorful bursts of flame. "When I catch you two, I swear I'll . . ."

Before he finished his curse, Johanna was running toward the multihued wagons that divided the tent camp from the performing area. Performers were a secretive people by nature, keeping the tricks of their trade private, sharing only with family members and apprentices. They didn't appreciate crowd members wandering through their camp and stealing the secrets that made their entertainment so valuable.

Johanna reached the boundary in time to see two blond heads disappear into the mass of people. She hesitated, remembering her father's warning not to go into the crowd alone, before plunging into the throng.

The entire township of Belem had turned out for the performances. Their duke, also known as Belem, hired a performing troupe to entertain his people at least twice each year. The peasants, dressed in their finery and drunk from a day of festival revelry, pressed close to the three raised stages trying to get a clearer view of the acrobats, Fireswords, and actors who entertained simultaneously.

I'll never find them in this mess, she thought as she shoved her way through the onlookers.

Where would they have run to? Where would she have gone if she was still eleven or eight?

To watch Father perform, of course.

Some long-deceased Performer had built small platforms in the highest branches of the araucaria pines. Unlike their triangular relatives, the araucaria's bristles grew in clumps at the top of the tree, giving an unobstructed view of the Performers high above the duke's fine home. It was one of the few places where a fall from the high wire was truly dangerous.

She searched the crowd for her father's crimson costume, hoping her brothers would be nearby. He stood at the base of the tree, deep in discussion with a person she couldn't see around the fat trunk.

If it hadn't been moments prior to his show, she wouldn't have been surprised. Her father was always in negotiation with someone—nobles and peasants, merchants and fisherfolk, blacksmiths and bartenders—to schedule another show. And yet he usually spent the few moments before every show doing a mental rehearsal of his routine.

It must be an excellent fee for him to do business now, she thought with a grin.

The cannon boomed, signaling the beginning of the main attraction, and her father ascended the tree.

Johanna turned, scanning the crowd. She still had no idea where her brothers had disappeared to. Perhaps they had continued beyond the performing area toward the rocky beach that bordered Duke Belem's property? Her stomach swirled with nerves as she imagined the boys splashing around in the choppy water. Both were strong swimmers, but even so . . .

The crowd bunched close, filling Johanna's nose with the stench of perspiring bodies and the sickly-sweet scent of pink guava rum. A hand pinched her bottom, but she ignored it, moving along with the press and drawing nearer to the ocean with each step.

Then, like fish caught in a giant net, the entire audience stopped. Every head tilted skyward, focusing on the man standing on a web-thin thread strung across the horizon. He waved bravely before edging his way across the rope, seemingly nervous and tentative.

It was all a ploy. In a moment his arms would windmill; the audience would gasp both terrified and thrilled that they'd see this Performer fall to his death.

Ten steps and her father did exactly as she expected.

The man beside her muttered an oath under his breath, and Johanna bit her lip to keep a satisfied smirk from appearing on her face.

The audience was locked in the moment; no eye blinked; no one shuffled forward. Then the arm actions propelled her father into a series of somersaults.

An enormous cheer rose to the sky, completely blocking out the waves crashing on the beach nearby. The crowd didn't mind that they'd been fooled. They loved the spectacle too much.

Her father finished his routine with a standing backflip and flourish. She couldn't see his smile but could tell by the confidence in his wave that he was proud—as always—of his performance.

The audience applauded, then laughed when Arlo's arms

whipped through the air again, one shoulder dipping toward the rope.

Johanna didn't laugh.

Her father rocked forward onto his toes, then back on his heels, throwing his hips out for balance. This wasn't part of the act, and he never, ever deviated from his routine.

Something was wrong.

One foot lifted high off the rope, extending far to the side.

"No!" The scream wrenched from her throat. She tried to force her way forward, but the crowd was too tight, the bodies too close.

His other foot left the rope and he pinwheeled through the air, disappearing from view. The shrieks of delight turned to shrill cries of terror, all muffling the thud of his body as it smashed into the ground between groups of onlookers.

Weeks later when Johanna woke from sweat-soaked nightmares, she was very grateful her brothers had disobeyed that night and gone to play on the beach.

No child should ever have to watch their father die.

Chapter 2
Jacaré

The doors to the Council Hall hadn't opened once in the three hours Jacaré had been waiting. Other petitioners had already filtered out of the antechamber, knowing their concerns weren't going to be heard that day.

But Jacaré stayed, sometimes pacing, his Guard-issued boots clicking on the stone floor, and other times staring at the source of his worries.

The few remaining supplicants probably thought it odd that a trained soldier, who wore weapons on his back and frustration on his face, would bring a piece of stained glass with him to the Hall. But it was this sharp-edged object, smaller than his two palms, that forced him to seek out the Mage Council's guidance in the first place.

The glass's honey-glossed surface didn't reflect the features of Jacaré's young face, his golden hair shaved close to the scalp, or the eyes that so many people called dangerous. Instead it acted as a window, showing glimpses of the land on the other side of the rugged mountain range that divided the continent into two unequal pieces.

The pictures changed irregularly, sometimes showing faces and people, sometimes vistas and cities.

Well, it was *supposed* to. The window had frozen on one image eight weeks earlier and never shifted again.

Jacaré held the square of glass so tightly that it bit into his palms, leaving angry red ridges in his skin. He prayed for the surface to move, begged it to re-form into a different scene, a different face, a different *anything*.

The security of Jacaré's people depended on a piece of glass he could shatter with his bare hands, and now the shoddy tool wasn't even working.

He'd faced the Mage Council when the glass had been frozen for two weeks, and his worries had been ignored.

It's probably just a hiccup in the magic, they'd said, rolling their eyes at his concern. Some members of the Council made it clear that the Elite Guard—the police force that kept the less-magically gifted in order—was obsolete and treated the High Captain with little respect.

It's not a perfect science, you know, they chided, as if he was unfamiliar with magic and magical objects.

Jacaré did know; he'd been responsible for the Keepers' protection for nearly three centuries. In that time, images had frozen for a week or so, but never longer.

This was no hiccup. Something had happened; the situation had changed. And there was more than the dysfunctional glass that gave Jacaré the constant feeling of unease.

"When will they see me?" he asked the uniformed attendant

standing guard outside the ornate oak door. The carvings were supposed to remind everyone who passed through that the Mage Council was guided by the goddess, Mother Lua.

Jacaré didn't have much faith in that.

"I told you, sir," the servant said patiently. "These meetings take time. Many issues need to be discussed and—"

Jacaré didn't wait to hear the rest, pushing past the attendant and throwing both doors open wide.

The Council sat behind a crescent-shaped table on a raised dais. One member argued his opinion at the center of the floor, where the large windows cast pools of light.

The man's words cut off abruptly at Jacaré's intrusion. "What are you doing here?" He turned to the flustered servant who hurried along at Jacaré's heels. "Silva, how did he get in?"

"I'm sorry, so sorry, Mage Cristoval," the servant said, rubbing his hands along the front of his green tunic. "He pushed me out of the way, sir."

Jacaré ignored the exchange and walked straight to the head of the Mage Council. He'd known Amelia for a long time and recognized the look on her weathered face. She wasn't happy to see him—though really, she never was.

"This is preposterous," Cristoval continued, taking in Jacaré's military uniform and the thin leather band he wore around his forehead that marked his station. "We're in the middle of an important debate. He can't be here. Our words are only for those sworn to the Council."

"Peace, Cristoval." Amelia stood, holding the wide sleeves of her robe away from the desk. "High Captain Jacaré must have a good reason to interrupt us. A very good reason."

Jacaré slid the glass across the scroll Amelia had been writing on. It smeared the fresh ink and clinked against a jar of sand before coming to a stop.

"Explain this," he commanded.

Amelia raised one white eyebrow at his insubordinate tone before picking up the glass. "How long has it been frozen?"

"Two months. I need to know exactly what it means."

She lowered herself slowly into her chair, the lines on her face showing every one of her five hundred years. Her arthritic hands traced the image, a bright blue glow emanating from her fingertips.

"The guardian is dead," she said in a near whisper, yet her words sent a ripple of murmurs through the Council room.

"You're sure?" Jacaré asked, his heart fluttering like a startled quail. "He could have taken off the divining pendant and put it in a box or—"

"No." Her mahogany eyes were solemn. "The man who received the pendant from the king died before passing it along to the rightful heir."

For centuries the pendant had been worn by the royal family of Santarem, the nation south of Donovan's Wall. It relayed images to the glass, offering the Keepers the wearer's view of the court and country. Before the last king had been murdered, he passed the pendant on to someone not of his direct line. It continued to function, but the magical link between the glass and pendant had grown weaker, the pictures coming less frequently.

Jacaré had wanted to climb through the mountains and cross the wall then, but his request had been denied. Because he'd always been a good soldier, he had obeyed.

"What will happen at the wall?" Cristoval asked, moving to stand at Jacaré's elbow. "Should we prepare Olinda to be invaded?"

"Of course not. Just because the guardian is dead doesn't mean the heir followed him into the grave." She covered the shining surface with her palm, hiding the image from sight. "The *chave* is still safe, as is the magic that keeps the wall protected."

Jacaré heard the nuance in her words. *For now.*

Arguments ensued. The youngest members of the Council fought with their elders; some suggested preemptive strikes. Others contended for preparing the city for war.

"Enough." Amelia brought her hands together and a clap of thunder reverberated around the room. All conversation ceased. "There hasn't been a single threat from Santarem since we crossed the mountains, and there is no reason to assume an attack will come now or anytime soon. We will discuss this as we discuss all other things: calmly and with consideration to all points of view."

"If there was ever a time for action, it's now," Jacaré said, ignoring her glare. "I'll take twenty men across the border, identify any threats, and seek out the pendant and the heir."

"You will do nothing without permission from this Council."

"My duty is to assure the safety of the wall, which is inexorably tied to the safety of the heir. You're not asking me to ignore my duty, are you?"

Amelia leaned across the desk, closing the distance between

their faces. Her *essência*—the raw energy she possessed and used to manipulate the elements—crackled around her like heat lightning. "I decide what your duty is. You will wait until this Council tells you what steps to take, or you will face the same fate as your predecessor."

He knew better than to engage Amelia; such a battle would be short and ugly for Jacaré. She was the head of the Mage Council because she was the most powerful magic wielder among the Keepers, capable of calling on any of the elements to do her will with devastating results.

"Yes, ma'am." Without being dismissed, Jacaré turned and left the Council room.

For weeks he'd been preparing to cross the wall, preferably with permission, but now it was time to defy them all.

Chapter 3

Johanna
Three Months Later

Johanna hopped over the creek, her boots slipping in the mud. She corrected her balance without a thought and dropped to a crouch.

And there it is, she thought proudly, a smile dimpling her pale cheeks.

One drop of blood, bright as a ruby against a glistening film of dew, was all the evidence she needed. Her aim had been true, the stag clearly wounded when it bolted through the mango orchard and into the forest of untamed walnut trees beyond.

The rabbits weighing down her game bag would help feed her brothers for the next few days. But the deer—*a buck no less!*—could be smoked and salted to keep all their stomachs satisfied through the slender fall and wicked winter creeping closer.

Johanna ignored the shivery sensation along her spine, too pleased with her success to recognize that no birds sang, no rabbits hopped, no bugs burrowed. All the smart animals had found a place to hide.

Her mind wrapped itself in an imagined conversation. *I know you wanted me to stay out of the woods by myself,* she'd say as she passed a steaming bowl of venison soup to her older brother. *But, Thomas,*

I'd rather go hungry than eat mango again. It doesn't matter how I cook it—boiled, baked, stewed—it still tastes like mango.

She immediately felt guilty, knowing her words would hurt his feelings. He'd worked so hard since their father's death and their subsequent expulsion from Performers' Camp. The accounting apprenticeship didn't suit Thomas in any way, but his miserly pay bought enough flour and salt to keep them from starving. He certainly didn't need his sister reminding him of his ink-stained fingers and threadbare clothes.

But her brother's warnings chafed like a pair of ill-fitting shoes. She cast them aside and sought out a new adventure: the tightropes, the trapeze, the fireswords (although her hair was still recovering from that endeavor), and even the lion cage.

If Thomas knew her at all, he'd know that cautioning her away from the forest was practically the same as marching her to its borders. Especially when there was food to be found and plenty of mouths to feed.

She followed the blood trail. The drops got larger and closer together, finally collecting in pools where the deer had stopped to rest.

Not much farther.

Something crashed in the bushes to her left, and she veered toward the sound. Her fingers tingled with anticipation as she slipped her hunting knife from its sheath. Johanna hated putting deer down, watching their liquid eyes turn opaque. It filled her with an awful sense of finality, but still, she couldn't let the animal suffer or her family go hungry.

The dense underbrush crackled, fallen leaves crunching as she eased toward her prey. The buck lay on its side, each breath leaving the animal's throat with a harsh gurgle.

Her shot had been too high, catching the buck in the neck. The arrow's shaft protruded from above the deer's breastbone, the fletching torn away during its mad dash through the densely packed forest.

Johanna refused to look at the deer's eyes, knowing she'd see its fear and be overwhelmed by guilt.

Thomas, Michael, Joshua, and even Mama need this, she convinced herself, and raised her knife.

Over her pounding heart and the animal's pained gasps, she heard another noise—a shuffle, a crack, the quiet tread of another predator. Johanna whirled, ready to slash and stab, to turn her tool of mercy into a weapon of destruction.

Too slow.

A heavy shoulder slammed into her ribs, knocking her to the ground. She grunted as a knee dropped onto her chest, forcing the air from her lungs and the knife from her hand.

Years of acrobatics prepared her for that moment. Ignoring the fear and breathlessness, Johanna kicked out with her right leg and looped it around the assailant's neck, forcing his hood askew.

The stranglehold would have knocked him out eventually, but strong fingers found the sensitive tissue alongside her calf. They dug in mercilessly, scoring her flesh and tearing skin.

Gritting her teeth against the agony, she relaxed her grip on the attacker, and he released her leg. She drew her knee to her chest and hammered the man in the jaw with her heel.

He cried out, and she scrambled to her feet. One step and she was flat on her stomach with the man's weight across her hips. Johanna threw her elbow, hoping to catch his nose, but received an explosive punch to the kidney.

Stars swirled across her vision, and she blinked to clear them, but another blow blasted across her ribs.

"Rafi?" a voice called from a few feet away. "Raf—holy mercy!"

From the corner of her eye Johanna saw boots.

"Help," she mouthed, unable to find the breath to project her voice. "Help."

Then . . . darkness.

Chapter 4

Rafi

Lord Rafael Santiago DeSilva pressed a hand to his bleeding mouth. He'd bitten his tongue when the poacher kicked him in the face.

His younger brother, Dominic, handed him a linen square to wipe away the blood. "I've never seen a boy fight with legs and limbs flying like that." Dom dug a leather cord out of one of his many pockets and began wrapping it around the boy's wrist. "A tiny thing too. Look at these knobby bones. It's pitiful enough to move me to charity."

Rafi grunted. "The only charity he'll get from me is a short rope and a long drop."

The summer had been cruel to the villagers and farm folk, with an unprecedented drought razing their crops, but the amount of poaching would leave the DeSilvas' land barren of all edible wildlife if left unchecked. Rafael would let his people hunt the animals to oblivion if he wasn't worried about the long-lasting effects. There was no guarantee that next year's harvest would be more abundant than this year's.

"Trial first. I'll take the evidence; you take the thief?" Rafi nodded toward the now-still deer.

"Giving me the heavy end of the deal, as usual," Dom joked as he hauled the poacher upright and slung him over his shoulder. He adjusted the load and froze.

"Our horses aren't that far. Surely you can carry that sack of bones a half mile." Rafi's forehead wrinkled in confusion as he watched Dom gently—much more gently than a poacher deserved—return the boy to the ground. "If you'd prefer the deer, then have at it. I thought to save you some bloodstained clothes, but if you insist."

Rafi stepped toward the poacher's prone form, but his brother stopped him, placing a hand at the center of Rafi's chest.

"Don't." Dom's face had gone pale, his lips compressed in a tight line.

"Why?" Rafi asked, concern beginning to churn in his belly. "That blow to the ribs couldn't possibly have killed him."

"Her."

"What?"

Dom edged closer, as if nearing a poisonous snake. Trembling fingers turned the thief's face to a shaft of sunlight that filtered through the branches overhead. Rafi looked past the short cap of hair and dirt-smeared cheeks. Dark eyelashes fluttered against porcelain fair skin. Pink lips parted slightly in sleep. Loose laces exposed a long slender neck, the hard slant of a collarbone and a soft mound of . . .

"May the Keepers steal my soul," Rafi cursed. "It's a girl."

CHAPTER 5

JACARÉ

Jacaré went straight from the Council chambers to the Elite Guard's barracks. Oil, sweat, and freshly molten metal flavored the air, all the comfortable scents of his home away from home.

The dark stone barracks were tucked behind Olinda's capitol building, where the Mage Council met, and were used by the soldiers who devoted their lives to peace and safety.

A stone balustrade separated the practice field from the stables, blacksmith shops, and armory. Jacaré rested his elbows on the edge, watching the fight that had most of the Guard forgetting their duties. One blindfolded fighter moved with smooth precision, whipping her metal-tipped staff to block the blows of three attackers.

A swordsman swung his weapon low, hacking at the back of her knees. It should have hit her and ended the practice, but she sensed the blow before it landed and dove forward, swinging her staff to catch the man in the throat.

Jacaré cringed when he heard the crunch, knowing it would leave an awful bruise later. The other two fighters redoubled their efforts, trying and failing to take the girl down. When she struck one in the sternum, the other shook his head and backed away.

Pira raised her blindfold, helped her opponents to their feet, and checked on the bruises she'd inflicted. Onlookers whispered about her uncanny ability to sense the location of any weapon.

Every Keeper had an affinity to at least one element, Earth, Air, Fire, Water, and Spirit. Those with one strong talent—like Pira's gift for Earth—were called *Saudade* and made up the bulk of the Keepers' society.

A rare few—called Mages—were blessed with the ability to manipulate all five elements with their *essência*. The Mages on the Council were the strongest of their people, capable of turning a breath of air into a wind tunnel and a spark into a blaze.

Jacaré should have been impressed both with Pira's skill and her sportsmanship, but as usual, watching her fight made him want to teach her a lesson.

He hopped over the railing and picked up two wooden practice swords from the bin of beginner weapons. Soldiers jumped out of his way as he crossed the field, pressing their fists over their hearts in salute to their commanding officer.

"Fight me," he said, tossing her the slab of wood.

She caught it out of the air and weighed the sword in her palm. "Aren't I a little old for practice swords, Jacaré?"

She never used his official title, no matter how many times he'd corrected her. The men she'd just defeated shifted nervously and took a few steps away to give the pair enough room to spar.

"You're never too old to do as you're told. Now raise your weapon."

Pira wiped the sweat off her shaved head with her blindfold, an unhappy frown tugging down her full lips.

"Throw that thing away." He waved to the strip of material. "If I'm going to beat you, I want you to see it coming."

A few gasps escaped the soldiers near enough to hear—but no one dared to say a word.

"Fine." She dropped the blindfold to the ground and sank into a fighter's stance. "Go to."

The fight ended in exactly ten seconds.

Pira lay flat on her back with the point of Jacaré's sword pressed against the hollow of her throat.

A slow applause started with the soldiers nearest and spread to everyone watching from around the practice field.

"You can't always use your affinity to save you, Pira." He threw the sword to the side, and offered her a hand up. "You never know when your gift will fail or when your opponent will come after you with something besides a metal weapon. You have to be ready to fight anyone, in any condition."

She bowed her head and looked at Jacaré through her lashes. The onlookers probably thought it was a sign of submission, but Jacaré knew better. He'd faced that blue-eyed glare a million times in the two decades he'd acted as her guardian.

"Thank you for the reminder, brother. I won't forget."

He hesitated for a moment, debating. He knew he could trust Pira, but if he involved her in his plans it could ruin her career for the rest of her life. And at only twenty years old, she had a very long life ahead of her.

"Was there something else?" she asked, her voice edged with anger.

Even after she'd been soundly beaten, she still couldn't manage to call him "sir." With that kind of an attitude Pira's future with the Elite Guard would be short lived, whether she helped him or not.

"Meet me at the house after first watch."

Chapter 6

Pira

The eighth chime of the watch bell was still ringing as Pira slipped out of the barracks. She didn't have to sneak away, plenty of people heard the High Captain command her to meet with him that night. But the fewer people who saw her leave her room the better.

She'd only been a commissioned officer with the Elite Guard for a few months, and there were still plenty of people who assumed she'd been promoted because of her brother rather than her own hard work.

The spectacle on the practice field hadn't helped matters.

She clenched her fists as she walked, feeling the layers of calluses that textured her palms. If they weren't a sure sign of her hard work, then the ink that stained the space between her thumb and first finger certainly should have been.

Pira didn't want to be a typical line soldier or even an officer. She wanted to command, and she spent every spare moment poring over tactical manuals, rewriting the very best concepts and rules in the tiny book she kept in her belt pouch. Nothing else mattered—not sleep, not family, not love. She'd given all those things up to pursue her career. And she was happy with the decision.

Until her brother found some way to humiliate her in front of her peers.

She wound through the hilly streets, skirting Olinda's entertainment district, to get to the two-story cottage tucked into the woods at the edge of town—the home where Jacaré had raised her after their father died.

They were half siblings—she was the only child of their father's very, very young second wife—but people couldn't get over the resemblance. They were both tall and long limbed with olive skin and pale blue eyes, but it was more than coloring and features. Pira spent her early years mimicking Jacaré's walk and fighting style.

Apparently she still didn't have it quite right.

A group of four men approached on the other side of the street, each of them stumbling drunkenly and laughing too loudly. They weren't breaking any laws, so she couldn't haul them off to jail, but she could sense weapons under their cloaks.

Three daggers, a belt knife, and a short sword to be exact. The steel sent a vibration through the air that pressed against Pira's skin like unseen fingers.

She wished one of them would stop, do something stupid, or even catcall her from across the street. She'd ached all day for a chance to break someone's face—a face she could mentally replace with Jacaré's—but the men moved on their way peaceably.

Mother Lua damn their souls to darkness, she thought with frustration.

Despite the strain in their relationship, Pira knew her brother. And she knew he wouldn't share his reason for the invitation if he could sense her temper. Jacaré never asked her to come to the house, and the request had piqued her interest. She'd barely been able to focus on her studies or drilling her unit that evening. Her mind tumbled with possibilities, rumors, and conjecture.

Lights spilled from the cottage windows, dressing the silver-barked aspen with dancing shadows. The leaves, already turning a late-summer golden, were gilded where the lamp's glow shined on them.

Pira took a few deep breaths, focusing on all the good memories of the tiny house, before turning onto the gravel path. She walked lightly, but the crunch alerted Jacaré, and he pulled open the front door before she reached for the handle.

"You're late."

"You said after first watch. You didn't specify when."

His broad shoulders were stiff, his body blocking the entrance so she couldn't see anything besides flames in the hearth beyond.

"Are you going to let me in?" She folded her arms tightly across her chest, wondering what in the world had her brother so on edge.

"If I do, will you swear that everything you see and hear tonight will remain a secret?"

Some part of her, the childish part that still sought his approval, leaped at the thought of being accepted into his inner circle. She smashed down that desire and forced herself to think critically. "Are you involved in something dangerous?"

"Probably."

That wasn't a surprise. She shifted her weight and saw a man-size shadow move closer to the fire. Whatever he was involved in, he wasn't doing it alone.

"Is it illegal?"

"Yes or no, Pira."

She drummed her fingers on her upper arm, thinking. There was only one question she needed answered, and she could already guess what her brother would say. "Is it for the good of the Keepers?"

"Would I do anything that wasn't?"

Pira paused before answering. Not because she doubted her brother's devotion to their people, but because she knew her hesitation would irritate him. "I suppose . . ."

He reached for the doorknob.

"Of course I'll swear!" she said before he could shut the door in her face.

Pira wanted to take the words back the instant she realized who else occupied the cottage's kitchen.

Chapter 7

Johanna

"I swear on my honor, and Dom's and your own, Mother. I did not know he was a girl."

"That doesn't matter," a woman's voice responded. "You know the law. We don't hand out justice with our fists."

"Look at the way he's dressed. It's completely inappropriate. And he was poach—"

"Referring to the girl as a 'he' won't change the facts, Rafael." The tone was a velvet-wrapped dagger. Johanna kept her eyes closed, hoping to avoid the woman who could wield it so potently.

Her location was foreign, the sounds of horses and scent of lilacs on the air proved that certainty. And good glory, the satin coverlet felt delicious against her palms.

"You beat someone into unconsciousness. You bloodied her leg and likely broke her ribs."

"I wouldn't have hurt her if I'd known—"

"So you'd annihilate a boy you outweigh by double?"

"He tried to strangle me."

"*She* defended herself."

The silence was damning, neither of them spoke, but the room filled with tension.

"Rafi." The woman's voice gentled. "What would you have me do? Shall I pretend it never happened?"

Fabric rustled, and Johanna opened her eyes a narrow slit. A woman and a man stood silhouetted against a large stained glass window. They were both tall and fine featured, but the man—*boy, really*—had dark hair that curled on the verge of wild.

"I would never ask you to ignore the law, Your Grace," he said with unusual formality. "I let my temper get the best of me. I'll take the punishment you deem worthy."

"Your Grace"? Where am I?

The woman raised her hand to her son's cheek. "We won't make it public knowledge. A few witnesses, perhaps the new weapons-master and the Captain of the Guard. Just enough people to satisfy questions, if there are any."

"And the girl, of course."

"It is her right."

Another hesitation, a heavy exhale. "Will she still be tried for poaching?"

Johanna, a consummate actress, could have feigned sleep for days to come, especially in a bed more comfortable than any she'd ever enjoyed. But she also knew the importance of dramatic timing. She'd been coached for years on perfect delivery, and this was her moment to make an entrance into the conversation.

She tried to push herself upright, but her head spun like a loose wagon wheel. The groan of pain was legitimate.

"Our fair thief wakes," the boy mumbled, stepping away from the window and nearer her bed. She saw then what the window's light had disguised: dark eyes framed with thick lashes and straight brows, a fine nose, and a strong chin. He was perhaps two years her senior, nearing naming age.

The face wasn't unfamiliar. It had been a few years since her troupe had performed for Duke and Lady DeSilva's estate, but she remembered their son as a smiling boy who applauded and cheered and begged for so many songs that her mother's infallible voice grew weary.

"I am many things, sir, but poacher is not a title I bear."

He coughed, a cold approximation of a laugh and likely the best this stern—*but unfortunately handsome*—young man could manage. "The stag hanging in the smokehouse begs to differ."

Johanna hated the way he loomed over her. She'd already spent too much time at his mercy and struggled to rise.

"Let me help, dear." The woman, an older version of the Lady DeSilva Johanna remembered, sat beside her on the bed and placed a supporting hand behind her shoulder.

Johanna nodded her thanks to the duchess. "I shot the stag in the public forest, not far from Farmer Milner's mango orchard."

"Liar," Rafi snapped. "You were well beyond the stream when I stumbled upon you."

Sow-kissing mud sucker. Johanna's eyes traced his perfectly tailored hunting gear, high-quality leather jerkin and breeches. "Send one of your retainers to follow the blood trail, my lord. I'm certain you employ *someone* who could track it to where I made my shot."

"You took it on my land." Fire burned in his dark eyes and blazed red spots on his cheeks.

"Should I have let it suffer?" Johanna raised a hand, grimacing at the bolt of pain in her side. "Never mind. It's apparent you enjoy punishing the helpless."

"Why you venomous—"

"Rafi." The lady called her son to heel. "Go. Send Snout to find the trail and follow it to its origin."

The anger Johanna felt at being termed a poacher sputtered. What if the grass had been trampled? What if the blood had washed away? Johanna licked her lips nervously, her tongue finding a tender split.

"Your Grace." She turned her gray eyes on the lady, offering a look that managed to be both humble and innocent. "I swear on my honor, on my family's, on my dear father's grave, that the deer was in the public forest when I took the shot. Please believe me."

Rafael gave another irritated cough-laugh. "How long were you awake and listening to our conversation?"

"Long enough to make sure I hadn't been tossed into the bed of a scoundrel." She touched her forehead where a fresh bruise hummed. It must have been the last shot of their brawl because she didn't remember receiving it.

"I'd never touch an ill-bred—"

"Enough!" The lady's voice cut through the argument. "I gave you a command, my son, and I expect you to follow it with haste. We wouldn't want a sudden storm to obliterate her claims."

"Yes, Mother." He gave her a half bow and glared vitriol at Johanna. "I'll be back in less than two hours with confirmation of one of our stories."

Chapter 8

Rafi

Rafi didn't like being proved wrong, but Snout pointed out the blood spatter from the initial hit and even tracked back to the place the girl had stood when she took the ill-fated shot. Both were on the public side of the river.

"It was a right fine shot, if I may say so," the tracker said as he scratched his perfectly average nose. His nickname hailed from his ability to sniff out any trail.

"It wasn't a kill, Snout." Rafi looked across the orchard but silently agreed with the tracker. With the low-hanging branches and shadows, it would have been a difficult mark for any man in his guard. "If she'd only waited for it to turn broadside."

Then she wouldn't be hurt, and I wouldn't feel such a fool.

"Dom, send riders to town. Have them spread word that we found a girl lost in the woods. Say she was injured and is under our care," Rafi said as he snapped a fallen twig in half. "I don't expect anyone to claim the figureless urchin, but I've already been wrong once today."

Dom snorted. "I'll mark it in my journal, for I'm certain it will never happen again."

Rafi punched his brother in the shoulder hard enough to knock the younger boy back a step.

"Careful with those fists, brother." Dom rubbed the spot theatrically. "They tend to get you in trouble. Right, Snout?"

The tracker held back a smile, but only barely. "Is there anything else, Lord Rafael?"

"If anyone does claim the girl, please escort them back to the manor."

"Yessir."

"Well . . ." Dom slapped his riding gloves against his palm as he watched Snout return to his mount. "I'd be happy to serve as your Punisher. I could pull my punches a bit, and perhaps save you some pain."

Typical Dom, always searching for the easiest way out of any problem. Rafi knew he could agree, that his mother would let him choose the Punisher. But it was a point of pride to select someone to dole out the blows—four times as many as he'd unjustly given—who could actually hurt him. Dom was strong for a sixteen-year-old, but he wasn't the Punisher Rafi had in mind.

There was a lesson in this, and Rafi wanted his stupidity to teach his younger brother the cost of mistakes. "If we don't uphold the law, then no one will."

"It's archaic. Can't we pay her off?"

"It's honorable," Rafi corrected. "No man should be able to take advantage of the weak. I'm going to ask Captain Alouette to serve as my Punisher."

Dom cringed. "I didn't expect to take your title, but if you're offering it up . . ."

"I'll survive."

"I'll pray for you."

I'll need it.

Chapter 9

Jacaré

"What is he doing here?" Pira pointed to the old man, who rocked his chair back on its hind legs and rested his boots on the hearth. "He's been *exiled*."

"Good to see you, too, Pira. Thanks for the warm welcome," Texugo said as he tossed another piece of kindling onto the blaze.

The light cast an orange glow onto the old man's pure white hair, as if it had caught fire. Jacaré almost laughed at the thought. Texugo had always been a hothead.

Adding Pira to the mix would be like throwing dry grass on a wildfire. Jacaré rubbed a hand over his shorn scalp, already doubting his plans and the inclusion of his sister. While great in a fight, an excellent hunter and scout, and generally trustworthy, she was a difficult person to manage. With both Pira and Tex aboard . . .

Pira gasped when the other person at the small table pulled back his hood. Whirling, she stepped in front of Jacaré.

"What is going on? Are these two even allowed in the same room together? If you're in trouble, then Tex is someone who might be able to help." She thumbed over her shoulder. "But *he* is practically on the Mage Council. Don't you think he'll run back to his grandmother and report exactly what's going on here?"

"Leão can be trusted."

"Leão is what . . . twelve years old?"

The boy cleared his throat, drawing their attention. "I'm almost eighteen. I make my own decisions, even if they're contrary to the Council's opinions."

"You can make decisions all by yourself without Grandma Amelia holding your hand?" Pira scoffed. "My, what a grown-up boy you are."

Jacaré grabbed his sister's upper arm, squeezing hard enough that she couldn't ignore it. "It's still early enough for you to leave, Pira." He yanked her toward the door. "We can do this without a fourth."

"Do *what* without a fourth?" Pira pulled her arm free.

"If you're in, no more commentary. I'm High Captain and you *will* follow orders." He folded his arms across his chest. "Agreed?"

Pira shot a dark look at the two other men in the kitchen. "Mother Lua knows you're going to need my help."

Such a typical response, always needing to score the last point. Jacaré held his tongue and let her sit down at the table between the two men.

"The magical barrier that separates our land from Santarem is in danger of falling," Jacaré said. His sister's eyes grew wide as the words sank in. "For the magic to remain stable, it has to have an anchor on either side of the wall. On this side, it's magically tied to Amelia and the Mage Council. On the Santarem side, it is tied to the line of kings. Sixteen years ago the king was murdered and the bond was passed to his closest living relative—an infant daughter who was smuggled out of the Citadel before it fell. We've been able to watch her and Santarem through a divining pendant that was given to her caretaker."

He set the glass down on the middle of the table. Tex didn't look at the image; he'd already seen it and understood what it meant probably better even than Jacaré. It had been in Tex's charge long before it became Jacaré's, and he had watched it pass from heir to heir during the two-hundred and seventy-five years he'd guarded it.

Leão leaned forward, trying to get a clear glimpse, but lurched back when Pira pulled it closer to her.

Jacaré explained his interaction with the Mage Council and their inability to make a decision about what should be done to protect their people.

"The heir—this princess—is the key to keeping the barrier stable. She's been away from the wall for too long." Jacaré pulled out the last chair from the table and sat on it backward. "Think of the magic like a piece of leather that's been stretched for a long time. Eventually it will develop a weak spot and snap. Our job is to relieve that tension."

"So we need to hop over the wall and find this girl and bring her closer to it." Pira shoved the glass toward Leão. "What's the Council's problem with that?"

Jacaré and Tex exchanged a look. The old man shook his head and turned back to the fire.

"They're scared. We crossed Donovan's Wall and erected the

magical barrier to protect ourselves from the influences of the people on the other side." Jacaré ignored Tex's grunt and pressed on. "The people of Santarem have short life spans, but they outnumber us by more than a thousand to one. Even without magic, they could overwhelm us. During the Mage Wars, our people were divided. We killed each other and the people of Santarem."

"It was an ugly, bloody mess," Tex interjected. "No one wants to see it happen again."

"Are they great fighters and strategists?" Leão asked, fingering the glass much like his grandmother had. The same blue glow emanated from his fingertips as he searched for a flaw in the magic.

Leão was a full Mage, gifted with the strength and ability to command all five elements, rather than just one or two like Pira and Tex. He'd chosen to become a soldier over the softer life of a diplomat. For that he had Jacaré's respect. And because of Leão's willingness to defy the Council, he also had Jacaré's trust.

"Some are violent. They harm each other much more frequently than our people do."

"I still don't see the issue," Pira said, stealing the glass back from Leão.

"There are several problems. Half the Council thinks that if the barrier collapses, the people of Santarem will attack us," Jacaré explained. "The other half thinks that Santarem has forgotten us, and we'd be better off forgetting them. The Council won't take action until they can come to a unanimous decision.

"It's been two months already, and I fear the princess may be in danger." He made eye contact with each person around the table.

"If she dies without passing on the bond, the barrier will fall, and then it won't matter what decision the Council makes."

"What makes you think she's in danger?" Pira asked, always looking for the fault in his logic.

"I believe her guardian was murdered, and whatever trouble found him will go after the princess next."

Chapter 10

Leão

Leão shifted his pack, moving the sword strapped underneath closer to his right shoulder. He prayed he wasn't going to need it for the rest of the journey, but something cold and venomous coiled in his belly. Death lurked somewhere nearby, waiting to strike.

He hoped to anticipate the bite and avoid its sting, but there were no guarantees for any member of their small group.

The sun had set on their third day of travel and with the failing light, the chilly air sank into his bones. Still, he held his position near the bramble hedge that hugged the mountain's feet and listened to the sounds coming from the fortress centered in Donovan's Wall. Jacaré called the square-shaped building the Citadel, and it was the first sign of civilization Leão had seen since they had left the borders of Olinda two days before.

Jacaré had been certain Pira would join their crew. The High Captain had four packs already prepared with foodstuffs, bedrolls, and weapons, and they left the cottage without a word to those who would miss them.

Defector, Leão's conscience had taunted. *You're leaving your post. You're disobeying orders. You're defying the Mage Council.*

The guilt waned as they passed the Elite Guard's last outpost. The men stationed there had grown lax with nothing to do besides hunt the occasional mountain cat that raided the sheep herds nearby, and the crew had breezed past the location without detection.

The outpost wasn't going to be much of a defense if something or someone did try to attack Olinda, and because of that Leão felt reassured by his decision to be part of Jacaré's incursion.

Passing the outpost had been their only chance of being detected or detained, and after that the trip had gone smoothly. They'd seen no signs of the dangerous predators rumored to haunt the narrow canyon that sliced through the mountain range. Not a growl or call or print.

Leão had been a bit disappointed that he hadn't faced any of the legendary creatures—pumas the size of horses and twice as fast—but as he turned his focus back to the Citadel, he realized there were plenty of challenges to come.

He used a trickle of his power to encourage the wind to blow in his direction, carrying the sounds of the fortress with it.

The men spoke harshly. If this was the quality of people that guarded the border, then Jacaré had been right to worry. From what Leão could tell, they spent more of their time swearing and spitting than doing any actual guard work. And their lack of concern showed.

The building they protected was falling into ruins. Two stone towers rose over the wall dividing the mountain range from the rest of Santarem. Portions of its crenellated ramparts had crumbled, leaving gaps like missing teeth in a sorry smile. The watchtower roofs under their hats of thatch leaned drunkenly toward each other, too weak to stand on their own.

It was a hideously constructed facility, but what it lacked in beauty it made up for with sheer immensity. Olinda didn't need fortresses, nor could the Elite Guard have manned one this size.

Not that the Citadel was full; he'd only heard four voices in the entire hour he'd crouched among the thorn bushes. Enough men to raise a warning if there was an attack, but not enough to stop even a small group of people hoping to cross into Santarem.

Hoofbeats drew his attention. They clattered across a stone courtyard Leão couldn't see. Two men, two horses, and a struggling captive.

From the sounds of the whimpers and occasional plea, he guessed it was a woman.

Mother Lua, these people are disgusting. He listened for a few moments more until he couldn't ignore her cries. *She may not be one of our own, but Jacaré will want to know. This is wrong, no matter which people she belongs to.*

Chapter 11

Johanna

A voice drew Johanna from a dreamless slumber. Her eyes popped open, expecting to see the beams of her wagon ceiling or perhaps a starry sky, but never a watered-silk canopy.

Images flashed across Johanna's mind like shadows on a tent wall: the deer, arrow, flying fists, arrogant prig, Lady DeSilva. Then she remembered.

There must have been something in the tea she gave me. Johanna stretched tentatively, feeling sore but not agonized. *Whatever it was, it worked.*

"Pardon, miss." A redheaded girl in a maid's cap held a bundle of pale blue fabric in her arms. "My lady asked me to attend to you. She sent this dressing gown for you to wear."

Johanna would have to get out of the bed soon if she planned to walk across the forest and through the orchards before her brother sent out a search party. She didn't want to leave the luxury behind but couldn't bear to worry her family. "Where are my clothes?"

"They were taken by the laundress and will be returned when dry."

"Oh." Johanna fingered her borrowed nightgown, feeling the lump of bandages that bound her ribs underneath it. "I was hoping to go home now."

The maid smiled sweetly. "Good thing your family has come here."

"What?" Johanna checked the window; the sun was still in the sky. Her mother probably didn't even realize she was missing.

"Your brother's come to claim you."

Johanna cursed.

The maid giggled, flushing as red as her hair.

"I'm sorry . . ."

"My name's Brynn, miss. Don't you worry, my brother's a sailor. I've heard worse language on his shore visits, and find myself directing those same oaths at him before he returns to his ship."

"Do you know which of my brothers is here?" *Please say Joshua.*

"I believe he gave the name of Thomas. Lord Rafael sent word to town to let your folks know you were well."

Except that if Thomas was at the estate, in the middle of a work day, all was certainly not well.

"He'll be up shortly with Lady DeSilva."

Perfect.

Johanna let Brynn slip the robe around her shoulders and tuck her back into bed. Moments later a knock sounded at the bedroom door.

Thomas rushed through, his face pale as Mother Lua in the night sky, and so similar to their father's that Johanna cringed. Lady DeSilva followed at a more stately pace.

He knelt next to the bed and took her hand. "Are you all right, Jo? The lady told me what happened." His eyes flitted to the bump on his sister's forehead, but the rest of her bruises were hidden. He pressed on, his voice worried. "What were you thinking? I told you to stay out of the forest by yourself. You know it isn't safe. Girls are kidnapped every day. What if you'd been caught by someone with less honorable intentions? I can't even . . . I don't even . . ." He ran out of steam. "I just . . . I can't protect you when you won't do as I ask."

Thomas rarely deviated from the script when it came to arguments. He asked all the questions without waiting for answers, his concern making Johanna feel guilty and foolish.

"I'm sorry." She meant it, but for so many other reasons.

He bowed his head for a few breaths, then looked at her with intense blue eyes. "Can you walk home? I'm sure Mother will be frantic when she realizes you are gone."

"No, no, no." The duchess waved away the idea. "She can't walk home, and she certainly can't ride home. She may have cracked ribs."

Thomas gave his sister a knowing smirk. "Johanna could walk on two broken ankles."

Of course, he'd bring *that* up. Another time when her disobedience had resulted in an injury.

"My ribs aren't broken anyway." Johanna swung her feet over the side of the bed, feeling sad to leave the cozy comfort. Her fold-down pallet in the wagon wouldn't be nearly as kind to her bruises. "If someone will bring me my clothes, we can be on our way."

"They won't be dry till morning," Lady DeSilva said, folding her arms across her chest. "You will both stay the night. We can make up the room for you next door, Master Thomas."

Thomas stood, his head barely coming to the duchess's chin, and yet he knew how to command a room. "I'm afraid that's impossible, Your Grace. I have to return to the accounting office by dawn." He held out a hand to Johanna, intending to pull her to her feet.

He'd probably lost half a day's pay to see to his wayward sister, and they certainly couldn't afford to lose any more. Johanna knew he'd carry her home if he had to.

Lady DeSilva put her hand over his. "Let her stay then. We'll have our physician check her bruises again in the morning and you can escort her home tomorrow evening."

All of Arlo and Marin's children knew when to bow their heads to authority, but Thomas's battle was evident on his face.

"Please forgive me for asking, my lady, but can you guarantee my sister's safety while a ward of your household?"

The duchess pressed her lips together in a tight line, and Johanna prepared to be tossed out of the room. "If I am not mistaken, you are Arlo the Acrobat's son and have visited this estate at least a dozen times. Correct?"

Thomas and Johanna exchanged a glance and nodded.

"As Performers, you've had a chance to compare our estate with those in Maringa, Belem, and Impreza. Would you say that I'm a tyrant or cruel or fail to uphold the laws of my land?"

"Of course not, my lady," Thomas said, looking as taken back by the question as Johanna felt. "Your estate and township are orderly, your tenants happy, and your staff voices no complaints."

It was true. The DeSilvas were known for treating their people as near equals rather than shoe-kissing subjects.

Lady DeSilva, at least. I'm still not sure about her lordling son.

"Will you let the words of my people serve as a testimony for my household, if my word of honor is not enough?" the lady continued.

Johanna mentally applauded the duchess. She worked Thomas like a pickpocket with a fat mark, taking control of the conversation without him noticing. The people of Santiago, the peasants and gentry alike, were prickly about their honor. Denying her request would have been a serious slight.

"Your word is enough, my lady," Thomas said, and bent his neck to her will. "My father always believed you and your husband were rulers worthy of our respect."

Lady DeSilva's smile lit her face. "Give my son the chance and he'll earn your respect as well."

Johanna rolled her eyes, but only Brynn—who stood forgotten in the corner throughout the entire exchange—seemed to notice.

"Well then, we'll see you tomorrow evening."

Thomas stooped to kiss Johanna on the forehead, just as he always did. "Enjoy your time here."

"I'll try."

Chapter 12

Dom

Dom always ate in the kitchen. There was no better way to start a morning than with *pão de queijo* hot from the pan, and milk fresh from the cow. He and Rafi used to sneak out of bed well before sunrise and wait under the kneading table. Cook would scream and rant and chase the boys out of her domain, but never before they got handfuls of cheese bread to tuck into their pockets.

It had been four months since they'd breakfasted together—and years since they could both fit under the table—but Dom still ate at the counter with the servants who stopped in for a bite. Rafi took a pannier of breads and meat with him to eat between visits with farmers and merchants.

Besides their weekly search of the forest for poachers' traps, Dom only saw his brother on the training ground. They hacked at each other with practice swords and foils, rarely exchanging more than a few grunts or apologies when one or the other landed a particularly hard blow. Dom secretly missed their morning conversations and the time when they were brothers instead of lord and second son.

Things had changed for both of them when the duke had died.

"Good glory, that girl can eat," Brynn said as she dropped a tray onto the counter beside Cook. "She said she'd like four *more* eggs and two *more* bowls of porridge and a few slices of bread."

"Do you think she's hiding it somewhere?" Cook asked as she stirred something with a rhythmic flick of her wrist. She was a lean woman for a chef, but strong as an ox. "The butcher's boy told me he hasn't sold them one slice of meat in all the time they've lived in town. I doubt they're eating well if they're hunting. It's been too dry for anything besides a few lean hares and bony pheasants."

"I watched her eat every bite," Brynn said, pulling a face. "It's almost unseemly."

"She's a Performer," Dom said, breaking into the conversation. "She's probably swallowed swords and balls of flame. I'm sure a dozen eggs wouldn't hurt her stomach."

"True." Brynn blushed to the roots of her hair; she was always red when Dom was around. "But she's also a girl. I couldn't possibly eat so much."

"Why don't you grab her meal and I'll go up with you and say good morning." Dom tilted his head subtly toward the pantry, and mouthed the word "custard."

Brynn ignored him. "Cookie, be a dear and fix our guest another tray? I've got to go check to see if her clothes are dry. Though it would be best for everyone if her pants got lost in the laundry. No girl in her right mind would wear breeches that tight."

"She's a Performer." Dom backed into the pantry, never taking his eyes off Cook. She didn't appreciate filching and could wield a wooden spoon like a mace.

"Still, she should have some decency, don't you think?"

"Have you ever seen what the Performers wear while they're swinging and flying and climbing on each other?" He spoke a little louder than normal, hoping his voice would carry beyond the pantry's door. Then he went to work, stuffing cookies, tarts, even an entire jar of blackberry preserves into the pockets that lined his pants from hip to calf.

"That's different. I've seen Performer girls after shows and they're all dressed like proper young ladies." Her eyes were wide, her face extra red. *Will you hurry?* she mouthed.

Where's the custard?

Cook turned, her eyes going wide, as her free hand patted the counter looking for her wooden spoon. "Dominic Marcello DeSilva, empty your pockets!"

Dom dodged wide, swinging around the kneading table and darting for the door. Cook brought her wooden spoon across his shoulder, but Dom made it into the hall without any further abuse.

The original portion of the estate was a sprawling three-level manor, but two stone wings had been added to form an open-ended triangle. As Dom rounded the corner and began pounding up the stairs, he heard Cook yell, "Your mother will hear about this!"

And she would, but when it came to cherry tarts, he'd accept any tongue-lashing.

Brynn huffed after him, a porcelain tray in her hands. "Must you antagonize her every day?"

Dom squinted at the ceiling as if mulling over a difficult sum. "Yes. I'm certain I must. Someone has to keep things interesting around here, or we'll all become straight-faced and grim like Rafi."

"Responsible, you mean," Brynn said as she hurried down the hall. The sun poured through the eastern windows, casting splotches of colored light on the floor. "Some people find responsibility attractive."

"People like you?" Dom asked and leaned against the doorframe, blocking her path.

Brynn's face pinked again, but she lifted her chin haughtily. "What if I do?"

"Then you're more a fool than I realized."

"At least he's not a little boy who steals treats from the kitchen." She gave the door a quick knock before shouldering it open. "Miss? I've brought the food you asked for."

Dom heard a girl's pleasant voice and tapped on the door quickly. "May I come in?"

"It's just Lord Dom," Brynn explained. "You can ignore him if you want. He'll likely talk you deaf if you let him in."

"I don't mind the company," she said. "You won't let me escape anyway."

He heard the rustle of bed coverings and clothes before he was admitted.

"Hello, I'm Dominic." He sketched a half bow in his best courtly imitation. "I'm the less responsible, less rigid, and more attractive younger brother of the lord who beat you into submission yesterday."

Chapter 13

Johanna

Johanna liked Dom immediately. Dom had the same dark hair and eyes as Rafi, but he had a mouth made for smiling and maybe mischief.

"It's a pleasure to meet you, sir."

"And you, my lady." He dropped into the chair next to the fireplace and stretched out his legs, stacking one boot on top of the other. Brynn kicked his foot out of the way as she arranged the tray over Johanna's blanket-covered lap. "They tell me you are a Performer."

"I was." Johanna steadied the plate with one hand and shoveled food into her mouth with the other. "We were expelled when my father died."

"They forced you to leave?" His voice squeaked a little in surprise. "That's . . . harsh."

"It's one of our laws," she said around a mouthful of porridge. "Death during a show is bad for business, and a sign of bad luck. A hedgewitch reviews each situation and reads each family's fortune, then she makes a suggestion to the Performers' Council. If bad luck follows us—and a family is usually cursed if one member dies while performing—then they ask us to leave before it spreads to the rest of our troupe."

Johanna didn't mention that her mother had been intoxicated during the review, and that Marin said nothing to convince the Council to rule in their favor.

"Bad luck is contagious?" Dom dug a cookie out of his pocket and offered it to Johanna.

"Like marsh fever."

Brynn had busied herself with a pile of silk, hanging it on the dressing screen and smoothing out the wrinkles, but stopped long enough to pull a face. Johanna didn't mind. Few people understood Performers and their lifestyle.

"That's very interesting," Dom said.

He squinted a bit at Johanna, and she wondered what he saw. A girl who might have been pretty if it hadn't been for her ridiculously short hair?

"What type of Performer are . . . or . . . were you?"

"I'm a jack-of-all-trades. I can swing on the trapeze and am a bit of an acrobat, but my father wanted me to focus on something a little less dangerous. So I'm mostly a singer and a Storyspinner."

Dom slapped one of his knees and said, "Tell me a tale then!"

"What would you like to hear?"

"Oh, I don't know if that's a good idea, miss," Brynn said, stepping closer to the bed. "What with your injuries—"

"I told you I'm fine. I've had much worse." Johanna tugged up her sleeve, baring a still-pink scar that stretched the length of her forearm. "I got this when I dropped a firesword. It was hot and sharp, and stung for days." She fingered her dark hair. "It was the same day I singed off all of this."

She spun the tale, explaining how she wanted to apprentice to the master Firesword, but they wouldn't take her after she'd burned herself.

Johanna's voice rose and fell, lyrical as a ballad, as she wove the details of a silly mistake into a story worth listening to. As she spoke she watched her captive audience, gauging their emotions and learning about them. Dom was perhaps a year younger than Johanna and seemed a little bit plush and lazy, but altogether likable. Brynn, on the other hand, worked and fidgeted, darting looks between Johanna and Dom.

She cares for him, Johanna realized. In Belem and Maringa relationships between the gentry and peasants were outlawed. In Impreza and the outer holdings of Roraima such unions were frowned upon. *But maybe here in Santiago there's hope for them.*

Then she thought of the conceited soon-to-be duke and knew there wasn't a chance.

Chapter 14

Jacaré

"So that's it?" Pira whispered, her eyes flashing. "*That* pile of stone kept the invaders out of our lands for so many centuries?"

The hulking fortress didn't look as impressive as Jacaré remembered it. No bright banners snapped in the wind. No polished armor reflected the stray bands of sunlight peeking through the clouds. There were no voices, no careful tread of patrol, no smell of horses or livestock. It looked defeated, lifeless, monochromatic.

"Not this empty structure, *criança*." He called her a child and watched her cringe at the nickname. "The people who once lived here. They protected the wall and kept others from entering our lands."

He closed his eyes for a moment, reliving the last time he'd been so close to the Citadel. Keepers lined the wall, each standing an arm's distance apart with their palms flexed toward Santarem. One hundred full Mages worked together, guiding the combined power of his people to construct the barrier. They poured their *essência* into the spell. The majority of them died, and the rest of them remained forever changed.

Jacaré had been deemed too young to participate, being only a year older then than Leão was now. But he'd been heartsore from too much war and loss and ignored the command.

He had stood directly at the center of the Citadel, not far from where Leão crouched among the brambles, and offered his *essência* to help create the barrier. He'd lived so much in those eighteen years, and suffered to protect his people. The thought of giving his life hadn't scared him, but living with the memories did.

Something had gone amiss; instead of killing him, the magic had rebounded, smashing into him with the force of a landslide. Instead of putting his total *essência* into the wall, the magic had changed him. He'd survived and aged perhaps two years in the three hundred since. A grown man, the High Captain of the Elite Guard, who looked like he should be Leão's best friend instead of his commanding officer.

At first it seemed like a cruel joke. He'd wanted to die but was cursed with more time. In the passing centuries he learned to put his loss behind him and live with the memories and nightmares. He hadn't disobeyed an order since that day.

Until now.

"We should never have relied on someone else to protect us," Pira continued. "We should have used our magic and destroyed them all."

"Enough, Pira." Jacaré didn't lose his patience often, but his sister pushed him closer to the bounds of his control than any other person. "Scout ahead. Leão should have a report by now. See if you can follow his trail."

She nodded and moved along the scree, her feet seeming to float above the loose rocks.

"They don't understand," said Texugo, once she was well out of earshot. "Their entire generation can't. They've never had cannon fire ringing in their ears days after a battle. The smell of burning pitch and the flavor of fear are all elements of a grand story. They don't believe there is anything more powerful than magic."

"That's a lot of words from you, my friend," Jacaré said, and wondered for the thousandth time since they'd left Olinda if dragging Tex on this task had been the wrong decision. The man had been old when Jacaré was young. Now wrinkles etched his skin like furrows in pale sand, and time had bleached all the color from his hair. Tex wasn't just old. He was ancient.

Despite his age and cantankerous attitude, Tex knew Santarem better than anyone. He'd traveled it from coast to coast, and from mountaintop to desert dune. But more than that, he remembered the people.

"I've got a few more things to say." Tex lounged against the boulder like it was a feathered divan. "Something's . . . not right."

It wasn't a very definitive statement, but Jacaré didn't need clarification. Traversing the mountains between Olinda and Santarem should have been a dangerous journey. But the peaks had been bereft of living creatures, both predator and prey. The deer herds had abandoned their valleys, the wild goats had disappeared from the slopes, and the giant cats had vanished.

"I know. I feel it too."

Tex studied his boots for a long moment before speaking again. "You know the barrier better than I do, Jacaré. If those creatures are getting across, doesn't that mean it's very weak?"

"Probably."

The older man grimaced. "Have you given any thought to what we'll face when we cross the wall?"

"It won't be like last time."

Tex snorted. "Don't be naive. It's always like that. There will be bloodshed. There will be loss. There will be no return for some." His thin white eyebrows rose. "Given the speed your scouts are returning to us, I think bloodshed will come sooner rather than later."

Leão made no noise as he ran; Pira made little. The only sign of their passing was a thin cloud of dust that puffed behind them.

The two came to an abrupt halt, their dust catching them with a whoosh.

"There are men in the Citadel—at least six—and one woman." Leão flushed and shot an uncomfortable look at Pira. "She's not there willingly."

"They don't change, Jacaré," Texugo said, levering himself to his feet and checking his weapons.

"Which is *exactly* why we're here."

Donovan's Wall provided the foundation for the lowest level of the Citadel's northern face. Miles of gray stone were blemished by an ironbound gate that led into the building. Only one man and the tiny baby he carried had exited through that gate and the dense bramble hedge beyond and survived.

The barrier hummed against Jacaré's skin, but no jolt of power tossed him back. Instead the magic seemed to welcome him. The bramble curled into itself; the sharp thorns tucking their points into the branches rather than snagging his flesh. The air grew bitter with the acrid sap that dripped from the plant.

His crew followed, unhindered, pressing against the wall on either side of the gate. Its hinges were rusted and broken, but it swung open silently under Jacaré's touch. He slipped through the door at a crouch, with Pira above him, short bow at the ready.

The rear hall was empty, but the smell of urine and rotting food scraps said it hadn't been for long.

Leão tapped his ear and pointed upward with four fingers, then pointed to the front of the Citadel with three more.

Jacaré nodded, and Leão and Pira peeled off, making their way through the hall and to the front entrance.

Tex headed for the central staircase, pulling his two-handed mace as he went.

The upper floor of the Citadel was in a slightly better state than the main floor, likely because the small contingent of guards slept on that level and occasionally patrolled on the third story when the weather was pleasant.

The soldiers threw dice on the once-fine rug in the center of the hallway, too involved in their game to realize death stalked toward them on silent feet.

They died as they sat. Dice and blood spilled across the slate floor with a click and splatter.

Jacaré stopped to wipe his blade on one guard's grease-stained uniform and searched the bodies for clues. He found what he was looking for almost immediately and cut free the coat of arms stitched above the man's heart.

He tucked it into his palm and entered the chamber which had once been the private quarters of a king. Everything of value had been stripped away except the enormous bed built into the Citadel's wall.

A body lay sprawled across the tangled sheets.

"Too late for the girl?" Tex asked as he surveyed the scene with casual distaste.

"Isn't it always?"

Tex didn't respond, and Jacaré should have known better than to wait for false assurances. Their mission had little chance of success, just as the poor peasant girl had little chance of survival in the hands of six repulsive soldiers.

He'd been too late to save her, but maybe he'd make it in time to save the princess.

"Take care of this," Jacaré nodded toward the bed.

"Of course." Tex reached into his belt pouch and pulled out one seed, glowing red against his fingers. With a flick he tossed it onto the bed, which instantly burst into flame.

They stood together in silence and watched the macabre blaze.

Chapter 15

Leão

The main hallway of the Citadel had once been a grand receiving area. Vaulted ceilings soared three times Leão's height. Delicate ribs of exposed stonework and intricately carved pillars gave the area a sense of light and openness. While it lacked the grand windows of the capitol building in Olinda, the interior of the Citadel was far less utilitarian than its rough-hewn exterior suggested.

Leão wondered about the people who had once lived there. They'd obviously been devoted to security—the arrow slits, watch-towers, and murder holes proclaimed that clearly—but they hadn't completely sacrificed beauty for safety.

On another night, when he didn't have murder on his mind, he might have stopped to study the soot-stained carvings, to see what types of things this people had valued enough to immortalize in stone.

Pira trotted a few paces ahead, bow in hand. She gave a cursory peek down the dark corridors that branched off the hallway, making sure each was clear. Leão was certain the remaining guards were at the Citadel's entrance, but Pira was sticky about protocol, which was probably why she'd been promoted to officer so early in her career.

They edged near the open portcullis. Outside a fire cast orange light into the hallway, making long shadows dance across the entryway. A fire so bright was foolish for men on watch. They would have been able to see much farther by the light of the moon and stars, but Leão guessed they weren't really watching for anything—especially not for something sneaking up on their backs.

Leão pressed himself into the nook created by the supporting pillars on either side of the portcullis and peered at the men beyond. There were three of them, two with their backs to the Citadel and one on the far side of the fire.

Besides their dirty uniforms, they didn't look like soldiers. Their hair was long and greasy and their faces sported uneven beards. The man Leão could see most clearly was thin to the point of skeletal.

"It's a 'festation, I tell ya. Snakes like these ain't right," one voice complained. "It's like they *wanna* bite us, always crawling in our boots and packs."

"It's not an infestation," another man corrected. "It's a curse. My gramma said this land was cursed because of what Inimigo did to the king and his kin. My gramma said—"

"I don't give a flying carp what your gramma says," the skinny man interrupted. "The only snake I care about is my own and if he's gonna get a turn with that girly upstairs."

Their laughs cut off abruptly as an arrow penetrated the thin man's eye. He toppled backward as Pira surged through the doorway, nocking a second arrow as she moved.

"What the—" The surviving soldiers stumbled into startled action, scrambling for weapons they'd discarded for the sake of comfort.

Pira's second shot caught another guard under the chin. He collapsed onto his side, his sword belt just beyond the tips of his fingers.

That left the third man for Leão. The soldier stood slowly, holding his hands out to the sides of his body, showing he was unarmed. "Don't hurt me," he pleaded. "I don't have a weapon."

Leão hesitated. These men were brutes, pillagers, rapists. They didn't deserve to die with any honor. Yet Leão couldn't bear to run a man through who was trying to surrender. It wasn't as detached as shooting someone from a distance. Stabbing a man was personal.

At least I can let him die with a weapon in his hands.

Leão kicked a sword belt toward the soldier. "Pick it up," he commanded.

"Leão, what are you doing?" Pira snapped.

He heard the whisper of an arrow sliding free of her quiver.

"Pick up your weapon." Leão stepped in front of her, blocking any shot she might take.

The man bent at the waist, moving with the careful precision of a person confronting an angry dog. His eyes darted nervously between Pira, Leão, and the dead bodies of his comrades.

"How's about you let me go? I never saw you. You never saw me." He stood, but didn't reach for his sword. "I'll walk out of here and not look back."

"Leão," Pira's voice sounded like it was coming through clenched teeth.

Bright orange light burst from two of the narrow windows in the Citadel's facade. Leão looked away from his captive for an instant—long enough for the man to draw a knife from his boot.

The small dagger never left the soldier's hand.

Before Leão's mind even registered the threat, his body reacted to its training. With a simple flick of his wrist, he sliced a clean line across the enemy's neck.

The man fell onto his face, blood spreading in a black pool around his body.

Pira released a slow breath before speaking. "What were you thinking?"

Leão wiped the tip of his blade on the dead man's uniform, obliterating the proof of its use. "I wanted to give him a chance."

"Like they gave that girl?" Pira shouldered past him, bumping him back a step. She rifled through the dead man's clothing with quick, angry actions. "They wouldn't have given you a chance. They would have run you through unarmed or not."

Leão relaxed his grip, the sword's point dropping into the dirt at his feet. He knew she was right. He'd acted foolishly, and yet he couldn't forget the look on the man's face when the blade had parted his skin.

"Have you done this before?" he asked quietly, eyes focused on the body. "Have you killed?"

"No." Pira found a bag of coins on the first body and slipped it into her pocket.

Her words surprised him. She was so calm, so focused, so decisive.

"You're very good at it." Leão meant it as a compliment, but Pira shot him a glare hotter than the fire that still flickered between the bodies.

She moved to the second corpse and resumed her searching. "Next time, you'd better be good at it too."

Leão nodded, not that she noticed.

There will be a next time.

Chapter 16

Jacaré

While Texugo refused to camp in sight of Donovan's Wall—mumbling something about it being too easy to go back to the Keepers' homeland if he could still see the way—Jacaré wanted to move on for entirely different reasons. The Citadel had once been a symbol of strength and security for the people of Santarem. The soldiers who protected it took great pride in their post. He'd counted some of them as friends.

Things change in three hundred years, Jacaré reminded himself. *And that change hasn't been for the better.*

That knowledge spurred him onward and confirmed his decision to cross the wall.

They walked south out of the mountain range, through the rolling hills that constituted the remnants of Roraima Township. The burned-out homes had fallen into piles of moldering lumber, providing perfect nests for rodents and at least one type of venomous serpent.

A burst of predawn rain forced them to seek shelter under the partially collapsed roof of an old stone inn. Tex found a scat-free corner, threw down his bedroll, and immediately went to sleep.

He didn't even offer to light the fire, though it would have been much easier for him than any of the others. Tex could turn a patch of wet sticks into a roaring bonfire if someone could motivate him to do it.

Jacaré had to remind himself that Tex had agreed to come on this sortie as a personal favor, and it was good to know he had someone with real experience watching his back.

Pira followed the old man's example, saying nothing as she rolled herself into a blanket, using it to hide her still-trembling hands.

Jacaré was impressed. He hadn't handled his first kill nearly as well as his sister had.

Leão, however, had thrown up after he killed the guard. No amount of training prepared a man for the hot spray of an enemy's blood across his knuckles, or the horrible gulping whine of a partially severed windpipe.

He sat near the small, smokeless blaze and sharpened his knife. He studied the blade by the fire's light, the glint of steel reflecting in his eyes.

"You did well today, Leão," Jacaré said, feeling obligated to say something, to offer some sense of understanding.

"Thank you, sir." Leão removed the woven leather band they all wore around their shaved heads. He rubbed his temples, finding the slight indent the *cadarço* left in his skin. Eventually he'd have a callus right at his hairline, as Jacaré and Tex had, and wouldn't notice the pressure against his scalp.

"Tomorrow, I'd like you to scout ahead and look for a place where we can purchase some horses. Tex is certain we'll find stables along the South Road before we get to Cruzamento."

"Yes, sir." Leão replaced his headband and checked the edge of his knife against his thumb. One drop of blood welled, and he flicked it into the fire.

"It gets easier, you know."

The younger soldier put down his weapon and regarded his commander over the fire. "The killing, you mean?" His voice was a fierce whisper that matched the emotion in his green eyes.

"One day, it won't bother you as much."

Leão nodded and sheathed his knife. "I was afraid you'd say that."

The next day dawned clear. The rain had washed away the low-lying fog that had settled around the Citadel and the Keepers' Mountains beyond. They covered the twenty miles between the Roraima rubble and the crossroads city of Cruzamento by supper. Tex entered the town alone and came back with four horses, a pack mule loaded with supplies, and a piece of gray-green silk.

He tossed the square to Pira.

"There isn't even enough to make a decent shirt." She held it up to her chest. "What am I supposed to do with it?"

Tex laughed, and Jacaré barely managed to keep his smile under control. "No women on this side of the wall shave their heads."

Their dusty traveling leathers, supplemented by a few linen shirts in bright colors, would allow them to go unnoticed, but Pira's bald pate would attract attention.

She eyed the two men, her face expressionless. "I'll dress as a boy instead."

They all laughed, even quiet Leão. With her perfect heart-shaped face, full lips, and heavily lashed eyes, Pira might have passed as an unfortunately pretty boy. But there was no way the rest of her body could ever be mistaken for male.

She crumpled the silk in her fist. "I'm not wearing this. I passed all the tests. I completed my training. I earned my *cadarço*."

"You can still wear it. Under the head scarf."

"But, Jacaré—"

"Put it on, and get on your horse."

She obeyed, swinging into the saddle, looping the reins around the horn. The scarf she folded in half and tied in a hasty knot under her chin. It looked ridiculous around her ferocious face, like a lion with a ribbon in its mane, but it would do for now.

"We can pick up a wig in Belem, if you'd prefer."

In response she kicked her horse into a gallop down the southwest road.

Leão watched after her for a moment. "I guess she'll serve as scout for the rest of the day?"

"Boy," Tex said between chuckles. "When a woman's in *that* mood, it's better for us all to keep our distance."

Jacaré knew he should have called her to task, reminded her to follow orders without question and show a little more respect, but going on this mission created a hardship for each of them. Pira had the most to lose, so he let her temper tantrum slide.

"At least she's riding in the right direction." Tex nodded toward the cloud of dust Pira kicked up on the prairie road. "And don't ask me again if I'm sure."

Jacaré had selected each of his companions for a specific purpose, and none of them could navigate like Tex. He could track a frog through water, find the quickest and easiest way between any two destinations, and hunt up a decent meal in a blizzard. If anyone could locate the heir with the few clues the glass offered, Tex would be the one.

The old Keeper pulled the cloth-wrapped bundle out of his bag and laid it across his saddle. With one hand he tugged away the string, revealing its shining surface.

The image still hadn't changed.

There were two faces, pressed close together in the left margin. The first—a teenage girl with wide, gray eyes and dark hair, cropped close to her head—seemed to be looking out of the glass. The second person appeared to be a woman, but it was difficult to tell from the angle. Jacaré could see the underside of a chin, unbound hair, and part of a tear-streaked cheek.

The faces were in focus, but it was the rest of the slightly blurry image that had provided Tex a few clues. On the right side of the image was the canopy of an araucaria pine.

"I hate looking at this thing," Tex said, covering the women's faces with his thumb, blocking out their expressions of suffering and despair. "Seeing through a dead man's eyes . . . It's plain morbid."

Jacaré had to agree, but he'd studied the shining surface thousands of times since he realized it had frozen on this image.

"What's this glint in the corner?" Leão asked, leaning across his saddle to point to the bottom of the glass.

Tex and Jacaré exchanged a smile.

"That, my fine observant boy, is how I know our destination." Tex rewrapped the magical tool. "It's the peak of a golden dome."

Leão nodded, understanding. "So, the uncommon trees and a glint are leading us to this city of Belem?"

"We have to start our search somewhere," Jacaré said, giving his horse a nudge. "And Belem is the last place we're sure she was."

Chapter 17

Johanna

"Wake up, miss!" Brynn hurried into the room and shoved back the bed curtains. She'd forced Dom out of the room after a second tale and made Johanna drink more of the medicine-laced tea. "Lady DeSilva will be here shortly to take you to Trial and Punishment."

Johanna's heart galloped like a pony in an open field. "Why didn't anyone mention it earlier?"

"The lady didn't know if she'd be able to make all the arrangements for a trial this afternoon, but with the young lord finished with his duties for the day, she decided there was time."

Trial. Did that mean they'd been unable to follow her trail, or had it washed away overnight? They wouldn't possibly have been so kind to her, offering a bed and food and conversation, if she was going to be convicted.

Unless that had all been some honor-bound oddity? Maybe they didn't treat criminals like prisoners in Santiago until *after* all the evidence had been gathered? Was that why Lady DeSilva hadn't wanted Johanna to go home with Thomas?

Johanna wasn't about to be tried for a crime she didn't commit, and she certainly wouldn't be Punished.

The window was an option. She'd been unconscious on arrival but had vague memories of an imposing yellow stone structure, dotted with jewel-toned windows in every color. It was smaller than any of the other dukes' residences—no towers or ramparts. She'd have no problem scaling the blocks, perhaps climbing to the red-tiled roof. It was sure to be slippery if there'd been rain, but Johanna knew she could manage it.

Although with the sun still up, she'd be too conspicuous on the side of the building. She could knock out the maid and sneak off the estate in disguise. Brynn's dress would drown her, but Johanna knew how to act like a deferential servant when the situation called for it.

"I'm really very sorry about this, Brynn." Johanna rolled to her feet, ignoring the flash of pain along her ribs. "I can't go to the Punishment for obvious reasons."

"But it's the law."

"I'm sure it is." Johanna's legs were weaker than she had anticipated. She'd need to gather her strength to take Brynn down with one smooth attack, and do it without drawing attention from other members of the staff.

The maid turned her back to pull the dress off the screen where she'd hung it earlier. It was the perfect opening.

Johanna took a silent step forward, hands outstretched, and was startled when the bedroom door swung open.

"Oh good, you're up," Lady DeSilva said as she hurried into the room. Her dark hair had been swept into a simple bun at the base of her neck. "Everything's been arranged, and I'd like to get this over and done with before your brother arrives."

"You wouldn't let me walk home with injured ribs," Johanna said, looking for a weapon, something she could use to threaten the women away. She backed toward the window, eyes darting around the room for a lamp, a chair leg, anything. "But you'll send me away with a brand or short a few fingers?"

"My dear, what are you talking about?"

"It's not a hand then? Perhaps you take a poacher's foot?" A horrible thought crossed Johanna's mind. "Please tell me you don't punish like Duke Inimigo. One deer isn't worth a life as a blind beggar."

The camisole the duchess held fell to the floor in a puddle of cream silk. "Johanna, we are not taking *you* to Punishment. Our tracker, Snout, found the trail just as you suggested and cleared you of any allegation."

Johanna's shoulders sagged with relief. "Then who's receiving the Punishment?"

"My son. He has to pay for his crimes against you."

"Crimes against me?" Johanna weighed the words. "In that case, I'll take fifty gold and be on my way."

The duchess's lips twisted into a grimace, and Johanna guessed she'd aimed too high.

"Thirty-five then, and we can consider it all forgiven?"

"We can work out some monetary reimbursement, but the law is the law, and no amount of coin will absolve him." The lady picked up the camisole and held it up for Johanna. "Though he'd appreciate your forgiveness, he couldn't accept clemency without incurring a mark on his honor."

"And I suppose honor is important to him?"

"Too important." Lady DeSilva nodded, and Johanna noticed the frown lines forming around the woman's mouth.

Johanna tugged the nightdress over her head. "Well then, let's get to your son's Punishment."

Chapter 18

Rafi

The girl practically skipped into the audience chamber. Perhaps skip was an exaggeration, but she certainly didn't stride with the contained elegance of Rafi's mother. She wore blue silk that clung to her chest and hips, revealing narrow curves that didn't belong on any boy. Even her short hair had been combed into gleaming waves, cupping her chin and showing a fine-featured face.

Thank you, Mother, for making me look like a complete and utter fool.

Not one word was muttered, but Rafi could see Captain Alouette's eyes darting between him and the girl who was most definitely a girl. The old retainer's lips pursed, making his blond mustache wiggle like a furry caterpillar.

Rafi withheld a sigh, knowing that his father would never have been in such a ridiculous situation.

The duchess led the girl to the second of five chairs arranged beyond the small drain in the floor, too far from the hearth for any warmth. A ring in the ceiling meant to hold up a chandelier had been outfitted with a rope and heavy leather manacles.

The girl's clear gray eyes studied the ring and the drain in the floor directly below it. Her nose wrinkled, but she didn't say anything.

Dom, Snout, and the new weaponsmaster, Raul Ortiz, entered a few moments later and barred the heavy door. It wasn't thick enough to stop stories from fleeing the room. The kitchen staff was probably already whispering about the broken girl, carried to the estate in the arms of the soon-to-be duke, and her angry family who'd likely raise a challenge for whatever virtue the girl still had.

What a wonderful way to start my legacy. I'll be known as the first lord in two generations who required Punishment.

"Thank you for joining us this day," his mother said, welcoming the group. "My son, Rafael Santiago DeSilva, has been accused of accosting Johanna Von Arlo in the forest. She received six blows at his hands, and as the law requires, he will receive four times as many for his abuse."

She turned to Rafi, her eyes wet, belying her steady voice. "Do you deny these charges?"

"No." His voice was low and flat. "I admit to the crime and accept the Punishment."

The duchess nodded. "Would anyone speak for you?"

"I will, Mother." Dom stood, fidgeting nervously. "Rafi—I mean, Lord Rafael—stumbled upon a poacher on our land and tried to stop him from killing a deer, but we didn't know the poacher was a girl. Johanna didn't look . . ." Dom's voice trailed off as he studied the girl from head to foot. "Sorry, but you didn't look like that."

"Only fools hunt in dresses, Lord Dominic," Johanna said. "And I was *not* poaching."

"That fact has been established." Lady DeSilva raised her eyebrows at Snout who nodded his confirmation. "Did Lord Rafael attempt to capture this alleged poacher and bring him—or her—to justice?"

"He did grab her, but she was sort of slippery—"

"Just say no, Dom." Rafi shifted his weight impatiently. He didn't need to be reminded when he should have stopped punching, when capture turned to assault, when he let his temper override his good sense.

"If there is no other testimony," Lady DeSilva said, searching the faces of her audience, "then we shall move to the Punishment."

No one spoke, as Rafi expected, and he began unlacing his collar with certain fingers. He tugged the linen from his back and handed the cloth to his mother, who folded it into a neat square.

Captain Alouette jerked on the rope and tightened the metal-studded manacles around each of Rafi's wrists. "Tight enough?"

There was no condemnation, no judgment, no disappointment on his face. Alouette was an excellent soldier and an honorable man. Someone Rafi's father had respected and trusted.

Rafi nodded and felt the rope go taut, pulling his arms over his head and stretching his frame to its full length. "I'm ready."

The captain cracked his knuckles and went to work.

Chapter 19

Johanna

Johanna felt ill. Her stomach swirled, her palms sweated, her throat burned, but none of those ailments were related to her injuries. Dom and Lady DeSilva were going to let a giant-of-a-man beat the conceited lordling. And he intended to take it.

She'd visited all the lands, studied in the libraries, and learned to accept many odd customs, some good, some bad, some disturbing, but this . . . this was brutal.

Lord Rafael stared at her with fire in his eyes, but his face remained calm as he handed his shirt to the duchess. He went willingly to his Punishment and shook the hand of the colossal Punisher like a trader in the marketplace.

His body bore a few scars, one arrow-straight slash above his hip bone and another across his left bicep, but otherwise it was unblemished and well defined. The corners of his chest muscles and the ridges of his abdomen stood out in shadowed relief as his arms were yanked above his head.

Not a perfect body, Johanna thought. She'd seen true perfection when she'd trained with the acrobats, their bodies thickly muscled in every imaginable location, but there was something poetic in Rafi's lean form.

The first punch took her by surprise. The Punisher exploded into motion like a Skylighter's rocket, blasting into Rafi's lower back. The breath whooshed out of his lungs, but his face showed no emotion. The second came to the right side of his rib cage, the third to the space above his navel.

Johanna cringed, her body reacting to the blows Rafi so pointedly ignored. Instead of grunting or mumbling or asking for mercy as the fourth, fifth, and sixth punches fell, his eyes stayed locked on hers, eyebrows peaked as if asking, *You see this? It's your fault.*

It wasn't until the tenth strike, a cracking blow against his ribs that the pain finally registered on his face. His mouth dropped open and he closed his eyes for one long moment.

What he received—methodical attacks to areas exposed and undefended—was a thousand times worse than what he'd done.

"Please." Johanna turned to the duchess and grabbed her hand. "Please make this stop."

The older woman's face was streaked with tears, and she gripped Johanna's hand tightly but continued watching.

The eleventh hit landed and Rafi's knees buckled. The rope swung slightly, supporting his weight, the top of his boots scraping the floor and catching on the drain. Captain Alouette didn't wait for him to regain his feet, winding up for another strike.

The muscles in the lordling's arms corded as he tucked his knees toward his chest, an unconscious effort at protecting himself.

"No more." Johanna came to her feet, but the Punisher pulled back his arm and slammed Rafi in the stomach.

“That’s enough!” she shouted, but was ignored. A hand grabbed her wrist but she wrenched away.

The Punisher didn’t seem to hear her, either locked into the moment or refusing to take commands from a peasant. He circled Rafi again, looking for a new place to damage.

Johanna leaped across the room, putting herself between the Punisher and his victim. “I. Said. Stop.” She wrapped her arms around Rafi’s torso, ignoring the sweat and bruises, and forming a human shield.

Voices were raised; the other men in the room and Lady DeSilva all called her back to her seat.

“Johanna.” Dom stood, looking between her and his brother. “He won’t thank you for your interruption.”

“I will not stand by and watch as he’s beaten senseless.” Rafi panted near her ear, each breath whistling with anguish. “Cut him down. Now.”

“No,” the lordling whispered. “Finish it.”

Johanna looked into his face, seeing the sweat that beaded his brow and the veins that had broken in his dark eyes. “You’re a fool. And I refuse to be responsible for the injuries of someone so mentally incapacitated.” She nodded to the knife sheathed at the Punisher’s belt. “Cut him down or I will stand here and block every blow you intend for Lord Rafael.”

Captain Alouette’s arms dropped limply to his sides and he looked between his liege lady and the strange, commanding girl.

“Alouette.” Lady DeSilva’s voice echoed in the stone room, a note of plea edging the sound.

Johanna wasn't sure if it was an appeal to continue or to quit.

The Punisher made the decision without a second thought. In one smooth move he raised his knife and sliced through the rope.

Rafi fell heavily into Johanna's arms, bearing them both to the cold stone floor. She grunted in pain as he crushed her bruised ribs.

"No," Rafi said, and raised one arm so the captain could help him back to his feet.

Captain Alouette shook his blond head, his mustache pulling down in a frown. "You owe her boy, twice over. Serve her and regain your honor."

Johanna could feel Rafi's heart pounding against the skin inside her elbow, and the heat from his fevered body seeped through her dress.

He made eye contact again, the fire in his gaze renewed. "I'd rather take double the Punishment than ever see you again."

Chapter 20

Leão

The five-day ride to Belem's estate was uneventful. Once they'd crossed out of the rugged terrain around Roraima and into the valley of Cruzamento, the landscape—rolling hills, prairie grass, the occasional vineyard or sheep herd—was beautiful in its relative monotony.

Leão was strangely disappointed. His mind had conjured images of a stark landscape, bereft of greenery and trees, as if it had been warped by the evil of the people of Santarem.

Jacaré tried to convince him that what they'd witnessed at the Citadel wasn't the norm, that he shouldn't base his opinion on a few wayward soldiers, but the girl's screams haunted his sleep.

He'd heard of such things happening, but he hadn't thought he'd ever witness them firsthand.

It wasn't that Olinda was completely crime free. He'd broken up fistfights and dragged a drunk or two to jail, but he'd spent the majority of his training patrolling the very quiet borders of the city and hunting predators that harassed their livestock. He remembered hearing about a murder a few years ago when some century-long feud had finally reached a head. The exact details were fuzzy in his mind, but he knew his grandmother had been involved in the trial of the killer. Eventually the murderer had been executed in a private ceremony.

He racked his mind for other examples of major crimes as he scouted ahead of the rest of his troop, but could only come up with two other situations. One Keeper was exiled for beating his own child and the other . . . was Tex.

The details of Tex's crime, whatever they were, had never been public knowledge. Besides Tex's ability with his mace, which was impressive for his advanced age, he never seemed particularly bloodthirsty or violent.

He was grouchy, that was for sure, but sleeping on the ground for days had that effect on Pira, too.

High Captain Jacaré seemed to trust Tex, and that was a pretty good testament.

Up ahead Leão saw dust, indicating mounted movement, and led his horse off the road. He left the animal cropping the long grass between two hills and crawled to the top so he could watch the road unseen.

A group of armed horsemen surrounded two ornate carriages and were trailed by a line of open-topped wagons. The guards wore a lightweight armor, polished to a high sheen and gilded with a clenched fist on the center of their chests.

Armor that's meant to be seen, not to be used, he realized with surprise. Still, they rode like men used to the saddle and watched the surrounding hills as if they expected something to attack them at any point. *Interesting.*

The two carriages were well built, with large wheels and springs to help keep their occupants from jostling around. Sheer material stretched over the windows, allowing a breeze in and a view out. It looked like a comfortable way to travel. The wagons, however, shook their passengers mercilessly.

Men and women were packed shoulder to shoulder, each wearing some sort of manacle around their necks. They kept their heads down and, unlike the soldiers, didn't speak.

As the wagons rolled past his position, he got a glimpse at the pasengers' blank-eyed faces. They seemed completely devoid of life, yet he could sense an odd energy pulsing around them.

Though Leão could command all five elements, he was particularly attuned to Spirit. It made him an excellent healer—the reason Jacaré gave for asking him to join their troop—and tracker because he could sense life before he could see it.

This energy was unlike anything he'd felt before. It left a residue on his skin like he'd fallen into stagnant water. He wanted to scrape away the remnant and hurry off.

Prisoners, he guessed. He imagined a list of heinous crimes he could attach to the group. *Murderers, rapists, thieves. They feel wrong because they've* done *wrong.*

"There's some sort of military group coming from the township," he explained once he'd rejoined the crew on the lee side of the hill. "They seem to be escorting someone of importance and transporting prisoners."

"Probably an underlord or landowner returning from a trip to the city," Jacaré said to Tex, who agreed.

Leão hesitated to say anything about the strange energy. Only another Keeper with a strong Spirit affinity would have felt it. Neither Pira nor Tex would have noticed it, and Leão wasn't sure what Jacaré's affinity was. It wasn't polite to pry into other Keepers strengths and weaknesses, so Leão let the feeling slide.

Maybe it has something to do with the people on this side of the wall. He nodded to himself and fell into position beside Pira. *Maybe it's something I'll get used to.*

Chapter 21

Pira

Pira didn't think she'd be grateful to see a Santarem city, but the outskirts of the Belem township were a welcome change to the blandness of the prairie. Inns, pubs, and shops had sprung up along the road with the irregularity of wildflowers in the spring, all clumped together around a central well.

A city also meant real food, something other than dried meat, dried fruit, and hard cheese.

"We should stop here," she said as they rode past one particular inn. Its windows were clean, the sign cheerfully painted, and the fragrance wafting through the door made her stomach grumble. "It smells good."

There was nothing magical about her senses, but she knew quality food when she smelled it.

None of the men offered an argument, and they dropped their horses and gear off at the stable before heading into the dining area.

Wet coastal air clung to every surface and coated every inch of bare skin with a dewy film. The wood sweated, the people sweated, and the glasses of chilled ale and cider puddled on the stone-topped bar. Just looking at the liquids made Pira's throat tighten with a desire for something besides the leather-flavored water in her canteen.

The serving girls, who'd been fluttering between tables with trays of bowls and cups, stopped where they stood and stared, their eyes lingering on Jacaré and Leão.

Pira didn't want to admit it, but she couldn't really blame the barmaids. Everything about Leão's appearance demanded notice.

She tried to remember that he was just a little boy—someone she'd helped train and who was younger by a couple of years—but the muscles across his chest and shoulders were anything but childish.

Blood rushed to her cheeks when she thought of the way the firelight had glinted off the hills and valleys of his abdomen the previous night. He'd scrubbed his shirt in the stream and walked around bare chested while he waited for it to dry. Luckily the stupid bit of silk tied around her head hid most of her face.

The closest barmaid pushed a damp strand of hair off her forehead and slinked over to them, her skirt swishing with exaggerated movements. Pira's fists tensed at her sides. She couldn't stand flirty girls, which was just one of the many reasons she had chosen a male-dominated profession.

"Welcome to the Mug and Mutton," the barmaid said to Jacaré with an inviting smile, and then directed another over his shoulder to Leão. "What's your pleasure?"

"Umm . . ." Leão stumbled, looking to Tex for help.

Had Pira chosen wrong? Had they come to the wrong type of inn? There weren't many pleasure houses in Olinda, but things were definitely different in Santarem.

Jacaré seemed equally surprised, turning to Tex for help.

"We need two rooms for the night, baths for four, and four plates of whatever you're serving," the older man said, with a smirk toward their *commanding* officer.

"Sure thing. That'll be ten bits up front, ten for each extra night you stay, and ten before you go." She wiped her hand on her apron and held it out to Jacaré, even though Tex was the one reaching for his purse. "I'm Miriam and I'll be happy to serve you tonight. Y'all can sit wherever you can find a spot."

Tex handled the cash, using what they'd taken from the soldiers' bodies in the Citadel until they could convert the coin they'd brought into local currency.

They chose a small corner table to wait for their stew. Pira sat rigid in the seat closest to the wall, wishing she could rip the damn headscarf free or that her hair would grow back for a few days. It wasn't out of vanity, of course. Pira didn't miss her blond locks all that much, but the silk was blasted hot.

Jacaré stretched his legs into the aisle and massaged a cramp out of his thigh. His eyes scanned the room's occupants, looking for threats. Tex lounged, angled toward the door, booted foot resting on the bottom of Leão's chair.

And Leão hunched with his elbows on the table, chin down, as if sensing the appraisal of every woman in the room. He wasn't far wrong. Every female between the ages of eight and eighty took a moment to covertly—or obviously—stare at his long, rangy frame and sharp-boned face.

Pira blocked his good looks from her mind and tried to focus on

Leão's other, negative traits. He was sheltered, inexperienced, and the grandson of the head of the Mage Council. All were good enough reasons to dislike him, but he'd won her begrudging respect with a dozen other abilities and a natural humility.

Miriam brought bowls of steaming soup and a couple loaves of dark brown bread. "If there's anything I can help you with . . . ," she said as she leaned across the table to pass Pira and Tex their food. She dragged her fingers across the back of Leão's chair. "And I do mean *anything*, please let me know."

Pira choked on her soup and Jacaré slapped her on the back a few times while she coughed.

"She may mean anything," Tex said as the barmaid walked away, "but all we need is a little information."

"I planned to scout around a bit after our meal." Jacaré dunked a piece of bread into the meaty broth, scented with garlic and onions. "The trees we're looking for are tall and tend to grow near a water source. I thought—"

"Why waste time looking when you can *ask*?" Tex nodded toward the bar. "Send Leão to ask one of those girls if they know of an araucaria grove nearby."

Leão put down his spoon, having finished the entire bowl. "Why me? Why not Jacaré?"

"They've already paired Pira and Jacaré in their minds, what with him sitting next to her," Tex explained.

Pira groaned and scooted her chair as far from her brother as possible, earning another laugh from Tex and a frown from Jacaré.

"Some of them may hesitate to speak with an attached man," Tex continued. "But any of them would sell their mother for a chance to talk to you, boy."

Leão's eyebrows disappeared into the white-blond fuzz of his hairline. "They sell their mothers on this side of the wall?"

"It's an expression," Pira explained with an eye roll. *And he's so gullible.* She wanted to be irritated but found him strangely endearing.

Leão darted a look at the group of girls, who stood close to each other, gossiping and glancing at their table. "What would I say?"

"I'd start with hello—"

"Tell them we're traders who use the pinecones for medicine—"

Pira cut both Tex and Jacaré off. "Swagger on up there, smile a bit, and say you're looking for the grove. They'll tell you what you want to know."

"Swagger," he mumbled, looking at Pira nervously. "Okay. I can do that." He wiped his mouth with his fingers and stood.

Leão held his head high and strode across the room with a lazy grace, leaned one hip against the bar, and tipped his head toward the nearest girl.

"*That's* his swagger?" Jacaré asked.

"No." Pira laughed. She hid a brilliant grin with her fist. "He's mimicking yours."

Chapter 22

Rafi

"I don't understand why you're taking this personally," Dom said, as they rode along the edge of the forest. The trees, thick with late summer foliage, blocked their view around the curves in the trail. "She didn't set out to wound your pride. It was bad timing and worse luck."

"I don't understand why you're constantly defending her." Rafi shifted in his saddle, trying to ignore the ache in his ribs. Even after two weeks, the bruises hadn't faded completely, and rides of any length made him miserable. "You said she was a singer and a Storyspinner. Are you sure she wasn't a hedgewitch who cast some charm over you?"

Dom laughed, startling a flock of black-capped tinamou into flight and sending Rafi's mood crashing even further. "She's just a girl, Rafi."

A girl who wouldn't accept any of the honor gifts Rafi had sent with his retainers. Not dresses, or silk, or bottles of excellent wine. Rafi had stormed into his mother's chambers the previous night after Johanna had sent back the latest basket of gifts—spools of lace imported from the Wisp Islands.

"Your honor isn't something you can bargain for, my son. Alouette said to serve her, and I agree," his mother had said. "You can't possibly determine what service she needs unless you get to know her."

Rafi didn't have time to worry about a lingering debt of honor when he had dozens of other tasks that required a future duke's attention. In a few weeks he could no longer rely on his mother for the responsibilities he was unable to address. Santiago, its township, the underlords, and merchants would be his sole duty on his eighteenth naming day, and he refused to let anything slip.

Even riding to meet with the Performer girl served dual purposes. He and Dom took the forest route to the back side of Milner's Orchard so they could check for any poachers' traps along the way.

"I think they're living in the next clearing." Dom pointed to a column of smoke rising above the trees.

Rafi racked his memory for a cabin so deep on the Milners' property but couldn't recall anything, and he knew the orchard as well as anyone. The smell of too-ripe fruit mingled with that of the knee-high grass, reminding him of sneaking away from his nurse to play among the reaching branches. He urged Breaker forward, and the horse picked up its pace through the last few rows of mango trees.

Bright flashes of color, wrong for late-season fruit, appeared between the branches. A red door, a yellow wall: the Von Arlos had painted their cabin like a—

"Wagon? They're still living in Performers' wagons?" he questioned Dom over his shoulder.

"Why wouldn't they be?"

Two tiny houses on wheels, perhaps five feet by ten, were parked near a fire pit. They each had domed roofs, narrow doors, and small two-paned windows on either side. Large rocks had been wedged under the wheels to stop them from rolling.

"Maybe I should offer her a house," Rafi said, thinking aloud.

"I don't think she'd accept that, either."

"Can you imagine living in such close quarters?"

Dom nodded to the people entering the clearing from the other side. "I doubt they spend much time inside."

Rafi blinked and looked again. Three people were coming through the trees, but they were walking on their *hands*.

A pair of long legs with toes pointed skyward led two smaller bodies toward the fire pit, moving easily across the root-ridden land. Some command was given, and they all began spinning with tiny prancing movements, lifting their hands high off the ground.

"Good! Now kick down and I'll show you your next combination."

It was Johanna's voice. Rafi watched as she continued her twirling, split her legs, and threw herself into a series of somersaults.

"Whoa," Dom breathed, and his horse stopped.

Johanna gave some instruction, and the taller of the two boys completed the same flips. The smaller hesitated, and she knelt close, offering encouragement.

The little boy—about seven years old—reached high above his head and tossed himself backward, stumbling slightly forward on the landing.

Rafi refused to be impressed. "Hello, Von Arlo family," he shouted as he stepped out from between the trees.

Johanna straightened at the sound of his voice and stepped in front of the boys. Her body was rigid, her hands in loose fists, her cheeks pink. "Oh, it's you," she said, but didn't relax. "Don't worry about him. Let's go inside and hope he'll go away."

The boys didn't immediately obey. The older one—whippet thin with a halo of blond hair—gave Rafi the stink eye. Johanna snapped her fingers, and her brothers hurried to the wagon's stairs.

"What about me?" Dom said as his horse tromped through the trees. He dropped off the saddle and looped his reins over a branch, not stopping to knot them.

Her face brightened. "Welcome to the clearing, Lord Dom. To what do I owe the pleasure of *your* visit?"

"I'm here to help my brother settle some business."

Johanna brushed off her dirty hands and filleted Rafi with her eyes. "You don't have anything that I want. I'm sure you can find your way home."

"You can't evict me from my own land."

"I could have sworn I was on the Milners' property." She kicked a wrinkled mango into the air; it fell into her outstretched hand. "Forgive me if I was wrong, my lord."

Rafi had never raised a hand against a woman—except by accident—but his fingers itched to slap the smug grin off her face. "The Milners have sworn their allegiance to the DeSilvas for generations. This property may not be mine, but—"

"Good enough for me. Good-bye." She turned toward the wagons, arms spread, ushering her brothers inside.

Rafi grabbed her wrist, intending to stop her, but she whirled toward him, trapping his arm under her own. Cold steel pricked his throat.

"Don't *ever* touch me again," she said with a growl.

He swallowed; the knife scraped his skin. *She wouldn't . . . she couldn't possibly.* He studied her narrowed eyes and saw cool certainty in their depths. This wisp of a girl, whose bones he could feel through her clothes, would slit his throat and not think twice.

Slow applause and a shrill whistle disrupted the moment. "That was incredible, Johanna!" Dom stepped closer. "I didn't even see you draw your knife. Where was it hidden? Show me how it was done."

She held Rafi's gaze for one long moment before releasing his arm and backing away. With a flourish she spun the knife and it disappeared.

"You know I can't share Performer secrets." Her lips quirked, a challenge in her smile, then she turned to his brother.

"But you're not a Performer anymore." Dom nearly pouted. "Please?"

Rafi felt rooted to the ground, like one of the age-old trees around him, as he watched the interplay between his brother and the girl. Dom walked backward, blocking her path to the wagon, but instead of threatening or pulling weapons, she laughed at his antics.

"I'm still honor bound to the Performers."

"Please," Dom pleaded, hands clasped under his chin. "Puh-lease!"

"You're as bad as my brothers." She hesitated, checking over her shoulder and eyeing Rafi in the distance. "I can show you the moves the street toughs use in the big cities, but no more than that."

Dom cheered and drew his belt dagger. Rafi cringed, expecting to see his brother disarmed and then disemboweled, but the girl simply took it out of his hand and weighed it in her own.

"This is a bit too long, and the cross guard is too heavy for trick work. You can use mine."

Rafi checked the knife at his own belt, a twin to his brother's. They had been the last gifts their father had given them before he died. The daggers were unadorned, but well made, and the length of the blade was perfectly balanced against the width of the cross guard. He knew it was ridiculous to feel affronted, but it seemed this girl could never simply accept what a DeSilva offered.

She demonstrated tossing the dagger from hand to hand, adding a little twist so that it landed blade-first in her palm. "It gives you a chance to dazzle your attacker. It also gives you the option to throw the blade if you don't want to draw them in close."

"Dom," Rafi huffed as he moved closer to the pair. "We don't have time for lessons in trickery. I've got other duties to attend to."

His brother flipped Johanna's dagger. It fell between his hands and stuck in the ground near his foot. "I thought part of your duties was to solve that pesky little honor issue."

"I've been trying to solve it for weeks, but she won't accept my gifts."

"Maybe that's because she doesn't want gifts," Dom said, trying the toss again and catching it successfully.

"Maybe *she* doesn't want anything." Johanna took the dagger from Dom's hand and flipped it up her sleeve. "Except to be left alone."

She hurried toward the wagon, but Rafi blocked her path just as Dom had done. She bristled like an angry cat.

"I'm not trying to harm you, but I can't have this debt hanging over me any longer." Up close he could see that the paint on the wagons was peeling, and the nearest window was cracked. "You're obviously in need of some basic commodities that I'm willing to provide."

Her eyes narrowed with anger. *"Basic commodities?"*

"Well, yes." Rafi eyed her fitted breeches and the black vest she'd laced over a cotton tunic. "You have needs, and I think I can take care of them."

The girl seemed to grow before his eyes, straightening her spine, raising her chin. Surely she was still the tiny creature he could toss over his shoulder, but she used some Performer trick that made her seem to fill the space between them.

"I have exactly what I need—"

"My brother means to say that he'd like to offer you a job," Dom said. Both Rafi and Johanna looked at him like he was a fable creature who'd appeared out of thin air.

Dom wielded his smile like a broadsword, using it and a few well-placed jokes to batter even his toughest opponents into submission. He turned it on Johanna then.

"Over the next few weeks we'll be entertaining several of the ducal houses, groups of merchants, some of the local guild people, and we could use someone of your veritable storytelling skill." Dom took Johanna's hands. "My father passed before he was able to arrange for troupe visits this fall and winter. Our guests will be bored senseless with Rafi for conversation and our woods too depleted for any hunting expeditions."

Bored senseless? Thanks for your vote of confidence, brother.

"We thought that you'd be willing to perform, for pay of course, until we can arrange to have a troupe come to the estate?"

It wasn't a bad idea—one Rafi wished Dom had proposed to him *before* they had come to the clearing—but it didn't fulfill the honor debt.

"Say you'll consider it." Dom gave her the grin that had all their maids swooning.

"She'll do it." A voice said from between the wagons. A diminutive woman, at least a half a head shorter than Johanna, strode into the clearing. She pushed her hood back, releasing a bounty of ash-blond curls liberally streaked with gray. "The Keepers know we could use the coin."

Johanna seemed to shrink as the new arrival joined their group. "Mama, meet Lord Rafael and his brother, Dominic. This is my mother, Marin."

Chapter 23

Johanna

"The Keepers are smiling on us," Marin said after the lordlings left the orchard. She folded the contract and tucked it into a slim metal box that fit neatly into the wagon's wall. "This is an excellent retaining fee for an apprentice-level singer and Storyspinner."

Johanna plopped onto a thigh-high pallet that functioned as her bed. Moments before it had been upside down, serving as a desk. Rafi had leaned over the smooth wooden surface, his lips moving as he reviewed the stipulations of the contract, and standing so close to Johanna's mother that he'd certainly been able to smell the liquor rolling off her skin.

Or perhaps he hadn't noticed, assuming it was some sort of odd perfume. Marin could fool anyone if she stopped after a few drinks; her hands were steady, her eyes bright; she spoke without slurring her words. Johanna wondered if it had something to do with her mother's years in front of an audience. Marin could slip on a sober face and play that role when necessary. She'd acted the part of master negotiator, bargaining for her daughter's performances and drafting a contract for Rafi to sign.

Johanna tugged down the netting that held the linens onto the bed and freed a blanket, tucking it over her bare feet.

"Don't pout, *cara*." Marin stroked Johanna's cheek with fingers as cold as a winter stream. "I'm so proud of you. Your father would be too."

"Can't you go instead?" Johanna didn't doubt her skill or her ability to provide quality entertainment, but she also didn't want to admit that Lord Rafael unsettled her. It wasn't fear, exactly. She knew he wouldn't physically harm her, but there was something in the way that he looked at her that made her feel . . . less. "You're so much better than I am. At everything."

"Johanna," her mother snapped, eyebrows drawn tight. "Stop this. You know I can't possibly take on an assignment if we have any hope of ever rejoining the Performers as a family."

Each of Arlo and Marin's children would be welcomed into Performers' Camp once they reached their naming days—Thomas was eighteen now and could return at any time—but Marin could only accept assignments approved by the Council. The Council guaranteed that each troupe adhered to a set of standards, moderated any disputes, and ruled on any Performer violations. If Marin or Thomas performed without the Council's approval, they would be banned from Performers' Camp for life, but Johanna was under age. Any performing she did in the next two years wouldn't count against her.

It was a harsh rule for those expelled like the Von Arlos, who had no other means of income, but it protected the community as a whole.

"This could open up so many opportunities for us." Marin reached into the cupboard above her bed and drew out a bottle of brandy and a small glass. She filled it to the brim and choked the liquid down in one gulp.

Johanna turned away so she didn't have to watch as the liquor burned its way through her mother's body, relaxing the tense muscles of her face and neck. Before Arlo died, Marin only drank the caramel-colored liquid for special occasions and celebrations.

Johanna didn't feel like celebrating, but that didn't stop her mother from drinking.

"Wipe that look off your face," Marin's voice snapped. "The DeSilvas are fantastic nobles to perform for. They treat us well—like equals instead of employees."

Unless, of course, they think you are poaching in their woods. Johanna kept that thought to herself, not wanting to see her mother's mood swing from mellow to livid. When Marin was really drunk—and swigging her fourth glass meant she was well on her way—she could only manage those two extremes.

"You were saying something about opportunities." Johanna fiddled with a fraying end of the quilt, pulling at loose threads till it started to unravel the entire hem. "You really think any of the visitors will be interested in hiring me?"

"They'll take one look at you and know your worth," Marin promised, her bright smile at odds with her glazed eyes. "They'll look at you and see *magic*."

Chapter 24

Jacaré

The wall around Belem's estate was only chest high. It would stop a horse and slow down a man, but it wasn't much defense against anyone determined to cross onto the duke's lands.

Two teams of guards and their dogs, however, were more of a deterrent, as was the moon that hung low and fat over the ocean.

The araucaria trees had become even scarcer in the three hundred years since the Keepers had crossed the wall. Only a few hundred trees still existed in small clumps across Santarem's five states.

"She said there was a grove, no more than twenty trees, close to Belem's manor." Leão pointed almost due south. "Duke Belem invites the townsfolk onto the estate for celebrations."

"How do they celebrate?" Pira asked, as she sank down next to the stacked stones of the wall. The shadows and a few scrubby brushes blocked them from view.

He shrugged. "They have some sort of performances. She didn't give specifics and I wasn't about to ask."

Tex and Jacaré exchanged a nod.

Leão had to spend ten minutes flirting—more like fending off the barmaid and her friends' advances—before he'd been able to ask the question. He returned to the table a little red faced, but with the information they needed.

"All right," Jacaré said, squatting beside his sister. "There's very little cover between the wall and the gardens. We'll wait for a break between the guards' rounds, and Leão and I will make a run for it."

"And Tex and I will, what, sit here and wait?" Pira asked, her voice rising a bit.

Jacaré bit his tongue to stop from reprimanding her on the spot. Not only was it an inopportune time, but she didn't respond well to public confrontation. "Yes. Hopefully that's all you have to do. If something happens, you can cause a diversion."

"Any suggestions?" Pira asked, sounding irritated.

"I'm sure Tex has a few ideas."

The old soldier snapped his fingers, sending sparks skyward. "Plenty."

Jacaré faced Leão. "Anything goes amiss, give us three trills of the red sparrow and we'll meet back at the inn."

They all nodded. Pira resumed her position at the wall, feet wedged between the moss-covered stone, just high enough to peek over the edge. She held out three fingers, slowly counted down to two, one. Closed fist.

Jacaré and Leão vaulted over the top in one smooth motion and dropped to the ground on the opposite side.

They sprinted across the open space, the grass barely disturbed by the speed of their passing.

A second, knee-high wall separated the gardens from the rest of the property; they hurdled it in stride and rolled into some bushes with tall feathery fronds. The ground had been divided from the stone pathway by a short filigreed fence and decorative shrubs.

The wind picked up, mixing the scent of the ocean with the night-blooming honeysuckle that draped over trellises and wound up the trunks of trees. The rushing waves masked the sounds of any approaching guards or animals.

They crept along a spiky hedge, moving away from the hulking manor house and toward a group of trees that swayed above the hammered-copper roof.

Voices rose from one vine-covered alcove, sounding a bit like a drunken brawl. Jacaré's senses hummed on the tense string of discovery, but no one came stumbling toward them.

The path turned from stone to gravel as they came closer to the coast. Jacaré cringed with every step. He wasn't terribly worried about overtaking the guards—they didn't seem particularly disciplined—but he preferred to go undiscovered.

The pathway widened into an open area filled with white silk tents, the bottom edges rolled up to admit the cool breeze from the sea. Candles burned in some, creating silhouettes of sleeping pallets, desks, and dining tables, while figures moved around in a strange dance of shadows, and voices murmured over the sound of the waves. All of it sat under the naked trunks of the araucaria and their crowns of pine fronds.

Leão tapped Jacaré's arm and pointed to the edge of the clearing. A large rectangle of wooden beams had been half buried into the rocky ground, with a few circular platforms interspersed over the distance.

Jacaré had sixteen years of images from the glass—some moving like he was peeking through a window and others frozen like a painting—to fill in the blanks in the girl's life. He had watched her train along with a family of entertainers, learning tricks and flips and stunts that seemed highly unsuitable for a girl of her value.

Of course he couldn't really pass judgment, as he dragged the future ruler of his people into a potentially hostile country.

They crouched behind the largest platform, putting the structures between themselves and the tents.

"What exactly are we looking for?" Leão whispered.

"An explanation." He looked toward the tree at the edge of the ring and gauged the space between it and the farthest platform. "This is where the guardian died."

Leão tapped his ear and pointed over Jacaré's shoulder.

Jacaré heard the near-silent tread of someone who knew how to move lightly on their feet. He slid a dagger out of his belt and duckwalked across the gravel, keeping his head below the platform's surface.

The footsteps came closer, but there was something off in the sound. The footfalls were too close together, like the person was taking very small steps.

Drunk, injured, or . . . Jacaré snuck a quick peek.

A child.

A small thing, perhaps four or five years old, skulked toward the ocean. Its blond hair, a circle around the child's head, swished as he—*yes, I think it's a boy*—cast furtive glances back the way he'd come.

"Paulo?" A woman's voice called in the distance.

The boy broke into a run, darting past Jacaré's position and straight to the water. He stripped off his shirt, tossing it onto one of the boulders that littered the coast, and bounded into the spray.

The tide rolled in, washing against his knees, his thighs, and then his chest. He laughed and whooped, holding his arms above his head in victory.

"Paulo, where are you?" the voice called again, sounding a little more frantic. "Come back. This isn't funny."

Leão nudged Jacaré hard in the ribs, then held up both hands, palms up.

"The tree has metal bars screwed into the trunk, like steps. I think it served as a launching-off point for a tightrope walker," Jacaré whispered. "From that vantage, see if you can come up with any reason he would have fallen. I'll keep watch."

The young Keeper disappeared into the shadow under the tree, and the child in the water continued to play.

The woman called for the boy again, but sounded a bit more distant. Only a few more minutes would pass before she recruited people to search for her son.

The water continued to rise, the waves slapping the rocky sand with a consistent rhythm, creeping farther and farther up the coast. The boy noticed none of it.

Get out of the water and go to your mother.

Jacaré watched the little blond head, the joyful face that reflected the moon's light, and his stomach wrenched.

A wave splashed the boy in the eyes. The next crested over his head and he laughed, enjoying the cool water on the humid night.

Jacaré wished he could enjoy the ocean with the same carefree attitude, but the horrible feeling in his stomach clawed its way up his throat, lugging a bit of dread with it.

Come in, Paulo. He sent his thoughts toward the boy, hoping they'd carry on the water.

The boy took a few steps toward the coast, dragging his hands behind him and waving them from side to side, the water perhaps hip deep.

Another wave crashed and Jacaré saw a hulking shadow, three triangular fins silhouetted against the moon's pockmarked surface.

Paulo spun in a circle, splashing as he went. Another surge and the shadow was nearly on top of him.

And the red sparrow trilled, once, twice, three times. Men were coming, likely looking for the boy, but they wouldn't make it in time.

Jacaré wasn't even sure he would.

Ignoring Leão's warning, ignoring the vibrating fear that filled his chest, Jacaré ran into the sea. He saw the beast lift its arrow-shaped head from the water, its maw gaping, teeth glistening like bone daggers.

With a snap it grabbed the boy's arm. His shrill scream rent the night air, then cut off as water filled his mouth. The beast slithered backward on its short fins, dragging the child along. Paulo managed to surface once more, gasping for breath.

The dark water turned darker still, blood pouring from wicked wounds, flesh shredded away.

Jacaré's knife sliced through the beast's neck. Its jaw worked convulsively, crunching bone, but if the boy screamed again, no one could hear it while his head remained under water.

The monster was huge, twice the size of a man and three times the weight, and its skin grated against Jacaré's with a thousand coarse bristles. He pushed the knife in deeper, feeling it strike bone. The mouth opened, releasing the crushed remnant of the boy's arm.

The animal slammed into Jacaré's legs, shoving him back several feet, but didn't follow with another attack.

Jacaré didn't wait for the beast to lick its wounds. He gathered the lifeless boy into his arms and hustled to a boulder a few feet out of the water.

Lanterns bobbed among the platforms, many voices and the barks of a dog joined the mother's frantic shouts, but the wounds were awful. If not for the faint flutter of the boys' pulse under his fingers, Jacaré would've given up, leaving the little body where it lay.

With a deep breath, Jacaré closed his eyes and reached for his *essência*. It had been a long, long time since Jacaré had performed such a major healing, and the effort hurt like torn muscles being forced into use.

In his mind's eye, he saw the boy's tattered flesh knit together, the veins and arteries reconnect. The blood flow eased, but didn't stop completely because Jacaré lacked the power to complete it as a strong healer would have.

"Paulo!" The woman screamed as she picked up the boy's discarded shirt, wading into the ocean. A few men dressed in armor sprinted closer, led by a thin dog.

The boy's eyes fluttered open, his little forehead wrinkled with confusion but not fear. Jacaré held a finger to his lips and slipped beyond the boulders and into the shadows. His arms shook as he hauled himself up the rungs of the tree's trunk, but he made it to the top before he heard a tiny voice.

"Mother?"

"Paulo!" She sprinted across the sand, tripping on her wet skirts. She gasped, seeing the blood that drenched the boy's pale torso. Her fingers traced over his body. "Where are you hurt?"

"My arm *was* hurt."

"What?"

The guards circled around, relief evident in their posture, lifting their lights high to study the boy.

"I got eaten by a *tubarão*." He touched the spot where the healing wound glowed livid under the lanterns' glow. "But a man saved me. He stuck my arm back on."

The mother pulled her child close, studying his eyes, his pale face, and the remnants of the injury. "But . . ."

One of the guards dropped to his knees; his light swung from his outstretched arm. "Thank the Keepers. It's a miracle."

Right there, around a boulder, three adults offered prayers of thanksgiving.

And for the first time in three hundred years, Keepers listened.

A steadying hand touched Jacaré's shoulder, and he peered farther into the darkness, where Leão had lodged himself between two branches. The young soldier passed something small and cylindrical to his commander.

Jacaré clutched his fist around the object and knew, without question, what had happened to the girl's guardian.

Chapter 25

Rafi

Death over dishonor. The family motto had been pounded into Rafi's brain since he was a child. His name and that phrase had been the first things he learned to write. Now it was working its way into his skull.

The family crest—a two-headed hawk with a sword in one claw and a candle in the other—had been cast in bronze and attached to the high back of his father's audience chair. The elder duke had been several inches shorter than his son, so the emblem showed over his head. Rafi had to bend his neck forward to keep the hawk's sword from drawing blood. It was a miserable way to sit, giving the impression of a childish duke too inexperienced to fill the seat of power.

"The pilin's for the dock are near rotted through. The whole thin' will come crashin' down one day soon. The catches have been poorer this season than any I've ever seen. We canna'ford to lose more product and men with it," Guildmaster Tolapia explained around the unlit pipe trapped between his teeth. He was a grizzled old fisherman, with bushy eyebrows and scarred hands. Three gold fishhooks pierced his left ear, identifying him as the chief of his guild. He sat with one foot rested over the other knee, looking incredibly relaxed.

"I understand that, Master Tolapia." Rafi nodded, trying to discreetly free a lock of hair that had wound its way into the hawk's feathers. "We can send someone to Impreza to purchase the wood we'll need."

"But the wood from Maringa—"

"We don't purchase from Maringa."

"Impreza's wood isn't as stron' and we'll have to replace it twice as often." The man freed his pipe and tapped it against his palm for emphasis. "It'll cost more in the lon' run."

"We don't trade for Lord Inimigo's products, no matter how high the quality."

The Guildmaster tugged at one of his earhooks. "Lord Rafael, I mean no disrespect. But your father's grudge against Inimigo . . . Don't you think it's time to let it go?"

"Would you have asked my father the same question?"

The color flooding the man's face was enough of an answer.

"Inimigo's troops slaughtered our king. They killed every man, woman, and child who lived in Wilhelm's Citadel and Roraima Township. Wilhelm was my father's best friend. His infant daughter was to be my betrothed. Inimigo hung their bodies over the stone walls and left them for the birds, then waged a war on this land that lasted *ten* years." Rafi was far from finished. "Tell me you didn't lose a friend, a brother, or a cousin in the battles?"

"Two younger brothers." The Guildmaster didn't meet Rafi's eyes.

"And you're ready to give Inimigo forgiveness?"

The man's pipe beat out a steady rhythm on the tabletop, bits of leaf floated on the air, filling the room with its sickly sweet aroma. "Forgiveness? Not so much," said the Guildmaster after a long consideration. "Peace and forgiveness are far distant things. You *can* have one without the other."

"We've had nearly seven years of peace, Master Tolapia. I don't imagine where we buy wood will change that."

"You're young yet, and I respect that you want to honor your father's memory and wishes, but I'd buy from my enemy if it meant my sons never had to see war." Done dispensing his wisdom, the fisherman rose from the table and offered the lord a respectful nod. The steward, Mortimer, showed him out.

Rafi rubbed his eyes, trying to remove the exhaustion that had settled under his lids like grains of sand. He'd been staring at piles of documents all day between meetings with Guildmasters, merchants, and the five underlords who'd ridden in from each of Santiago's country manors.

And he hadn't slept well, his thoughts plagued by the Performer girl with her knife tight against his throat and her breath soft on his cheek.

"May I get you something, sir?" Mortimer asked, chafing his thin hands together. "Perhaps a late lunch, or I can have your page prepare a bath so you'll be fresh for dinner with our guests?"

"I have a few more things left to address before I can finish for the evening." Rafi shuffled a handful of papers, attempting to ignore the envelope at the bottom.

"If you insist, my lord."

Rafi tried to read a report on the state of the city's sewage system, but the lines and curls of Mortimer's spidery handwriting began to crawl together.

He stepped away from the table and watched the men in the practice yard. Dom was locked hilt-to-hilt with the weaponsmaster, Raul. The younger DeSilva had good speed and agility, but he lacked patience and finesse, often dropping his guard as soon as he saw an opening. Raul feinted, Dom took the bait, and the match was over.

On the field, Rafi was rarely defeated. His moves were meticulous, his foot placement precise, but he couldn't say the same for his statecraft. He always seemed to be stepping into political muck and struggling to get himself out.

He ran a hand through his hair, loosening the knots that had formed, then returned to his chair and dug out the letter.

CHAPTER 26

JOHANNA

Servants dressed in blue-and-silver livery bustled around the dining hall. The tables had been draped in matching linens, and leaves and eucalyptus branches were woven around the gilded candelabras. It lent the cavernous room a festive air and covered the scent of the freshly mopped stone floor.

Johanna had come early to test the room's acoustics and to pace the distance in front of the raised head table and the lower tables to determine how much space she'd have to perform in.

The roof of the dining hall featured two large windows; the glass had been stained a rose color and cut into a simple pattern of repeating diamonds. She stepped into the space between the windows' light, fidgeting with the silk-covered buttons on her bodice, and took a few deep breaths.

Johanna had sung and spun stories for large audiences since she was a small child and had never been plagued by stage fright. But as she stood in the DeSilvas' dining hall, her stomach knotted like a drying line in the wind. Unwilling to lay her nerves at Lord Rafael's feet, she closed her eyes, imagined the tables full of an adoring crowd, and began to sing. Her voice filled the room with the sound. Johanna hadn't inherited her mother's range, but each note was clear and rich.

Johanna gave the simple lovers' lament her best effort. She wrung emotion out of the lyrics, hoping to lead her audience through the range of anguish, betrayal, loss, anger, and finally vengeance.

As she reached the last stanza, she opened her eyes and cut off with a squeak. The entire staff had frozen in their places, hands hanging idle as they listened.

"From the looks on all your faces, I assume I sounded awful?" Johanna offered them a nervous grin.

"Oh no, miss!" Brynn's round cheeks were slightly pink, her pixie face alight with pleasure. "Please don't mind us. We'll get back to work and let you get back to singing."

"Would you like me to sing something less woeful?" Johanna launched into an upbeat pub tune. The words were a little inappropriate for most of her performances, but the serving staff enjoyed it, tapping toes and bobbing heads to the rhythm.

Drink up, my boy! Lift up your cup!
Tell the bartender to keep it filled up.
Blow off the foam. Take a big sip.
Find a nice girl with cherry-red lips!
Dance a few steps. Kick up your heels.
Gulp down your beer and like how it feels!
Oh-la-la. Oh-la-la. Oh-la-la. Eh!

"Promise you'll sing that tonight," a voice said from behind Johanna. "I can't wait to see my brother's face."

"Lord Dom," Johanna said with a dramatically deep curtsy. Might as well practice before she actually had to use it. Her dress was tight through the chest and hips, flaring at her thighs. It gave her enough room to move, while still flattering her wasplike waist. "I'm not certain your guests would appreciate that type of music."

"Sure they would." He offered his brightest grin. "The visiting duke and the underlords go slumming all the time. I've heard that when Belem is in his cups, he's been known to kick up *his* heels and dance a step or two."

"And what about you?" Johanna raised an eyebrow at him. "How do you act when you go slumming?"

He gasped, pressing a hand to his heart as if she'd wounded him. "I'll have you know, I never go *slumming*."

"Well, of course not," Johanna quickly amended, surprised at his affront. "Certainly someone like you—"

"Never has a free moment with a mother and brother like mine." A smile curled the corner of his mouth. "But if you can think of a way to sneak me out, I'd love to go slumming with you."

"I'll think on it." She didn't mention that she had a mother and older brother who kept her far from the pubs and inns, fairly trapping her at their wagon.

"Although," Dom said, his face suddenly serious. "We couldn't really call it slumming. I bring the quality of everyone up a few notches."

Johanna laughed and caught a glimpse of Brynn's grim face as she added scented oil to the lanterns bracketed around the room. The maid kept peeking at Dom when she thought he wasn't looking.

Oh dear. I believe I've made someone a bit jealous.

Chapter 27

Jacaré

"They pray to us," Leão said, his voice laced with awe and revulsion. He sat on the inn's floor next to the bedroom door, his knees tucked to his chest, looking every bit the confused seventeen-year-old he was. "Why?"

Jacaré leaned against the headboard, sinking into the pillow. Healing the boy after the *tubarão* attack had drained his *essência.* His head pounded and his chest ached, as if he'd taken a beating. What he'd done was dangerous for someone who lacked the power of a full Mage.

"I think we should worry less about this convoluted religion, and more about what *this* means." Pira held up the metal cylinder no longer than her thumb. It was light in both color and weight and tapered to a needle-sharp point at one end. "You found it stuck in the branches?"

"But they *slaughtered* us." Leão wasn't about to be dissuaded. "How could they go from hating us to worshipping us? Can so much change in three hundred years?"

Tex took the cylinder out of Pira's hands. "There are two scratches on the shaft, and it's poison-tipped. It's got a tangy scent, like nightshade."

"Someone wanted the guardian dead." Pira sat on the floor between Tex's chair and the bed, the top of her fuzzy head—free of its scarf—in Jacaré's line of sight. "This was murder, not an accident."

"Yes, but the motive may be completely unrelated to the heir," Tex said, poking the nearby washstand with the dart's tip. The lightweight metal scratched the wood, leaving a pale line on the dark surface. "The guardian could have made enemies along the way."

"We're not going to talk about this?" Leão interrupted again. "It doesn't bother any of you that these people *pray* to us?"

Jacaré rubbed his eyes with a finger and thumb. The chatter made his headache worse, and to be on the road at sunrise he needed to get some rest. "Everyone listen up." All heads turned toward their commander. "Leão, make a list of questions. Tex and I will answer them tomorrow."

Leão's mouth opened, but he knew better than to disobey his commanding officer.

"Pira, can you determine where that metal was mined or who it was made by? That may give us a clue as to who wanted the guardian dead."

At least I hope it will.

"Definitely." She held the dart in the lantern's light, looking for a maker's mark.

"Leão, go down to the common room. See if you can use your connection with the barmaid to find out what happened at Belem's estate. She may know the name of the guardian and where his family has gone."

Leão gave a resigned sigh, and rubbed a hand over the blond stubble on his head.

"If she doesn't have the answers, ask her where we might get a map," Jacaré continued.

Tex rocked onto his chair's back legs, balancing it effortlessly. "We don't need a map. I've got one in my head."

"Things change in three hundred years. The major roads will probably still be intact and mountains will be the same, but new towns will have been built, some abandoned, or their names changed."

"So you're going to doubt my skills now? Even after I've brought you this far?"

"I'm not doubting you. I want a map so we can update what you already know," Jacaré snapped, his patience growing thin. "Get to work. I want you ready to ride at sunrise."

They all rose without a backward glance or murmur.

"Not you, Tex." Jacaré called back the older man before he could leave. "Sit down."

"Jacaré, whatever it is can wait till morning. You're as pale now as you were the day we first crossed the wall, but then you were bleeding from a dozen wounds."

"I don't need the reminder." Jacaré dammed the rising tide of memories, refusing to let them wash over him. "Now sit down. I have three things to say, and you'll sit in that chair and hear them all."

He'd never spoken to Tex with disrespect, always overly concerned with impressing his mentor, but he was too tired to moderate his tone.

Tex sighed and dropped into a chair that creaked under his weight.

"First, stop questioning my orders. Pira has a hard enough time following my commands without your example."

"I didn't agree to be your subordinate." Tex didn't raise his voice, but his tone was lined with iron. "I agreed to come as a consultant and a friend."

"Stop questioning my orders. At least in front of them." Jacaré tried to wipe away the spiderwebs that spun across his vision. "If you have a problem with something I do or say, you can approach me privately."

Tex considered for a minute. "I'll try."

Jacaré knew it wasn't in the white-haired Keeper's nature to be second in command to anyone. Tex had demanded autonomy from the Mage Council, leading the Keepers' military during the Mage War and guarding their people as they crossed the wall. Once over the wall, he challenged the Council on every decision, from the fortifications of their new settlement to the traditional colors of the Elite Squad's uniforms. Eventually they forced him into retirement, hoping his successor would be more biddable.

Jacaré had been a disappointment.

"Next, we have to assume that whoever killed the girl's guardian either knows her identity or at least that he smuggled the child to safety."

"We don't know that. He could have been a gambler or a cheat—"

"Not the guardian. Surely I don't have all the information, but every image on that glass showed him as a well-loved and trusted man." Jacaré remembered a few moments from early in the girl's life, where she looked at her adoptive father with sheer adoration. He'd seen the same expression on the guardian's wife, friends, and other children.

"All right," Tex said with a nod, and rocked back in the chair again. "I'll defer to your character judgment."

Jacaré's temper flared, but he managed to hold it in check. He was too exhausted to do anything about it anyway. "We will operate under the assumption that the heir is in danger. She's been away from Donovan's Wall for too long, and we need to return her to her rightful home if we intend to keep the spell on the wall intact."

"It's falling, isn't it?"

With a deep sigh, Jacaré nodded. "The balance of power is shifting every day, and it's having side effects the Mage Council never anticipated."

"Are you talking about those nasty little snakes in Roraima?"

"It's more than that. Tonight with the *tubarão* attack, the lack of predators in the mountains, and . . ." He paused, trying to put his thoughts into words. "The city of Roraima has been abandoned for sixteen years, yet it wasn't overrun with weeds and saplings. The land is sick. It's not recovering from the destruction."

"Have you thought about the implications of what you're saying?" Tex waved in the general direction of Roraima. "What, exactly, are we restoring her to? Do you honestly think the four of us can give her back her kingdom?"

"Of course not, Texugo." Jacaré sat up straight. "We don't have to return her to the throne, just to the proximity of the wall, before whatever is infecting Roraima has a chance to spread to the rest of Santarem."

The chair legs thumped to the floor. "You'll return her to a wasteland? What will you do to keep her there? And her children and her children's children?"

"I don't know yet," Jacaré's voice crackled with frustration. "Why don't you tell me what I should do?"

"This is your mission."

"I'm tired of coming up with the answers."

Tex smirked. "Welcome to the world of command."

Jacaré closed his eyes again and rested against the pillows. "I only care about keeping the barrier standing."

"I know." Tex ran a hand over his face, looking drained. "Do you remember the day it was cast?"

Jacaré nodded slowly, allowing the memory to float to the surface of his mind. "It's something I'll never forget. This new generation . . . if they knew that the people of Santarem worship us . . ."

"It would be the Mage Wars all over again," Tex finished for him.

The silence between them stretched, only punctuated by the tread of feet in the hallway and the slamming of a door. Both men were lost in blood-soaked memories, remembering the crumpled bodies of the innocent, sacrificed in a war over pride and power.

Tex cleared his throat. "What was the third thing?"

"When Leão approaches us with questions, I'm going to tell him the truth. He needs to know the history as we remember it, not the history the Council has sanitized."

A slight smile crinkled Tex's lips. "Finally. A decision I agree with wholeheartedly."

Chapter 28

Rafi

The cream-colored paper had a grease stain from the sealing wax. It was an odd thing for Rafi to notice, but his mother had been holding the letter for ages, reading and rereading the words as if trying to decipher some foreign language.

"Do you have any advice for me, Mother?"

Her face had gone bloodless, her lips as gray as the widow's gown she'd donned for the dinner party. The paper crumpled under her fingers, seams appearing across the carefully scripted words. She mashed the letter with a violence Rafi never imagined from his mother. Then she rose, walked calmly across the room, and tossed the paper into the fire. "What I'd like to advise you to do and what you should do are two very different things."

"Give me options."

"I have a contact who can help us hire an assassin—no, several teams of assassins so we are certain the job is done correctly—and do away with Inimigo forever." She rubbed her hands together like she was trying to rid herself of the letter's filthy author. "The Keepers know we've all prayed for some calamity to befall him—"

"Mother, I can't believe you'd say that!"

Lady DeSilva gave a cold approximation of her usual smile. "Oh, come now! You've heard about how Inimigo treats his peasants, and the tales the merchants spread after they've delivered their wares to his palace. Inimigo is an evil, power-hungry devil. Santarem would flourish without his infectious presence."

Rafi didn't disagree, but it wasn't a plausible solution to his problem. "Assassins aside, what *should* I do?"

Lady DeSilva considered, folding and unfolding a pleat of her dress. "Invite him to join us for your naming celebration. If you send a carrier pigeon tonight, he'll have a few days to prepare and enough time to get here before your birthday. He'll see the invitation as a sign of good faith that you intend to honor the treaty."

"He'll see it as a sign that I'm biddable." Rafi scrubbed a hand through his hair. "He knows I'm young and untested. He's looking for a weakness he can exploit, so he can plunge Santarem into war and put himself on Wilhelm's throne."

There was no clear heir to the crown after the king's death, and the states of Santarem chose to function as four separate entities. The surviving cities of Roraima—Cruzamento and Vicente—remained unallied. At first it worked, each state managing its own commerce and taxes, but over time the trade routes fell into disrepair and bandits threatened caravans, robbing and pillaging as they traveled between the states. Road maintenance and security had been one of Wilhelm's primary duties, as well as acting as an arbitrator for disagreements among the dukes, and between the dukes and their people. He was the highest judge of the land and was considered his country's greatest protector from threats both without and within.

"I don't care how Inimigo sees it. We want the rest of Santarem to see that you tried to keep the peace, Rafi. They need to know that you made the effort, so that when Inimigo starts building his armies and hoarding iron from his mines, they'll know whose side they want to fight on."

"You think it will come to that?"

"Inimigo will never be satisfied with a mere dukedom while the throne is empty. We knew it was only a matter of time before he made a grab for power." She gave a little shiver and edged closer to the hearthstone. "Your father's death expedited Inimigo's plans."

Rafi leaned back in the chair, forgetting for a moment the hawk and its damnable sword. The pain to the back of his skull was a swift reminder of the dozens of reasons he wasn't suited to serve as duke. First and foremost that Rafi was nothing like his father.

Camilio DeSilva had been a bulldog of a man. Short and barrel-chested, he had a laugh that could shake down a mountain and a battle cry that would bring an army to its knees. He was like Dom, funny and quick-witted, a soldier's soldier, and everyone's friend. But unlike his younger son, Camilio also had an explosive temper.

Rafi had inherited that unfortunate attribute. It took him a little longer to blow his top than the senior DeSilva, but once Rafi lost control, no one dared stand in his way.

His blood boiled, thinking of the contents of the letter and the potential of hosting Inimigo in his home. "Maybe he'll give me a reason to kill him."

"I'm sure he'll give you dozens, but you can't take the bait. You have to be unshakable, the perfect host, if you don't want this to devolve into civil war."

"What about the rest of the letter? Do you honestly think he'd name me heir to the throne if I married his daughter?"

"Never. He'll want you close and then poison your wine at the nearest opportunity." She tilted her head, considering. "Although murder is a dual-sided blade. You could wait for him to name you heir, then stab him in the back when he least expected it."

Rafi laughed. "When did you become so bloodthirsty, Mother?"

"After you handed me that letter." Her brow creased. "Would you want to be king, son?"

"Never." His answer was immediate. "I can't imagine a more Keeper-blasted punishment. I hate being duke. The responsibility must be a thousand times worse for a king."

"Good. A man who wishes for power is the most likely to misuse it." She reached for his hand. "Rafi, if you could choose anything for your life, what would it be?"

He considered for a moment, biting the inside of his cheek as he thought. "Honestly, I'd like things to go back to normal—to the time before Father died. I don't think I'll be a bad duke, but I would have been better prepared if I could have spent more time with him. I knew this would be my duty someday, but I thought I'd be an old man when the title became mine."

"You're doing a fine job." She patted his arm. "I am proud of you."

Mortimer knocked at the door. "Pardon, Lord Rafael, Lady DeSilva, the guests have gathered and are waiting for you to be announced."

Twenty minutes later, Rafi wished he'd spent the evening reviewing the sewage report. The murky water under the city flowed with less stops and stutters than conversation with Duke Belem. He'd been seated at the head table between Rafi and Dom, and across from Lady DeSilva. Forty or so lower nobles and merchants had come for the supposed honor of dining with the two dukes.

It had been years since Rafi had seen Belem, and the time had not treated him kindly. Belem had a large belly that dangled over a pair of chicken-thin legs. His face seemed swollen. His lips were like two fat earthworms, pink and glossy, against florid cheeks.

He seemed to have only two interests: wine and women. And he had plenty of both, keeping the serving girls hopping to refill his cups and then pinching their bottoms when his glass was full.

"Who's the lovely little tart at the far table, in the pink dress?" Belem squinted his small brown eyes in the lady's direction.

Rafi set the roll he'd been buttering on his plate. "That's Isabella Rodrigues, the *wife* of a wool merchant."

"Huh," Belem grunted around a mouthful of food. "Nice apples."

"They're mangoes, actually."

Dom choked, wine spraying out his mouth.

Rafi held back a grin and scooped a sample of the brown-sugar-covered fruit onto his platter.

The exchange went unnoticed by the duke. "Call them up here. I'm always interested to hear what wool merchants have to say."

It was a lie. Belem wanted a closer look at the merchant's attractive wife, but Rafi couldn't deny the request. The young couple approached the head table with barely contained excitement, bowing and curtsying profusely.

"Lord Belem, it's a pleasure to meet you, sir." Master Rodrigues shook Belem's hand then bowed over it. "I work closely with one of your underlords. Leandro? From Alegre?"

"Leandro, of course," the duke said, but his smile was for the lady only. He raised his eyebrows at her a few times and received a demure grin in return.

"He speaks highly of you, my lord," Rodrigues continued, either oblivious or ignoring Belem's flirtation. "I'd hoped he'd accompany you on this visit, but given the unfortunate circumstances . . ."

Belem's joviality faded. "Yes, quite unfortunate."

"I know Leandro," Lady DeSilva interjected, concern wrinkling her forehead. "He's our closest neighbor over the western border. What's happened to him?"

"Oh! Not to him. To his stepdaughter." Isabella regained everyone's focus and seemed to blossom under the attention. "It was awful, really. She was murdered after a dress fitting. Her mother found her, throat slit ear to ear, in a dressing room. Blood was everywhere, and there was an awful burn on her neck. Her maid is a close friend of mine. She said—"

"I'm sure we don't want to speculate over dinner," Belem interrupted, reaching for a fried plantain. "It upsets my digestion."

"Oh dear. Oh dear!" Isabella twisted her hands together. "Forgive me, my lord."

Belem wiped a bit of grease off his chin with his knuckles. "Perhaps I'll let you make it up to me later."

Rafi scooted back his chair, causing it to squeal against the stone. "Please excuse me for a moment," *so I don't gag on my food.* "I'm going to go check on our . . . entertainment."

Leaving the table midmeal was improper, but Rafi had to get away from Belem before his temper took control.

Nodding to the waitstaff, Rafi entered the kitchen and found he wasn't the only member of the gentry who'd escaped the dining hall.

A girl in a deep emerald dress stood with her back to the kitchen door. Her hair had been pinned in a myriad of tight curls around her head. Her pale shoulders, bare across her back, seemed to reflect the kitchen lanterns like she'd been dusted with gold powder. Rafi's protective sense surged, wondering if she was another woman trying to avoid Duke Belem.

Then she tilted her head back, laughing at something Brynn said, and his concern dissipated.

"Johanna."

She turned, startled. It wasn't just her back that looked different. She'd done something to her face that made her look—

"It's still a bit early, but my guests seem a little more boisterous than usual." Rafi shifted his feet, trying not to notice the angle of her collarbones or the smooth scoops of flesh beneath. *Damn Belem. My mind's a muddle.* "I'd like to start your performance before dessert."

"Certainly, my lord." She took a towel off the counter and dusted her hands, and then dabbed at invisible spots on the front of her dress. "Am I presentable?"

He offered a sharp nod. "I'll make the announcement now."

Chapter 29

Johanna

Johanna stood inside the kitchen arch, while Rafi strode to the center of the room, and waited for him to make his speech.

He flashed a smile to his guests—it made him look more like Dom—and accepted the applause with humility. His voice was clear, his diction excellent, his message simple. He didn't offer any flowery praise besides referring to Johanna as local talent and welcomed her to take the stage.

As was tradition, Johanna offered him a swan-neck curtsy. She bent her knees deeply, tilted her chin to her chest, and held up her hand. It was an awkward position, and it seemed like hours passed before Rafi took her hand and tugged her gently upward.

He bent and brushed the back of her hand with a kiss. "The floor is yours, milady." He managed one more smile, closer to the cold smirk she was used to seeing on his face.

"Thank you." Johanna resisted the urge to wipe the hand he'd kissed on the skirt of her dress. It was the first time they'd touched without one or both of them smothered in blood or bruises, and the contact made her skin grow uncomfortably warm.

She turned and offered curtsies to each of the tables. Some members of the audience watched; others chatted; most ate.

Johanna allowed herself a grin, knowing that before the end of her performance they'd focus on her alone.

With a quick lick of her lips she started the show with a jaunty hunting ballad that was a favorite in all of the dukedoms.

Heads turned; food stopped halfway to mouths; voices cut off. Their interest spurred her on, and she sang more difficult variations of the same melody, watching the faces, judging reactions, choosing the next song by their interest level and responses.

Rafi barely looked at her the entire time she performed, seemingly more concerned with his plate or the ceiling.

Johanna tried not to doubt her performance, chalking up his disinterest to his personal dislike of her and not a lack of skill.

She finished the songs she'd prepared and took requests for stories or tunes from the head table. The ladies wanted lovers' ballads, darting looks at the men that held their interest. The young men wanted songs of great battles. The Duke of Belem wanted a tavern song and even sang a few bars when Johanna was unfamiliar with the tune.

Finally it was Rafi's turn.

"My lord, is there anything particular you'd like to hear?"

"I suppose," he said, and dabbed at his mouth with a napkin. "How about 'The Lovers' Lament'?"

His request was met with a few cheers from his female guests, but it took Johanna by surprise. It was a dark, mellow song about a love that reached beyond the grave, and seemed out of character for the lordling.

"Certainly." She bobbed a small curtsy.

Johanna turned her back to her audience for a moment, digging out the right emotions for the tale of unconquerable love.

She began singing, still facing the hearth at the front of the room and slowly rotated, reeling her audience in by degrees. Women reached for their beaux's hands. Men draped their arms around their lady loves' shoulders. Duke Belem leaned back in his chair and folded his arms across his paunch, ignoring his dessert for her entertainment.

But then there was Lord Rafael, watching her with cool disinterest.

It was infuriating.

Johanna was determined to impress him.

You asked for this.

Chapter 30

Leão

Leão leaned against the bar, exactly as he had earlier that night, but the dark-haired girl he'd flirted with was nowhere to be seen. The crowd in the common room had grown a little quieter as the moon set. It was late, but a few rougher-looking men sat in a corner playing a game that involved several small cubes and wooden cups.

"What's your pleasure?" The girl who'd welcomed them to the inn—*Miriam,* Leão thought—rested her elbows on the bar. Her rounded cleavage seemed ready to pop out of her low-cut corset.

Leão gaped for an instant and then looked away. Keepers didn't openly display their flesh like the people of Belem, and it made him uncomfortable.

"I had a few questions, and I hoped that the other girl could answer them for me."

"Lessie?" Miriam eyed Leão openly. "She went home hours ago. Her da doesn't let her work after dark. Says it puts wrong ideas in a gentleman's head to see an unchaperoned girl on the street by herself."

"A wise man."

His comment earned a bright grin. "Then perhaps you'd be willing to walk me home as I'm without a chaperone?" She paused and tilted a shoulder toward him coyly. "Unless, of course, you're the type of gentleman to get wrong ideas."

Leão was naive, but he didn't miss the nuance in the girl's body language. He gave her a smile that had received positive responses before. "When can you leave?"

"I'm off now." Miriam shouted to someone in the kitchen and received a grunt in return, then slipped under the bar to join Leão.

He politely offered her his arm, and she took it and giggled.

"Which way do you live?" he asked as they passed through the inn's front door.

"My house is on the block directly behind us." She waved to the west. "That route is quicker, but the neighborhood is a little dangerous. A girl I know was killed walking home from work late one night." She shivered and pressed her body against Leão's. "We'll take the longer route to be safe."

"Are murders common here?" he asked, remembering the prisoners in the wagon.

"There are a few every year." Miriam led them closer to the stable where the Keepers' horses were kept. "Duke Belem's guards do a pretty good job keeping the streets safe, but that night the township was packed with visitors here for the festivities. Those nights are always more dangerous with that Performer riffraff in town."

"Performers?"

"Yes. At first the guards thought maybe one of the Performers snuck away from their camp and killed poor Elise, but they all banded together and said that none of them had left Duke Belem's estate."

"Oh?" It wasn't that Miriam needed prompting to keep talking, but he felt like he should say something since her feet weren't really moving anymore. They stood a few steps from the stable's doors.

"You know how those Performers can be. They always stick together, keeping each other's secrets and spying at every town." She lowered her voice and Leão had to lean closer to listen. "People say they kidnap children and tempt young girls to leave respectable jobs to wear those scandalous costumes."

"Was Elise the kind of girl who'd run off to join the Performers?"

"No. She was real close to the aunt and cousins she lived with." Miriam frowned and shook her head. "When they found her body, neck slit and marked up, the whole family was devastated." She tightened her grip on his bicep and tipped her head up to look into his face. "Just talking about this makes me so, *so grateful* you were willing to walk me home."

Leão's mouth went dry; he wasn't sure what he was supposed to do next, but there was a promise in her eyes. Maybe if he could keep her talking, he could learn more from Miriam. About a lot of things.

"Why don't we find a place to sit down and talk for a few more minutes? Unless you have to get home right away?"

Miriam rewarded him with a broad smile. "I know the perfect place." She wound her fingers through his and dragged him into the stable.

CHAPTER 31

RAFI

Rafi had chosen "Lamento de Amantes" because it was his mother's favorite. He had heard her sing a few lines at his father's funeral and knew it had special meaning to her.

Johanna sang it beautifully. Her voice arched with the high notes and plummeted with the low ones, weaving passion and heartbreak into every tone. Dom was perfectly still, his mouth slightly open as if in constant awe. His mother leaned her elbow on the table, resting her chin on her palm. A sweet, wistful smile curved her lips.

Duke Belem's eyes never left Johanna, locked on to her like she was meat and he was a starving man.

Johanna raised her arms slightly, appealing to the audience, and took slow, dramatic steps toward the head table. The moonlight poured through the windows, playing across her cheekbones, giving her face a pale, ethereal glow. Two steps, she was in shadow. Two more she returned to the light. Two more and she stood directly in front of Rafi, only the table separating them.

Her voice was powerful, mesmerizing, as she came to the song's conclusion. He couldn't look away even if he wanted to. She pleaded with her eyes, her palms out begging for his love and protection.

Yes. Anything for you. The thought sliced through the connection between them like a knife through a taut rope. Rafi sat back in his chair, shaking off the power of her gaze.

After her last word, there was no sound for a moment. Then Duke Belem stood and began clapping. Everyone soon followed.

But Rafi felt frozen solid. He didn't stand; he didn't applaud. He stared.

She held his eyes for a few moments, then lifted her chin up and turned away.

Duke Belem leaned over, patting Rafi on the shoulder. "Send her to my rooms tonight. I should like to get to know her better."

Chapter 32

Johanna

Johanna tore through the laces on her dress. She wanted it off. She wanted to get out of the estate. To get as far from Rafael DeSilva as soon as possible and never, ever, see him again.

She wasn't sure why his approval—or lack thereof—of her performance even mattered. Everyone else had been effusive with their praise as she tried to leave the dining room. The Duke of Belem had kissed her cheeks and slipped a small purse into her palm.

"What would it take to receive a private performance?" he'd whispered, his lips wet against her ear.

Johanna had never met the duke before, but she'd heard the nasty rumors that trailed his name. "I'm sorry, but I'm slated to Storyspin for tomorrow's meal. I need to rest my voice till then."

"Perhaps just to talk." He'd clamped hard fingers around her wrist. "I'm a man of the world. I might be able to interest a girl from Santiago in a few tales of my own."

Dom and Lady DeSilva came to her rescue, assuring the duke that Johanna would be back the next evening and he'd have the chance to speak with her then.

Rafi didn't seem to notice, deep in conversation with a merchant of some sort. The lordling could manage a laugh and a smile over some wool-related joke, but he couldn't put his hands together for her performance.

It was offensive. It was rude. Johanna should have been used to those responses from the gentry, but from Rafi, who still *owed* her an honor debt it was . . . exasperating.

He wore the same stoic expression during her performance that he had during his Punishment!

I'll find something that will draw some sort of emotion out of him.

She slipped into her hunting clothes, tore the pins from her hair, and hung the dress over the screen. Lady DeSilva promised to have it freshly pressed for her performance the next day, and that meant Johanna didn't need to bundle it into a saddlebag and haul it back to the wagon.

"Miss?" Brynn's voice came through the door. "Your brother is here to escort you home."

With Thomas's income and the money delivered prior to her performance, they'd been able to buy a bit of extra food and a horse so he didn't have to leave before dawn each day to walk into town. They'd be riding double, but it would still be faster than walking along the forest road in the dark.

"Good. I can't wait to leave." Johanna threw open the door before her vest was properly laced over her tunic.

Brynn's mouth dropped open, and Thomas's forehead crinkled.

"Did the show go badly then?" He pushed off the wall he'd been leaning against.

"Oh no, Master Thomas," Brynn said. "Miss Johanna was fantastic. The applause went on and on. I don't know why she looks so . . ."

"Crazy?" Thomas suggested.

The maid blushed. "I was going to say frazzled."

Johanna marched back into the room and gave herself a quick once-over in the mirror. Her face and neck were flushed. Her hair crimped, corkscrewing in all directions. She'd missed a few notches in her vest and it was laced askew.

"I do look particularly heinous." She tucked the loose strands of hair behind her ears. "I'll have to wash and pin it again in the morning."

Thomas's face appeared over her shoulder. He attempted to smooth down her mane, but it simply bounced back. They both laughed at the reflection.

"How did this happen?" His eyes raked over her, taking in her rather haphazard appearance. "You look like you've been—" He cut off as Brynn followed him into the room to gather Johanna's dress.

"What?"

"Nothing." The worry lines in his forehead returned. "We'll talk about it on our ride home."

A groomsman brought around their mild-mannered pinto mare. Michael had named her Splotchy due to the splashes of brown on her otherwise white coat. She looked small and dirty compared to the rich coaches and thoroughbreds waiting for their owners to finish up their revelry.

The party had spilled onto the balconies, taking advantage of the fresh evening air to continue their business or flirtations. Lord Rafi stood with a group of people, mainly girls, listening to some story the Duke of Belem told.

Johanna pulled up the hood on her vest, hoping neither duke noticed her departing, and swung up behind Thomas.

They trotted off the estate and into the forest before either spoke.

"Jo, what happened tonight?" Thomas looked over his shoulder at her, as if he could make out her face by starlight.

"Nothing. I don't want to talk about it."

"I *need* you to talk about it. My imagination . . . It's being very brotherly."

"What?"

He patted Splotchy between the ears, although Johanna suspected her brother needed the calming more than the horse. "The last time you had a run-in with Lord Rafael, you ended up bleeding and broken. Tonight, when you stepped out of that room, with your hair wild, your cheeks pink, your shirt half laced . . . well . . . you looked like you'd been tumbled."

"Tumbled?"

"We got that lecture the same day, so don't try to play innocent. You know exactly what I'm talking about, and you know the consequences." His back went tense where her fingers gripped his shirt. "I saw the way you watched him as we left the estate, but none of that duke's promises mean anything. They all say what you want to hear, take what you have to give, and toss you out when they're through. Other Performer families may not have a problem with such behavior, but our parents would never sanction such a . . . a . . . tryst."

Johanna burst out laughing, startling a potoo from its perch. The nocturnal bird swooped across their path, a murky shadow against the darkness. Splotchy trotted a couple of steps before settling back into a smooth gait.

"How is any of this funny? Father would have galloped back to the estate and demanded an explanation, and I'm considering doing the same thing."

"Only one person in that entire household has helped me out of my clothes, and I assure you that Brynn is not a threat to my virtue."

Thomas sighed. "I did it again, didn't I?"

"You mean racing forward and making assumptions without letting me get a word in?"

"Yes. That."

She squeezed his tight shoulders. "You can't help your vivid imagination. You're the son of two Storyspinners."

"I suppose," he said after a long moment. "Are you going to tell me what really happened tonight if it didn't involve a tumble?"

The frustration returned, laced with a tingling sense of inadequacy. "You're going to think it's stupid."

"Probably."

Johanna could hear the dry humor in his tone and flicked his ear.

"Ow." He put a hand over the offended spot. "How am I supposed to listen to your complaints if you leave me with no hearing?"

With a pent-up breath, she explained exactly what had happened. Rafi's request, her excellent performance, the long-lasting applause.

"But Lord Rafael didn't even blink. It's like I bored him to sleep." Her shoulders slumped.

"Hmm."

"I love how long-winded you are when you're angry and how you're so very silent when you don't really care."

"I care, Jo," he said, looking over his shoulder again. "I'm just surprised that it upsets you."

"Why? It's courteous to clap for a Performer even if you didn't love their act, and he didn't."

Thomas smiled, his teeth flashing white in the dark. "Perhaps I *should* ride back to the estate and have a chat with DeSilva."

"I doubt he's going to accept an etiquette lesson from you."

"Not that." He laughed, sounding so much like their father that Johanna pinched her eyes shut for a moment. She tried to block out the rush of memories, but it was like standing in a river during a rainstorm. There was no way she could avoid getting wet. Her last conversation with her father had been punctuated by laughter. And then he'd kissed her good-bye and hurried off to his show.

She saw it again—his arms swinging, his body shifting, before finally getting too far from the rope. The crowd's scream and the thud of his body as it smashed into the ground seemed to happen simultaneously.

While everyone else mourned, she checked the wire, the platform, the supports ten times. She even climbed up and walked across the rope herself, to test the tension, but it was perfect. Still, Johanna believed *something* made her father fall.

"You want his approval," Thomas said, completely oblivious to the detour her thoughts had taken. "I worry about what you may be willing to do to get it."

“Don’t,” she managed around the emotion that clamped down on her voice. “Don’t worry. I’ll never let Lord Rafael lay another finger on me.”

“I wish I believed you.”

She flicked his other ear.

Chapter 33

Pira

Whoever made the dart had done an excellent job disguising their identity. It had been poured into a mold and sharpened to its wicked point by a right-handed metalsmith. That much Pira could tell.

It narrowed down the field, but, she couldn't determine the basic metal composition without more research.

Donning a hood, she left the inn without drawing any attention. Leão had been deep in conversation with the barmaid who was trying to seduce him. Pira stifled a laugh at the thought. Proper Leão, grandson of the head of the Mage Council, wouldn't lay a hand on the girl.

But that didn't mean the trollop wouldn't put her hands on Leão. Pira's feet ground to a halt, and she almost turned back to rescue him from an inappropriate education.

Who are you to decide what he should and should not learn? You have no hold on him.

Pira shook away the thought and hurried toward the blacksmith's shop she'd seen as they'd entered the township. Jacaré had issued a command, and she intended to follow it. Even though he wouldn't necessarily condone her methods.

The shop was long closed, so Pira picked the lock on the door in less than three seconds. It swung open on silent hinges.

Horrible locksmith, decent hinge maker.

The front of the store featured a selection of daggers—likely the smith's showpieces—and some more mundane items. Buckets of hoes, scythes, and pitchforks lined the area behind the counter and divided the room into two spaces. She crossed into the workshop and crinkled her nose against the smell of metal filings and the stink of man sweat.

The forge was cold, but the smith had banked coals in a small brazier near the rear wall. She tossed them into the hole, squirted a little fire starter over them to encourage the blaze and pumped the bellows a few times.

Flames licked the air, and Pira leaned over the stones that lined the lip of the forge, letting the heat wash over her. She wasn't cold, no one could be in the blasted humidity, but the fire warmed her like a welcome embrace. Pira wasn't at home anywhere like she was at the forge.

Pira's gift was slightly more specialized than other Earth affinities because she was specifically attuned to metal. She could sense the location of ore and minerals. No one would ever be able to stab Pira in the back.

If she hadn't succeeded in becoming a member of the Keepers' Elite Guard, she would have apprenticed with a weaponsmith and spent her time honing steel instead of using it.

The metalsmith who owned this shop was organized and neat. His tools were pegged along a side wall, grouped by type and size, and a selection of leather aprons hung by the shop's rear door.

She dropped the dart inside a heavy cast-iron bowl, sure to withstand the heat, and selected a pair of tongs. The bowl began to glow as red as the coals around it, but the dart looked unchanged. Pira donned one of the smith's heavy gloves and used the tongs to rotate it a few times.

Nothing.

Frustrated, she threw more coals into the pit and pumped the bellows until sweat dampened her shirt. She swept an arm across her forehead and pushed back her hood to let her head breathe.

Pira leaned across the pit's mouth, her skin tightening at the heat, and checked the dart. Still no visible change, but the *feel* of the metal was different. She rolled the dart with the tongs and realized why she hadn't been able to sense the type of metal. It was dual layered. The inside was copper, but it had been coated with something unfamiliar.

Then the air shifted, a slight disturbance in the vibration of the metal around her. Spinning, she raised the tongs in time to stop the hammer that had been aimed at her head.

The tongs crunched, bending sideways, and the blow sent a painful tremor up through Pira's shoulder.

Her attacker—likely the blacksmith by his build—swung the hammer again, but she threw herself sideways, scuttling around the forge.

"Stop!" she said, raising her glove-encased hands. "I'm not stealing anything!"

"Not stealing! You're using my coals, my forge, and my tools. You cost me an excellent set of tongs and—" His eyes widened, and the hammer dropped to his side. "You're a girl. What's a girl doing working at my forge?"

"Look, I'll pay you for the cost of your tongs and coal." She shook off one of the gloves and reached toward her pocket. He raised the hammer. "I'm trying to get to my coins."

"I don't think so." He waved his makeshift weapon menacingly. "Take off the other glove and put both your hands on top of your little bald head."

"You don't want to do this," Pira promised. Even without a weapon, she would be able to seriously maim the blacksmith, which would be a shame. Despite his powerful build, he was a friendly-looking fellow, with short dark hair and a freshly shaved face. "I just needed a little help and your shop was already closed."

His eyes trailed down to the bowl among the coals, and his forehead wrinkled in confusion. "What were you trying to do? Melt down an assassin's dart?" He shook his head, and his mouth quirked with humor. "Good luck with that."

"Assassin's dart? Who makes them? Where do they come from?" She edged toward him slightly, drawing his attention, and he raised his hammer again. "I know it's copper on the inside, but it's coated with something I've never seen before."

The blacksmith regarded her over his weapon's head. "Why do you need to know?"

Pira debated for a moment, biting her bottom lip. What should she say?

"If a girl like you has an assassin's dart, you're likely in trouble." The man waved to the shop's back door. "Get out."

"No! A friend . . . a friend of mine was killed. And we . . . I mean . . . I found this dart near him." She allowed her shoulders to slump. *Men like women who are helpless. Be helpless.* "I want to know who killed him and why."

"If you have a *friend* who was killed by an assassin, it's best if you stay out of that business."

Helpless was not working.

Faster than his eye could follow, Pira's right hand reached into her left sleeve and drew a throwing dagger. "Look. It's obvious you know something about assassins. Tell me what I need to know, and I won't use this on you. And in case you're thinking of doing something stupid, I have excellent aim."

His mouth dropped open in stunned surprise. "Are *you* an assassin?"

"Definitely not."

"I don't know any women who know how to work a forge, or throw a dagger, or shave their heads for that matter." His hands dropped to his sides. "Who are you?"

"*I'm* asking the questions."

"I'll answer them if you lower your knife." The blacksmith took a confident step toward the forge. "I'm not stupid enough to assume that's the only knife on your person, but I'd like to believe that you won't kill me when we're done here."

Blast it. He was likable. Pira lowered the knife and laid it on the edge of the forge as a promise of peace.

He nodded. "Good enough. I'm Ricketts, by the way."

"All right." She put her hands on her hips and waited. "The dart. Tell me about it."

"Well . . . I don't know much about assassins, but I've heard that dukes and the richer underlords hire them on occasion. To take out a rival or some such." He motioned at the wall, where similar hammers hung. She nodded permission to put it away. He flipped it in the air, caught it by the head, and slipped it between two pegs.

"Names, specifically?"

"Our own Duke Belem, for one. But you're right about this." Ricketts grabbed a set of tongs and picked up the dart from its bowl. "I'd bet my shop that it's coated in beryllium."

"I've never heard of it."

"That's because it's rare. It's not minable, that I know of, but is found in streambeds and so forth." He dunked the dart in a brine wash. It sizzled, and a puff of salty steam wafted across the room. "There's only one state that has the capability to smelt it: Maringa."

"And the Duke of Maringa, do you think he'd hire an assassin?"

Ricketts regarded her like she'd said something completely ridiculous. "Where are you from?"

"No questions." She snatched the tongs from his hand and pulled the dart out of the wash. "I still can't feel it."

"It's light." His eyebrows drew together. "That's what you meant, right?"

"Back to the Duke of Maringa," she deflected, setting the still-hot dart on the worktable. The beryllium gave off no vibrations; it was like it wasn't there, completely masking the copper underneath. When it had been heated, the bond between the layers loosened enough that she could feel it, but now that it was solid again, it was like one of her senses had been cut off.

A nervous flutter started low in Pira's belly. If weapons were coated in beryllium, she might not be able to sense them at all. It would take away one of her strengths and weaken her as a fighter—just like Jacaré had done with the wooden sword on the practice field.

"How can you not know about Inimigo? His name is synonymous with 'butcher' in our land and *'Finalreinar'* in his own."

Reign ender.

"Inimigo was responsible for the last king's death." She tried to say it without making it sound like a question.

"And the Ten Years' War, and the obliteration of Roraima." Ricketts studied her again, as if looking for a lack of mental acuity, but didn't find anything but a pretty face and a trim figure.

Roraima, at least, was a name she recognized. She'd slept among the ruins.

"Thank you, Ricketts." She pulled out her purse and dropped a couple of coins on the edge of the forge and retrieved her dagger.

He picked up the first coin and gasped in surprise. "Where did you get these? They must be ancient. . . ." He looked from the golden disc to Pira and back. "The *cadarço*. I thought it was an odd headband, but you . . . you're a *Keeper*."

She flipped the knife into her hand and held it against the blacksmith's neck. "Do not speak of this to anyone."

"But—"

"Your silence. Promise it to me now."

His mouth opened and closed a few times. "You really *could* feel the metal, couldn't you? That's part of your magic."

"Don't make me cut out your tongue."

Instead he lowered himself to his knees in front of her. "I've never been a believer, and now I'm sorry for that—"

She hit him behind the ear with the butt of her dagger before he could finish his sentence. The blacksmith crumpled to the ground, narrowly missing the edge of the forge.

Pira pushed through the back door and hopped the fence around the yard. The whole way back to the inn, she hoped the information she'd gained would be worth the cost of their exposure.

Chapter 34

Rafi

Rafi dripped wax onto the tiny letter, pressing his father's sigil ring to seal it.

The guests had finally made their farewells or retired for the evening, but Rafi had to get the missive off to Duke Inimigo before dawn if he wanted the bird to reach Maringa in time.

He rubbed his tired eyes, but it didn't help. He was exhausted, worn to the bone, and anxious. Having people in his home, strangers and friends alike, always made him feel slightly off-kilter. The constant scrutiny, the whispers, the false smiles, the lurid invitations, and the thinly veiled threats were like pebbles in his shoes. He tried to deal with it all, but eventually it blistered. He suffered it quietly and nursed the irritation in private.

Such was his duty.

The house was silent as he walked to the staircase that led to the bird roost. The pigeons cooed and clucked as he opened the lock on the bamboo cage. He attached the scroll to the bird's foot before tossing it into the air.

He leaned across the railing, watching till the bird disappeared into the night and long after. From the roof he could see the entire estate, the lands around it, and the Santiago township in the distance. Beyond that were his underlords' holdings, one in each compass direction. Each duke had four underlords to help oversee their state and divide the territory into manageable parts. Since Santiago was the smallest state, Rafi's underlords were closer and constantly underfoot.

He rotated in the direction of the Milners' orchard, wondering if Johanna and her brother had made it safely home. He'd have to warn her about Duke Belem's interest—or have Dom do it. The girl would probably take the warning more seriously if it came from anyone but Rafi.

Or maybe I should let her cut out Belem's heart with her little dagger, he thought. Rafi grinned at the thought of her knife against the man's double chin. *I wonder where she keeps it in that dress. No sleeves, no pockets. It'd be difficult to fit in a bodice laced so tight—*

Stop.

Rafi pushed her out of his mind, headed for his chambers, and nearly broke his neck when he stumbled over the body at the bottom of the stairs.

Chapter 35

Pira

The stable was dark, the hands long abed, by the time Pira and Tex pushed through the doors. It suited their purposes perfectly. No one would be around to witness the four Keepers fleeing Belem in the middle of the night.

Three Keepers, she mentally corrected. Leão hadn't returned from his *assignment* with the barmaid yet, and Pira had been forced to gather his things and haul them out of the inn.

The only upside was that the boy hadn't been around to hear the epic dressing-down she'd received from her brother. It was never pleasant to be reprimanded in front of a subordinate. Especially perfect Leão, who never disobeyed, never made a mistake, never questioned orders.

Pira was still a little bit shocked that he'd agreed to come on this assignment. It was easier to tag Leão as some obedient Council toady than a thinking, calculating member of their mission.

"How long can it possibly take to walk a girl home?" Pira asked as she dropped her saddlebags on her horse's stall door.

"Quite a while, when you're young." Tex wagged his eyebrows at her, which earned him a disgusted glare in return. "Don't you worry about Leão, though. He'll find his way back soon enough."

"He better be grateful when . . ."

"When what?" Tex asked, as her voice trailed off.

She held her finger to her lips and pointed to the loft. She heard the noise again, a giggle and a hushed whisper.

"I told you we'd find Leão soon enough." Tex cupped his hands around his mouth and yelled, "Boy! Get your bony arse down here. We're moving out. Now."

Pira took a quick step back to avoid being smashed by the body that rolled out of the loft.

Leão landed with a cat's grace, barely making a sound as his feet hit the packed-dirt floor. He straightened, revealing that he was shirtless. Again.

"What's going on?" Leão asked, oblivious to his state of undress.

Tex smirked as he leaned a shoulder against one of the stable's supporting beams, looking amused. "I could ask you the same thing. I bet you've got a story for me."

"Nothing happened, sir," he answered quickly.

Pira looked from Leão's bare chest to the loft, where a dark-haired girl leaned halfway over the ladder.

"Don't leave yet," the trollop crooned, the bodice of her dress tugged aside to reveal one pale shoulder. "We just got started."

In a minute you're going to get started looking for your teeth, Pira thought.

The stable doors swung inward, and Jacaré entered. Sweat slicked his skin, and he walked with a slight hunch to his shoulders.

Pira's anger at the barmaid abated, and she opened her mouth to voice her concern. But one scathing look from her brother made it shut with a click.

"Would you please throw down whatever he left up there?" Jacaré asked, the sharpness in his voice reminding Pira of the tongue-lashing she'd received.

A shirt, vest, and a small satchel plummeted down, nearly hitting Pira in the face. She snatched them all before they hit the floor.

"It got hot up there," Leão explained as Pira shoved his shirt into his bare arms and dropped his saddlebags at his feet.

"I bet it did." She shook her head and turned away, saddling her horse with quick decisive movements, the tack jingling. *What did you expect? You saw the way she hung on him. What does it matter anyway?*

Leão shrugged into his shirt, then helped Miriam out of the loft.

The strumpet leaned against him, running a finger from his chin into his unlaced collar. "I look forward to seeing much, much more of you when you come back through Belem."

Pira yanked on the girth strap, earning an irritated huff from her horse. She took a deep breath and loosened it a notch, giving the animal an apologetic pat on the flank.

"Jacaré, Miriam says that when the Performers aren't traveling, they congregate at a camp northeast of Santiago," Leão explained, his voice sounding slightly hoarse.

"Not that you should go there. I don't know what business you have with the Performers, but they aren't welcoming to outsiders," Miriam said with a delicate shiver. "Some say that they harbor outlaws, assassins, and spies among their ranks. And they're certainly thieves. Whenever they come to town, houses are burgled, and last time they were here a girl was killed."

More likely the Performers are easy scapegoats, Pira thought.

"Is their camp far from the east road?" Jacaré asked.

Miriam shrugged. "I don't know, but I doubt they can take those wagon houses of theirs far from any path."

"And they always travel in the wagons?" Jacaré asked.

"Always," Miriam confirmed.

Pira saw the look Tex and Jacaré exchanged, and the older man offered a subtle nod.

Jacaré had once told her that if you gave Tex a general direction, he could find anything.

As Pira led her horse from its stall, she knew they'd be testing his abilities.

Chapter 36

Rafi

"Blast and damnation," Rafi said, using the wall to keep from falling on Belem's prone form. "Why aren't you in your room?"

The man raised a half-full wine bottle and belched. "Came to see you. Saw you walk out, but was a bit too slow to catch ya." He reclined against the bottom stair, thin legs kicked out in front of him. "I'm not exactly in a good way to take stairs. They're a bit too twisty."

And you're a bit too drunk. "Here." Rafi offered the man a hand.

Belem batted it away, his grin morphing into a scowl. "I'll get up when I'm ready."

"All right." Rafi shifted his weight and wondered if he should gather some of the staff to help get Belem to his rooms.

"I said I came to talk to you, boy."

"It will wait till morning."

"'Twill," he slurred, taking another big swig from his wine bottle. "My mood won't, though, so listen up." He gave Rafi a glassy-eyed glare. "Inimigo's going to come here."

"Yes. I know. I read the letter you delivered. He'll be here for my naming."

"He'll be here in three days or so."

Rafi leaned a little closer to the drunken duke, hoping he'd misheard. "What?"

"Inimigo stopped over at my manor. For a rest he said. I was already in the courtyard ready to leave when he comes marching in with dozens of retainers and guards." Belem wiped his mouth on his sleeve. "I left my wife behind to serve as hostess. We don't get along all that well anyway."

No surprises there.

"Inimigo thinks that since you killed your own father—"

"I didn't have anything—"

"That you might be a different sort of duke than your old man was." Belem squinted at Rafi in the half-light. "I think Inimigo might be right, but he might be wrong, too."

"My father's heart stopped," Rafi clarified, his own pulse pounding in his ears. Rumors had circulated after Camilio DeSilva's untimely death, the worst of the gossips blaming an upstart son who wanted his father's place. "The doctor said it was natural."

Belem belched, ignoring Rafi's protests. "Take Inimigo's offer, when he makes it. It'll be better for all of us." He held out his hand for Rafi to pull him up.

"Which offer?" *The offer to be his heir? The offer of his daughter? Something completely different?*

Belem slapped Rafi on the back hard enough to make him stagger. "Don't let your blasted honor stand in your way. You DeSilvas are so sensitive."

The duke swayed slightly, but the forward momentum got him moving, and he took several teetering steps down the hall.

"Why did you tell me?" Rafi yelled after him.

Belem waved over his shoulder as if he was swatting away an irritating bug.

Is this a part of some convoluted plot, or did Belem tell me out of honest concern?

Rafi wasn't sure either way.

Chapter 37

Johanna

Michael was asleep in Johanna's pallet when she returned to the wagon, one fist pressed against his still-chubby cheek, and the fingers of his other hand laced through the netting. Her mother snored softy in her own fold-down bed.

The wagon door swung open and Thomas peered in. "Do you want me to move him?"

"No. He looks so sweet. Plus, Joshua will thank me for having a bed to himself for one night."

"All right." Thomas hesitated on the wagon stairs.

"What?" Johanna asked, too tired to wrestle her brother's thoughts free.

He shifted his weight, the wood underneath his feet creaking. "If you don't want to go back, there's probably some loophole in the contract. Mother always writes in an escape clause."

Johanna tugged off her boots and shrugged out of her vest. "Honestly, it wasn't that bad, and if I keep it up we could buy a second horse so we could get out of here."

"You still think we're going back to Performers' Camp, don't you?"

"Why wouldn't we?" One of the pallets behind her creaked, and

Johanna prayed their conversation wasn't waking up Michael. Once up, he was difficult to get back to sleep, wiggling and squirming until he found the perfect position, which usually involved his bony elbows digging into Johanna's back. Their mother, however, could sleep through everything. The alcohol certainly helped with that.

"I just . . . don't think it's going to happen." He seemed so downcast.

"You're eighteen. You could go tomorrow."

He snorted. "I'm not going anywhere without my family. You couldn't feed Michael and Joshua with your talent alone."

"Ouch." She raised her eyebrows at him, waiting for the apology.

"You know what I mean. They're like a pestilence; they eat everything in sight."

She held up a finger, forestalling him while she dug into her pocket. "Look at this." She tossed him the coin purse that Duke Belem had given her after the performance.

He dumped the coins out into his palm. There were about thirty bits of silver. Enough to feed them all for ten days if they were careful. "I guess I underestimated you," he said with a smirk. "Put that in the safe before you go to sleep."

"I will. See you tomorrow."

"Evening. Tomorrow evening." He hopped off the stair with his usual grace, stretched a few times and kicked up to a handstand. "Mama's riding into town with me in the morning. She's working at the seamstress's shop again. So it'll be just you and the boys tomorrow."

That was pleasant news. Her mother had gone into town almost every day, looking for work, and generally coming back soused. If she'd found someone to hire her a few days in a row, maybe she was finally recovering from Arlo's death. It was an optimistic thought, one Johanna hoped to hang on to. She missed her mother, their easy banter, the way they stuck together when outnumbered by the boys.

"Will she be back before I leave?" Johanna leaned out the door to watch him.

Thomas did a few inverted push-ups, then climbed up and down the stairs of the wagon all on his hands. He didn't get to use those muscles very much as an accounting apprentice. "She'll have to leave a bit early, but should be back here with enough time that you'll make it to the estate without having to run."

"If you say so," she said as she crept into the dark wagon. "Good night."

Johanna felt along the edge of the pallet to the center carving and slid the slim metal box free. Their few coins shifted slightly, hissing against the metal box.

"Jo?" Michael asked, his voice sleepy.

"Go back to sleep. I'm putting my money away."

"Did you get lots and lots?"

She smiled in the dark, loving the childlike sentiment. "Enough that mother could bring home some meat pies tomorrow."

"The pork ones with sugar on top? They're my favorite."

"We'll tell her in the morning." Johanna pulled back the metal latch and rifled through documents until she found the section designated for coins and dropped the purse in. Her fingers brushed something cold and sharp. Then her thumb caught the edge of a thin chain.

Ah, she thought. *Father's necklace.* She lifted it out of the box and held it to the moonlight that peeped through the tiny window. The stone glistened green, seeming to glow with its own light.

It was a surprise to find the pendant among their few valuables; everything else had been sold after her father's death. Johanna wondered if her mother had held on to it for sentimental reasons, or if it wasn't worth the trouble to sell.

She dropped it back in the box and crawled over her brother to the largest strip of pallet and wedged herself against the wall.

Chapter 38

Jacaré

They'd been on the road for four days with little sleep and cold food.

Jacaré ignored the ache in his chest, instead funneling his still-replenishing *essência* into his horse to keep the beast galloping long past the time when a normal animal would have collapsed. Leão did the same for Tex and Pira's horses, as neither of them were capable of very much healing.

The information Pira gleaned from the blacksmith, coupled with the dry weather and odd animal behavior, fueled Jacaré's sense of urgency.

Pira's mouth, still turned down at the corners, had been blessedly silent since their night in Belem. Jacaré knew Pira's attitude was a result of the reprimand he'd given her, but he didn't think that was the only burr in her backside.

He saw the covert looks Pira shot at Leão. Had their mission been any less serious, he might have pulled her aside and sought out the source of her feelings. Was it just attraction, or was there more to it? Not that it mattered. A relationship between them would be doubly damned with Leão destined for the Mage Council.

His brotherly concern made him shake his head. The world

tilted at the action, and he gripped his horse's mane for support.

"Jacaré?" Pira's voice was high with worry.

"I'm fine," he said, without looking back.

"You're not." She rode up alongside him, peering at his face from under her headscarf. "You look like you're going to vomit."

"I said I'm fine."

"We're stopping at the next town. We'll get some hot food, and you can sleep for a few hours."

He couldn't be weak. He couldn't slow them down. Jacaré felt trouble building on the horizon, stirring with the gray clouds. "No. We're going to keep up this pace. We can't be far from Performers' Camp now."

They rode cross-country, over the rolling plains of Belem, through a scrub forest, and into the low mountain range that divided Roraima from Santiago. Avoiding main roads, they trusted Tex's senses to provide them with the shortest routes, but they hadn't stopped for fresh supplies.

Leão returned from scouting the road ahead, slightly out of breath. "There's a town about a quarter mile to the south."

"I didn't tell you to look for a town."

"I know, but I thought maybe . . ."

"I also didn't ask you to think." Jacaré knew he was being harsh, but he was beyond exhausted. "You were instructed to ride ahead and look for Performers' Camp."

"Yes, sir, but—"

"Oh Light," Pira cursed, cutting him off. "I think my horse just threw a shoe."

Jacaré ground his teeth. "That's a bit convenient, isn't it Pira, given that we're so close to a town?"

She dismounted and made a show of checking her horse's hoof. "It certainly is." She clicked her tongue dramatically. "Mother Lua's luck must be with us."

"Can't you repair it?" He'd seen her use her skill with metal to do similar things before.

"Nope." She started shifting bundles from her horse to Tex's and Leão's waiting hands. "This horse can't be ridden another step."

All the brotherly concern he'd felt moments before fled in the face of her defiance. He knew, without question, that Pira had pulled the nails loose.

Tex smirked, and Jacaré wondered if they were plotting together behind his back.

Jacaré wanted to be angry, to tear into both of them, but he should take the situation for what it was.

At least they had enough respect to let him make the decision, even if it was only to save face in front of Leão. "Six hours. We'll take two to resupply and four to sleep, then we'll be on the road again."

The town was well appointed, with stone buildings and slate roofs rather than thatch. Small fenced-in yards featured herb gardens and flowering bushes. A villa, slightly larger than the other homes in town, sat astride a small rise at the end of the main road.

The steady bustle of villagers suggested that it was a profitable holding and a good place to stop for a few hours.

A garland of white flowers stretched over the road as they entered town. They were a few days old, the petals dried to a dingy yellow. Smaller wreaths of white flowers hung on every door.

Jacaré recognized the symbol—someone of importance to the community had died, and the entire village was in mourning.

He doled out assignments, sending Tex for supplies, Pira to the blacksmith, and Leão to care for the other horses.

As he moved across the town square, he felt eyes follow him. He looked over his shoulder, noting that his troop had drawn plenty of attention. It wasn't a surprise. A place so far from the main road probably saw the same merchants year after year and had few other visitors.

The stares shouldn't have bothered him, but there was something wary and fearful in most of the gazes he met.

He ignored them and entered the town's only inn. The innkeeper looked up from wiping the bar, and his eyes grew wide at Jacaré's riding gear and the sword visible over his shoulder.

"What can I do for you, traveler?" the innkeeper asked, tossing his washcloth into a bucket of water.

"I need a couple of rooms for the evening and a hot meal."

The innkeeper's eyes flicked nervously toward the door, but Jacaré didn't need the tell. He could feel the vibration of footsteps through the floorboards—footsteps of someone who didn't want Jacaré to know he was there.

Jacaré turned to the side, and the hand that had been reaching for his shoulder sailed past.

"Excuse me," Jacaré said, pretending to just notice the man who'd snuck up on him. "I didn't see you there."

The man was short with a large belly undisguised by a deep-green jacket. The gold buttons, which seemed to be a sign of some office, strained against his bulk.

"Yes, yes. Quite so." He tucked his hand in his front pocket, as if that had been his intent instead of reaching for Jacaré's shoulder. "My name is Quimby. I'm the Captain of the Guard here in Vicente. You're new in town, but you didn't register at the main gate."

"I apologize," Jacaré said, donning his least threatening smile. "My friends and I must have entered through the other side. We didn't see any notification to register."

Quimby rocked onto his toes and back onto his heels. "The other side of town you say? So you came from the west?"

"Yes, we did." Jacaré leaned against the bar, trying to show he was relaxed, but Quimby twitched like a rat's nose in a garbage heap.

"No one enters town from the west. That's why there isn't a guard-house on that side." Quimby narrowed his eyes at Jacaré. "Where are you coming from and where are you headed?"

Jacaré had found the truth usually worked better than a lie. He hoped his crew remembered that lesson. "We came cross-country from Belem and are headed toward Performers' Camp."

"So you didn't come on the main road?" Quimby rocked back onto his heels again and patted his belly with both hands. An odd little smile quirked his lips. "Why wouldn't you take the main road? It's an easier passing."

Easier maybe, but not faster. "My friends and I have never seen this part of the country, and we wanted to do a bit of exploring."

"In this part of the country? There's nothing very interesting here. Unless . . ."

A small group of people, five men including the bartender, had meandered closer to listen to their conversation. Jacaré's *essência* was still weak, but hostility flavored the air like spoiled eggs, the stench too potent for anyone to ignore.

Jacaré didn't take the bait Quimby offered and left his "unless" hanging. "Like I said, we're just passing through. We'll be gone by dawn tomorrow."

"Are you sure you weren't looking for something specific? Maybe another girl to kill?"

"Excuse me?" Jacaré's body didn't shift, but the elbow resting on the bar could be moved swiftly enough to draw a dagger. Not that he'd need it. Even in his weakened state, he could defeat all five townsmen. The innkeeper, the most threatening of the group, wouldn't be a match for Jacaré's speed and training.

"You heard me." Quimby stepped forward, nearly bumping Jacaré with his paunch. "You match the description of the man who killed our Rosalinda."

Jacaré had to give Quimby credit for his bravery. He wasn't afraid to challenge a man twice his size and who looked half his age.

"I've never been to your town before. And I'm sorry if you've suffered a recent loss, but I'm not the man you're looking for." Jacaré nodded out toward the village, where the rest of his troop was fulfilling their assignments. "My friends can vouch for me."

"Your *friends*," Quimby snorted. "Take him, boys."

Jacaré weighed his options. He could take out the five townsmen, gather his crew, and try to escape, but they'd have to steal a horse for Pira and would have some angry people chasing them. "I won't fight. Tell me where you want me to go."

The men didn't listen and grabbed on to Jacaré like they expected him to flee.

"Our Lord Venza is waiting for you."

It would have been too easy for Jacaré to break away, but his gut told him to stick around and listen.

Chapter 39
Leão

Leão handed over the coins to pay for their horses' food and care and ventured back to the inn, but froze before he could get to the building's door.

Jacaré, surrounded by five local men, was being half dragged, half marched through the town square. He caught Leão's eye and gave a subtle nod to follow along.

What is going on? he wondered. Jacaré didn't appear to be in any danger. The men who held his arms didn't look very fit or well trained, so Jacaré had to be going along with them willingly.

Shoppers and hawkers, washerwomen and errand boys, merchants and craftsmen stopped mid-activity to watch the odd procession. Their eyes flitted over Leão and back to Jacaré, weighing and measuring, before returning to their conversations.

"Have they caught the murderer?"

"Is that him?"

"Could be. Nothing that looks that good ever is," one woman said, eyeing Leão over the top of her laundry line.

The neighbor over the fence shook her head. "I thought Lady Venza said he was older—too old for Rosalinda to have been cavorting with."

"Not Rosalinda. That girl couldn't see a stray dog without wanting to take it in."

Both women clicked their tongues, and Leão felt their gazes follow him up the road. He didn't worry about the gossip or the stares, but the word "murderer" trailed after the group.

The men herded Jacaré toward the large house at the street's far end. The smallest man, the one who seemed to be in charge, opened the gate and ushered them all through.

"Just a moment, Captain Quimby," Jacaré said. "One of my traveling companions is just outside. Don't you think it would be fair to have him join us? To vouch for my whereabouts when this crime was committed?"

Quimby gave Leão a dark look before opening the gate. "Lord Venza will want to talk to him anyway. Who says this young buck wasn't involved?"

He gave an irritated flick of the hand for Leão to join them.

The whole situation made Leão want to laugh: the overweight leader, the mishmash of guards, the accusation with no foundation, the fact that they didn't even take away Jacaré's weapons. But Jacaré's brow was drawn in grave lines, so Leão knew he should take the situation seriously.

The door to the villa swung open, and a man with gray-streaked hair and a matching mustache stepped out.

"What's going on, Quimby? Who are these people?"

The little man offered a hasty bow before speaking. "Lord Venza, these men entered the city without registering at the main gate. And this one," he said, pointing to Jacaré, "matches the description Lady Venza gave of the man seen with your daughter."

Color flushed Lord Venza's face. "Bring them both into my office. I'll send one of the maids to fetch my wife."

Leão and Jacaré were ushered into a tiled foyer. A table on the room's right was draped in a red cloth and displayed a dozen bouquets of white flowers. The potent scent of gardenias and camellias filled the small space with a rich perfume that didn't quite cover the stench of death.

There was a body somewhere nearby.

The lord led the group to a room with a large desk and a few wooden chairs. The furniture was simple, but well made, and Leão's seat didn't shift as he was shoved into it.

"I can see why you think this man could be my daughter's killer." Lord Venza stood behind his desk, supporting his weight with his hands. Dark pockets of skin hung below his eyes. "He does seem to match the description and has the look of a fighting man."

Quimby preened, pulling the hem of his jacket down. "Exactly as I thought, my lord. He's tall, lean, and he moves like someone who's used to using a weapon." He flicked the sword still strapped across Jacaré's back. It gave a dull ping in response. "He carried this into the inn."

"Hmm." The lord's eyes landed on Leão. "Were you with your companion five days ago?"

"Yes, sir. We were at an inn in Belem," Leão answered with confidence.

"Which inn?"

"The Mug and Mutton, sir. The barmaid, Miriam, can verify that we were there."

"Ha!" Quimby punched his fist into the air, a wide smile breaking his face into two round parts. "That's an eight-day ride away. You couldn't possibly have covered that amount of ground in five days. They're lying, my lord."

"But we rode—"

"Cross-country, I know." Quimby hovered in front of Leão's face, reminding him of a bloated mosquito looking for one last bite. "It still should have taken you longer."

Leão looked to Jacaré for guidance but couldn't read the look on his commander's face. "We have an excellent trail finder," he said weakly.

"I saw your horses when you rode in. Besides the one that had thrown a shoe, they were worn but not heaving. No animal could have galloped that far and survived." Quimby's smile turned to a sneer. "To have made it from Belem to here in five days, you would have had to run the entire way."

Leão opened his mouth to explain that they'd done just that, but Jacaré's hand turned to a clenched fist.

"And what in the Good Keeper's name would have made you travel that hard?" Lord Venza lowered himself into his chair.

Wouldn't he find it interesting to know that we are the Good Keepers?

"Lord Venza," Jacaré spoke up. "What my friend says is true. We have ridden hard, stopping along the way to change mounts whenever possible. We, too, are hunting a murderer."

Leão tried not to let his surprise register on his face.

"Hunting a murderer?" The underlord blinked a few times, obviously as stunned as Leão felt.

"We're headed to Performers' Camp to seek out more information, and because of a thrown horseshoe we stopped in your town," Jacaré said as he leaned forward. "Perhaps we can be of assistance to you. As you ascertained, we are fighting men from far to the north."

"You look more like pirates from the far south." Quimby pouted, folding his arms over his paunch.

"We have no reason to believe your words," the lord said. "What proof can you offer? Who hired you to seek out this murderer? What references do you carry?"

"Venza?" a soft voice called from the doorway. "One of the girls said you had reason to see me."

At first Leão thought the woman who entered the room was a statue. Besides a dark lock of hair that had slipped from her veil, she was completely devoid of color. Her clothes, skin, even her eyes, seemed to have faded to a pale and lifeless gray.

"I'd like to sit with Rosalinda for a few more hours before . . ." Her lip trembled. "Before you take her away tonight."

"I'm sorry, my love." Lord Venza crossed the room and draped a protective arm around his wife's shoulders. "These men entered town this afternoon without registering, and this one seems to fit the description you gave. Quimby brought them by so you could have a chance to look at them."

She visibly composed herself, tucking the stray hair under her head covering. "Stand," she commanded in a voice brittle as ice. Her eyes traced over their bodies, taking in their heights, clothing, and the weapon Jacaré wore over his shoulder.

Her eyes, so sorrowful in her washed out face, made Leão ache with empathy. This woman's suffering was a raw wound, seeping with anguish.

Even with all his skill, with all the healing power he supposedly had, there was nothing Leão could do for that kind of pain.

She raised a finger and pointed to Leão's chest. "This one is much too tall."

Her head tilted to the side, and her tongue dampened her bottom lip. "Do you, sir, ever wear your sword at your hip?" she asked Jacaré in a soft monotone.

"Never, my lady." He touched his hip where his daggers hung. "As you can see, my belt is made for one hunting knife and pouches only."

"He could have worn a different belt," Quimby suggested with an irritated huff.

She nodded. "Will you turn around so I may see your back?"

Jacaré rotated slowly, the glares from all the men in the room tracing his every move.

The woman moved to Jacaré's side. "My daughter was very petite. She wore her hair piled on top of her head to give her more height. That night, she danced with a stranger half a head taller." She reached out and touched Jacaré's shoulder with one finger. "She wouldn't have reached your chest. You are too tall as well."

"My lady! Don't base your decision on what you *thought* you saw during the festivities!" Quimby's jowls vibrated with anger. "He could have been slouching, or perhaps Rosalinda was wearing higher shoes that night."

"No, Quimby. I know what I saw, and this man is not him."

"But—"

"This is not the man." Her tone turned sharp. "The man who murdered my daughter was not this tall. He wore his sword on his hip, and his hair in a queue at the base of the neck."

Quimby took a breath, probably to protest again, but Lord Venza dropped a hand on his shoulder.

"You heard my wife. While I appreciate your help," he said nodding to the knot of men, "all of your help, pinning the blame on any stranger who enters town will not bring the murderer to justice."

He excused them to leave and they followed the lady out of the office. "I apologize for your inconvenience here in Vicente. As you can see, we're quite overwrought. Your appearance seemed like a stroke of luck, though I don't suppose any murderer would walk back into town unless he knew he couldn't be identified."

"We're truly sorry for your loss," Leão spoke up, his mind awhirl with the details of another murder. "Your daughter . . . she was killed in town?"

The lord nodded, wiping a hand over his tired face.

"I'm sure it's difficult to speak about." Leão hesitated, taking a breath before pushing on. "Would you mind telling us what happened? I only ask because as my friend said, we too are seeking a murderer."

Jacaré's eyebrow twitched, but he didn't stop Leão from speaking.

"About four months ago, a young barmaid was murdered as she walked home from work." Leão laid out the details of the story Miriam had told him between their kisses. "The girl, Elise, didn't return when her aunt expected. They found her two streets from home with her throat slit and a brand burned into the side of her neck."

All the color in the lord's face faded away, and his hands shook on his desk. "How old was she? This Elise?"

"Just sixteen," Leão said softly.

"And she lived with her aunt, not her parents?"

"That's what I understand, my lord."

"Oh Light," Venza cursed, wiping a tear from his eyes. He took a few moments to gather himself. "Few people know, but our daughter, our Rosalinda, was a foundling. My wife and I were never able to have children of our own."

Jacaré's hands tensed on the arms of his chair. "I know this is an awful thing to ask a mourning father, but your daughter's body, it's still laid out in the house. Isn't it?"

"Yes," the lord breathed.

"May we see her?"

Lord Venza only hesitated a moment before nodding. "Follow me."

He led them deeper into the house, where the smell of death was poorly masked by flowers and fragrant oils. A small room, cold even though sunlight poured through a west-facing window, held an altar and some artwork featuring Mother Lua.

On the stone lay a young girl, her dark hair fanned around her head like she was floating in water. Even in death, with her cheeks beginning to sink in, she was lovely. And though the resemblance wasn't perfect, her height and coloring were close enough.

The dead girl could have passed for the girl whose sorrow had been frozen on Jacaré's glass.

She was dressed in a rich blue silk, a matching scarf hiding most of the wound on her ruined throat. With hesitant fingers, Leão pushed the material aside. Below the gaping slash a red burn marred the pale white flesh. Two small lines, one straight and the other jagged and broken, had been branded into Rosalinda's skin.

Two girls murdered and marked. Both sixteen and of questionable heritage. It couldn't be a coincidence.

Chapter 40

Johanna

"Come on, boys. We've got to go." Johanna had waited longer than she dared. The sun was too high in the sky, and her mother still hadn't returned. Johanna forced down her disappointment. Her mother had a difficult relationship with punctuality, which had become even worse after her father's death. "Put on your shoes and we'll run a bit."

"But," Joshua said, studying his filthy feet with chagrin, "I don't have any that fit."

The boy was in that horrible stage between eleven and twelve where something that had plenty of room yesterday was guaranteed to pinch tomorrow. He'd become all knees and elbows, sharp pointed chin, and hollow cheeks.

Johanna rubbed her forehead, feeling overwhelmed. Her brothers would probably be fine in the clearing by themselves, but she hated to leave them unattended. What if a panther roamed the woods or they stumbled on a poisonous snake? Or worse, that their mother came home drunk and angry?

"Can you make it through the forest barefoot?"

"Sure. I walk around here all day without shoes."

The ground was littered with small stones, nettles, and the

twisted roots of age-old mango trees. The forest couldn't be much worse, and really, what other choice did she have?

She paced for a second, before grabbing the satchel that held her Storyspinner's cape and a small collection of cosmetics. "All right. Let's go."

They started off at a jog. Little Michael clung to her hand but never complained or slowed them down. At least for the first mile.

One-third of the way into the run, he stared at Johanna with tear-filled blue eyes that begged for a rest. So she slung him across her back, where he gripped with an acrobat's strength, making himself the lightest burden possible. The satchel hung around her neck. It thumped against her hip, but she couldn't find a more comfortable position for her brother and the bag.

Carrying his weight, even up the hills wasn't so bad. There was always a down slope after, and they stuck to the soft grass that grew along the side of the path. It didn't jar as much as the hard, hoof-trodden trail.

They'd almost crossed the halfway point when Joshua stubbed his toe, splitting the nail and bleeding all over the place.

"Keeper-cursed scum sucker," Johanna growled as she bound the toe as quickly as she could with a strip torn from her shirt.

"I'm okay," Joshua insisted, limping forward a few steps. "I can make it."

But despite his sweet attempt at bravery, she could see the pain on his face. Even worse was the knowledge that her efforts to protect the younger boys had failed. Joshua and Michael both realized how much their family needed money from this job.

"I can run for a while," Michael offered. "Let's go."

Johanna picked up Joshua. Even though he was thin, his extra weight made her legs burn and arms cramp. Still, she and the boys pushed forward, until Michael's breath came in ragged pants and Joshua's arms trembled around her throat.

"It's . . . not that . . . much farther," she said, but each word hurt to speak. She offered Michael the best smile she could muster. His bottom lip quivered, but he trudged forward.

She managed to put one foot in front of the other until her knees turned to jelly. Johanna and Joshua tumbled, somehow taking Michael down as they fell.

They all lay in the grass for a moment, panting and probably crying, at least two miles from the manor.

"We're okay, Jo." Joshua pushed himself to his feet and limped to her side. He held out a shaky hand, as if he could pull her up.

She wanted to lie in the shade under the walnut tree, to rest for a while, but for her brothers she stood and stumbled along.

This has got to change, she thought as sweat dripped off her forehead and soaked through her shirt. *We're good people. We work hard. We don't deserve to live like this.*

Chapter 41

Rafi

"Mother's going to kill us if we don't get back soon," Dom said as he marched toward his horse. "And by kill, I mean actual murder."

"We've got plenty of time," Rafi whispered, stalking toward the rabbit den. He carried the bag of vegetables to the hole they'd been watching and dropped a few carrots into the tunnel. "I hope they eat those and get fat and have thousands of babies, so we can eat them next year."

The hunting had gotten so slim, the forest so brown as a late-season heat wave dragged on, that Rafi worried all the small creatures would die without human intervention. He'd already dropped off sacks of grain and a salt lick to a meadow a small deer herd frequented, but leaving food for rabbits was something unheard of.

"*I* have plenty of time, because no one will be sitting close enough to smell me." Dom sniffed his armpit. "You, on the other hand, will have Belem in your lap all night."

Rafi didn't need the reminder. He'd spent half of his sleeping hours worrying about the amount of food the dukes and underlords, their retainers, and hangers-on were glutting through. Why couldn't they all have stayed at their own estates and simply sent letters of congratulations and a nice gift? Maybe something that would fill their larders? Winter wasn't even upon them, but Santiago would soon be relying on the salted stores the Fishermen's Guild put up during the spring run.

But food wasn't his only worry.

The conversation with Belem and Lord Inimigo's imminent arrival had Rafi's mind spinning till dawn. When Rafi finally dozed off, the Performer girl's voice had provided the accompaniment to his nightmares.

It was that damn lament I requested. Rafi shook his head, trying to dislodge the echo of his dream. *Next time, I'll ask for dancing tunes.*

The song made him think of the only time he'd seen his father, Belem, and Inimigo together in one location. Rafi had accompanied his father to witness peace brokered between the allied states Santiago, Impreza, Belem, what remained of King Wilhelm's outlying holdings, and Inimigo's state of Maringa.

You can never trust Inimigo, his father had cautioned. *It doesn't matter how many plans I thwart, he already has four more in play.*

Rafi had ridden knee to knee with his father to the treaty table, surrounded by heavily armored men. He remembered watching Inimigo cross the field on foot—his charger had been put down the day before, after the final battle—but the man's gold armor and red tabard were fine as any king's, and he held his head high and proud.

I thought he was coming to agree to peace, Rafi had said, confused by the man's pompous appearance.

As long as the throne is empty, peace with Inimigo will be uneasy.

His father gave Rafi a hard look. *Mark my words, son. This treaty will not last.*

Why don't you take the throne then, Father? I've heard the other lords say you earned it.

His father shook his head; the lightweight mail at his neck jingled as he moved. *It would take a better ruler than I to hold that throne.*

Fingers snapped in front of Rafi's face, drawing him out of the memory. "Where'd you go?" Dom regarded him through narrowed eyes.

"I'm sorry. I was thinking of Father."

"Father wouldn't have minded the horse sweat, but he'd have sent you home too, for fear the ladies would be appalled at your stench."

"The ladies that flirt with you won't notice that you smell just as bad?"

Dom scoffed. "Never. They're so overwhelmed by my good looks that the rest of their senses stop functioning completely."

Rafi couldn't help but laugh. "Dom you are—"

"Shh!"

"No, really, your self-confidence boggles."

"I said, shh!" His face had gone serious—a rare look on Dom. "I hear something over there."

"Like what?" Rafi whispered.

Dom shrugged and moved toward the noise, unhindered by any concern for his own well-being. Not that the forest was rife with predators, but after their father's death Rafi saw danger in unexpected places.

Rafi drew his belt knife and followed his brother through the brush.

Three boys—*correction, two boys and a filthy Johanna*—struggled forward on the edge of collapse.

"Hey!" Dom yelled, stepping through the brush and letting it snap in Rafi's face. "What are you all doing out here?"

"Oh, Lord Dom. I'm so glad to see you," Johanna said, sounding breathless. "My mother didn't return to our wagons and the boys and I have been running, but Michael got tired so I carried him, then Joshua fell so I carried him, too. Please, I need to get to the manor in time to change so that I can—"

Her mouth dropped open when Rafi stepped through the bushes.

"Our horses are just over that way," Rafi said, ignoring the expression on her face. "We'll be happy to give you a ride to the manor."

"I . . . I don't—"

"I'll take the boys," Dom said, digging treats out of his pockets. Johanna's brothers didn't seem to mind that the cookies may have been in the company of pebbles and random bits of snakeskin. "They can ride double on my horse. Rafi, you take Johanna back on Breaker so that you can both clean up before dinner."

"That's not necessary," Johanna said, managing to stand up straight.

"Sure it is." Dom knelt next to the older of the two boys. "You can't possibly expect—you're Joshua, right?"

The boy nodded.

"You can't expect Joshua to walk on that foot."

Joshua turned bright eyes on his sister, and for the first time Rafi saw Johanna off balance.

"Well . . ."

"Dom, don't you have something in one of those pockets that could mend up that toe a bit?" Rafi walked backward, hoping that Johanna would follow. "Your brothers will be in excellent hands."

The little one smiled around a bite of cherry tart, and Rafi felt his heart twinge.

"Go, Jo," Michael said. "He has treats."

Chapter 42

Johanna

Johanna didn't like the idea of being alone with Rafi. And by Mother Lua's light she was such a mess. Sweat made her now-torn shirt stick to her body, and she was certain her hair stuck up all over her head. Why did Rafi always catch her when she looked her worst?

Not that he cares. And, of course, I don't either. It doesn't matter if he thinks I'm ugly. Still, she couldn't stop herself from fidgeting with her vest and wiping her face on her sleeve when his back was turned.

Rafi walked a few steps in front of her, too high-and-mighty to walk beside her.

"So I guess this clears your debt?" she asked as they neared the horse. "It must be nice not to have that hanging over your head."

"No, my honor debt still holds," he said as he swung into the saddle. "I couldn't possibly leave three weary travelers in my woods alone. That would be wrong."

"Wrong? How?"

"Part of being a duke requires me to take care of all my subjects. Typical courtesy doesn't free me of my mistake."

"I'm not one of your subjects. I just live here." She was too blasted short to get into the saddle unaided and unwillingly accepted the hand he offered. "In my opinion, this counts."

Rafi yanked her up behind him, as if she weighed nothing. Johanna couldn't help but remember the hard lines of his body at Punishment. He'd been hung up like a side of beef at the marketplace, all the curves and corners of his muscles on display for her perusal. She tried not to the think of the press of his body against hers as he fell when Alouette cut him free, and his bare chest against the tender skin inside her wrist.

"If you live in Santiago, you're my responsibility." He kicked the horse into a trot, and Johanna gripped his leather jerkin with as little physical contact as possible. "And your opinion doesn't really count."

"Of course not. Why would it?"

He didn't argue, and Johanna fought the urge to flick his ear like she did to her brothers when they irritated her.

They didn't talk, and the ride to the manor was blessedly short with the horse trotting along a worn game trail.

The DeSilvas' estate appeared over a rise, yellow stone walls a stark contrast against jewel-toned windows and bright white balconies. A few underlords had already arrived for the evening's festivities, eyeing Rafi and Johanna as they rode under the main gate.

And probably assuming awful things.

"I'll drop you off at the kitchen entrance," Rafi said as they rode toward the stable.

She hoped that if he dumped her like baggage in front of the manor there would be less speculation. "No need to trouble yourself. I can walk the rest of the way, my lord."

He looked into Johanna's face. "When you say 'my lord' like that, I wonder what words you're replacing my title with in your head."

"I have no idea what you're talking about." *Hooflicker. Flea-eating dung monkey,* Johanna's mind supplied. Blood crept into her ears, but she made herself meet his gaze.

"Of course not, you're a perfectly trained Performer. Quiet, biddable, always thinking the very best about your benefactors."

Johanna did not like the teasing note in his voice. "Always the *very* best."

"I'm glad to hear it," he said, his mouth twisting into an arrogant, sarcastic smirk. "I wouldn't want you to think poorly of me."

"And what if I did?" She issued that challenge as she slid off the horse.

He leaned over the side of the saddle, narrowing the gap between them. "I'd find a way to change your mind."

She laughed and walked away. "Good luck with that, *my lord*."

Chapter 43

Jacaré

Jacaré didn't get the rest he needed in Vicente. When they left the city, they'd replenished their supplies and rode new horses, but he also carried a new burden.

"Swear to me that if you find this man, you will spare him no mercy." Lord Venza had held tight to Jacaré's hand. "He killed my child, left her in an alley to bleed to death. Swear that you will avenge her murder and the girl from Belem too. I expected to go into the ground long before my child, not have to bury her before . . . before she even experienced life."

Lord and Lady Venza's pain was too familiar for Jacaré to ignore. He knew the anguish of a life cut short, and his conscience wouldn't allow him to disregard their plea.

"If I find the man responsible, he'll pay for his crimes." It was the best promise he could make under the circumstances. Finding the heir came first.

Performers' Camp lay half a day's hard ride from Vicente. Leão had ridden ahead, scouting the trail Tex said would take the crew in the right direction.

The hills were pockmarked with quarries, some abandoned,

some still functioning. Shadows dripped into one of the scarred pits, disappearing into its stony depths, before they saw Leão again.

He stopped midtrail, waiting for the crew to catch up.

"Did you find it?" Jacaré asked.

Leão nodded, the late afternoon sun casting his cheeks and forehead with a golden hue. "There's a narrow path through a stretch of boulders. It's barely wide enough for us to ride on two abreast. Over the hill is a small valley, farmland on the outskirts, and tents and wagons grouped in the middle."

"Anything else?" Jacaré asked.

Leão took a long swig from his canteen before he answered. "I . . . I felt something." He shivered, but he couldn't possibly have been cold. Sweat beaded his forehead, and the sun blazed against his back. The unclaimed land north of Santiago wasn't nearly as humid, but summer clung to their skin and tickled their noses with the smell of horse sweat and lush undergrowth. "It was like someone in the valley was working magic."

"That's impossible," Pira said. "The people of Santarem don't have *essência*. They can't—" She suddenly realized that neither Jacaré nor Tex had disagreed with Leão's claim. "They can't use magic, right?"

Jacaré shifted in his saddle, having mentally prepared for this conversation and the related questions for days. "The quick answer is no. The people of Santarem cannot work magic." He looked at the next hill, knowing the girl they'd been searching for could be on the far slope. It was tempting to push off the discussion for later, but he knew that both Pira and Leão deserved the truth. Actually, they both had deserved to know before they had crossed the wall.

"They can't work magic unless they are descendants of Keepers." The words fell like a rock in a pond, ripples widening and washing over them.

"That's not possible," Leão said. "The law expressly forbids copulating with anyone other than another Keeper."

"That didn't seem to stop you in Belem," Pira said smugly.

"I did not—"

"Your shirt was off!"

"That doesn't mean—"

"Enough!" Jacaré's voice cut over all of them. "It wasn't always the law. Once there were Keepers who took people from Santarem as mates. Many of these Performers are descendants of a Keeper-Santarem bonding."

Leão shook his head, shocked and dumbfounded.

"They may have a remnant of *essência* and some of our other traits, but after three hundred years most of our influence has been bred out."

"Maybe soldiers like you three, but full Mages . . . we couldn't," Leão said with a dismissive shake of his head. "There would be an imbalance of power, and eventually the Mage would be able to control their mate's free will."

"We don't have time for a history lesson. We have an heir to save," Tex reminded them, his voice low and gruff. "Quick version: Everything you've been taught about why we crossed Donovan's Wall was false. Yes, the people of Santarem rose up and slaughtered a good number of our people. The war was ugly, but it wasn't unfounded."

"What?" Pira and Leão said at the same time.

Jacaré took over. "Some Mages were using their power to turn non-Keepers into slaves. Our people divided into two factions: The Nata, who wanted to use their power to dominate the people of Santarem, and the rest of the Keepers, who felt it was wrong. The Nata were ultimately defeated. The remnants of us crossed the wall to keep the people of Santarem safe."

Leão's face went pale. Pira, on the other hand, was flushed with anger.

"The barrier must remain standing," Jacaré continued. "There are Mages in Olinda who might be tempted to rule, to reestablish the Nata, if they realized it was an option."

"But . . . ," Pira started, looking at each of the men, seemingly unable to finish her thought.

Leão spun his horse and trotted back the way he had come without another word. Pira followed, casting her brother a glare over her shoulder.

"That went well," Tex said, turning in the saddle to face Jacaré.

"They've been lied to their whole lives. All that matters now is that they believe us," Jacaré said, watching the distance between him and the younger members of his crew expand.

"They have to. We were there."

Chapter 44

Rafi

Rafi didn't want to hand Breaker's reins to the waiting groom. Going into the house meant facing the frivolity and flirting, the subterfuge and schemes. He wanted to get back on his horse and ride until Breaker's stride drove a certain Performer girl out of his thoughts.

She was infuriating, prideful, and rude. She hadn't murmured a word of thanks for getting her back to the manor before she had to perform. Not that he expected it; but still, the courtesy would have been nice.

"Walk him a bit before you take him into the stable," Rafi said, patting the horse fondly on the neck. Breaker's black coat was hot under his fingers, but the well-conditioned animal wasn't blowing and sweating. "And an extra scoop of oats, if you please. He deserves it."

The groom nodded his assent and led Breaker into the paddock.

"You can judge a lot about a man from the way he treats his mount," boomed a voice from the barn door.

Rafi whipped toward the sound, a smile already tugging at his lips. "My father used to say the same thing."

"Your father was smart." An old man with a curly cap of steel-gray hair stepped onto the walkway separating the two grazing yards.

He limped a bit more than Rafi remembered, his steps crunching unevenly over the gravel. But the face was the same as always, and as familiar to Rafi as his own: the hard jaw, the dark eyes, and the hair that had to be kept short or it would turn wild. "He was also one of the best men I knew."

"I've heard you say that before." Rafi took a couple steps toward his uncle and caught the man in a tight embrace. "Or you wouldn't have let him steal my mother away."

"Steal?" Fernando, the Duke of Impreza and Lady DeSilva's elder brother, said with a half laugh. "I couldn't have kept Liliana out of your father's arms if I'd poured an ocean between them."

Rafi's throat tightened at the slight hitch in his uncle's voice.

"I expected Camilio to come thundering down the path to greet me. It's hard to believe I'll never ride with him again."

Three months earlier, Rafi, Dom, and their father had gone to an underlord's property to hunt an abnormally large panther that had killed two farmers. They'd been midhunt when the duke keeled over. He was dead before he hit the ground. All signs pointed to heart failure, though his father had always been a healthy man.

"I wished you could have been here for the burial, but we all knew it was impossible to leave during Salting Time."

Impreza's main export was fish and other things harvested from the ocean. Early summer was their busiest season, and every man, woman, and child packed, prepared, and shipped the harvest. Even the inland farmers sent whomever they could spare to the ports to help with Salting Time. For several years, Rafi, Dom, and their mother made the trip to the southern state to work alongside Duke Fernando and his people. Rafi stood shoulder to shoulder with fishwives and underlords and learned how to process fish, seaweed, and ocean animals into dozens of different products. In Impreza the gentry were expected to work alongside the peasants, and Fernando could not leave his state even to attend his brother-in-law's interment.

"But you're here now."

Fernando gave Rafi's shoulder a tight squeeze, and they began moving toward the house.

"I saw Belem's carriage outside the stable. I guess we'll get your naming out of the way soon?"

Rafi stopped and faced his uncle. "Inimigo's coming."

"What?" Fernando said, sharp as a stiletto.

"Belem said he'll be here the day after tomorrow."

The older man's hand dropped to the sword at his belt. "Good. I'll finally have a chance to fulfill that promise."

"The treaty has held for years. Any action you take against Inimigo—"

"The treaty was political. Between me and Inimigo, that's personal." Fernando's dark eyes had gone hard, his jaw was set.

"It was personal for my father, too," Rafi reminded him.

"Inimigo's troops killed my *son,* Rafi." His hand clenched his weapon's hilt. "I know it was war. I know Diogo was a trained swordsman, but he was a boy—no older than you are now."

Rafi choked back the rush of memories brought on by his cousin's name. As a child he worshipped Diogo, following the older boy like a shadow.

"No promise, no piece of paper, no words will stop me from seeking out retribution for that man's crimes," Fernando continued. "I will bring down war upon all of us if I see Inimigo's face." He spun on his heel and headed back to the barn. "Tell your mother I'm sorry."

Fernando called to the retainers milling about the yard. They looked at one another with confused faces but made their way toward their lord.

"You'll leave before you've even seen her?" Rafi yelled at Fernando's retreating back. "Stay the night at least! You can be halfway to the border before Inimigo sets foot in Santiago."

Fernando stopped.

"Please. Stay the night." Rafi jogged across the space that separated him from his uncle. "Your horses have earned one night's rest, don't you think?"

Fernando turned slowly, an unwilling smirk on his lips. "They do deserve one night off the road I suppose. And you deserve to be duke for turning my words on me like that."

Chapter 45

Johanna

The maids took one look at Johanna and dropped everything—an empty tray in Brynn's case—and rushed to her aid.

"We've been worried sick about you, and it looks like we were right to worry." Brynn grabbed Johanna's hand and dragged her toward the main hall and the room she'd used to dress the night before.

Johanna explained the situation, as Brynn poured buckets of not-quite-warm water over her head.

"Don't you worry one bit about Joshua and Michael," Brynn said as she helped Johanna step into her layered skirt. "We'll all keep an eye on them."

The door to the bedroom swung open, and a rather pale Lady DeSilva stepped into the room. Brynn's fingers froze as she laced up the back of Johanna's dress.

"L-lady, we—"

"I heard," she said, not unkindly. "Cook needs you in the kitchen. I'll take care of Johanna."

"Yes, ma'am." Brynn marched away, leaving the ribbons from Johanna's bodice hanging loose.

Johanna steeled herself for the reprimand she deserved. She'd been late to arrive, brought her two younger brothers with her, and her attitude toward Rafi bordered on unprofessional.

He did come to your rescue today, Jo. You don't have to like him, but you don't have to be rude, either.

"Thank you, my lady." Johanna found her manners. "I can manage the rest myself."

"Nonsense. We have hungry guests who are looking forward to a skilled Storyspinner." She urged Johanna toward the silk-covered stool in front of the dressing table. "Sit. Let me do your hair. I never had a daughter to practice on."

Johanna dropped onto the stool without an argument and spread her skirts wide, trying not to wrinkle them.

"To be honest, I have a few things I need to speak with you about." Lady DeSilva's eyes were solemn as they met Johanna's in the mirror. "I must start with the hardest part first. I fear that if I held this till the end of the night, you'd assume I was more concerned with your performance than your well-being."

Johanna didn't know what to say, so she nodded, pulling a strand of hair out of the duchess's hands.

"Your mother was arrested this afternoon."

"*What?*" The word was more air than sound as it leaked out of Johanna's mouth.

"She left her job at the pub—"

"There must be some mistake, my lady. My mother works for a seamstress," Johanna said, ignoring the tight ball of dread in her stomach. "She's an excellent tailor and embroiderer. She made this dress."

The lady's hands stopped fussing with Johanna's short hair and settled on her shoulders. "The seamstress let her go last week. She caught your mother drinking at work and fired her after she spilled some alcohol on a pile of valuable fabric."

Johanna's eyes dropped to the tabletop, studying a knot in the oak surface. It seemed to go around and around in an oblong whorl. She wished it were a magical whirlpool that would open up and swallow her whole. Maybe it could whisk her back to the day before her father died, when the bottles in the cupboard above his bed had always been full.

"One of Captain Alouette's men realized who she was and brought me the news." Lady DeSilva resumed her pinning. "Marin is being escorted to your wagon right now. The man she accosted, some outrider for a merchant camp, isn't seeking retribution of any sort."

Oh, Mama. What were you thinking?

Johanna allowed herself ten seconds of self-pity and sadness before putting on her Performer's face. This job was more important than ever.

"Thank you for the information and your help with my hair." Johanna spread the contents of her satchel over the dressing table. She needed rouge for cheeks. They were much too pale after the run and—

She cut off the thought and applied the color to her cheeks with a soft rabbit's-foot brush.

The lady finished her hair while Johanna coated her lashes in a coal and aloe mixture. She only wore it when she was

Storyspinning, so that her audience could better make out her expressions.

Johanna heard a quick intake of breath and caught Lady DeSilva's stare in the mirror.

"I'm sorry." She shook her head and gave a little half laugh. "You reminded me of someone else with your eyes made up like that."

Performers got that all the time. "You said you had a few things you wanted to talk to me about? Besides . . ." Johanna bit her bottom lip to stop its trembling, then picked up a tub of color like she intended to apply it. "Besides that incident with my mother?"

Lady DeSilva's face blanked for a moment. "Yes. We're going on a picnic tomorrow afternoon. Rafi and I hoped you'd be willing to do a bit of singing for the group. We'd, of course, pay you for an additional show."

"I'd love to, but I care for my brothers during the day." *While my mother lies about where she's been.* The sadness and embarrassment she'd been feeling ignited in a flash of anger, like a match struck in a dark room.

"That'll be no problem. We can put them up for the night, and I know some of the maids would love to have a change from their normal duties."

"I couldn't possibly ask you to . . ." *But we really need the money.*

"Johanna, I've got a house full of guests that need entertaining." She offered a gentle smile. "You'd be doing us a favor."

"If you're certain it wouldn't be an imposition. My brothers can be—"

"Have you met my sons? This house and staff are accustomed to rough-and-tumble boys."

"I'll only accept half of my regular fee to cover the cost of their care."

"We'll see." Lady DeSilva patted Johanna's cheek with motherly affection, and Johanna felt the anger at her own mother grow from a flicker to a searing flame.

Chapter 46

Leão

Four men, armed with short swords, blocked off the main trail into Performers' Camp. They were all thinly muscled, their arms bared by multihued vests, but not malnourished.

"State your business." The speaker was a bit taller than his companions. He wore a bright red strip of cloth tied around his brow and another around his bicep like a band of office.

The Keepers' Elite Guard wore the braided *cadarço* to signify an advanced level of training. Leão cringed inwardly, hoping the similarity was a fluke, and not proof of Jacaré's story. "We're looking for someone," he said, signaling to Pira, Tex, and Jacaré, a few horse lengths away.

"Got a name?"

"No, but I can describe her."

The men on either side of the leader shifted, hands edging toward the weapons slung through the wide sashes at their hips.

"Son," the leader said, stepping closer to Leão's horse. "You wouldn't be the first man to lose his heart to a Performer girl, but don't claim she stole your coin purse. We Performers are flighty by nature, and as you don't know her name, she certainly won't remember yours. I'm sorry for your long journey, but you and your"—he studied the approaching group, eyes lingering on Pira's face—"people need to move on. We don't allow strangers into Performers' Camp."

Leão's cheeks flushed red. "This isn't about hearts or purses, this is about—"

"A debt unfulfilled," Jacaré said. "A Performer once saved my life, and I heard that he was recently killed in a fall. We rode from Impreza to offer a boon to his wife."

"He must be talking about Arlo." One of the younger guards elbowed the man next to him.

The leader wasn't so easily taken in. "That's a long ride to offer a boon to a Performer. Why not wait till the next time a troupe made it to your town?"

"There was no guarantee that she'd be with them, and I don't know her name. But I'd recognize her face if I saw it and would know my debt was fulfilled."

"Are you sure you're not from Santiago?" The leader said with an arrogant smirk. "I didn't know men from Impreza were so committed to honor."

"Arlo saved my life. Don't I owe his family a personal visit?"

The leader shrugged. "You can give me the boon and I'll be happy to pass it along."

"It's not that I don't trust you, friend," Jacaré said, sounding decidedly unfriendly. "But fifty gold pieces is a lot of money to put into the hands of the wrong person."

"Fifty gold," the youngest guard whispered, eyes wide with awe.

"That is a lot—" His words cut off when the leader smacked him on the back of the head.

"I'll talk to our Council and see what they make of your claims." He pointed to a narrow trail, branching off into some pine trees. "Head that way and make camp. I'll send someone back with word on the Council's decision by dawn."

"Thank you for your assistance. Can you give me a name to call you by?"

The leader turned, walking backward down the rocky trail without a stumble. "I'm Benton, the Firesword. These lads are members of my troupe. They'll stay nearby if you need anything."

"We don't need anything except to see Arlo's widow."

Benton offered a self-confident smile. "Don't get your hopes up."

Chapter 47

Rafi

Lady DeSilva held tight to her brother's arm as he escorted her into the dining hall. To Rafi, it looked like she was gripping too tightly, hoping to hold Fernando in Santiago by her fingernails alone.

She'd been ecstatic to see her brother—slipping into a fishwife patter and begging all the details of her native state—and angry that he planned to leave before Rafi's official naming ceremony. She called him a fish-swiving fool and several other curse phrases that made Rafi's ears burn. Ladies did not speak like that, especially his lady mother.

Fernando took it all in stride, waiting for her tirade to end, before saying simply, "Inimigo killed my son."

That one simple statement ended the argument abruptly, though Rafi could tell from the calculating look on his mother's face that their discussion was far from over.

The serving staff set an extra plate, between Rafi and his mother, so they wouldn't have to ask the Duke of Belem to move down a chair. Lady DeSilva fretted a moment that her brother would feel slighted to sit on his nephew's left-hand side rather than his right.

"Good glory, woman!" Fernando said as he dropped into the chair.

"Living in Santiago has made you soft. If it's going to make you blue in the face with worry, I'll sit on the floor with the dogs."

"You certainly are filthy enough," she said, much to the amusement of everyone within hearing distance. "We could have waited till you had time to change."

"No need to hold dinner for me."

"Hear! Hear!" Belem said, waving a greasy chicken leg above his head. "My stomach couldn't wait a moment longer, and the Duke of Impreza can impress us with his fine southern silk tomorrow."

Rafi exchanged a look with his uncle, letting the older man determine whether or not to address his planned departure.

"I'll be leaving in the morning, Belem." Fernando sliced a piece of chicken into small precise bites. "I have matters to address at home."

Despite having already swilled three glasses of wine, Belem wasn't drunk enough to believe that excuse. He nodded a few times and wiped his oily fingers on the linen he'd tucked into his collar. "Heard Inimigo's coming, eh?"

Heads at the lower tables turned with interest to the dukes' conversation.

"Among other things," Fernando said, eyeing his sister sharply.

Rafi guessed his mother had kicked Fernando under the table. Rafi had been the recipient of bruised shins and crushed toes when his mother wanted him to change the topic or hurry along a conversation.

Fernando cleared his throat. "We've had some pirate attacks along our coast. I came with only a small guard so we could travel light and fast, as not to diminish our troops at my southern port."

"That's most unfortunate," Belem said, reaching for the pudding that had been set in front of him. "The girl they've hired to sing for us is exquisite, and I'm not talking about her voice. She's a petite thing, and young, but there's something about her mouth that makes me forget I'm a married man."

Rafi's hand tightened around his cutlery till the metal grip bit into his palm. "It doesn't take much."

Belem laughed, slamming Rafi across the shoulders with a meaty hand. "Too true!"

While they ate, Lady DeSilva carried the conversation and carefully sidestepped all of Belem's crass comments. She handled them smoothly and with a skill Rafi knew he lacked.

She should be duchess in more than name, he thought as he scooped fried yucca into his mouth. *Maybe a few more years with her as regent would do all of Santiago well.*

"As the first round of desserts has been served, why don't you announce our entertainment?" Lady DeSilva gave her son a wide-eyed look in warning.

Rafi wiped the frustration off his face and pushed away from the table.

The kitchen was a flutter of activity as always, but most of it seemed centered around the two little boys sitting at the kneading table. Someone had washed them both up, though Michael's hair stood up straight in the back, and his mouth was circled with powdered sugar.

Johanna clucked at them, every bit the mother hen. She wiped her youngest brother's face and placed a kiss on his forehead, leaving a smear of lip stain.

"Ew, Jo!" Michael rubbed at the spot, making it worse and earning a smile from his sister.

She does have a pretty mouth, Rafi realized as she applied a matching kiss to Joshua's forehead. He bore it with more patience than Michael, ignoring her attentions and popping a pastry into his mouth in one bite.

"Chew, Joshua." She pulled the basket away from him. "It's not going to disappear. No one is going to steal them from you."

On impulse Rafi snatched the basket from under her arm and pushed it back in front of the boy. "I don't know if I'd believe that. Have you met Dom and seen all his pockets?"

Both boys nodded, eyes wide with interest.

"Where do you think he gets the food he fills them with?"

Joshua hugged the basket to his chest as if he expected Dom to appear and steal all the remaining rolls away. Michael's little hand wedged under his brother's arm and grabbed as many rolls as he could hold.

Cook smacked Rafi on the shoulder with her wooden spoon. "Don't you listen to him. There's plenty. You eat your fill and then eat some more."

Rafi grinned at the murderous look on Cook's face, but his smile faltered when he realized Johanna was also giving him the evil eye.

Her neck had turned red and her pretty mouth was pressed flat.

I'm always stepping in it with her. She gets so blasted angry when

I'm around. Though she probably had good reason to dislike him. He had beaten her to a bloody pulp.

"Dessert has been served. Are you prepared to Storyspin, Miss Johanna?" He offered her his arm.

Johanna reached for the long cloak that hung on Michael's chair. She tied the cloak's thread across her throat and tossed the sides behind her shoulders, leaving the majority of her green gown exposed. It looked heavy and uncomfortable, but Rafi had seen many Storyspinners and knew their capes were much like Dom's pockets: full of surprises.

"The question is, are you ready, my lord?" she asked with a smirk that spoke of a secret.

They repeated their walk into the dining hall as protocol dictated: the welcome, the announcement of the performance, the curtsy—and then Rafi had to kiss her hand.

He hesitated a moment, the intensity of her gaze a lash across his bowed neck.

She hates me.

Rather than offend her further, his lips barely grazed her knuckles. An actual kiss from him, even on her hand, would not have been welcome.

She finished her curtsies to each of the tables in turn, but Rafi didn't watch. He was too confused by the look on his uncle's face.

"Where did you find her?" Fernando asked, grabbing Rafi's arm as he sat down. "Where did she come from?" A deep line furrowed the man's forehead, but he only had eyes for Johanna.

What was it about the girl that had the dukes, even the

long-widowed Fernando, panting like dogs in late summer? She was attractive, but there were a lot of beautiful women in Santarem. There was even a decent selection in the dining hall.

"She's much too young for you, Uncle." Rafi forced humor into his tone.

"Oh, I disagree there. Women are not like wine. They're better before they age." Belem winked at Lady DeSilva. "Present company excluded."

The lady ignored the comment and answered her brother's question. "Johanna is the daughter of two Performers. Her father was killed in a tragic accident, and she lives near the Milners' mango orchard now."

"Unfortunate," Belem mumbled as he shoveled a bite of dessert into his mouth. "A girl like that needs a man in her life. Or a duke."

Fernando and Lady DeSilva didn't seem to hear Belem, too involved in their whispered conversation.

Rafi leaned back in his chair, waiting for Johanna to begin her story and to dispel the horrible mental picture of her snuggled in his uncle's arms. Or Belem's for that matter.

She reached into her cloak and threw a fine black powder high into the air. It hung like a glistening sheet of fog, hiding her from the audience's eyes. She lowered her voice, speaking softly, but it still carried to every corner of the room.

The story was that of a huntsman, lost in a dark forest. Awful beasts stalked him, and Johanna's pale hands danced across the fog, giving the impression of a great chase.

A spark appeared off to the left, her arm held far from her body.

She tossed the glowing fleck into the cloud of dust. The entire thing ignited, illuminating Johanna like some sort of nymph in a fairy tale, a perfect illustration for the story. The huntsman was pulled to safety by a woman of indefinable beauty and strength—a goddess.

Bits of burning ash fell, like stars tumbling from the night sky, but nothing caught flame. Rafi had heard the story before, and had even seen it done with the same effects, but Johanna told it with a fresh passion.

The huntsman offered the golden goddess everything to repay her for his life, and she took it.

Johanna tossed two more handfuls of powder into the air, one golden, one purple. As they swirled together, they gave the impression of two shadows locked in an embrace.

The story didn't have a particularly happy ending: The huntsman died, and the goddess roamed Santarem with the child of their union as her only company.

But Johanna managed to twist the words into something heart-achingly beautiful and poignant. Rather than sadness, Rafi felt the goddess's joy in her child—the first Keeper. He had his mother's ability to tap the elements for power, but it was tempered by his father's humanity and mortality.

Johanna raised her hands above her head, and a bright ball of white light seemed to appear in her hands. The goddess, in the form of Mother Lua, looked down on her people every night and watched over her child's progeny.

Rafi tried to look away, to ignore Johanna and the spell she wove over the audience, but there was something hypnotic in her eyes.

He felt like she told the story for his ears alone, that some invisible thread connected them.

"I should like to meet her," Fernando said softly as the story concluded.

The thread snapped with a harsh recoil. Rafi gasped as if he hadn't drawn breath since the first word spun off Johanna's tongue.

"I told you she was exquisite," Belem said in an overloud whisper.

Chapter 48

Johanna

The applause was thunderous. Johanna reveled in the audience's reaction, knowing she'd affected them all. The women dabbed tears; the men clutched their lovers' hands during the romantic tales and the laments. They laughed when the story called for it and cheered and gasped at all the right moments.

Except Rafi.

He leaned far back in his chair, long legs stretched out in front of him, seeming the relaxed lordling. But unlike Belem—who lolled to one side of the chair with his ever-full wine cup dangling from his fingers—Rafi's act was incomplete. His arms were folded a bit too tightly across his chest, and he shot measuring glances at the men on either side of him.

He'd never make it as a Performer. His real feelings are too evident.

Rafi managed to bring his hands together in an unenthusiastic applause as Johanna finished the last story she'd prepared for the evening. She planned to take a few requests, sing a bit, then return to her room with her brothers.

"The evening grows late, but perhaps the head table has a particular selection they'd like to hear?" She posed the question to Rafi, hoping his answer might give her a hint at his interests and what her performance lacked in his eyes.

He waved to the man on his left. "I'll defer to my uncle. He won't have the pleasure of hearing your lovely voice as frequently as I."

Lovely voice. Johanna hid her look of disgust with a curtsy to the Duke of Impreza.

The man, an older, more distinguished version of Rafi, exchanged a look with Lady DeSilva before speaking. "I do have a request. An odd one perhaps." He laced his fingers together and rested his elbows on the table. "I had a Performer visit my estate after the treaty was signed. He told an incredible tale called 'The Survivor of Roraima.' Do you know it?"

Johanna hoped her cape disguised the goose bumps that rose along her arms and her too-stiff spine. She knew the tale; it was the last story her father had ever spun.

Most of the stories she told were old, embellished and elaborated. But that story was fresh, the words bleeding from wounds not-quite healed.

"It's not a particularly pleasant story, my lord," Johanna said, imagining the pall that would fall over the dining room as every person thought of their lost king, his kindhearted wife, and their angel baby, or perhaps a loved one or friend who'd been trapped inside Roraima's walls as the township burned.

"I've never heard it," Lord Belem said, for once sitting in his chair rather than draping himself across it. "I should like to hear it as well."

Rafi quirked his dark eyebrows—black peaks sharp with curiosity—and her decision was made.

"Once there was a beloved king," she said, taking a few backward steps to the center of the floor. "He was a hardworking man who toiled alongside his people. In the spring, he harnessed his mighty war horse to the plow and prepared his people's fields. In the fall, he wielded a scythe and helped them harvest. In times of peace, he hosted feasts where all, even the most humble peasant, were invited to dine at his side. And in times of war"—she paused and made eye contact with several members of the crowd—"he welcomed his people inside the walls of his fortress and protected them.

"Many years passed, but the king had not found a suitable bride. His people were concerned, and they sent girls and women, young and old, from every state and from the isles to gain the king's hand, but none could earn his fancy.

"Then, one night, a girl appeared at his gate. Her clothes were torn and filthy, her hair a matted mess. She trembled from fatigue and hunger, but nothing could disguise her beauty. People who met her said she seemed to shine from within."

A few heads in the crowd nodded their agreement. Some of them had certainly met Wilhelm's queen.

"The kingdom rejoiced, for their king had finally found a woman whose heart was pure and who wasn't afraid of hard work. They had one year of blissful happiness, and the queen gave birth to a lovely daughter.

"But all was not well. One lord was unsatisfied with his station in the land. He sought more power, riches, and glory."

The double doors to the dining hall burst inward, slamming against the stone walls. Two men with shining breastplates strode into the room, escorting a broad-shouldered man in a deep crimson cape. Diamonds twinkled in both of his ears, and a narrow band of gold wrapped around his brow, pressing flat his black hair.

There were gasps, and a chair clattered to the floor.

"Fernando!" Lady DeSilva said, grabbing her brother's arm, but his sword was already sliding free of its scabbard.

Rafi jumped up from his seat and stepped in front of his uncle. "Stop," he commanded.

Dom, Captain Alouette, and the weaponsmaster appeared at Duke Fernando's side, all with hands on their weapons, ready to draw.

The man in the doorway watched the scene with a smile that only reached his lips. "I didn't expect such a welcome." He pressed his hand over his heart. "Perhaps I should offer my apologies, Lady DeSilva. I sent an outrider to announce my early arrival, but it appears the message didn't reach your ears."

The duchess extracted herself from the group of men, shooting one concerned look at her brother. Rafi stood close, nearly nose to nose with his uncle, speaking in a tone too low to reach Johanna's ears. Not that Fernando seemed to be listening; he only had eyes for the richly appointed man in the doorway.

"Duke Inimigo," Lady DeSilva said as she approached the group; her tone was just south of frigid. "This is a surprise."

Chapter 49

Leão

"They have a council and wear *cadarço*," Leão said as he and Pira curried the horses. "It could be a coincidence."

He waited for her to toss a sarcastic remark or eye roll his way—she couldn't get through any conversation without some caustic observation—but she didn't respond, her hands moving efficiently over the horse's coat.

With currying combs still in hand, he walked to the next horse down the line and started on its far side so he could see her over the animal's back. He liked to watch her face when they talked. She tried so hard to seem implacable, not letting anything affect her, but her eyes gave her away. They were bright and fiery, revealing every time she thought he said something stupid and tilting up a bit at the corners when she tried to hide a smile.

He hadn't been able to make her smile in days, and he'd finally figured out why.

"I feel like I owe you an explanation for my actions in the barn," he said, watching her. She wouldn't make eye contact, but her hands hesitated for a moment. "I'm not sure what you thought, but I wouldn't break the law. Not even to get information about Performers' Camp."

She met his gaze with a flat stare, then resumed her brushing with an irritated head shake.

"You have to know me better than that. I don't break the laws," Leão continued. "I'm a member of the Elite Guard. I live to uphold them."

"You honestly think I'm upset with you over a matter of the law?"

Upset was a mild way to describe her attitude toward him, and Leão didn't think he'd done anything else to deserve her ire. "If it's not the law, then why are you mad at me?"

He dodged the currying brush she chucked at his head.

"I don't give a fig about the law, Leão. We've broken the law dozens of times just to get here." She rounded the tail end of his horse and pressed a hard finger into his chest. "It's about *using* that girl to reach your goal."

"I don't have much experience with kissing, but she seemed to enjoy it."

She slapped him too fast for him to react, then spun on her heel and marched away.

"I don't understand why you're angry," he mumbled, pressing a hand to his stinging cheek.

Pira continued her trajectory beyond Tex and Jacaré, who were spitting rabbits over the fire.

"Where are you going?" Jacaré said as she stepped out of the circle of stones that delineated the camp's boundaries and headed into the woods.

She didn't answer.

Jacaré stood, but Tex put out a restraining arm. "Let her go. She may find out something helpful."

Chapter 50

Rafi

"Let me go," Fernando said through clenched teeth. He gripped his sword with white knuckles, but the men on either side of him weren't going to let him use it.

"Uncle, please. Don't start anything here," Rafi asked, placing a hand on Fernando's chest. A vein in the man's neck hammered in time with one above his eyebrow.

"I'm not starting anything, Rafi. I intend to finish it."

Lord Inimigo, Duke of Maringa, raised empty palms. "I come unarmed, bearing gifts, accompanied by family." He waved, and a girl stepped into the dining hall. Behind her stretched an endless line of servants, all in matching livery and wearing thick, silver bands around their necks. "I wanted to welcome your nephew into manhood. I bear you no ill will, Lord Fernando. I know I'll never earn your forgiveness, but perhaps we can dispense with the hostility between us." He offered a smile, his teeth so white they reflected the light. "Let's put aside the past and move toward the future."

"You're a butcher and a murderer. Your men hung our king from the ramparts of his castle and killed every man, woman, and child within the walls of Roraima." He turned suddenly, pointing his finger at Johanna. "This Performer was telling us the tale to remind us of your nature. Finish it, girl. Tell them about the screams of the dying."

All eyes focused on Johanna, and for once she looked uncomfortable under the scrutiny.

"Enough," Rafi shouted. "I will not allow my naming day to result in war. In Santiago, we uphold the treaty and expect all of our guests to do the same, or they will be asked to leave this state."

Duke Inimigo sketched a half bow in acquiescence. Fernando shook his head. "Then I shall leave. I warned you that I wouldn't sleep under the same roof as this Keeper-blasted excuse of a man."

"Fernando, please." Lady DeSilva held out a beseeching hand, which was ignored.

"Escort me out, Rafi."

"Dom, you and Master Ortiz stay here and make sure all of the men from Impreza follow us out," Rafi commanded. "Captain Alouette will accompany us."

The men stepped away, allowing Fernando to return his sword to his hip and, without another word, they all turned for the dining hall's far doors.

"Good-bye, Fernando," Duke Inimigo yelled. "I had hoped to meet you under different circumstances."

"The next time I see that man, I hope he's on the end of my blade," Fernando responded, loud enough to draw a few gasps.

Rafi's jaw tightened, as did his grip on his uncle's arm.

The grooms in the stable yard were manic, running to the barracks, saddling horses, adding foodstuffs to panniers. In this case, the eavesdropping servants had done Rafi a favor.

"Send them away," Fernando commanded, signaling to the grooms and men nearby. Rafi shooed the onlookers back and helped his uncle prepare to ride.

"I have two things to speak with you about, and I'd hoped to have more time to do it. But now . . ." He threw his saddle over his horse's back. Fernando pressed his thumbs into a notch in the saddle horn, and the section slid aside. The compartment hid a small linen bag. "We can work out the details later, but I intended to name you heir to my estate at your naming ceremony."

He pressed a sigil ring into Rafi's palm. Rafi knew the emblem without looking. He could feel the fins of the great fish cutting into his skin.

"I know it would be too much land for you to manage alone, but I hoped you would train up Dom and send him to me to act as your regent."

"Uncle—"

"I don't have time to debate this. Just agree for now." He pressed on, not waiting for an answer. "The second thing is that girl, that Performer. I think she could be in danger. Someone is hunting girls that match her description. My lieutenant's daughter was murdered after attending a performance last year. Another, a maid from my own estate, has been missing for five months."

"What happened to them? Why were they targeted?"

"It could be a sick infatuation with a specific type of girl, or . . ." Fernando shook his head, eyeing all the people in the yard. "Your mother has her own suspicions. I'm not sure if I believe them, but post a guard on Johanna's rooms and at her house." He gripped both of Rafi's shoulders.

"Of course. I'd never let harm come to any of my people. I'll do everything I can to protect her."

"Make sure you take care of yourself, too." Fernando opened his mouth to say something else, but shut it as one of his guardsman approached.

"We're ready to ride when you are, my lord."

"Mount up. I'll be with you momentarily."

The guard nodded and called to their small contingency. Fernando waited until the man had moved a fair distance away. "With Inimigo and Belem under your roof, you must tread carefully," he said, eyes searching out a threat. "Don't let Belem's laziness fool you. He may look as harmless as a jellyfish, but we both know their sting is deadly."

"I'll be careful."

Fernando's face broke into a fierce grin. "I'll miss you, boy, but I hope to come back before the first winter storm."

"All right."

The man gathered him into a tight hug. Rafi held on, wishing that his uncle was willing to stay.

No chance.

Fernando swung into the saddle, whistling to his men, and they left the yard at a gallop. The horses' hooves thundered like the threat of rain in the distance, and Rafi wondered if perhaps the storm was already upon him.

Chapter 51

Johanna

The gentry whispered, shooting nervous glances at Inimigo as Fernando was escorted out of the dining hall.

"Forgive me for interrupting your meal, sirs and ladies," Inimigo said, offering another half bow to the room. "If someone will direct us to our suites, we'll leave you all in peace."

Lady DeSilva seemed uncharacteristically flustered. Her staff hung against the back walls waiting for her to issue a command, but she didn't act.

Johanna coughed and shot a look at Brynn.

"I'll go get some fresh place settings, my lady," Brynn said with a curtsy.

It worked, spurring Lady DeSilva into action. "Yes, please do. Join us, Duke Inimigo." She eyed the crowd, silencing a dozen conversations around the room. "We extend hospitality to all our guests."

"Thank you for your generosity, but my daughter and I are road weary. Tomorrow, perhaps, we'll be more fit company."

That's doubtful, Johanna thought. The duke, his men, and his daughter fairly glistened as if fresh from the bath. The girl's hair hung to her tiny waist like a solid sheet of black silk. They must have stopped outside the township to don their best clothes. There was no way the girl could have ridden comfortably in a dress cut so close to the skin. It had a high collar and long sleeves, but there was no question of the girl's shape. She had a beautiful figure, tall and well rounded with a generous bust and hips.

"Before we retire," Inimigo continued, "I'd like to introduce my daughter, Maribelle." He held out a hand, and the girl curtsied deeply to Lady DeSilva.

Johanna could hear the seams on the dress screaming, expecting them to pop under the strain, but the material shifted without tearing. Pity.

"I hope she'll find friends among the DeSilvas."

"I hope she will as well." Lady DeSilva's words lacked conviction, but she gave the girl a polite head nod.

Johanna used the distraction to sneak into the kitchen, earning a wink from Dom as she went.

Brynn and Cook were deep in conversation, heads tilted together, voices low as they dried the huge stack of dishes at the end of the washing line. The smell of lemon-scented soap hung heavy over the vats of boiling wash and rinse water.

"Johanna, did you hear?" Brynn asked as she rubbed a plate dry. "Inimigo brought *slaves* with him. Thirty of them."

"How do you know they're slaves? I thought Inimigo had to release all his captives as part of the treaty."

"He did, but rumor says he buys people from the Wisp Islands. All the servants he brought with him have got collars around their necks. They remind me of the dogs in Lord Rafi's—" She cut off with a squeak, eyes focused on something over Johanna's shoulder.

"Pardon me." The voice was feminine, deep and sultry, but there was something in the sound that made Johanna twitch like someone had run their fingernail from the base of her skull to her tailbone. "I'm looking for the housekeeper."

Johanna took the towel out of Brynn's hand and stepped into her place beside Cook, studying the newcomer in her peripheral vision. The woman stood a head taller than Brynn, making her as tall as Rafi. Her blond hair had been swept away from her face into a tight twist, highlighting dagger-sharp cheekbones and a pointed chin. A few lines radiated from her dark brown eyes. Taken individually her features were a bit too angled for true beauty, but somehow the collection resulted in a stunning face. She was dressed in Inimigo's colors, but not in anything you could call livery. Her dress draped across her body in delicate folds, baring one shoulder, and was belted at the waist with wide golden links. Whoever she was, she had access to plenty of coin.

"We don't have a housekeeper," Brynn said as she untied her apron. "I'm the head maid. How can I help you?"

"No housekeeper? It's impressive you manage so well." The woman said it so it wasn't quite a compliment.

If Brynn noticed the derision in the woman's tone, she was too well trained to comment. "Was there something you needed?"

"I'm Vibora, Duke Inimigo's steward. We brought a large staff—servants, personal dressers and so forth—but it seems there isn't enough room." She gave Brynn an almost smile. "If there aren't enough beds here in the house or in the barracks, perhaps there is a place where the servants can put up a few of our traveling tents."

Johanna shivered despite the hot plate in her hands and the humidity of the room. Something about this woman made her skin crawl.

"I'm sure we can find some accommodations, if they don't mind sleeping several to a room." Brynn pointed to the doorway that led to the living areas.

"Just a moment."

Cold fingers touched the back of Johanna's neck, and she followed them to the face of Inimigo's steward.

"I heard the DeSilvas hired a Performer for this occasion." She tapped Johanna's bare neck twice before dropping her hand to her side. "I so enjoy a good performance, and look forward to seeing more of you during my stay."

Johanna resisted the urge to step out of the woman's reach. "Thank you, my lady. I'm always pleased to have a receptive audience."

"I'm sure you are."

Vibora let herself be led away by Brynn, and Johanna scrubbed at her neck with the drying cloth. The feeling of *invasion* remained.

Cook grunted and handed Johanna another plate. "I'm shocked a woman like that is Inimigo's steward."

"Because she's a woman?" *A strange, disturbing woman?*

"No, because she's so lovely." Cook began stacking the dishes in a hutch near the kitchen's entrance, peeking around the corner so she could see where Brynn had taken their guest.

"Do you think I'll need to clear my brothers out of my room? Would it help if we went back to the wagons tonight?"

"Goodness! Didn't anyone tell you?" Cook eyed the serving staff, searching for the failed messenger in their midst. "Master Thomas came and took the boys home after you began Storyspinning. He said there was some business with your mother and thought it was best if you all went home for the evening."

Of course he did. Thomas was nothing if not the peacemaker. Marin had likely returned to the empty wagons, angry and embarrassed, and sent her eldest son scurrying to bring back her children.

Johanna's shoulders drooped. She'd have to walk to the wagons tonight and leave early enough the next morning to arrive in time for the midday meal.

And I'll have to drag my brothers with me. Through the forest. Again.

Cook's face wrinkled with concern. "What do you need, miss? What can I help you with?"

The amount of dishes and pots and pans was daunting, and even though it would make her journey stretch even later into the night, Johanna wanted to help. These people had been good to her. She reached for the next dish. "Nothing. It's just that I'll probably need to get home before too long."

"Out with you! Performers don't clean anyway." Cook pushed Johanna toward the kitchen door. "You go and get some rest."

When Cook wouldn't relent, Johanna changed into her hunting clothes. She slung her satchel over her back, waved good night to the gate guards, and walked into the woods.

Johanna wasn't afraid of the forest at night. The animals created their own music of rustles and chirps. The cicadas and crickets added the descant, and the three-quarter moon danced on a stage lit by stars. It was peaceful, and Johanna needed to enjoy the calm as she intended to raise hell when she got home.

A titi, its white face a bright splash in the shadows, scolded her from one of the trees. The little monkey hooted and chittered, protecting its family, till she was far beyond its territory.

Animals instinctively knew how to care for their young. How could her mother have forgotten? What had happened? How does a respected Performer fall so far?

Johanna cringed at that turn of phrase. She'd seen her father fall. One instant off balance had sent him to his death. But her mother's condition, self-inflicted as it was, had sent them all tumbling. If Marin had been sober the day the Performers' Council ruled, maybe she could have convinced them to let the family stay.

Johanna had kept that nugget of anger close to her heart, carrying it with her for all these months without saying anything, and it had finally worn a hole she couldn't ignore.

Perhaps if Johanna hadn't been completely wrapped up in how the scene with her mother would play out, she would have heard the horse hooves before they were too close.

Chapter 52

Pira

The three remaining sentries built themselves a large fire at the head of the trail. The night had cooled, but not enough to warrant such a blaze, so it seemed they were trying to remind their visitors of their presence.

It also served as an easy way to identify each of their positions.

Pira snuck through the trees and rocks that bordered the trail, watching as two of the men tossed blades between them with practiced precision. She hated to be impressed, but she was. A little. Even with her excellent eyesight, she could barely make out the gleam of the metal in the firelight. The men seemed to know exactly where each blade would land and continued the pattern, making a rhythmic hiss and thump as blades slapped their palms.

She made no noise, not even crunching the dry leaves underfoot, and yet the third man turned away from the fire and his friends. Pira froze, feeling his eyes on her. He stopped a stone's throw from the tree where she had hurriedly crouched.

"James, whatcha doing?" one of the men asked, continuing to toss his blade without hesitation.

The man shifted his weight, stones grinding under his feet. "I thought I heard something." He took a tentative step toward Pira's position.

"A squirrel, probably."

In the light of the waning moon, Pira saw confusion on James's face. He looked around, studying the shadows right over her head. After a moment he rubbed his forehead and turned back to his friends.

"Maybe it was a skunk. They creep around at night sometimes."

Pira waited till she was sure the sentry was distracted before moving down the hill, through the farmland, and to the tents and wagons. The shadows of the bonfires danced along each home's sides, bobbing and swaying to the cacophony of instruments and voices. Even after dark they were still violent with colors and pattern.

There was something about the camp and its dwellers that felt almost wild with activity. People danced and sang and flipped and shouted, while children darted between wagons, chasing dogs or walking on their hands. Even the small cluster of farm animals seemed a little too unsettled in their pens; they paced and munched. And bleated in Pira's direction.

She moved away from the goats, hugging the sides of the manger—one of the few permanent, wood-framed buildings in the entire valley. There were other low-roofed cottages and barns, but she'd bet her best pair of boots that the two-story hall at the center of camp was where this so-called "council" met.

Pira hoped to sneak close to the building and listen to their conversation. They'd have to say something about Arlo and his family. If she was lucky, they might reveal where the princess was hiding.

The wagons and tents were laid out in orderly spokes, radiating from the hall. She'd have to work her way around the circle, keeping low to the ground and hugging the shadows, moving slightly inward when the chance presented itself. She darted to a stable, and from there to a large chicken coop.

Scouting out her next move, she saw a small cottage with herbs drying above a railed porch. The door to the cottage swung open, and a cloth-shrouded shape stepped onto the porch. The person's head—Pira couldn't tell if it was male or female—turned in her direction.

"Come out, come out, little Keeper!" a wavering voice called. "I've been waiting for you all day. And bring that pretty boy with you. He's on the other side of the coop."

Pira peeked around the corner and watched as a long shadow detached itself from the coop's back wall.

"Are you coming?" Leão asked as he walked past her.

Chapter 53

Rafi

"What is wrong with you?" Johanna shouted as she dusted off her clothes. "Don't you know how stupid it is to gallop your horse down a dark trail? Feel free to break your own neck, but don't break mine!"

"You're dressed in dark colors. I didn't see you till I was almost on top of you." Rafi slid out of his saddle and picked up Johanna's satchel, which had sailed into the nearby bushes. "Breaker wouldn't have run you down."

Rafi had returned to the dining hall, hoping to get to the bottom of his uncle's mysterious words, only to find his mother in a panic.

"Go now. Use the gate on the south side of the estate to avoid drawing any attention. There's only one guard on that part of the wall." Lady DeSilva had practically shoved him out the door that opened onto the yard. "Find Johanna and make sure she's safe."

Rafi wanted to argue, but there had been real urgency in his mother's tone and he jumped to obey.

He'd saddled Breaker without calling a groom, then led the horse behind the barn to keep them hidden from view. He rode hard, both because it was what his mother wanted him to do and because it felt good.

The stars and moonlight had been enough for Breaker to make his way safely down the well-known trail, but neither of them had expected Johanna to appear out of the darkness.

He held out her bag, but the strap was broken. "It looks like your satchel didn't survive the fall unscathed."

"Neither did my hand." She held her scraped palm up for him to see. Blood ran down her pale skin and disappeared into the sleeve of her tunic.

Rafi's gut clenched like he was anticipating a kick to his midsection. "I'm sorry. I was trying to make sure you were safe."

"A lot of good you've done me." She rolled her hand up in the hem of her shirt and held it tight against her chest. "Whenever you're around, I seem destined for injury."

"I said I was sorry."

Johanna snorted and started down the trail toward the orchard.

"Where are you going?"

"I'm trying to get as much distance from you as possible," she said without stopping.

"I'm supposed to bring you back to the estate with me."

"Ha! I won't go anywhere with you willingly."

Has there ever been a girl so stubborn and pigheaded in the history of Santarem? She marched along a dark forest trail, head held high, a slight limp in her gait, but with no concern whatsoever about things lurking in the shadows.

"Johanna, don't be stupid about this." Rafi jogged to catch up with her; Breaker followed as he was trained to do. Rafi grabbed her uninjured arm, pulling her to a stop.

She shook off his grip. "Are you going to throw me across your saddle if I won't agree to ride with you? Is that the kind of man you are, *Lord* Rafael?"

"No," Rafi said, shocked at her words. "Never."

"Then let me go." She turned for the trail again, but this time her back was hunched and her limp more pronounced.

Rafi felt sick, like that blow he'd been expecting had landed. She looked so pitiful and small, dwarfed by the trees.

"You're hurt. Let me help you."

"I don't want your help."

What choice did Rafi have? He mounted Breaker and trotted after Johanna. Giving her a bit of space, but still close enough to protect her if any danger was going to present itself.

She ignored him. The sound of her scuffling footsteps and Breaker's hoofbeats made him uncomfortable. He started to talk, hoping the sound of his voice would loosen the knots that coiled in his chest.

"It's a nice night. The days still hold plenty of summer heat, but it cools off in the evenings."

She ignored him and picked up her pace.

"Soon the leaves will start changing and this whole forest will look like it's on fire."

He continued on, speaking about the weather and the lack of hunting, and finally shifting to the drought and the state of the farms. Saying it all aloud, hearing the words float off into the night—rather than in whispered conversations with his mother and private meetings with his other advisors—was a pleasant change. He aired his worries about his people not having enough to eat and being forced to import commodities from surrounding states.

"I know Inimigo will sell to me at a good price. He's willing to do anything to secure a better relationship between our states, but I hate the idea of trading with him." Then without thinking, he admitted the thing that weighed on him the most. "I wish my father were here."

Embarrassment and sadness choked Rafi, and he couldn't say anything else for a few moments. He slid the reins between his fingers, noticing the rough spots where he'd bent and looped the leather over and over again. That too reminded him of his father.

"Me too."

He cleared his throat. "My father always knew exactly how to handle every situation. There was never a question about his honor, and no one doubted his decisions were the right ones. I'll never be as good of a duke as he was." He laughed humorlessly. "I've already made such a mess."

Chapter 54

Johanna

"My father always said it wasn't how you started, but how you finished that really mattered." Johanna felt a twinge of sympathy. She understood the weight of responsibility, how it could bow your back with worries and clutter your mind so you couldn't think of anything else, and Rafi had many more people depending on him.

"I liked your father," Rafi said quietly. "His stories were a good balance to your mother's beautiful voice."

"Thank you." Johanna meant it, but the compliment also made her feel self-conscious of her own skills.

"You have her gift."

"If that was true—which it's not," she said, and looked at him over her shoulder, "then why are you always so bored during my performances?"

"Who told you I was bored?"

"You didn't have to *say* anything!" She faced him while she spoke. "You don't clap; you don't smile; you don't laugh. Everyone else is completely absorbed, but you look like you can't wait to get out of the room."

"I clap!"

"Like you have to, like you're being polite." She turned back around, disgusted with herself. Performers never beg for adoration, and she had no idea why she wanted it from Rafi.

"You don't understand," he huffed. "I feel like I always need to apologize to you for something or other."

She stopped, and Breaker took a step to the side to avoid riding her down. "When have you *ever* apologized to me for anything?"

"I just did!"

"No. You said you felt like you needed to, but you haven't actually done it."

Rafi jumped off Breaker's back, landing next to Johanna. "I said I was sorry about almost riding you down tonight."

"You didn't mean it. It was a forced apology."

"Well . . . I was trying to help you!" He stepped closer to Johanna, towering over her petite frame.

"Well nothing! You're not sorry you don't like my performances, you're not sorry you almost killed me tonight, and you're not sorry about that day in the forest." Johanna didn't mean to bring it up, but once she got started, she couldn't quit. "You're only sorry that there's a mark on your honor. In my opinion, you'll never earn it back until you feel honest . . . remorse . . . for attacking me in the woods. I don't think you ever will because you don't think you were wrong."

"It looked like you were poaching, and game has been so slim this year that stopping you was the first thing that crossed my mind."

"You could have stopped me without knocking me out."

"You fought back and I defended myself."

A victorious smile curled Johanna's lips. "And you still are."

Rafi closed his eyes and let a long slow breath out his nose. "You're right. I'm not sorry that I tried to stop a poacher."

She opened her mouth to counter, but Rafi held up one finger. "I am sorry, so terribly sorry, that I hurt *you*, Johanna Von Arlo." He touched the back of her hand lightly, a gentleman pleading his cause. "The moment I realized how badly I'd hurt you was one of the most awful of my life. I've never felt so much raging guilt, and I *beg* you to forgive me."

Johanna was hyperaware of the feel of Rafi's warm fingers on her skin, the gentle touch, true regret in his eyes.

"I know I haven't earned it yet," he said, stepping toward his horse and breaking the contact between them. "I hope someday I will."

The hard feelings she'd been harboring fled, replaced by something soft and fluttering.

He swung into the saddle and stretched out a hand toward her. "Would you allow me to offer you a ride home?"

Johanna took his hand and mounted behind him. "You better. At this rate, I'll have to start walking back to the estate as soon as I get to the wagons."

Rafi laughed, and Johanna tightened her grip around his waist just a bit.

Chapter 55

Jacaré

"They've been gone too long." Jacaré set aside the saddlebag he'd been repairing.

Tex, relaxed as always, reclined against a large log they'd rolled near the fire. His eyes were closed, his arms folded behind his head, legs crossed at the ankles. Pure, undiluted calm. "They're fine. No one down in that camp is going to attack them."

Jacaré wished he could believe that, but the memory of Lord Venza's daughter laid out on a cold slab of stone was too haunting. "Did you forget that we've discovered two dead girls who could have passed as the heir's doubles? And just a few months ago, Arlo was murdered. Doesn't that worry you?"

"Talk this out with me," Tex prompted, though he left his eyes shut. "We found an assassin's dart at the site where the guardian was killed. You assume that it was meant for the guardian, yet his death was the result of a fall from the high wire we could see stretched across the top of the glass."

"Assassins don't typically leave weapons behind." Jacaré stood, needing to pace. "If he shot at Arlo during a performance, and missed . . ."

Tex nodded reaching the same conclusion. "He wouldn't have been able to retrieve the dart while so many people were around."

"Right." Jacaré stopped walking. "I think he missed, but succeeded in making the kill. Arlo saw the dart or the shooter, lost his balance, and fell."

"Lots of assumptions," Tex said with a grunt.

"Think about it: The dart was poisoned. Whether Arlo died from the poison or from the fall, the assassin guaranteed the kill."

A crackle on the trail alerted them that someone was approaching. Tex dropped his arms to his sides but didn't come to his feet. He still looked relaxed, but was ready for whatever was coming their way.

The Firesword, Benton, nodded to the men as he joined them at the fire. "Evening, men. Where are your younglings?"

He asked the question politely, as if for the sake of conversation, but his eyes darted to the picket line where the horses were hobbled, and to the bedrolls near the fire.

"You know how young ones are. Always looking for an excuse to be alone." Tex waggled his eyebrows suggestively.

"I surely do. I remember those days." Benton sketched a smile. "Too bad, though. I was hoping to take care of all of you at once." With the last words, he threw two knives, each on a direct path for the men's hearts.

And yet that was where Benton failed. Tex and Jacaré were more than men.

Benton found himself staring at the night sky, his own knife at his throat. Jacaré knelt on the would-be assassin's chest.

"Assumptions, eh, Texugo?"

"Hmpf."

Chapter 56

Pira

Pira was on guard, her fingers itching to draw the dagger in her boot, but Leão walked toward the cottage without looking back.

What other choice did she have but to follow? Leão was the closest thing the Keepers had to royalty.

The door stood ajar, and Pira peeked inside. A small cot hugged one wall, a cheerful fire crackled at the hearth, and at a tiny table in the corner Leão sat with the oldest woman Pira had ever seen.

"Come in, dear thing." The woman waved with a gnarled hand. A face grooved like maple bark smiled out of a bright yellow hood. "Close the door behind you. It gets awfully cold in the evenings."

Pira hesitated in the doorway, but the smell wafting from the hearth drew her in. "Is that *maracujá* jelly?"

"And fresh scones to put it on." The woman nodded to a plate on the table and to Leão with a half-eaten pastry in his hand. "I knew you'd come today, but I didn't know when, besides after dark. Seems you've got good timing, as the scones are still steaming."

Pira didn't have many issues with self-control. It was a trait her brother possessed and she'd worked hard at achieving. But *maracujá* on *anything* was difficult for her to turn down. Her mouth watered, thinking of the sweet-tart flavor and the way the heat from the scone would make it slide across her tongue.

"They're good," Leão said with a near groan, and held up a second one, a bit of preserves ready to drip off the side. He caught it on his finger and licked it clean. "Best thing I've eaten in weeks."

"How do you know they're not poisoned? For all you know, this woman wanted to lure us here for that purpose."

The old lady raised her eyebrows but didn't argue her innocence.

Leão took another bite. "Then I'll die full and happy."

Pira restrained the urge to dive across the room and snatch the entire jar of jelly away. Instead, she sniffed the contents, held it up to the light—not that any alchemist worth their salt would leave visible evidence—and finally smeared a bit on the inside of her wrist.

"Don't feel obligated to eat, dear." The woman lowered herself onto the hearth, leaving the other chair empty for Pira to take. "I wanted to offer you Keepers something you might enjoy."

"How do you know who we are? How did you know we were coming?" Pira asked, feeling the short hairs on her head prickle with suspicions.

"You may call me Elma." She smoothed her shawl, like it was some rich piece of silk rather than a scrap of homespun wool. "I see many things. Sometimes the future, sometimes the past, always the truth."

It had the ring of a phrase well rehearsed. Pira was not impressed.

"And . . ." Leão prompted as he reached for another scone from the half-full plate.

"She can't sense it," Elma said, eyeing Pira. "She's not like us."

"She can sometimes. If she really tries."

Pira did not like being the center of a conversation she wasn't taking part in.

"What are you talking about? Sense what?"

"Elma's *essência*. She's one of us."

Pira leaned against the fireplace, the heat of the stones seeping through her hunting leathers and warming her back. She felt full and relaxed, and just a bit sleepy.

"I couldn't possibly leave them behind, no matter what the Keepers demanded," Elma said, wrapping up her tale. "So I didn't side with either group. My husband and I moved to this little valley, insulated from the battles and bloodshed, and raised our children and grandchildren." She let out a long tired sigh. "Then I lived on to help raise their children and grandchildren and whoever else found our little sanctuary. I'd never do anything to hurt the Performers. They are my people, more so than the Keepers. They are my family."

A fist pounded on the cabin's door, shattering Pira's calm and shaking the small windows on either side. Leão's scone fell with a liquid plop as he drew his weapons.

"Relax," Elma said, pressing a gentle hand to Pira's. "It's one of the sentries."

The Keepers exchanged glances and remained ready.

"Elma! Wake up!" a voice yelled as its owner jiggled the door. "The men camping on our boundaries have captured Benton and are holding him hostage."

"Just a moment, Didsbury." The old woman limped across the room.

She opened the door wide, allowing a clear view into her home.

The young man on the porch, one of those who'd greeted the Keepers on arrival, blanched. He fumbled at his sash for the hilt of the short sword, his fingers missing the grip.

"Oh stop, Didsbury. Leão and Pira are my friends." She shook her head in disgust. "You young people always reach for weapons instead of asking questions."

"But . . . but . . ." He pointed at Pira and then Leão, who was scraping his jelly off the table and licking his fingers. "How did they get in here? We were watching their camp."

"They walked, obviously." Elma reached for a tall stick behind the door. It was a knotted piece of wood, but it shone with evidence of frequent use. "I told you they were my *friends.* They have skills similar to my own."

Didsbury nodded, as if Elma's answer made perfect sense.

"Let's go rescue the rest of your group." Elma held out her arm for Didsbury to take and beckoned with her stick for Leão and Pira to follow. "Or more likely rescue my Performers from them."

Chapter 57

Johanna

Thomas sat near the fire, a book from their small collection clutched in one hand. He jumped to his feet as Breaker trotted into the clearing.

"Lord Rafael." His look of surprise shifted to amused suspicion. "Thank you for delivering Johanna home. I hope it wasn't *inconvenient*."

Johanna heard the insinuation in Thomas's tone and sent her brother a glare he wouldn't miss.

"Oh no. It was my pleasure." Rafi helped Johanna slide out of the saddle, holding her hand till she was steady on her feet beside the horse. "There has been word of . . . brigands on the roads again, and we—my mother and I—decided it would be in Johanna's best interest if she wasn't alone in the forest."

Thomas's forehead bunched at the words. "Really. I'm surprised they'd stray this far from the main roads."

"Yes, well, we wouldn't want to risk Johanna's safety." He looped his reins around his saddle horn, and then unwrapped them again.

"Of course, my lord."

"Good night, then." Rafi gave Johanna a quick smile and nod before riding away.

Johanna watched him disappear into the darkness before turning to face whatever her brother had in store. She couldn't ignore the scathing look.

"It was his *pleasure* to bring you home?"

"Stop it, Thomas. He didn't mean anything." She took her cloak out of her satchel and gave it a few good shakes. "He was just being polite." *I think.*

"The way he looked at you wasn't polite." Thomas patted the log beside him.

"What does that mean?" Johanna wanted desperately to go to bed, but the opportunities to talk to her oldest brother were too few for her liking.

"There was . . . longing in his eyes." He set his book down, and Johanna knew she was in for a grand admonishment. "Is there something you haven't told me? Because if he didn't care for you at all he would have sent one of his guardsmen to escort you home, but he did it personally. Mark my words: That means something."

A small smile crept onto her face at the thought. *It might be pleasant to mean something to someone. Even if that someone is Rafi.*

Especially if that someone is Rafi.

She could feel Thomas's appraisal. "What?" she asked.

"If I didn't know better, I'd think that maybe you liked him, too."

"Oh please," Johanna said with a laugh. "Matters of the heart are the least of my concerns."

Thomas's face fell, and their conversation turned to uglier topics. "I'm assuming you heard about Mama?"

"Lady DeSilva told me herself." Johanna stared into the flames, her cheeks reflecting their heat. "I've never been more embarrassed in my entire life."

"I won't pretend to understand what happened or what she was thinking, but could you maybe go easy on her? She's having a hard time."

"Aren't we all?" Tears pricked Johanna's eyes. "You should've seen the boys at the estate, Thomas. They ate and ate till I thought they'd be sick. I hated to stop them from getting full. Who knows when we'll have enough to feed them like that every day? But we would be closer if she'd stop swilling away every extra coin."

Thomas folded his hands together and rested them on his knees. "She's broken, Jo. When we committed father's body to the flames, there was a moment when I thought she was going to throw herself on the pyre. But she didn't. She looked at each of us and stepped away from the edge." Leave it to Thomas to make their mother look like a martyr. "Give her a little leeway. She lost the love of her life and the profession she lived for all in the same week."

Johanna held on to her anger with iron claws, trying to ignore her brother's calming influence.

"She's selfish! That's what she is." The tears spilled over Johanna's cheeks. "She is so absorbed in her sadness that she can't see how hard we're working."

The wagon door creaked, and Johanna knew without looking that her mother was standing right behind her.

"Mama." Thomas stood quickly. "We—"

"I wanted to let Johanna know I laid out a different dress for tomorrow." Marin's voice rasped like tree branches against a house.

"I didn't think it was right for her to wear the same gown day after day, especially as *she's working so hard*."

Johanna closed her eyes, ignoring the two-pronged stab of guilt and shame.

"I'd better get some rest so I can find a new job tomorrow."

The slam of the wagon door didn't cover the sound of Marin's quiet crying.

Rather than facing her mother, Johanna crammed into bed with Michael, and Thomas wedged himself into the narrow space on the floor. It wasn't a restful night, with images of her mother and a dark-haired lordling flitting through her dreams.

CHAPTER 58

JACARÉ

Jacaré kept their attacker immobilized while Tex took the man's belt pouch and searched his pockets.

"Where I'm from, people who kill without warning or reason are called assassins," Tex said as he dumped the pouch on the ground. "As far as I know, you haven't given us a warning and we haven't given you a reason. So that makes you an assassin."

Benton's smile was too bright for someone being tied to a log. He turned his head and yelled, "Help me! Didsbury! James! They're attacking me." He added a high-pitched scream that cut off when Tex cuffed him across the mouth.

The blow was hard, but Benton laughed. "That wasn't very nice."

"Neither is killing people," Jacaré said as he finished off the knot.

"Jacaré," Tex called. "You need to see this." In his palm lay a sigil ring. The metal had been scorched black, making the emblem at the top difficult to see. Tex tilted it to the light of their fire. "When I saw those lines on the dart, I thought they were just scratches . . ."

Jacaré took the ring and gripped it till he felt the metal dig into his skin. He opened up his hand, knowing what he'd see: a straight line and a jagged one. Mirror images of the mark branded onto Elisa Venza's neck.

He felt a sense of relief. *We've found the man who is murdering teenage girls simply because they fit a type. Killing for money. Killing because he can.* The feeling was replaced by a primal, savage thirst for vengeance that could only be quenched with blood.

"Stop," Tex said, his gentle tone at contrast with the firm grasp on Jacaré's forearm. "Assassins kill for money. We need to know who's paying him."

There was a knife in Jacaré's hand. He didn't remember drawing it and he didn't remember forcing it against Benton's throat.

"I know where your mind is, son, and you need to come back," Tex continued, his hold tightening. "Leave the past in the past."

Jacaré blinked a few times, reconnecting with his surroundings, leaving the memories of another murderer behind. "I'm fine." He cleared his throat and tried to make the words more convincing. "I'm fine."

There was a commotion on the trail, a brief argument.

"You can't go in there by yourself."

"Didsbury," said a feminine voice. "I've been handling matters like this since well before your father was born."

"But Elma . . ."

"Get out of my way."

Tex grunted. "This should be interesting."

At least two pairs of feet crunched along the gravel that led to the small campsite. Pira entered first, her shaved head reflecting dimly in the firelight. She raised her eyebrows at the captive. Leão followed, supporting a woman whose limp defied the authority in her voice and in her *essência.*

"Stop where you are," Jacaré shouted, wondering if this was the power Benton had referred to. "Who are you and why are you here?"

"A friend. Don't you take one of your own at her word?"

"Not on this side of the wall." Jacaré looked between Elma and Leão who had so politely escorted her into camp. The boy was as much a hostage as Benton, though he didn't seem to recognize the danger on his arm. "Only traitors stayed behind, and only the youngest or those who siphoned power from others could still be alive today. And what place would be better to steal *essência* than a camp of half-breeds?"

The woman grunted. "Go to your commander, boy. Show him I mean you no ill."

Leão steadied her before leaving her side. She thanked him with a head nod.

"Now you can release Benton. Performers don't take kindly to having their own attacked."

Tex snorted. "How do Performers feel about assassins murdering their visitors?"

"Assassins?" She took a few steps closer to the fire. The light made canyons of her wrinkles. "There must be some mistake."

"I'm afraid not." Jacaré held up the throwing knife. "He said he came to 'take care' of us."

"He's captain of our guard here at Performers' Camp. He thought you were a threat," Elma countered.

"If that's the case," Jacaré said, and raised his other hand displaying the sigil ring they found in Benton's belt pouch. "Explain why this mark was found on the bodies of two murdered girls."

Elma leaned heavily against her stick, as if Jacaré's words were physical blows. "Oh, Benton. I knew you'd been in a street gang before you joined our camp. I thought you left that life behind."

To Jacaré she sounded like a parent, questioning the actions of a wayward child. Her tone surprised him. "That's not all. The same mark was on a dart we found at the site where Arlo fell to his death."

The old woman bowed her head for a moment. "Are these charges valid?"

"Elma the All Powerful." Benton eyed the old woman with contempt. "Haven't you *seen* all of this already?"

"Of course not. You know that's not how my power—"

"Power! Bah," Benton spat, ignoring the armed men around him. "Your *mystical abilities* never protected the Performers from harm! You couldn't even protect them from me."

The color drained from her face. "Benton, what are you talking about?"

"You're supposed to be our wise, powerful leader, but you're just as blind and stupid as the rest!" The assassin raised his bound hands, pointing a finger at Elma. "I earned your trust, I guarded your camp, I watched your children, and no one ever suspected." Benton smiled as his words sank in. "You let me become a part of your community, and it's protected me from suspicion for years."

Elma's voice was barely audible over the crackling campfire, but there was a dangerous undertone to her words. "Explain yourself."

"Can't you do something *magical* to discern the truth?"

"I wouldn't tempt her," Jacaré cautioned.

"Ha—" Benton's laugh cut off abruptly, his body twitching as if it had been shocked. "What was that?"

"Your warning." Elma lowered herself to a log on the far side of the fire. "Next time I'll make you squeal like a stuck pig. Now explain yourself."

The assassin's grin returned. "That was a good trick for an old charlatan."

Benton jolted, his limbs going rigid for a few seconds. His mouth popped open and he groaned.

"Answer me," Elma prompted. "Were you paid to kill Arlo?"

He licked his lips, eyeing Elma with a new sense of wariness, but the arrogance returned to his posture and the set of his jaw.

"Not exactly. He became a target by association." Benton focused on Elma. "I was supposed to kill a barmaid from Belem. There was nothing particularly redeeming about her tavern, the food was mediocre, and the people were low class, so it was quite a surprise to find Arlo drinking a cup of ale in their common room."

"Why would anyone want to have a barmaid killed?" Elma asked.

"At first I didn't know and I didn't care. Teenage girls are such easy marks and they die so beautifully—their skin parting as my knife glides across their flesh." He turned to Jacaré, a cold smile growing on his face. "I'm not stupid. After my third assignment, I realized my employer was eliminating girls who fit a specific description and had a dubious background."

Realization dawned in Elma's eyes. "You were hunting the lost princess." She looked at the Keepers ringing the fire. "That's why *you're* here."

Jacaré and Tex exchanged a glance but didn't acknowledge her statement.

"Everyone knew about Arlo's longtime friendship with the king." Benton shrugged as if the connection was obvious. "If the princess had survived, who better to know her location? Performers travel to every state. He could stop in and check on her periodically, and keep the secret of her heritage until she could ascend the throne.

"Arlo was one more loose thread." He made a cutting gesture with two fingers. "Killing him during his high-wire performance was brilliant. Everyone assumed it was an accident."

Jacaré shook his head, confused. "If you were sure the barmaid in Belem was the one, then why did you keep killing?"

"I kept getting assignments," he said with a shrug. "The money was good, so why would I quit?"

"Who's paying?" Tex asked, spinning his belt dagger around his forefinger. "Inimigo? Belem? Who?"

"If only things were that simple," the assassin said with a laugh. "I could be *persuaded* to answer your questions, but I'd like to live for a while longer with all my body parts intact."

"I say we kill him now," Pira said, from the far side of the fire. "We can send the pieces to Venza."

"I'm inclined to agree," Tex said, nodding to Jacaré for approval.

"Don't." Elma used her stick to push herself awkwardly to her feet. "Murderer or not, you can't dispense justice to a Performer."

"Why not?" Tex asked.

"You have no authority—no matter how important you think you are." She raised her hand and thick bands of air wrapped Tex from neck to knees, trapping his dagger to his side.

"Elma, what are you doing?" Jacaré asked.

"Benton is one of *my* people. He needs to face our laws and *our* punishments." She took a few uneven steps forward. "Besides, do you really want to challenge me?"

Jacaré drew on his *essência* till needles of pain stabbed the back of his eyes, but it wasn't enough to break Tex's bonds. "I need answers."

"We'll get them. My way." Elma offered them a gap-toothed grin that held a hint of malice. "We'll take Benton down to camp, find out everything he knows, and allow our Council to determine his punishment."

Jacaré released his grip on his *essência*, feeling energy flood back into his limbs and breath return to his lungs. "We'll follow you."

Chapter 59

Rafi

Rafi rubbed his eyes with his thumbs, trying to force away the grit of fatigue.

He stumbled into his room and nearly jumped out of his skin when he realized the chair in the corner was occupied.

"Mother!" He returned his dagger to its sheath. "What are you doing here?"

She slid her needle into the fabric she'd been embroidering and met his eyes. "What I have to say couldn't wait another moment."

Rafi dropped onto the edge of his bed and began tugging off his boots. "Does this have something to do with Uncle Fernando's command to keep Johanna watched? I sent two men to guard her camp, even though I doubt she's in danger."

"I hope two will be enough." She abandoned her embroidery and sat beside her son.

"You talk about Johanna as if her demise is imminent." He loosed his dagger belt and held the knife between his fingers for a moment, remembering how deftly Johanna had tossed and flipped the one she owned. She could handle herself in a dangerous situation. He smiled at the thought and dropped the dagger on the bedside table.

The grin fell off his face when he saw the lines of worry etched on his mother's. He placed a hand over hers and asked, "What's going on?"

Lady DeSilva took a breath, and a deep sense of unease washed over Rafi.

"Do you remember the story Johanna was telling before Inimigo burst in? 'The Survivor of Roraima'? Have you heard that tale before?"

"Once or twice. It's a fable about a man who survived the razing of Roraima—which we all know is impossible—and how he smuggled out Wilhelm's greatest treasure."

"What if I told you the story was loosely based on truth?"

He eyed his mother askance. "Someone made off with the king's bounty? Congratulations to him, but I still don't see how this has anything to do with . . ."

A picture began forming in Rafi's mind. Wilhelm and his family had been killed sixteen years ago, after he failed to diplomatically encourage Inimigo to give up the siege and go home. Wilhelm sent birds to his allies, but Inimigo's troops shot them all down. One eventually got through and reached Rafi's father, but by the time Camilio marshaled his troops, they were too late to save Roraima. The township had burned to the ground.

Rafi remembered how his father's eyes had clouded over and his voice had rasped as he recounted the scene. His best friend strung up alongside his infant child over the gate, warning any who approached to stay away. Camilio had cut down the bodies himself and brought them back to his estate for interment. There had been no mention of the queen, but everyone assumed her body had been in one of the mass graves.

"How could someone have gotten out?" Rafi asked, finding his mother's gaze. "The Citadel was surrounded on three sides and backed up to the mountain and the brambles. Even if someone had escaped onto the mountain, Inimigo's troops would have shot him down."

"I suppose that's true." She covered her mouth with her hand for a moment. "It's just that Johanna bears such a remarkable resemblance to the queen. Fernando saw it too. With her hair so short, it was easy to dismiss, but when she stands in front of an audience, her presence feels so familiar."

"Fernando said someone was hunting girls that matched Johanna's description." Rafi flopped back on his bed. "All because they resemble our dead queen? That's insane."

"It's not only Johanna's looks, Rafi. Her father—"

"Arlo the Acrobat, *not* Wilhelm the King."

Lady DeSilva's lips pressed into a flat line. "Arlo was a close personal friend of King Wilhelm's, Rafi. He performed at the Citadel several times each year."

Rafi rolled onto his elbow. "Roraima is near Performers' Camp. I'm sure they had more performances than the other states."

"Your father once told me that Wilhelm used Performers as spies, to keep tabs on the happenings in every dukedom."

It was a genius idea. The Performers had a perfect excuse to be in every state and had access to the gentry. They could pass messages to members of other troupes without attracting suspicion. Rafi wished he'd thought of it first.

"You believe that Arlo smuggled out the princess while Roraima was under attack?" Rafi ran his fingers through his hair. "It's a lovely fairy tale, Mother."

"There's one more thing."

Her voice had dropped to a near whisper, as if she worried the shadows were listening. "I prepared Wilhelm and the baby's bodies for interment, Rafi. The baby we buried was a boy."

Rafi sat up so quickly his mother shied back. "Why didn't you say anything before?"

"What was the point? There was no guarantee that Princess Adriana had survived the attack, and then the war started. It was more important to bring peace to Santarem than return an infant monarch to a throne she couldn't maintain."

"But why string up the wrong baby, Mother? Why would Inimigo do that?"

"So all of Santarem would believe his victory was complete, and to banish any hope that Wilhelm's heir survived."

Rafi rested his elbows on his knees and clutched at his hair with both hands. He couldn't believe a person could be so repugnant, so disgusting, so consumed by victory.

I should have let Fernando kill him, and damn the consequences.

"For the sake of argument, let's believe Johanna is . . . who you say she is. How can she pose a threat? She doesn't have any people. She can't marshal troops. She's no danger to anyone."

Lady DeSilva shook her head. "None of that matters. She's the last remaining heir to a throne Inimigo has been coveting for decades. He's not using aggression to seek it out, but a possible betrothal between you and his daughter would assure him your support. Belem is his closest ally, which leaves Wilhelm's surviving underlords and Fernando to stop Inimigo from taking exactly what he wants."

There was a weight in Rafi's pocket, something so heavy that he was amazed he'd been able to push it to the back of his mind. He pulled out Fernando's ring, and his mother gasped.

"Even less would stand in his way if I'm the heir to Impreza."

His mother's eyes welled with tears. "Fernando's still young enough to produce another heir. Why would he . . . That fool."

"Until we can convince him otherwise, I'm the heir to two dukedoms. And if we're going to keep Inimigo off the throne, we'll need to avoid a betrothal with his daughter." Rafi smiled at the thought. "That shouldn't be a problem."

"I know that look, Rafael Santiago DeSilva. I see it on your brother's face ten times every day." She gathered her embroidery supplies, packing up for the night. "In a few days, you will be the Duke of Santiago. Every decision you make now weighs on your future."

"I couldn't possibly forget." *Even if I tried.*

"As your advisor, I think it would be best if we entered into negotiation with Inimigo for his daughter's hand." She held up a finger forestalling Rafi's complaint. "If nothing else, it could give us a hint at what intrigue is afoot."

She was right. As usual.

"It's not like any betrothal between you and Inimigo would be legal anyway," she continued. "If Johanna is Wilhelm's heir, then you're honor bound to marry her."

Chapter 60

Pira

Pira didn't want to be welcomed as a guest. She didn't want to go down into Performers' Camp, though the smell of roasting meat and fresh vegetables made her salivate. She didn't want to abandon the little camp they'd made upslope and spend the night in the valley.

But into the odd little community she marched because her brother commanded her to.

"Stable the horses, see that they get some oats, and try to rest," Jacaré had ordered as he propelled a bound Benton down the hill. He followed Elma and Tex into a two-story building known as the Council House.

Elma assigned Didsbury to take Pira and Leão to the camp and make them comfortable. The young Firesword stopped at a bell-topped pole that marked the official entrance into the camp. He pulled a worn rope and rang the bell three times.

All movement in the camp ceased, children halted their games, women stopped stirring their pots, conversation died, and every head turned in Pira and Leão's direction.

"We have guests!" Didsbury yelled.

The stillness broke like a rogue wave as all the Performers in camp rushed to greet their visitors. Someone took the horses' leads out of Pira's hand. "Wait!" she shouted, trying to follow their animals.

"Don't worry about them," Didsbury said at her shoulder. "They'll be well cared for."

She looked to Leão for help, but he had a child in one arm, several others clinging to his legs, and was carrying on a conversation with all of them at once.

Pira wasn't quite sure how it happened, but she found herself sitting on a low padded stool with a bowl of steaming soup in one hand and a chunk of fresh bread in the other. On her right a young man, probably in his early twenties, described his acrobatic skills and on her left someone in a floor-length cape sang a battle song.

It was too much. Too much noise. Too many colors and textures and smells and people. She didn't know who to answer, who to thank, which person to watch practice, or which of the dogs at her feet to kick.

Leão didn't seem to have the same problem. He was shown to another stool across the fire. He ate, carried on two conversations, and applauded at the appropriate moments. His green eyes sparkled, and he flashed his dimples at every girl who spoke to him.

How can he handle all this attention? Pira thought as she took a bite of her bread, using it as an excuse not to answer the questions of a child kneeling in front of her.

Growing up, it had usually been just her and Jacaré. Their meals had been quiet, tucked in their little cottage. Even the noise of the barrack cafeteria on its worst day couldn't compare to the jangle of instruments and voices clamoring over one another.

Chapter 61

Leão

Leão shouldn't have had any problem falling asleep. The bed was comfortable, the bedding fresh, and having walls and windows was an improvement over bugs attacking him all night long.

And yet, the soft breathing of the person on the wagon's other pallet—just a scant four inches from his own—was enough to keep him awake.

He should have said no, should have turned down the Performers' offer of shelter for the night, but he'd been afraid to offend them.

What difference did it make anyway? He and Pira slept side by side almost every night. Sure, her brother was usually on her other side, but being alone with her shouldn't have made a difference.

But, oh Mother Lua, tonight it did.

He'd coerced her to dance, holding her tight so she couldn't escape to a quiet seat on the side. Once he had her in his arms, he couldn't pretend she was another soldier with a wicked jab and sharp tongue. She was a woman with long legs and full, pink lips.

Bedding down with his horse or even in a rank pigsty would

have been more restful. No relaxation technique, no breathing exercise, no amount of sheep counting could wash away the memory of her body pressed close as they danced.

Light, how could I have been so blind?

The dance had ended and he hadn't wanted to let her go, his palms aching to smooth down the length of her spine, to feel the texture of her skin, to—

She turned toward him in her sleep. Leão smothered his thoughts, afraid that perhaps she sensed him thinking about her. Not that it was possible, but members of the Elite Guard all developed an awareness of when they were being watched.

Pressing his forearm over his eyes didn't block out the sweet torture of her nearness and the heat he could feel rising off her sleeping form.

Green grass. Blue sky. Boats on the water. Pira's smile when she laughs. Pira's eyes when she's mad. Pira pinning me to the floor during that training exercise last year. Me pinning her back.

He rolled over, trying to create as much space between them as possible. The pallet's hinges squealed as he moved.

"Leão, are you awake?" Her voice was low, husky with sleep.

"Umm-hmm." He didn't trust himself to speak.

"Have Jacaré or Tex stopped in yet? Have you heard anything?"

The men had disappeared with Benton, Elma, and the rest of the Performers' Council before the meal. There had been a few whispers of some sort of broken Performer Code, but no one had speculated about what was happening behind the Council House doors.

If they were anything like the Keepers' Mage Council, a month could pass before they heard any word of Benton's fate.

"No. Not yet."

"Oh." She stretched, her arm brushing against his as she reached high above her head. "No matter what happens tonight, I bet Jacaré will expect us to ride at dawn."

"Yes." He pinched his eyes shut tight, trying not to measure the distance between them, but his body knew she was right there.

Pira rolled onto her side, propping herself onto one of her elbows. "You aren't getting sick, are you?"

Oh, I'm some sort of sick all right.

When he didn't answer immediately, she pressed her hand against his cheek. "You feel a little feverish." Her fingers trailed down his face, finding the pulse at the side of his neck. "Your heart's beating fast."

And with her words it leaped into an even faster pace.

"Pira." Her name rolled off his tongue like a groan. Couldn't she tell that every move she made, every little touch, incited a battle within him?

She's a commanding officer. She looks at me like I'm a child.

"I'm not good at healing. I have very little affinity for Spirit." Her hand quested down his chest, pressing her palm over his heart. "But I can try."

"Stop." He grabbed her wrist gently, holding it in place. "I'm fine."

He opened his eyes, finding her surprised face hovering near, but he didn't release his grip.

"Are you sure?" Her breath was warm and minty against his skin.

And the war was lost.

He raised his head, pressing his lips against hers once, hesitantly. He expected her to jolt and then to slap him. She gasped, but didn't move away.

So he kissed her again, with more intent. To his surprise she responded, her mouth softening against his.

Chapter 62

Pira

Leão's hand was on her side, his lips tentative against hers. Pira paused for the length of one thought—one moment of *what in the Light am I doing?*—before giving in. The brush of his mouth wasn't enough. She needed to measure the breadth of his shoulders with her hands, to feel the crush of his arms, to taste him on her lips.

Whenever they'd sparred, Leão fought her with skill and intensity, never holding back. His kiss was the same, fueled by desperation, all tongue and lips and gasping breaths. Hands searched her body, strong and certain as they ran down her back, finding her belt loops, using them to pull her closer.

The muscles of his chest flexed and tensed under her fingers. She traced the lines of bone and sinew she'd spent so much time staring at, finding the valleys between his ribs.

This is so wrong. So wrong, so wrong, she thought as the heat from his body scorched her own, singeing her palms with a touch that had been forbidden. And yet she didn't do anything—didn't *want* to do anything—to make it stop.

Tex took care of that for her.

"I'm not going to ask what you two think you're doing because it's quite obvious there isn't a whole lot of *thinking* going on." His gruff tone filled the tiny space.

They lurched apart, each hugging the wagon's opposite walls.

The old man shook his head, and Pira wasn't sure if he was amused or disgusted. "Jacaré wants to ride in three hours. I suggest you use that time to sleep."

With that he slammed the wagon's door and marched down the stairs.

In the sudden silence their breathing rattled like loose shingles in a windstorm. Pira could see the rapid rise and fall of Leão's chest and the bare skin of his abdomen where his shirt had ridden up.

"Pira . . . I . . ." His mouth hung open for a moment. "I'm sorry. I didn't mean for things to—"

She heard shame in his tone and didn't wait for him to finish his sentence. "It was a mistake. We're both tired and not thinking clearly."

"I know—"

"It's late. We'll just chalk it up to stupidity and pretend it didn't happen."

"A-all right."

She turned her back to him, tucking her knees close to her chest and the blanket up around her ears. "Go to sleep. I know Jacaré's going to want to ride hard tomorrow."

"Yeah."

Pira covered her mouth with her hand, feeling the tender skin of her lips. She pressed them together, savoring the flavor of Leão as it lingered on her tongue. *He doesn't have any feelings for you. It was a mistake. He agreed. It was stupid.* I *was stupid.*

Chapter 63

Johanna

Johanna woke to the sound of male voices. Rafi's face immediately popped into her mind. She rolled to her elbows, peeking over the sill, and saw two men in DeSilva livery sitting near the fire pit. For one ridiculous moment Johanna was disappointed that the lordling hadn't come as her personal escort. After his apology, which had been surprisingly sincere, something changed in the way she saw Rafi.

Under the brooding, arrogant facade was a boy—not much older than herself—who was fettered with responsibility. He feared failing his family, his people, and disgracing the memory of a deceased parent. She knew the weight of those chains.

He's doing the best he can, she thought as she climbed over Michael's sleeping form. *I have to respect him for that.*

She tried to ignore the bubbling sense of something else, something a little stronger than respect.

The sun peeked above the horizon, but it was so early. She wanted to clean up their small living spaces before she left for the day, but that meant facing whatever beast may be asleep in the other wagon.

Instead of a mess of bottles, a bucket of sick, and the lash of her mother's drink-sharpened tongue, Johanna found the space empty and everything in perfect order. The wooden surfaces gleamed, the floor was freshly swept, and across Johanna's bed lay a dress of pale green damask.

It had always been one of her mother's favorites.

Tucked into the laced bodice was a single sheet of paper and her father's necklace. Johanna brushed it aside and read the words on the note.

My Dearest Johanna,

Your father wanted you to have this necklace when you were old enough. Tonight, I realized that time has come. The casing is bent and the stone is flawed, but I promise it's worth far more than it appears. I hope it will bring you more luck than it brought my dear Arlo.

You are a better daughter than I deserved to have.

Love Always,
Mother

Johanna's chest ached like she'd been shoved into a corset five sizes too small, and she knew the feeling wouldn't abate until she was able to speak with her mother.

She slipped into the dress and attempted to comb her hair so it somewhat resembled a lady's and not the overgrown mop of a boy. The gold chain dropped over her head, and the warm pendant slid under the neckline.

She checked her reflection in their small mirror and was pleasantly surprised at how well the color suited her.

"All right, boys," she said as she stepped out the wagon door. "Let's get ready to go."

Chapter 64

Tex

Far to the north, a glass glowed bright enough to wake a sleeping man.

Tex stumbled to the saddlebag on the floor, finding the leather-wrapped bundle. Frantically, his fingers tore through the ties that covered the glass's surface. He was too late to catch the image in action, but he hurried to the window to determine what he could see.

The picture was frozen again and horribly murky. A bright beam of light fell across a crisscrossed lump. Tex could make out a square window, a splash of washed-out color.

And then it made sense. He was looking at a crazy quilt of some kind, a tiny body asleep in a narrow bed—a bed terribly similar to the one he'd just climbed out of.

Someone had touched the stone and activated it.

The question was who. And where.

Chapter 65

Rafi

"My lord! My lord, wait!"

Despite Rafi's desire to ride into the meadow and leave the rest of the servants and underlords behind, there was something compelling about the voice.

Ugh. So this must be Vibora. His staff was all abuzz with discussion about Inimigo's kind, pleasant, thoughtful, beautiful assistant. Even Rafi's steward Mortimer—a notoriously difficult person to impress—said Vibora seemed "relatively intelligent for someone in Inimigo's employ."

Rafi could ignore her, and whatever she needed. No one would stop him. If he rode Breaker at a gallop, no one would even be able to catch him. But that would be running, and a responsible duke never ran from anything. Especially not from high-ranking staff members of a visiting duke.

"Yes? What can I do for you?" he asked.

The crowd of servants—busy attaching panniers of picnic goods and other necessities to saddles—parted for her, nodding hello and offering smiles as she went. Whoever she was, she'd certainly made friends among the maids and couriers quickly.

"Good morning, my lord." She stopped at his stirrup and bowed her neck in deference. "Forgive me for interrupting you, but Lord Inimigo wanted me to make sure you'd received his invitation to join him for breakfast."

Rafi took a deep breath, hoping to calm his temper. Who was Duke Inimigo to invite Rafi to breakfast? Visitors waited for invitations; they didn't issue them.

"I'm afraid I've already eaten. Please give Duke—"

"Your mother also requested that you join the duke and his daughter." Vibora offered Rafi a square of paper between two outstretched fingers.

Rafi's heart sank. He'd been looking forward to a morning away from his guests, to give him space and a chance to put his thoughts straight about betrothals and intrigue and too many secrets.

Dom urged his horse closer, so he could see over his brother's shoulder. Rafi tilted the paper so his brother could read his mother's missive.

"Tell them you already ate, and that you couldn't possibly stomach a bite in Duke Inimigo's company," Dom suggested. "Because you're already full, of course." He smiled at Vibora and received a flat-eyed stare in return.

Rafi crumpled the paper and tossed it into the goat pen. "Tell my mother and the duke that I'll be along shortly. I have a few arrangements to make."

The woman nodded, and Rafi watched her return to the house at a slow, gliding pace, as if all the world would wait for her. Halfway back to the house, Vibora froze as if a poisonous snake had slithered across her path.

Her head swiveled toward the line of horses, eyes scanning the servants who laughed and chatted as they waited.

Was she looking for someone specific? Perhaps she needed something else. Rafi opened his mouth to shout after her, but she blinked and continued into the house.

"Can you manage this on your own?" Rafi wanted Dom to say no, to tell him he couldn't possibly direct the servants without assistance.

"I intend to stay out of Brynn's way," Dom said with a grin. "She's quite capable of handling this, as you are well aware. I'll lie in the shade all day, listen to the birds sing and the wind blow through the meadow."

Dom was right. Accompanying the servants to prepare for that afternoon's picnic wasn't necessary, but Rafi liked having an excuse to be close to Johanna. He turned in the saddle, searching for her. She sat shoulder to shoulder with Brynn, the two of them laughing lightheartedly. Two guardsman in DeSilva livery loomed behind her like shadows at dusk.

"Oh." Dom followed his brother's gaze. "So the rumors *are* true."

Rafi stiffened. Had his brother somehow discovered his mother's suspicions about Johanna's identity? If he knew, who else did?

Dom dismounted and freed the pannier from behind Breaker's saddle and tied it to his own. "If you don't want people to know, you should really make your interest less obvious."

Rafi leaned across his saddle and snatched Dom's reins, holding both horses steady. "What are you talking about? What rumors?"

"Brother, relax." Dom gave Rafi's knee a playful shove. "Gossip follows every lord around. Especially when he and an attractive

Performer girl disappear at the same time." He shook his head, as if slightly confused, but a smile still creased his face. "I can't say I understand her taste in men. Surely she knows that in a few years I'll be the brother everyone will want."

The knots in Rafi's neck loosened a bit, and he allowed himself one more fleeting glance in Johanna's direction.

"If you want to keep your romantic rendezvous private you have to be sneak—"

"It wasn't like that," Rafi insisted, his voice low. He felt honor bound, among other things, to protect Johanna's reputation. She'd suffered enough at his hands and was a prickly person to apologize to. "I wanted to . . . to make sure she got home safely."

Rafi doubted every action he'd taken regarding Johanna. Perhaps it would have been better to send her away—to where, he wasn't sure—but it would have been too easy for someone to attack her en route.

No. It was better that she was where he could keep on an eye on her personally, and where guardsmen he trusted could provide her protection when he was unavailable. And if she was supposed to be his future wife . . .

"You're doing a horrible job *not* looking at her."

Rafi realized that he'd been staring, feeling a twinge of jealousy as she chatted with a few of the visiting underlords. Then one man touched her elbow, and Rafi's jealousy shifted to concern.

Any one of them could be an assassin. It would be so easy to slip a knife between her ribs, or poison her food, or snatch her into the underbrush. In that moment he made a decision.

"Dom, I need your help."

Rafi didn't tell his brother everything—there were some secrets better left unspoken—but he needed another person he could trust to keep an eye on Johanna. He laid out a plan that he hoped would protect her while still allowing him to treat with Inimigo.

"She's not going to like it." Dom scuffed the ground with his boot. "She may not play along."

"She'll do it. If she's in danger, her family may also be at risk. A man intent on killing every girl who matches her description wouldn't let a couple of little boys stand in his way."

Rafi hesitated outside the small dining room's door, trying to make out the voices on the other side.

"You said the men of Santiago were honorable, or at least a little more circumspect about their dalliances."

"He's a man, or will be soon, Belle. You can't expect more from him than that."

"But she's a Performer!" The girl's voice rose in pitch. "Some gutter-whelped entertainer who isn't even talented enough to be sanctioned by the Performers' Council. If she were another high-bred lady with taste and class, perhaps I'd be willing to share him—"

Her voice cut off with a thump and a gasp.

"Enough," Inimigo said, sounding dangerous. "I don't care if he brings a trollop, or a man, or a horse to his bed, as long as he brings you to it as well. I've fought too long to lose it all because my daughter doesn't want her husband to act like a man."

There was another pained intake of breath before Inimigo

continued. "You will obey me. You will flatter and sway him. You will convince him that you are the only choice for a betrothal, or I will ask Vibora and her friends to help you. You wouldn't want that, would you?"

"N-no, Papa. Please."

Vibora? She hadn't seemed particularly threatening, but she did work for Inimigo. That alone made her a woman with secrets.

Rafi didn't want to get caught listening at closed doors. "Good morning, Duke and Lady," he said as he entered the room. "Forgive me for delaying your meal. I'm glad your steward caught me. I couldn't imagine breakfasting with a more . . . lovely companion."

He took a moment to study the girl's form—as he supposed Inimigo expected him to do. Maribelle's dark hair had been swept off her neck, which was bare, as were her shoulders and a generous portion of her chest. Two large cutouts exposed the girl's abdomen from her rib cage to her hip bones. Smooth, tawny skin stretched over sinuous curves. Rafi knew dress styles in Maringa were more revealing, but this gown had to border on scandalous even there.

She offered her hand and Rafi pressed his lips to it, noticing a series of fingerlike bruises ringing her wrist.

A coconspirator in this plot, but an unwilling one.

"She is something to be proud of," Inimigo said, eyeing his daughter like a prized mare.

Maribelle returned her father's smile without a blink or tremble.

And a good actress.

Rafi waved to the table laden with an assortment of breads, cheeses, sliced meats, and fresh yogurt, not that he had any inclination to eat while his stomach broiled with disgust. "Tell me the news from Maringa." Rafi schooled his features into pleasantness and hoped that neither of his guests would realize his smile was fake.

"Lord Rafael, we both know that Maringa's economy, its people, its textiles and commodities are far richer than Santiago will ever be." Inimigo leaned forward, resting a fist on the table beside his plate. "I want to expand trade from my state beyond Belem, but your people and those of Impreza hold me in no great esteem. I'm here to attend your naming ceremony as a gesture of goodwill, and I'm offering you my daughter's hand to create a greater connection between our states."

At least he didn't spend the entire meal making small talk, Rafi thought as he set down his goblet. "While your daughter is beautiful," he said, nodding to Maribelle, who blushed prettily, "and a new trade route between our states would be mutually beneficial, I'm not certain the people of Santiago are prepared to forgive you for the deaths you sanctioned during the Ten Years' War. What reason can you possibly give me—and I them—that would clear those memories from their minds? And why would they believe you when you arrive at my home with thirty *slaves* in tow?"

Rafi leaned back in his chair, trying to appear more calm and controlled than he felt. A drop of sweat rolled down his back and puddled at his belt.

Inimigo considered Rafi with pursed lips. Rafi hoped he saw a confident, educated man and not a boy spouting his mother's words.

"Yes, Vibora said there were rumors circulating about my

prisoners." Inimigo drummed his fingers on the tabletop as he spoke. "Rather than incarcerate all petty criminals in Maringa, we give a select few the opportunity to work off their debts as members of our household staff. The collars are to help us delineate between regular staff who have access to every room in my house, and those who have limited access."

"You brought these criminals into my home."

Maribelle spoke up. "They aren't criminals in the usual sense. They're rehabilitated street people, mostly. Isn't that right, Papa?"

"They aren't dangerous." Inimigo placed a hand on his daughter's bare shoulder. "I wouldn't let anyone evil near my child."

Except yourself.

"Perhaps the people of Santiago would be swayed by the opportunities I give the lowliest of mine," Inimigo continued. "If that's not enough, there's always Maribelle's dowry."

"Twenty thousand in gold, shares in two of your mines, a selection of jewelry." Rafi shrugged as if unimpressed. "I'm sure an underlord in Belem or Impreza would be happy with those terms."

Maribelle crumpled her napkin between multiringed fingers. "It's not enough for you?"

Rafi rested his elbows on the table and narrowed his eyes at the duke. "I was once betrothed to a princess. Her dowry was an entire kingdom. Why would I give up on that when there are rumors that she survived and is on the Wisp Islands, massing troops for her grand return?"

"People love romantic notions of missing heirs returning to claim their thrones. It's something straight out of a Performer's tale." A vein ticked at Inimigo's left temple, but his face showed no other sign of emotion. "I *know* the princess is dead. Unfortunately, a group of overzealous soldiers strung up her body. I executed the lot for their actions."

It wasn't the confession Rafi hoped for, but it also didn't eliminate Inimigo as a threat to Johanna.

"A dead girl can do nothing for you, Rafael. *I* can fill your grain silos. *I* can feed your people, this year, next year, for ten years to come. But food isn't what you really need."

"Then what is?"

"Protection." A small smile crept onto Inimigo's face. "There's a storm coming, and the two hundred men in your garrison aren't going to be enough to stand in its path. You could call in the men from each of your outposts and force your underlords to marshal their troops as well. They won't be enough."

Rafi's throat grew dry, but his back continued to sweat. "Is that a declaration of war?"

"From me?" Inimigo placed a hand over his chest, clearly offended. "Of course not. I was offering a piece of advice."

"Tell me then, where will this great threat come from? The Wisp Islands? The Pirates from beyond Impreza?" Rafi tried out one of Dom's smirks. "Or perhaps you expect the Keepers to appear and take back this land."

"No need to be flippant, my boy. There are people who see the future of Santarem as one united country, rather than five divided states."

Inimigo's neck had gone red, but Rafi continued to push.

"I assume you're one of these people? The one ready to wear the crown of a united Santarem?"

"Those are your words, not mine." Inimigo grabbed his daughter's wrist and pulled her to her feet.

"I'm not certain this country would ever accept you as a king."

"Consider my offer. Consider your position in the new Santarem."

And as the duke vacated the room, Rafi wondered what, exactly, Inimigo had been holding back. There had been some undercurrent of tension, something that even the implacable duke had been unwilling to discuss.

What was it? Rafi wondered. And how much danger were his people about to face?

Chapter 66

Johanna

Three gazebos nestled in the shade of towering balsa trees. Their silver branches, frothy with heart-shaped leaves, whispered with the breeze that blew through the meadow. Late summer asters bloomed in jewel-toned clumps, each a bright spot of color against the blue silk curtains draped from the gazebos' eaves.

The scene was peaceful and private, a perfect place for the nobles to put aside old arguments and hash out new agreements.

It was that element of perfection that made Johanna nervous. Her brothers had the ability to turn the most idyllic settings into disasters.

"Promise me," she said for the fiftieth time since they had left the estate, "that you two will be on your best behavior. No tumbling, no wrestling, no yelling—"

"No fun," Michael added. He sank down against one of the fat tree trunks and rested his sulky face on his fist.

"You can have fun." She ruffled his blond curls. "Just make it *quiet* fun."

"We'll stay out of the way and not snitch any treats," Joshua promised, his blue eyes wide and serious. "We'll be so good that you won't even know we're here."

Guilt burned bitter at the back of Johanna's throat. She didn't mean to leech the enjoyment out of the day, but Lady DeSilva had been so kind, so understanding. Johanna didn't want to do anything that would disappoint her employers.

"But Lord Dom said we could have cake. Lord Dom said—"

"Michael, I don't care what Lord Dom said. I'm here to perform and you're here to stay out of trouble."

"Did I hear my name and 'trouble' in the same sentence?" Dom's boots crunched over the undergrowth as he approached. "Whatever it was, I didn't do it. Unless you're referring to some missing *dolce de leite*. I might have had something to do with that."

Dom reached into his pockets and pulled out two paper-wrapped packets, presenting a caramel treat to each boy.

His words were light, but his smile seemed a bit too forced. "Did I tell you boys about the fish I caught yesterday? There's a stream not far from here. The water is lower than usual this year and some big fish have gotten trapped in the deeper pools."

"Why don't you go see if you can find them?" Johanna straightened from her crouch and dried her suddenly damp palms on her dress. "Stay where you can see the gazebos. I'll come find you in a minute."

Neither of her brothers questioned their sudden freedom and darted off in the direction Dom pointed.

"Is something wrong?"

He hesitated, shuffling the dirt between his feet before he spoke. "Rafi believes you're in danger. That someone among one of the visiting groups may be planning to hurt you."

"Me? Why?"

"I don't know all the details," he said, checking to see where the closest servant stood. "Rafi needs an excuse to stay close to you. For your protection."

"Oh please. Rafi *wants* an excuse to stay close to me." She meant it as a joke, but her face flushed as brightly as the asters.

"I wish that's all it was, Johanna, for all of our sakes, but he is deadly serious about this."

"No one is going to hurt me, and Rafi is certainly not responsible for my safety." She rotated her wrist, letting him see the gleam of the dagger she kept there. "I can take care of myself."

"He was afraid you'd say that. So . . ." Dom stopped, licked his lips, and then continued. "He's letting everyone believe that something happened between you last night, when he chased you into the forest. I've spent most of the morning confirming the rumors."

"You *what*?" She'd seen him joking with the servants and underlords who'd come out with the first wave of picnickers, but Johanna never imagined she was the subject of their conversations.

"Rafi thinks the best way to keep you safe is to make sure his interest in you is known." He checked over his shoulder as hoofbeats neared. It was the remainder of the party led by Lady DeSilva. "No one is going to hurt you or *your family* if they know it will draw Rafi's anger."

"No one wants to hurt us. We're nothing. Nobodies." She turned in the direction her brothers had run, wishing she could call them back.

"Johanna, I don't know why anyone would want to do you harm, but I do know my brother." Dom frowned, and Johanna realized that underneath all the charm and laughs, he could be as intense and serious as his sibling. "If Rafi says you're in danger, then I believe without question that you are."

Perhaps it had something to do with her mother's confrontation in town, or maybe someone among the nobles carried a long-standing dislike of her father.

"You don't know anything else?"

"Nothing."

Johanna worried her bottom lip between her teeth. Was there some way to use her so-called relationship with Rafi to figure out who intended to harm her?

"What do I need to do?"

"It's simple. Flirt. Innocent touches." Dom dug a trench in the dirt with his boot. "That sort of thing."

"I can do that." And watch the reaction of everyone who noticed.

Chapter 67

Jacaré

Jacaré pushed his crew hard. They rode at a breakneck pace out of Performers' Camp, headed toward the Santiago estate. Elma was certain the girl and the Von Arlos had settled there after Arlo's death.

"She'll be safer there than anywhere else," she assured them as they entered the Council House. "The DeSilvas are the best kind of people in Santarem. They were devoted to the king and his family, and were the first to muster troops to come to the Citadel's defense. If they realize that they're harboring Wilhelm's heir, they'll protect her fiercely."

Even with that knowledge, Jacaré couldn't ignore the warning bells sounding in his head.

Yes, they'd caught Benton, but he had been a tool used to accomplish a task. Someone else was in control. Someone Benton wasn't willing to identify.

"I only met the person once. No name, no face. Just a cloaked and hooded shadow in a dark corner of a bar in Cruzamento," he had said.

They'd chained the assassin to a chair in the small, two-story building. Five other chairs, carved out of dark wood, and a wall of bookshelves were the only furniture. Two elderly men, both retired Performers and members of their Council, joined Elma, Jacaré, and Tex for Benton's trial.

"Was it a man or woman?" Jacaré pressed.

"Oh, I don't know," Benton said with a grin. "The person was taller than me, but so are a lot of people."

"How do you get your assignments?"

"I get them and my payment from the barkeeper in Cruzamento. He's just a middleman."

It took every ounce of self-control not to break the assassin's fingers, but Jacaré had promised not to touch Benton without Elma's permission. "Tell me something."

"Promise me I'll live."

"I can't do that." Jacaré nodded to Elma. "I need . . ."

The old woman waved off his words and stepped close to the assassin. She pressed one crooked finger against Benton's chest. Smoke began rising from his shirt.

"That's good, Elma," Benton said with a laugh. "But not good enough."

The smell of burning flesh filled the room. The Council members shifted uncomfortably in their chairs but made no remark.

"Who are you protecting?" Jacaré asked with a growl.

Sweat beaded on Benton's forehead, but he kept his lips sealed.

"People who hold out under torture only do so for two reasons." Tex leaned against one of the supporting posts, arms folded against his chest. "Love or fear."

"He's an assassin," Jacaré said, pacing around the chair. "He's not motivated by love. So who could he possibly fear more than one of us?"

The question was the answer.

"It's another Keeper."

Chapter 68

Rafi

The cold snap Santiago had suffered a few weeks earlier seemed a distant memory. The sun beat upon the roofs of the gazebos with heavy fists of heat. The silks provided shade but stopped the breeze from stirring the air inside.

The ladies from Maringa—including Maribelle in the little material that stretched over her—wilted like delicate morning flowers by noon and retired to one of the gazebos to escape the heat. Rafi had helped Maribelle from her horse when they'd arrived. Her bare skin skimmed across his palms and left a layer of sweat he wished he could wash off.

Belem and Inimigo lounged on padded sofas in the gazebo most shaded by the balsa trees, sipping on wine the servants chilled in a nearby stream. That is, Inimigo was sipping. Belem had given up the glass and held a bottle against his chest, where its condensation mixed with the sweat stains on his tunic.

Lady DeSilva was completely unfazed by the heat and led a conversation about water rights. The rest of the southerners, local underlords and a few of the braver souls from Belem, enjoyed the pleasant sunshine, kicking a ball in the meadow, tossing horseshoes, and chatting.

"Oh for Keeper's sake!" Belem sat up suddenly, knocking over a bowl of grapes as he went. "Go get that Performer girl so we have something to think about besides how blasted hot it is!"

"She wasn't planning to perform till later this afternoon," Rafi said, straightening from his slouch. He could ignore the heat, but he had been uncomfortable for other reasons. Every time he passed Johanna, she gave him a come-hither smile that he struggled not to return.

The tilt of her chin, the set of her mouth, the extra sway in her walk were all so blatantly flirtatious that no one could overlook the new attraction between them.

Rafi found himself wishing it wasn't a ruse.

He suspected Johanna, and the gossip circulating about their relationship, was the real reason Maribelle hid in the other gazebo. As a duke's daughter, Maribelle rarely had to share anyone's attention.

"If it's a matter of money, I'll pay her myself." Belem reached into a pocket and threw a small bag of coins on the table.

"That's unnecessary," Rafi said as he rose from his seat. "We have other forms of entertainment. Perhaps we could play a round of Strategy? I'm sure both of you could teach me—"

"Get the girl, Rafael." Inimigo looked at Rafi through heavy-lidded eyes. "I understand her appeal transcends her ability."

Rafi's heart stuttered; he hated to introduce Johanna to Inimigo at all, but he knew he couldn't avoid it forever. "She is very talented."

A lecherous grin quirked Inimigo's mouth. "As I'm sure you're well aware."

"She does put on quite a show," Belem said as he rolled back onto his sofa, looking every bit like a cat, fat and lazy after devouring a plump mouse.

"Send someone to fetch Vibora while you're out there. I need a few words with her."

Rafi was pleased when his mother nodded for him to go. He should have insisted on staying—gleaning every bit of intrigue from their conversation—but his mother was more adept at political maneuvering.

He took a circuitous route through the picnic area, speaking with his guests and observing Inimigo's collared servants as they huddled in the shade beneath the trees. They didn't appear to suffer, all healthy and well fed, but there was something odd about them.

They weren't talking, he realized. Rafi tried to think of a time when he'd seen a collection of servants who didn't use their free time to chat and laugh. This group sat silently, studying the woods around them, a tenseness in their muscles that suggested preparedness to act.

Either they were very well trained, or . . . Rafi didn't know what. He was tempted to pull one aside, but the call of two high-pitched voices drew him away.

"Did you see how far I spit that one, Jo?" Michael grabbed Johanna's shoulder, shaking her.

She lay on a scrap of tablecloth in the cool grass, her feet in the stream and her dress pulled up high enough to be improper. Her bare legs were pale and well shaped against the dark gray river rocks.

"All the way across the stream?" she asked without sitting up.

"And farther!"

Joshua shook his head. "It landed in the water."

"Did not!"

As Rafi got closer, he could see that Johanna's eyes were closed against the dappled sunlight poking through the branches above. Without opening them she said, "There's a wider bit of stream farther down. The first one of you to spit five grapes clear to the other side wins a prize."

The boys exchanged a grin and broke into a run, blowing by Rafi without a hello.

Two guards lurked by a tree a few paces away. Rafi waved them off, and they clunked up the river a ways.

Johanna seemed to have dozed off, her lips slightly parted in sleep, one arm thrown across her forehead, half blocking the light. She was vulnerable and completely relaxed, enjoying a lazy afternoon.

Guilt overwhelmed Rafi, knowing that her untroubled sleep would soon be something of the past.

His shadow fell across her face and her eyes opened slowly. She studied him sleepily, then burst into motion, jumping to her feet and smoothing down her skirts. "Do you always lurk over girls while they sleep?"

"I try not to," Rafi said, hoping wit would disguise his nerves.

"Are you here to make the rumors your brother has been spreading look real?" She stepped into plain leather slippers, holding her skirts modestly so she could see her feet. "*Lovers* would never stand so far apart."

"And you would know because . . ."

She didn't answer, pinning him with a glare sharp enough to flay the scales off a fish. "Why do you believe I'm in danger?"

Rafi did step closer. He wanted to be able to whisper so there was no chance they could be overheard. But Johanna did the same. They stood, nearly chest to chest, not touching, but near enough that he could smell the sweet scent of acai berries rising off her skin.

He had plenty of experience flirting, sneaking kisses in shadowed corners, meeting in the gardens or in the barn for a few moments of unchaperoned bliss. Before his father died and so much responsibility had been dropped on his shoulders, Rafi could imagine a moment like this. A reckless moment. Where he'd put his hands around Johanna's waist and pull her close and kiss her till they were both breathless. Now, things were different. Johanna wasn't a maid or visiting underlord's daughter. She was a girl in danger, and maybe the only surviving heir to Santarem's throne.

More than that, *Rafi* was different. He could see this moment replayed in a thousand different lights. What would his mother think? What would his people think? That he was the rapscallion lord who'd suffered Punishment before his naming day and in whose hands no girl's virtue was safe?

"Johanna, how well do you know your parents? I mean . . ." He stumbled, searching for the words that would put into question everything she knew about her life, about her station, about her family. "Would they ever have lied to you? Even if it was to protect you?"

Her forehead creased; her gray eyes showed confusion. "What reason would my parents have to lie to me? What would they have to protect me from?" She shrugged slightly, and it seemed to move her even closer. "We led a simple life, traveling, performing, resting at Performers' Camp when we were between jobs or needed time off."

"There was never a time when you doubted you were—" He cut off that line of questioning. Rafi had no intention of hurting Johanna again, and making her question her relationship with her family would do just that.

If I could talk to her mother first . . .

"One of the dukes has expressed an inappropriate interest in you." It wasn't a lie exactly. Wanting to kill her could certainly be considered inappropriate.

"And so you've appointed yourself the defender of my honor?" She jabbed him in the chest. "I have brothers, you know, and, when all else fails, I'm handy with a knife."

Had she forgotten the beating he gave her? Yes, she put up a fight, but it hadn't been enough to save her then and it wouldn't be enough to save her from a man bent on murder.

The voices in the distance seemed to grow louder. If someone discovered them, this secret meeting needed to look authentic.

Rafi had no choice. He had to touch her. Lightly he set both of his hands at her waist, his thumbs over her hip bones. She was thin, small enough that his fingers spanned the distance all the way to her spine. There was a moment, a craving, to use his grip to pull her closer, to press the entire length of his body against hers. He forced the impulse aside, trying to focus on the words he had to say.

"Please, Johanna. Let me take care of you."

Chapter 69

Johanna

Johanna's breath caught in her throat. Rafi's words were honest, his dark eyes sincere. She wanted to lean against him, to let someone else bear her concerns. But what would it cost her to take it all back on later?

"I will. On two conditions."

He nodded for her to continue.

"First, that your care extends to my family."

"Of course. I'd never let harm come to them."

"And second, that protecting me from whatever this threat is will clear you of your honor debt toward me."

"But—"

She covered his mouth with her palm. Being so close to him, having his fingers at her waist, made her forget that the connection between them was all an act. She slowly lowered her hand. "I want to be able to leave Santiago when this threat is cleared and not worry that a lordling with a misplaced sense of honor is chasing me across the countryside." She smiled to soften the words. "You've done more than enough for me and my family. All debts between us are forgiven."

Johanna expected a sigh or Rafi's shoulders to slump in relief, but instead he studied her eyes. She didn't know what he was looking for, but she couldn't turn away. She'd never been kissed—not when it wasn't part of a performance or a game—but she'd seen enough kissing to know what was supposed to be done.

If he'd bend his neck a bit and she went up on her toes, they'd be perfectly aligned. She could hold on to his shoulders or wind her fingers into the curls at his neck to pull him closer.

She tilted up her chin and his thumb drew unconscious circles on her hip. From that point her skin seemed to ignite, like he'd laid a path of Skylighter's powder all over her body. She pressed tingling fingers against his chest, feeling the heat of the solid flesh underneath.

"Rafi . . ."

He licked his lips; his dark gaze flickered to her mouth. There was an instant when everything went still, where nothing stirred except the breaths they shared.

He took a step back, releasing his grip on her waist.

"Duke Inimigo and Duke Belem are miserable in the heat and would like you to divert their minds with a story or a song." He offered his arm with complete formality. Only the lingering warmth at her waist gave any indication that something had nearly happened.

"Let me gather my brothers, and I'll come straightaway," Johanna said, turning to hide her disappointment.

Michael and Joshua stood knee-deep in the stream, arms in the water, trying to catch trout the way their father had done dozens of times.

Joshua's blond hair was wet, standing up around his head like a porcupine in a pique. "You have to be quieter," he whispered to Michael. "You scare them away with all your noise."

"You're quiet enough for both of us." Michael spun a circle in the water, stirring up dirt and pebbles.

Johanna smiled at the twist in Michael's words. Their father always said that Michael was loud enough for all the boys in their family.

"Hop out." Johanna found one shoe and followed it to a sock, and then another shoe. Both of Joshua's shoes—a new pair she didn't recognize—sat on a rock side by side with the socks tucked neatly inside. "We need to get back to the gazebos. I've got some singing to do."

"But why?" Michael said as he waded to the side. "Everyone's up the stream a ways."

"Surely not everyone." Rafi shaded his eyes, looking for people ahead.

Michael nodded vigorously. "I'm pretty sure it's everyone important. Dom, Brynn, bunches of girls in dresses, the fat duke, the mean—"

"Michael!" Johanna snapped. "You can't talk about the dukes like that. It's not . . ."

"Inaccurate," Rafi mumbled, struggling to keep his lips from curling.

"Polite," Johanna finished, shooting a glare in his direction.

"Well . . . it's what Josh said when he came down out of the tree." Michael thumbed at his brother who hunched his shoulders at the accusation. Then, as if sensing a chance to shift the blame, Michael said, "He climbed that big one all the way to the top, where the branches are thin and wiggly. I thought he was going to fall."

"Oh, I'm certain you were terrified with worry." Johanna held out her brother's shoes.

"Perhaps Joshua would be willing to climb the tree again, and see if all my guests are still upstream," Rafi suggested. "Not all the way to the top, but enough to get a good view."

Josh was half up the trunk before Rafi had finished his sentence. He edged onto a stout limb, holding on to the one above to secure his position. "They're still there. At the pool."

"Come down and we'll go meet them." Johanna watched as he dropped from branch to branch, never checking his balance or grip. Her brothers' talents were innate, their ease of movement, their fearlessness with heights. Those were all things Johanna had had to learn, after much practice and focus. It wasn't fair that the boys got all the natural talent.

Michael and Joshua skipped ahead, the two guards followed behind, and Rafi and Johanna walked side by side. Silence draped between them like a sheer curtain, transparent but impossible to ignore.

The young lords had stripped off their outer layers and splashed around the pool in their linen shirts and breeches. The ladies demurely dabbled their toes in the water.

"Oh, Lord Rafi! I'm glad you're back." Lady Maribelle reclined on a blanket, her skirts spread like frosting on an ornate pastry. Other young ladies and at least one lady's maid speckled the ground around her like cupcakes fallen from a tray. Their dresses were bright in late-summer colors, but all paled in comparison to Maribelle's silk-and-lace embroidered confection. Her maid's finger frantically plaited the lady's black locks into a crown around her head.

Maribelle shook the maid away and ran her fingers through her hair, letting it cascade down her back.

She was beautiful. And exotic. And noble.

Maribelle offered a hand to Rafi. "Help me up, won't you?" She held tight to him, pressing against his side as she stood. "I had the most splendid idea. Your brother said there are wild raspberries blooming all over the forest. Let's hunt some up. They'd be a perfect addition to dinner. I absolutely love raspberries, and I'm sure you know exactly where all the good ones are."

"I suppose," Rafi said hesitantly.

Johanna skirted the group and headed to the gazebos with her brothers lagging behind.

"We'll make a game of it," Maribelle continued. "The teams who come back with the most berries will get a prize. My papa will be sure to give something good."

That had both Joshua's and Michael's attention.

"Can we go, Jo?" Joshua asked, hope brightening his eyes.

Johanna hesitated. Would the boys be in danger? Could someone possibly hurt them in this crowd? With the bright sun and laughing nobles, it was a scene too perfect for anything amiss.

"You may go, but the prize isn't meant for one of us. It's a game for the nobles."

"But Jo—"

"Michael, do you want raspberries or not?"

He scuffed at the plants and didn't respond.

Joshua held out a hand for his brother. "Come on, Michael," he said, disappointment evident in his tone, "we better hurry before all the berries are picked."

She watched the group head toward the forest—Joshua tugging Michael, and Maribelle draped on Rafi's arm.

Rafi looked in Johanna's direction and she stopped, her heart stuttering with hope for the words he might say.

"Johanna." He ignored the clawed grasp on his arm and Lady Maribelle's frown. "If you see Inimigo's steward, Vibora, tell her that he wished to see her."

Fool. What did you expect to hear? He's a duke and you're a Performer.

"Of course, my lord."

Johanna chided herself as she returned to the gazebos. *What happens on stage, stays on stage.*

She finally understood why her father avoided her mother's plays. If every scene had looked as real as those moments in the forest had felt, she could certainly imagine how difficult it would be for Arlo to watch.

She spied Vibora standing with one of Rafi's housemaids, their heads tilted together as they whispered. What sort of secret could two servants from such different stations share?

"Mistress Vibora?"

The woman straightened, a slow uncurving of her spine, and Johanna was struck by how the woman seemed to loom over everyone. Not that the maid noticed; she smiled up at Vibora like her mind had gone simple.

"You may go, Beatriz." The maid skipped away, grinning as she went.

Everyone seemed to like Vibora, despite the fact that she worked for Inimigo. Brynn had raved about the woman's beauty and kindness on their ride to the picnic that morning. But as Johanna got closer, a feeling of *wrongness* rubbed against her like a chemise made of nettles.

"Did you need something, Johanna?"

"Lord Inimigo requested you join him in the gaz—"

With one pointed nail Vibora tipped Johanna's chin to the light. "*Both* of your parents were Performers, correct?"

"Why?" Johanna took a step back, but Vibora followed.

"Answer the question."

"Let go of me." Johanna could reach into her sleeve and have her dagger out instantly, but pulling a knife on another duke's servant would have consequences.

"Something about you is very strange," the steward said, and pushed Johanna's face away. "Tell Inimigo I have to see to one of the servants and I'll be along shortly."

"I'm the strange one?" Johanna whispered as Vibora left the clearing. A half-moon indented in Jo's skin. She rubbed at the mark, hoping it would fade by the time she entered the gazebo.

Not that it mattered. The silk draperies made the interior dim, but the structure was hot despite the shade. Wine and citrus fruit almost covered the smell of Duke Belem's sweat, but not quite. He snored like an unhappy hog and twitched in his sleep. Lady DeSilva and Inimigo spoke quietly, but neither of their faces reflected Belem's serenity.

"Excuse me, my lord and lady." Johanna offered a curtsy. "Mistress Vibora will be here shortly. Would you prefer me to entertain later?"

Inimigo raised a hand to stop Johanna from leaving. "Of course not. Lady DeSilva and I would like to relieve our ears of that awful growling."

Belem snorted and rolled to his side, cushioning his fat cheek with one hand.

"Of course, sir. Is there anything specific you'd like to hear?" Johanna rolled her foot from side to side as a strange sense of nervousness overtook her. She'd performed for hundreds of people from all classes, but singing for two of the highest rulers of the land in such an intimate setting made her stomach do acrobatics.

"Sing me something . . . victorious." He pressed a finger to the band of gold he wore around his brow, tapping his temple a few times.

Lady DeSilva turned her knees away from Inimigo, tucking her dress tight under her thighs.

He certainly hasn't made friends here. Johanna moved near the gazebo's door and began singing a battle tune so old no one remembered its history.

Here the war begins.
Here is where I stand.
Cross my sword, slam my shield, but never take my land.

Hear the call of men,
Coming to my side.
Their voices raise; their call is clear; my law they will abide.

Inimigo's fingers ticked on the chair's arm, beating out the rhythm. As the chorus came, the war cry of an ancient king, Inimigo clapped along, the sound reverberating in the small space.

Lady DeSilva rested her chin on her fist and stared at a point over Johanna's head. It wasn't Johanna's favorite song either, but it was the first to come to mind.

The story ended with the enemy retreating, leaving behind their dead and injured in their haste to escape.

"I forgot how much I enjoyed that song. Thank you for reminding me." Inimigo tilted his head to the side, regarding Johanna like a vulture choosing the juiciest parts of a carcass. "There's something about you—"

"She looks very similar to Underlord Ronaldo's latest wife, don't you think?" Lady DeSilva offered, leaning forward in her chair.

Inimigo looked at her askance. "Ronaldo from Sulciudad?"

"Think of Lady Ronaldo twenty years ago. The resemblance is there."

Johanna hoped her face didn't reveal her thoughts; in her opinion Lady DeSilva couldn't have been much more insulting. The Von Arlos performed at Sulciudad, Maringa's most southern holding, prior to their final trip to Belem. The lady of that house was at least sixty years old, had stark white hair on her head, and black ones springing from her chin.

"She was always small framed and wore her hair short." Inimigo pursed his lips. "I suppose . . ."

"I know exactly who she looks like."

Johanna whipped toward Belem, who was no longer snoring or asleep. His eyes were nearly hidden under swollen lids. His tongue appeared between his lips, moving slowly like a bloated slug over rough terrain.

He pushed himself upright, smoothing down his sleep-mangled hair. "It's not even how she looks. It's how she *teases*." He nodded toward Inimigo, seeking a compatriot. "It's the way she smiles, and the way she leans close to you when she talks."

"I've never—"

"That's enough, Lord Belem. You are drunk and the alcohol has made you forget your manners." Lady DeSilva trembled with anger. Her face was pale when she turned to Johanna. "You're excused for the day, Johanna."

Without a word Johanna backed out of the gazebo and melted into the woods.

Chapter 70

Rafi

Rafi hated to send Johanna to face Inimigo and Belem alone, but he also couldn't choose her over Maribelle with everyone watching. A slight like that would not be ignored. His only consolation was that neither of the dukes would make a move against Johanna with so many witnesses.

The nobles broke into groups of four or five and headed off into the woods. As if on cue, all the retainers faded into the trees, leaving Rafi alone with Lady Maribelle. She stood a few feet away, a basket she'd finagled from one of his servants draped over her arm.

Rafi's hands were full, raspberry juice staining his palms. He ate a few to free up a hand, and paused to wipe his fingers on the grass.

"I wanted a chance to speak to you without interlopers." Maribelle held out the basket for his other handful.

"Lady Maribelle, we probably shouldn't be seen without a chaperone—"

"Let them talk. Rumors have a tendency to become truths." She popped a raspberry in her mouth. "A rumor about us would only hasten our betrothal, and that would suit me perfectly."

Her candor froze Rafi for a moment. "I wouldn't want to be responsible for untruths whispered about you."

"Don't give me any tripe about upholding honor." She snorted. It was an oddly horselike sound coming from such a fine-featured face. "Your reputation is even darker than mine."

A fist of guilt clenched in Rafi's stomach. *And now Johanna's is sullied too.*

"Accosting your peasants, taking a Performer as a lover, killing your own father," she continued. "All bold moves."

"I didn't kill my father."

She looked at him through her lashes, a knowing smile curving her lips. "Of course not. And I haven't contemplated dozens of ways to dispatch mine."

Rafi could deny it again, knowing his words would fall on deaf ears. "What do you want, Maribelle? Or are you a pawn in one of Inimigo's grand schemes?"

"Not this time." She hesitated, and Rafi saw something nervous and shifty under her arrogant facade. "Marrying you is the only way to escape from my father, and without my help you won't live long enough for that to happen. My father is committed to putting himself on the throne at any cost. He'll lie and betray and kill to get what he wants, but . . ."

"But what?" Rafi prompted when the silence stretched too far.

"He's not in this alone. He's made some friends, powerful friends, who want to help him achieve his goal." She folded her arms across her chest, the basket resting against her hip. "They are very dangerous."

"Who are they? Pirates? Slavers? What can they offer your father that he doesn't already have?" Maringa was the richest state in both natural resources and economy. It could survive with very little trade from the other states.

She stepped close and put her mouth next to his ear. "Magic," she breathed.

Magic? The girl had to be completely unhinged. The closest thing to magic was Performers' tricks—all sleight of hand and simple science. Only in the stories of Mother Lua and the Keepers were feats of magic ever possible.

"You don't believe me." Maribelle studied his face, as if doubt was written plainly across his forehead. "I don't blame you. It sounds ridiculous, but if you'd seen them, you'd know they were a threat. Vibora is a mouse by comparison."

"So you're saying Vibora can do magic?"

"She can do *things* . . . She makes things happen." She rubbed mindlessly at her wrist where a purple bruise blared against her olive skin. "Things that aren't natural."

Rafi wondered what other damage Inimigo had done to his daughter, maybe to her mind.

"Thank you for telling me," he said, trying to placate her.

She offered him a haughty smile. "I thought it was best you know. Then you can be prepared for whatever treachery my father has planned."

That was a truth Rafi couldn't ignore, despite its messenger. Maribelle may have been mistaken about magic, but Inimigo likely had allies beyond the obvious ones.

"I appreciate the warning and will . . . take it to heart." Rafi offered her his arm, hoping to lead her away before the rumors spun out of control.

There was a shout in the woods, and both Maribelle and Rafi jumped. Dom and two guards came crashing toward them.

Apprehension washed over Rafi, making his skin prickle from head to toe. "What's going on?"

"We lost her," the first guard said without preamble. "We were trying not to be obvious about who we were following, so we mixed with the servants outside the gazebos. She must have snuck off after she performed."

Rafi snapped into action. "Dom, go get Snout."

Chapter 71

Johanna

Joshua and Michael had a lifetime's worth of experience picking berries and finding nuts to supplement their meals while traveling between performances. Johanna followed their tracks to a sunny rise in the opposite direction all the other people had traveled. Within minutes she spotted them; both had full hands and stained lips.

"I thought I told you to stay with the group!" she yelled up the hill.

"They'd be all picked if we followed everyone else," Joshua explained.

She tried to be angry, but Michael stuffed his cheeks full of berries, and she found herself laughing instead.

"Don't eat too many! They'll make you sick."

Johanna stopped at the tree line to fill a handkerchief with raspberries. She'd save a few for the next morning when the boys were hungry. Again.

Once her square was filled, she knotted the top and followed the noise her brothers made into the trees. It was cooler under the branches, the ground littered with twisting ivy and ferns that crunched under her feet. She checked over her shoulder to see if the two guards had followed her from the gazebos to the woods but found someone wholly unexpected.

Duke Belem.

He smiled when he saw her surprise. "I apologize if I frightened you, Johanna. I'd like a word with you, if I may."

Rafi's words echoed in her ears. *One of the dukes has expressed an inappropriate interest in you.* After her performance, she couldn't say which of the lords gave her the worst impression. Inimigo stared at her with creepy interest, and Belem . . . Belem was vile.

"Of course, my lord." Johanna measured the distance between them. She could run, but the ground cover and her skirts would slow her down.

"I have room in my house for a girl such as you." His gaze traced down her body and back up. "I could use someone of your veritable talents."

Every time she saw Belem, he had a bottle in his hand and was either drunk or well on his way. There was a drying wine stain on the front of his tunic, but he stood balanced on the balls of his feet, as if expecting to burst into motion. Johanna shifted the raspberries into her left hand, freeing her right so that she could reach for her dagger if she needed it.

"I'm sorry, my lord, but I've signed a contract with the DeSilvas, and my family is settled here. I couldn't take any offer that forced me to leave them behind."

"Those sweet little boys I saw earlier?"

"I have an older brother, as well. He should be along any moment." The lie came smoothly, but Belem clicked his tongue in response.

"You mean the one who has an apprenticeship in town? I'd be surprised to see him now, given that he doesn't generally leave till after sunset."

Shivers ran along Johanna's skin like an army of ants. "I'm surprised you know so much about my family."

"I don't know everything, Johanna, but I'd like to." He took a step forward and she matched him with one backward. "My estate is beautiful, and wealthy. We make a healthy profit on the items we buy from Maringa and sell to the rest of Santarem at a premium price. Such fools they all are, holding to their honor and misguided principles."

He reached toward the belt hidden under his paunch and Johanna drew her dagger. "Put your hands down."

Belem laughed, his jowls wiggling with amusement. "Relax, girl. I was reaching for my purse."

"Don't bother. I'm not interested in your money."

"Come now, you can't honestly tell me this is how you saw your life turning out? Performing in a tiny state rather than Santarem's biggest cities?" He lowered one hand slowly, untied his purse, and tossed it at Johanna's feet. It split open and gold coins spilled out the top, cascading over her foot and rolling under the vines below.

Then she was flat on her back with a knee pinning her knife hand and strong fingers at her throat.

"Performers are always distracted by money." Belem exhaled into her face, his breath reeking of wine fumes and rotten cheese. "It appears you are a fool as well."

He was so heavy, his weight pressing her into the soft dirt. Her skirt was trapped under his legs and she couldn't get them free.

"Get off of me!" She swung her left arm, dragging her nails across his face. He caught her wrist and slammed it into the ground.

"That will come out of your salary." Belem spit blood from a split lip. "I came to you with an honest proposal and then—" His words cut off with a sharp intake of breath, his eyes wide with shock. "Wh-what is that? Where did you get that necklace?"

She could feel it then, the green crystal pressed against the hollow of her throat.

Belem broke the chain holding the pendant, cradling it in his meaty fist. Johanna struggled and bucked her hips, but the duke didn't seem to notice. He swatted her hands aside and stood up, still staring at the necklace.

"Mother Lua, it can't be." Without another word, he walked toward the pond, swaying like a drunk as he went.

Johanna sat among the pile of coins, feeling the sting of the broken chain across her neck and grateful she hadn't suffered worse.

Chapter 72

Jacaré

Something had changed among Jacaré's troop members. Strained silence drifted around their camp with the smoke from their small cooking fire.

They were tired and worried—he knew that and felt it too—but there was something more in the dark looks Tex sent both Pira and Leão. Pira kept her distance from the men like they'd been skunked.

Scrapes between soldiers were common, but they were a small, tight-knit group and needed to focus on something other than their disagreement.

He'd chosen to stop in the late afternoon so that everyone could catch a few hours' sleep without anyone having to stand watch. They'd eat, rest, ride on at dusk, and be at Santiago by the following afternoon.

Leão returned from the stream with a string of cleaned fish in his hand. He stepped wide to avoid brushing against Pira as she pulled the saddle from her horse.

Yes, there was definitely something going on.

"Help me get these wrapped," Jacaré commanded Leão, pointing to the wide leaves he'd gathered to bake the fish in. "The coals are ready now."

"Yes, sir."

"Hold up a moment," Tex said. He held the glass on his palms, the wrappings dangling from either side. "The image is frozen again." He shook it as if that would make the magic start working.

Jacaré snatched it out of the old soldier's hand and studied the image. It showed a canopy of trees with late afternoon sunlight creating streaks of golden fog across the glass surface. There was something brown—*maybe a thatched roof?*—at the bottom of the image. "How long has it been like this?"

"I checked it this morning and it showed a wagon like the Performers live in, and then there was a stream of images changing every half hour or so, but it's been stuck like this for two hours." Tex leaned over Jacaré's shoulder. "But I can't figure out why she'd be lying on her back for so long unless . . ."

He couldn't finish the sentence and Jacaré didn't need him to. The last time the image had frozen, the person wearing the necklace was dead.

"She's not dead," Jacaré said with conviction. "Everyone back on your horses. We ride without stopping until we find her."

"But—"

Jacaré cut off Pira's complaint and kicked dirt over their fire and the fish. "Leão, heal the horses at steady intervals. I don't care if their legs break. You heal them while they run." He turned to Tex. "What do you remember of the last images? Can you find where she was living?"

"A mango orchard. From the angle of the sun, I'd say on the southwest corner of the Santiago township."

"We'll ride there first. If we're lucky she'll have dropped the necklace somewhere in the woods."

Mother Lua, Jacaré thought. *I've gone insane.* He replayed his instructions in his head but had no time to doubt anything he'd said. They had to get to the girl before. . . . Then the image made sense.

The bit of thatch at the bottom of the image wasn't a roof. The texture was too smooth and orderly. It was hair.

Someone had attacked the princess.

Jacaré kicked his horse's flanks. He'd ride the animal to its death if that meant saving the heir and Santarem.

Chapter 73

Rafi

Rafi had no problem following the trail Johanna and her brothers had laid. Broken sticks, trampled grass, toe digs in the soft dirt were all there for those who looked, but in the end he didn't even need them. Michael's voice blasted from over a rise and Rafi sprinted to the sound.

"I'll kick him in the shins! I'll bite off his nose!" the boy yelled, his face red in his frenzy. "No one knocks my sister down!" He demonstrated exactly what he wanted to do, spinning and thrashing, little fists swinging in anger.

Joshua stood nearby, snapping the heads off wild wheat and crumbling them as he walked.

Rafi jogged past both of them and straight to Johanna. "What happened? Who knocked you down? Are you hurt?" He grabbed her elbows to study her face. Her hair was a bit askew and the back of her dress had picked up some dirt, but otherwise she looked uninjured.

"It was Duke Belem," she said, and Rafi could feel a slight tremble run through her. "He didn't hurt me, not really. At first it seemed as if he had . . . intentions." She tilted her head toward her brothers, and

Rafi knew that he'd have to wait for a full explanation. "He knocked me down and stole my necklace."

"Your necklace?" A thin line of blood, fine and bright, showed against her pale skin. "Why would he want your necklace?"

"I have no idea. It was just a flawed crystal on a chain." She pressed her hand to her throat. "It was sentimental in value because it belonged to my father."

Michael jumped between them. "Whatcha' going to do, Lord Rafi? Are you going to punch him in the face? Throw him in jail?"

Flog, beat, castrate him. The law in Santiago required no less, and Rafi wanted to hand out the Punishment personally.

"Nothing," Johanna said.

"What?" Rafi asked.

"I'm unharmed. Lord Belem was confused, and likely drunk. He made a mistake."

"Johanna, that's ridiculous. There has to be some recourse—"

She squeezed his arm hard. "We'll discuss it later. Let's get back to the group, and have a nice afternoon."

"You don't intend to perform now. Not after this."

"I *intend* to act like nothing happened, draw no further attention to myself, and then go home." To end the conversation, she turned and followed Joshua up the hill, draping an arm around the little boy's hunched shoulders.

There wasn't much of a party to return to. Dom and Snout rode back from the estate announcing that Duke Belem had fled with only three of his retainers in tow.

"Did you see him? Did he say anything?" Rafi asked.

"I did, my lord," offered Snout. "He didn't even stop to pack. Simply grabbed the first few men he saw and headed due north like he had a hurricane on his heels."

The two underlords who'd accompanied Belem to Santiago didn't know what to make of their liege lord's strange actions.

Lady DeSilva took control. "Duke Belem must have had a reason to return to his estate. Perhaps he received a missive we are unaware of or had an ominous feeling that he should go home." She patted arms and offered smiles as she moved through the crowd. "Given the strange circumstances, I suggest we retire to the manor for the rest of the evening and I'll have my staff provide you each with private meals. You can send birds to the towns he may pass through or pack for your own return journeys if you choose to leave."

This appeased most of the guests, though it didn't stifle the murmuring. Heads were bent together, nervous questions filled the air. Why had Duke Belem left? Was he offended? Was there an emergency? Was war on the horizon? Eyes darted between the DeSilvas and Inimigo, judging and deciding based on the lords' actions what their next steps should be.

Rafi was happy to let his mother handle it all, to whisper in ears and calm nerves. His mind festered with a question he couldn't answer: What happened between Belem and Johanna that sent the duke running?

Chapter 74

Rafi

Rafi's hands gripped his reins too tightly, causing Breaker to toss his head irritably. The horse recognized his master's feelings and pranced a bit in response. Rafi wanted to relax, but he couldn't forget what had nearly happened to Johanna that afternoon. He patted the horse's neck in apology.

"We're ready to ride, my lord." Captain Alouette already had Michael mounted on his horse and a bedroll attached to his saddle.

Dom hauled Joshua up behind him. Rafi wasn't going to leave Johanna's care to the two guards who drew the short straws for the duty, who could so easily be distracted by a cherry tart or a tart in a dress. Captain Alouette was the best soldier on the estate and someone he trusted implicitly. He and Dom had agreed to stand guard at the Van Arlos' camp—though Alouette had raised questioning eyebrows at the order. With these men, Johanna would be safe until different arrangements could be made.

Arrangements Rafi was certain she wouldn't like.

"Here she is," Dom said as Johanna walked out of the estate dressed in her hunting leathers.

They fit better than Rafi remembered, hugging her like an

acrobat's costume. She'd been eating well since she'd started working for his family, and it showed.

She held up a hand and Rafi tugged her into the saddle without a word.

Rafi let Dom and Captain Alouette lead the way to the forest trail. Breaker wanted to stay close to the other horses, but Rafi held him back, trying to maintain enough space to keep their conversation private.

"How are you?" he asked quietly.

She sighed, her breath warm on his neck. "I'm fine. Grateful. Confused." She snorted. "My mother said that necklace never brought my father good luck, but I can't help but think it saved me today. Though I have no idea why."

Rafi had explained the situation to his mother, who was equally dumbfounded by Belem's strange actions. Rafi wanted to send a group of men to ride after the duke and drag him back to face justice. As usual Lady DeSilva cautioned him to do the opposite. "Any action you take will have political repercussions. Right now, with things so unstable and so much in question, I suggest you send a letter to his estate expressing your displeasure—"

"I'm not displeased, Mother. I'm livid." Rafi had stomped around the lady's sitting room, wanting to drive his boots into Belem's face.

Lady DeSilva considered him for a time before asking, "At Belem or at yourself?"

The answer, of course, had been both.

The rest of their conversation—discussing his feelings toward

Johanna—wasn't something Rafi wanted to revisit, especially with her sitting so close to him now.

"I have a proposition for you," he said, tracing the horn of his saddle idly.

"I've already been propositioned once today, thank you."

Rafi smiled. If Johanna was in full command of her wit, then she was probably fine.

"It's not that sort of proposition." He paused, knowing that if he didn't phrase his request just so, Johanna would balk and he'd have a fight on his hands. "I'd like to extend the terms of your contract, to make you my estate's official court performer. The title would offer your family a sense of stability, a constant income, and room and board.

"There's a small cottage that generally belongs to the Captain of the Guard and his family, but Alouette is not married, so it's currently vacant." He pressed on through her silence. "It has two bedrooms on the main floor and a loft above. It's not large, but it's comfortable."

"I can't," she said simply, her fingers tightening in the sides of his vest and pulling it taut across his chest.

"Yes, you can." Rafi tried to peer at her over his shoulder. "You don't have to stay with us forever. When you turn eighteen you can return to Performers' Camp, and they won't hold any of your actions against you."

"I just . . . can't."

Rafi bit down hard enough to make his teeth hurt. Couldn't she see that he was trying to protect her? Couldn't she see that he cared?

He turned halfway in the saddle and grabbed the poorly tied strap of Johanna's satchel.

"What are you doing?" She shied back a little, her eyes wide and frightened.

He yanked the bag off her shoulder and threw it into the bushes.

"Are you cra—"

"Oh blast!" Rafi yelled loud enough to catch both Dom's and Captain Alouette's attention. "Johanna's lost her bag somewhere along the trail. You ride on ahead and we'll be right behind you."

Dom grinned and wagged his eyebrows. "Sure thing, brother. Catch up to us when you can."

If only.

Chapter 75

Johanna

Rafi had lost his Keeper-cursed mind. She dismounted by herself, shaking off his help, and headed toward the bushes where she *thought* he'd tossed her bag.

"Do you have any idea what that cape cost? It's not like I have an eternal stock of powders and props, unless I go to Performers' Camp and purchase more." She swatted away a thistle bush. "And not only that, but my cape was specially made by mother as a wedding gift for my father. I can't believe you just—"

She turned from her search to find Rafi standing right behind her, the satchel hanging from his outstretched fingers.

"I threw it next to that walnut tree, and I'm sure you'll find it still serviceable." There was no levity in his words, no smile on his face, as if he hadn't played some mindless joke. "I have several similar satchels and you can pick a new one tomorrow, or I'll buy you one if none of mine are satisfactory."

Johanna had the oddest sensation that her skin had shrunk, compressing her breath, her movement, even her thoughts. "Rafi, what's wrong?"

He stepped closer, close enough that she had to tilt her head to look up at him. The evening stars crowned his dark head with pinpoints of light, casting a shadow over his eyes. The effect was stunning, highlighting his straight nose and full mouth. The memory of his hands at her waist, of the way her arms fell naturally at his biceps, made her stomach quiver.

"What happened with Belem today . . ." He hesitated and pushed the satchel into her arms. "I think—and my mother does too—that it was just the beginning of the danger you're in."

She gave a humorless laugh. "That's ridiculous. I'm certain no other lord will corner me in the forest, except perhaps you, and be . . . and try . . ." She waved her hand, hoping he'd finish the sentence. "I seem to have a knack for being in the wrong place at the wrong time. Perhaps I should take Thomas's advice and stay out of the woods."

"Probably, but it's more than that." He ran a hand through his hair, tugging at the curls. "Johanna, has anyone ever told you that you look like Wilhelm's queen?"

"No." She shook her head, hoping the movement would loosen all the parts of her that had grown uncomfortably tight. "Why would they? My mother says I look exactly like *her* mother. My hair, my eyes, my build, everything."

"Did you ever meet your grandmother?"

"She died years before I was born."

He nodded, as if this was confirmation of something she didn't understand. "Give me a moment to explain before you interrupt." He placed his hands on her shoulders. "Someone has been hunting girls who match your description: dark haired, pale eyed, beautiful.

Fernando told me that two girls have been murdered in Impreza this year, and we've heard rumors of other similar murders. All the girls bore a resemblance to the dead queen.

"The issue is that my mother—who was a close friend to Queen Christiana—sees the resemblance in you. There's something about your eyes and the way you talk that my mother can't ignore. You're exactly the age of Wilhelm's daughter. Your father had a very close relationship with the king, perhaps even as his spy. 'The Survivor of Roraima' was a story that came from Performers' Camp. It may have originated with your father, and could have been based on his escape—"

"Stop!" She shoved his hands off her shoulders, and then followed with a push to his chest. "My father was not a spy. He was an acrobat and a storyteller. He traveled *everywhere*. Not just to Roraima. I was born at Performers' Camp. I. Am. A. Performer."

"I'm not disagreeing with you." He reached for her hands, trying to soothe her. "There are others, dukes like Belem and Inimigo, and Mother Lua only knows how many others, who will look at you and see a threat—as someone who could make a bid for the throne of Santarem and shatter their plans to take it for themselves."

"But it's not true!"

"They don't care. Inimigo fought a war for ten years, and only quit when his army was depleted. Do you think that after all of that, one more life would make a difference to him?"

Johanna backed away from him, backed away from his words, backed away from the doubts that surged into her mind.

Why don't I look like my brothers? Why can't I sing like my mother? Why do I have to work twice as hard at everything that comes to them so naturally?

She only got a few steps before her hip collided with a tree. She slid down the trunk, tucking her knees to her chest. "I'm not the princess."

Rafi sat on the ground beside her, his shoulder against her knee. "That may be true, but until the threat has passed, I'll keep you safe. If you move closer to my estate, we'll be able to keep guards around you and your family."

"For how long? For a year? For ten years?" She took a breath, but her lungs wouldn't expand. "Till Inimigo gives up? Till Belem dies?"

He cupped one of her knees and gave it a gentle shake. "I'll talk to him. I'll tell him you're not who he thinks you are."

"Because I'm not. I'm just a Performer girl, who wants to live a Performer life."

"I'm not sure I believe that either."

Her forehead crumpled. "Why not?"

"When people talk about you, they do it with a sense of awe." Rafi's hand moved from her knee to her arm. "You are so much more than *just* a Performer."

No obligation, no lingering debt of honor, made him say those words. His tone was warm, not forced or faked.

Johanna leaned into his touch, wanting more contact, to feel his mouth over hers. She took a deep breath, expecting the scent of wood and leather that lingered on his skin, but all she smelled was smoke.

She turned toward her family's camp. "Rafi . . ." She bolted to her feet. "Look!"

Above the trees, licking the night sky with tongues of yellow and orange, were flames. They shot and twisted in the breeze, sending sparks into the orchard.

"The wagons!" she shouted, sprinting down the forest road.

Chapter 76

Rafi

She stuck to his back like a tick, holding tight to his body, her breath rasping in his ear. They rode Breaker faster than any sane person would have.

The horse pulled up short when they neared the smoke-filled orchard. Breaker whinnied and pranced, but Johanna leaped off his back and ran ahead.

Then she tripped and tumbled, disappearing out of sight.

Her name burst from Rafi's lips as he followed at a dead run, nearly falling over the same obstacle.

Captain Alouette.

Four arrows protruded from his chest, one more from his neck. His eyes were open, but their glazed surface didn't see anything around him. His sword still hung at his hip.

Ambush. Rafi crouched, keeping his head low, and drew the dead man's sword.

He heard Johanna's voice, keening for her mother and brothers. She ran toward the wagons, both of which were burning.

As Rafi passed Alouette's body, the roof of the farthest wagon collapsed inward, tearing at the air with the screams of wood.

Johanna threw her arms over her head, protecting it from the bits of flaming lumber that fell like rain around them.

"Mama!" She spun in a circle, searching for any sign of her family. "Joshua! Michael! Thomas!"

"There!" A dark mound blocked the trail leaving the clearing. Rafi ran past her, ducking under the low branches of a massive mango tree.

He dropped to his knees, skidding across the dirt, and stopped next to the body. *Bodies,* he realized, as he rolled Dom onto his side. Joshua lay underneath the younger lord, and even in the half light, Rafi could make out their blood-blackened clothes.

"Dom," Rafi whispered, sliding his fingers up his brother's torso. They came away warm and sticky. He reached for his brother's neck and found the flutter of a pulse. Rafi ripped his vest over his head and pressed it against his brother's chest, trying to stem the blood flow from a wound he couldn't see.

Chapter 77

Johanna

This isn't real. This is a nightmare. Joshua's hands were cold, his face a white smear in the smoke-filled darkness. She felt his ribs rise and fall, his body shuddering against her legs.

"Josh," she whispered. She turned him over, and he cried out against the pain. "Where does it hurt?"

She wished she hadn't spoken when she saw the sword wound that crossed him from shoulder to hip. *Oh Keepers, save him. Mother Lua, make this bleeding stop.*

"Jo?" His voice was soft; blood bubbled across his lips.

"Shh, Josh. Don't talk. Everything's going to be fine." She pulled her Storyspinner's cloak from her satchel and covered his abdomen.

"I wanted to be brave," he mumbled.

She leaned against the worst part of the wound, but his blood soaked through the layers of the cloak instantly.

"I saw what happened today in the woods. I saw him knock you down."

"Hush, Joshua. Don't try to speak." She folded the cloak again, pressing her body weight against the gash, but it didn't make a difference. Her hands were wet; his face was gray.

He covered her hand on his stomach. "Michael."

Johanna's eyes searched the darkness, praying all the while that she wouldn't see another body lying somewhere in the distance.

Joshua's lips moved, but he didn't make any sound. She leaned close, putting her ear against his mouth.

"Mmmm . . . safe." He gasped once, then all the air wheezed out of his lungs.

"Joshua?" She knew, but didn't want to believe. She touched his mouth, feeling for breath. Touched his chest, but felt no heartbeat. "Josh. No, no, no, no."

A hand closed on her arm; she shook it away. She knelt over her brother, pressing her forehead to his. Her tears pooled in the hollows below Joshua's eyes and dripped off the sides of his face.

"Wake up, Josh," she whispered to his still form. "Wake up."

"Johanna." The grip returned, fingers digging into both of her arms. "We have to go. Whoever did this could still be out there."

"Let me go. I can't leave him like this!" She tried to shake free. "He's my little brother. I've always, always protected him. I have to stay with him."

Rafi pulled harder, dragging her backward. "You can't do anything for him now—"

She turned quickly, slashing her fingernails down Rafi's cheek. He let go for a second, enough time for her to crawl back to her brother's side.

Then Rafi was on her again, grabbing her forcefully, restraining her arms, hauling her backward against his chest.

Chapter 78

Rafi

Rafi hated to manhandle her. Hated the way she kicked and flailed, hated the way she used her nails against him like talons, tearing at his throat, making his face bleed. He had sworn he'd never do anything to hurt her again, but he had no choice. Tossing her over his shoulder, he pinned one of her arms awkwardly around his neck and tried to stop her from kicking him in the chest and thighs.

They had to find Breaker and ride back to the estate. He didn't believe Dom would still be alive when he returned, but he had to give it his best shot and he couldn't leave Johanna behind if murderers were still in the woods.

Rafi ran as fast as he could under her weight, calling and whistling for Breaker.

A horse whinnied and another answered. Dom's and Alouette's mounts had taken off through the woods toward home. Perhaps when someone saw the riderless horses, they would send soldiers out to investigate. He prayed someone was already on their way.

Johanna finally stopped fighting, but he could feel her sobbing, head down against his back.

He shifted positions so he could cradle her in his arms. She tucked her face into the curve of his shoulder and locked her arms around his neck.

I failed her again.

In that moment of inattention four shadows detached themselves from the side of the trail. They were tall, taller even than Rafi. The planes of their faces were painted golden by the flickering firelight of the still-burning wagon.

Rafi had never seen them before and knew they weren't there to help.

"Put the girl down," the man in the lead commanded. He held a sword pointed at Rafi. Two people behind him held bows at ready.

"You can't have her." Rafi clutched her tighter, his heart hammering against his ribs. Could he take on four? They all wore boiled-leather armor and handled their weapons like soldiers. There was no way. No way he could defend her and survive, but maybe he could give her time to run.

"Johanna," he said, his lips against her brow. "Run. Run to the Milners' house. Run for help."

She stiffened in his arms. Her gray eyes searched his as he set her on her feet.

"I don't think so." She whirled in his arms, a dagger flying free of her sleeve and out of her hands instantly. It caught the closest soldier in the shoulder, and he grunted in surprise.

She flipped another dagger into the air, catching it lightly in her palm.

"This is for my brothers." She sprinted toward the surprised group, holding the dagger like a sword.

Rafi drew his own weapon and waded into the fray. He'd barely raised it to block the first blow when something hit him in the head.

The trail rushed toward him. He saw dirt. Then he saw nothing.

CHAPTER 79

LEÃO

"What happened here?" Leão asked as he surveyed the scene. The fire from the Performer's wagon was spreading to the trees. He raised a hand and sent a burst of wind to blow it out. It didn't stop the wagon from smoldering, but at least the entire forest wouldn't go up in flames.

He'd used the same power, a thick rope of air, to knock out both the boy and the girl. They'd fallen almost on top of each other. Her head rested against his back as if she'd been using it as a pillow.

"Ambush, obviously," Tex said, as he held a swath of linen against Jacaré's shoulder. "At least six mounted men, and there's something about the way that fire is burning. Doesn't feel natural."

"Six mounted men who may be on their way back when they realize they didn't get the girl." Jacaré's tone was harsh. "Pira, get the horses. See if you can find an extra to carry the princess. We'll travel faster if we don't have to ride double."

Leão started forward, his hand held toward Jacaré's wounded shoulder. "Do you want me to heal that?"

"No. Check the camp for survivors, not that I expect there will be any. Then see if you can determine which way the attackers fled or who sent them." He let Tex wrap a strip of cloth around the wound. "Leave things as they lie. The boy won't remember much of this in the morning, and we don't want to give anyone a reason to come after us."

"You don't think they'll chase us when they realize she's missing?" Leão asked as he hurried toward the camp.

"We'll cover our tracks and make sure the attackers' are clear. They'll have no reason to follow us."

Leão jogged into the smoke-filled camp, avoiding the body of a man pincushioned with arrows, assessing the scene as he went. The windows on the still-standing wagon had shattered, and the door had been barricaded shut before the fire had been lit. Someone had died in that blaze.

If only they'd arrived a half hour sooner.

They'd pushed the horses to lameness and to foaming, and even with healing they'd ridden four mounts to death. It had been an awful thing, to feel the animals give up their will to live. Without the horse's own energy to assist in recovery, Leão could do nothing for them.

The replacements they stole—there hadn't even been enough time to pay for them—wouldn't last much longer if they kept up the pace.

And neither will I.

The weariness had sunk into Leão's bones, making every part of him ache like he'd been trampled in a stampede. The constant riding, the lack of sleep, the drain on his *essência* wasn't at all what he'd expected when he'd agreed to follow Jacaré over the wall. None of his training had prepared him for what he'd seen and done.

He followed the footprints, past the second wagon and into the trees beyond. He heard a whimper. It was a quiet sound, easy for him to have ignored if the tracks hadn't led directly to it.

Two bodies lay side by side beneath a mango tree, and stationed between them was a crying child. His face smeared with ash and dirt, his eyes swollen from the smoke. He sat with arms locked around his knees, rocking back and forth.

"Boy," Leão said, holding out his hands, showing that he was unharmed. "I'm here to help."

The child didn't listen, bolting to his feet and climbing the tree as fast as a monkey with a panther on its tail. Even Leão, with all his speed, wasn't quick enough to catch the boy before he disappeared into the branches.

"Come down. I can help you."

There was no response beyond panicked breathing and the rustle of the wind through the trees.

What horrors the child must have seen. It was no wonder he was frightened.

Stooping, Leão checked the pulse of the two bodies on the ground. The smaller was already cold; the blood pooled around it was too much for anyone to have survived. The second body was still warm and . . .

Leão pressed his hand against the chest, feeling a faint heartbeat. It was weak, fading under his touch. It was an impulsive decision, more instinct than thought. He'd been trained to take life, but also to save it whenever possible. And with this boy, it was still possible.

His *essência* sought out the wounds, binding the horrible injuries, knitting flesh and organ and tendon back to its original form. His arms started to vibrate, the muscles shaking beneath his skin; his back spasmed violently with the effort to stay upright.

Completely drained, on the verge of blackout, Leão felt the chest rise and fall.

Thank the Light.

As he staggered to his feet, leaving the child in the tree and the bodies on the ground, Leão knew that despite his personal weakness he'd done the right thing.

"Anything?" Jacaré asked, already mounted. A lead rope had been tied between his horse and a large stallion. The girl lay limply over the animal's neck, her wrists tied together to keep her mounted.

"They went north," Leão managed to say without panting.

"Then we'll head west for a while before breaking north on the main road," Tex said, turning his horse onto a narrow trail that led into the brush.

"Can we overtake them?" Pira asked as she tossed Leão his reins. "We may be able to learn who they are and why they've been—"

"We don't need to know anything else." Jacaré followed the path Tex was taking. "Our only duty now is getting her to the wall."

Leão missed the stirrup the first time he lifted his leg. Had it always been so far from the ground? He managed to pull himself up on the second attempt.

If Pira noticed, she didn't say anything, sticking close behind the girl they'd searched for for so long.

With one last look, Leão peered into the darkness, wondering about the boys and hoping they would make it through the night.

CHAPTER 80

RAFI

A hard slap brought Rafi back to consciousness. He blinked, trying to clear the haze from his vision, and pushed his palms to his ringing ears. An image appeared—a face streaked black like a demon from the lowest hell, its eyes swollen to narrow slits.

Rafi took a deep breath in surprise and choked on the smoke in the air.

Smoke.

He stood up too quickly and the world spun. Rafi staggered a few steps before regaining his balance and felt a small hand press against his side, as if to steady him.

"Michael."

The memory rushed back. Joshua dead, Dom close to it. The sword in his hand. Johanna with her dagger. He searched the ground frantically, expecting her to be nearby.

"Where is she?" Rafi dropped to his knees in front of the boy, holding his small shoulders tightly. "Where did they take her?"

Michael's mouth opened, but the only sound that came out was a sob.

Rafi's stomach plummeted into his boots. "Is she hurt?" He was terrified to ask any other question.

"Don't know," the boy whispered, his voice rasping. His lips trembled, his body shook. "They took her away."

Oh Mother Lua. Rafi's mind worked in reverse; soldiers appearing on the trail, Joshua and Dom under the tree, Alouette dead outside the camp. He'd been hurrying, praying that Dom would live long enough for help to arrive.

The sky was still dark, but dawn brightened the horizon with shades of purple and magenta. Too much time had passed, but maybe by some miracle his brother lived.

Rafi swung Michael into his arms, feeling the boy's salty tears sting the gashes Johanna had inflicted on his neck.

The fires in the wagons had burned out. The first had collapsed completely, its axle resting on the ground. The second's roof had fallen in, and smoke still poured around the cracked and splintered door. The bright paint had melted, leaving streaks of red and blue that dripped down the wagon's walls like tears.

"Lord Rafi," Michael whispered. "I think someone's coming."

Sure enough hoofbeats pounded up the trail. Rafi set Michael down. "Where did you hide?"

"Over there." He pointed toward the tree that stood guard over the place where Joshua and Dom had fallen.

"Go. Climb it and be silent."

The boy ran, his breath wheezing through burned lungs.

Rafi darted into the underbrush on the side of the trail and found a fallen tree. It afforded him a clear view of the road and of the mounted specter that rode into camp.

"Stop here!" Dom shouted to the stream of men who followed him, some in DeSilva livery and some in Inimigo's. His shirt was filthy and bloodstained, and he held his left arm pressed against his side as he dismounted. "We don't want to ride over any trail they left."

Snout stood next to Dom, offering him a supporting hand, which was ignored. Raul, the weaponsmaster, drew both of his swords as if expecting an attack any moment.

"Search the forest to either side of the trail. There may have been a chance—" Dom stopped and cleared his throat. "They might have been able to make it into the woods."

The soldiers followed his command, but Snout stuck close to Dom's side.

"Can you tell me, my lord, where you were when you heard the first shout?" Snout asked, his voice gentle.

Dom's face blanked; his eyes were haunted. "Alouette was in the lead with Michael behind him."

Rafi stood up, drawing a startled gasp from the nearest soldier.

For a moment the brothers stared at each other, as if expecting the other to dissolve with the smoke.

"I thought you were dead," Rafi said quietly as he stepped onto the trail.

"I'm fairly certain I was." Dom fingered a tear in his shirt, the edges crusted and stiff with blood. "When I didn't see you out here, I could only assume . . ." He couldn't manage another word and the brothers embraced, pounding each other on the backs and swallowing tears.

"Did any of the others go with you? Did you see anyone on the trail?" Rafi hoped that Johanna would appear from among the searchers.

"No one." They followed Snout into the camp, being careful to step where he stepped. "Alouette and Michael entered the clearing and then I heard a scream. Michael tumbled off the back of the horse, and I rode forward, unsure what had happened. Right into a trap." He looked at the wagons and shook his head. "I've never seen something burn so quickly. They went up in flames the instant I crossed into the clearing. Michael ran between the wagons, and I rode after him, hoping I could make it through to the other side. But arrows were flying, and Nudger spooked."

He covered his mouth with a fist and shook his head. "Joshua fell off and darted for the trees, but two men stepped out from behind the wagons. They cut him down. Blessed Keepers, he was just a boy."

Dom filled in the rest of the details, how he tried to protect Joshua, but there were too many men. They pulled him from his saddle and stabbed him through the chest.

He pulled his shirt aside, showing Rafi the raw, puckered scar. "I felt myself dying," he whispered, pressing his hand over the spot. "I felt the world fading away, and then there was so much heat. Like my blood was boiling in my veins. I thought perhaps I was on fire . . . or maybe the fire cauterized the wound."

"That man fixed you," a gruff little voice said from a tree. Michael swung down from the branches. "He made you better, but he didn't save Mama or Thomas or Joshua, and he took Johanna away."

Chapter 81

Johanna

Johanna regained consciousness one sense at a time. She heard the clop of hooves first, then she felt the pain. Her hands tingled from being tied together around a horse's neck, and her back ached like she'd been in that position for a long time. A bruise was forming on her chest from the constant friction of the saddle horn.

She opened her eyes, taking in the forest that pressed close, the sun rising behind her, and the family of *bugios* racing through the treetops. The monkeys swung hand, foot, and tail, keeping pace easily with the trotting horses, howling their displeasure at having humans in their territory.

I'm still in Santiago, she realized. The ground hadn't turned marshy or hilly yet, and the forest was thick. *And I'm riding Breaker.* Tears welled in her eyes, knowing that Rafi wouldn't have let the animal go willingly.

Joshua was certainly dead, and she held little hope for her mother, Thomas, or Michael. Adding Dom, Captain Alouette, and Rafi to the death toll made bile rise to her throat. Choking it down, she forced herself to stay in control, knowing without question someone would come hunting these murderers soon.

Not that Johanna intended to lie around playing the delicate captive. She'd escape, run back to the estate, and help lead the group that would bring her family and friends' killers to justice.

The ropes binding her wrists around Breaker's neck weren't painfully tight, but the only way to get free herself would be to flip them over the horse's head. There wasn't enough length to make that happen.

"She's awake, Jacaré," a female voice said from behind her.

The man guiding her horse looked over his shoulder and met Johanna's gaze. The sun glinted off the planes of his high cheekbones, kissing his face with morning light. "Pardon the accommodations, Princess. We'll untie you in thirty minutes when we rest."

"I'm not a princess," Johanna said through gritted teeth. "You *slaughtered* my family and friends for no reason."

"We had nothing to do with the deaths at your camp. We arrived just in time to rescue you."

"Rescue me?" she shouted loud enough to make Breaker's ears twitch. "What kind of rescuers tie you to a horse and drag you away from your home?"

Johanna jerked on the rope, lashing it back and forth. Breaker shied and she used the movement to slide out of the saddle. She ran alongside the horse, trying to flip the tether over his head, but it was too tight.

The man appeared at Johanna's side, hauling Breaker to a halt. "Calm down. We mean you no harm." He sliced through the rope, grabbing Johanna's elbow as she took one stumbling step forward.

"Then let me go." She failed to yank her arm out of his iron grasp.

"I'm sorry, but I can't do that. I—"

Johanna whipped her elbow toward his jaw. He dodged the blow, but his grip loosened enough for her to break free.

Praying the mass of trees would hide her, she darted for the forest. At the edge of the trail something caught her feet and sent her sprawling into the spiny branches of a *palo barracho* tree. The conical thorns raked her from arm to hip, leaving bloody gashes in her flesh.

Rough hands rolled her away from the trunk. The pain fueled her anger; she kicked and thrashed against her captor.

"Please don't fight me," he said. "I don't want to keep you tied up or chase you down. If you understood how important our mission was, you'd come along without question."

"I'll never stop fighting," Johanna growled, and redoubled her efforts.

"We don't have time for this." He knelt across her thighs and pinched her knees. Her skin burned at his touch, and then went cold like a million frozen pins had punctured her flesh. She couldn't move her legs. They were dead.

"What did you do to me?" she shrieked, trying and failing to wiggle her toes. She'd once misjudged a trapeze release and smashed her thigh into the platform. It hurt and had been hard to move, but after a few moments she'd regained the feeling. This was different—the loss of sensation was complete.

He ignored her question. "Look around, Princess. The forest is unusually dry. Predators sneak into villages and attack people instead of livestock. Something is amiss in this land and the problems will only get worse." He hefted her into his arms, unfazed by her weight. "You are the one person who can save Santarem."

"You're crazy. I'm just a Performer. My family was all Performers."

"You're wrong. Your name is Adriana Veado Von Wilhelm, and you are the heir to a power that will save your people."

Johanna shook her head, denying his claim, but there was something deadly serious in his blue eyes.

"My name is Jacaré, and I am a Keeper."

Chapter 82

Rafi

Servants scurried from the kitchen and barracks to the horses in a controlled panic. Everyone had an assignment they needed to fulfill, a job that needed to be done before the riders could pursue the attackers.

"They have a six-hour head start," Rafi said as he strapped a bedroll behind the saddle of his borrowed horse, fingers fumbling in his rush. "They'll probably stop at sundown to rest, especially if they're unfamiliar with this area, and then we can press on. Our knowledge of the landscape will give us an advantage."

Dom caught the roll before it hit the ground and handed it back to his brother. "She's fine, Rafi. If they wanted her dead, we would have found her body already."

"I know, but . . ." His voice faded as horsemen approached. Snout and a small group of soldiers entered the courtyard. Two packhorses carrying canvas-wrapped bundles trotted at the end of the line.

The tracker's face was grim as he approached. "Lord Rafi, we recovered two bodies from the wagons. Marin and Thomas, sir."

Rafi pressed his forehead against his horse's flank, not caring who witnessed his moment of weakness. *I promised her I'd protect her family. I promised and I failed.* "Thank you," he said, once he pulled himself together. "I know that couldn't have been pleasant."

Snout shifted, looking around the yard. "There's one more thing, sir." He held out a cloth-wrapped package. "I wouldn't open it here. Marin was holding it when she died. I think that makes it something important."

Underneath the canvas Rafi could feel a rectangular box, perhaps ten inches long and two deep. He tucked it into the saddlebag, hoping to give it to Johanna personally. Soon.

"I'll be ready to ride shortly, my lord."

As soon as the tracker walked away, Lord Inimigo approached.

"I'd like to offer you some assistance in your search," he said, dispensing with all courtesy.

Rafi's eyebrows jumped in surprise. "I could use a man with campaign experience to ride with the other group." It was a lie. Rafi didn't want Inimigo anywhere on either trail. If Inimigo was involved—and despite Belem's strange actions Rafi wasn't convinced he'd acted alone—he'd likely hinder the group as much as help.

Inimigo gave a snort. "I have too many ducal duties to ride off after a group of brigands, though I do envy *your* youth and position." He patted Rafi on the shoulder, as he would a small child. "However I'd like to lend you one of my best trackers and bowmen."

Two linesmen, Rafi could accept. If they got in the way or caused problems, he could order them home.

What other choice did he have? Inimigo would likely send someone to trail after them. At least by accepting the soldiers into his group, he'd know where Inimigo's people were.

"I'd appreciate your assistance. See that they're outfitted with everything they need from my stores and are ready to leave in the next ten minutes."

"I knew you'd agree. They're ready." Inimigo raised two fingers in the air and signaled for some people to join them.

Rafi gritted his teeth when he saw who approached. *Father said Inimigo was a master schemer, and I stumbled right into his game.* "I can't possibly accept your steward. I'm sure you can't afford to lose Vibora's assistance."

Rather than a split skirt or breeches, Vibora was dressed head to foot in slim-fitting leathers. They looked accustomed to wear and were tailored like Rafi's own. She approached with a long-legged stride her shorter, collared companion had difficulty keeping up with.

"Before she came to my service, Vibora was a tracker of some renown."

Rafi scrambled for a way to rid himself of Inimigo's aid. "Raul's group could use another experienced—"

"No, no. She'll be traveling with your group." Inimigo leaned close to Rafi and lowered his voice to a whisper. "As will this servant, Lucas. He's an excellent archer and completely obedient to Vibora. Their skills are my *gift* to you."

Damn him. Rafi couldn't refuse a gift without slighting Inimigo.

The young man, perhaps five years older than Rafi, kept his head bowed, eyes focused on the ground. If not for the thick collar around his neck, Lucas's chin would have rested on his chest.

"What was his crime?"

Vibora answered. "He was a pickpocket, Lord Rafael." She put a finger under the servant's chin and raised his face. Dark circles ringed eyes that matched the defeated slump of Lucas's shoulders. "He's completely reformed now. Subservient, quiet, and skilled."

"And you trust him?" Rafi asked.

"Of course, my lord." She released Lucas's face, and it drifted down to his chest.

Excellent. A conspirator and a criminal riding at my back. "If there is anything either of you need, please see to it immediately."

Inimigo waved the two servants away.

"Your affection for the Performer hasn't gone unnoticed, son."

The hair on the back of Rafi's neck stood. Even if some unforeseen disaster occurred, and Rafi was forced to marry Maribelle, this man would never be his father.

"I want you to find her and get her out of your mind." He squeezed Rafi's shoulder. "Marrying Maribelle is the quickest path to secure peace for our states and the rest of Santarem. I know you. I know this honor debt will hang over your head for the rest of your life. It would be a shame for you to spend weeks and weeks looking for this girl, when your estate so desperately needs your presence."

Rafi wasn't surprised that Inimigo knew about the obligation he had to Johanna. He wouldn't be surprised if Inimigo knew all the details of the Punishment and the events that had led up to it.

"Search for these kidnappers. Bring them to justice, if you can, but don't spend more than a month on this chase or Santiago could suffer from neglect," he said, accenting his words with a nod. "Rafi, my son, think on my words. Do the right thing for you and your people."

Four weeks. Search for Johanna, determine if she's truly the heir, prepare for a war or a wedding. Rafi felt it then, the exhaustion, the strain, the responsibility.

"That's reasonable." He stepped away from Inimigo's touch. "If you'll excuse me, I have duties of my own to attend to before I leave."

Rafi walked away, feeling Inimigo's eyes following him, and decided he'd better get used to it.

Chapter 83

Jacaré

Besides finding the heir, nothing had gone according to plan. Yes, they'd managed to save her from meeting her family's fate, but not without earning her distrust.

I handled this all so poorly, Jacaré thought as he drove his horse forward. *If she hadn't run, if there wasn't someone chasing us, if that person wasn't a Keeper . . .*

Tex hadn't said it plainly, but the fire that burned the Von Arlos' wagons had been magically fueled. The support beams should have taken hours to collapse and the windows had melted in their frames. *Nothing burns that fast naturally.*

Johanna leaned over Jacaré's horse's neck, coughing against the dust their travel kicked up, her thin shoulders shaking as she cried. Her shirt was torn, blood soaking through in places along her arms.

With a sense of self-loathing Jacaré tightened his grip around her waist and used the contact to heal a few of her injuries. He didn't dare mend them all or revive her legs, fearing she'd run again.

She shivered as the magic worked its way through her body, closing wounds and easing the worst of the aches.

"I'm sorry I can't do more," he said next to her ear. "I'm sorry we didn't arrive earlier, Princess."

"Don't call me that. My name is Johanna."

"When we stop, I'll explain everything. I promise."

"I don't want your promises," she said, shouting to be heard over the horses. "I want my family back."

Tex had stopped in the middle of the trail and waited for Jacaré to ride up beside him. He looked over the top of Johanna's head like she wasn't there.

"We need to rest. The horses have been running for twenty-four hours straight; Pira and I are exhausted. Leão's about burned out." His white eyebrows danced together, creating harsh lines on his face. "He's not powerful enough to raise animals from the dead, especially when he looks like he's got one foot in the grave himself."

They all turned to look at the two riders behind them. Leão rested his forehead on his horse's neck and ignored Pira's efforts to hand him a drink.

"He shouldn't be so drained. With his level . . ."

"Even when you had—" Tex cut off his words and frowned at Johanna.

She wiped her eyes. "If you don't want me to listen in, just let me off here. I'd be happy to walk back."

Tex ignored her. "Even *before* it would have been hard for you to push on like Leão's doing now. Let's find a safe spot, rest for a few hours, and push through the night."

Jacaré's instinct was to keep moving. Whoever killed the Von Arlos would soon realize—if they hadn't already—that Johanna wasn't with her family when they'd been killed.

He didn't want to slow down for anything, but he accepted Tex's advice.

"Fine. We'll rest for four hours."

Chapter 84

Johanna

By the time Jacaré called for them to make camp, the sun hung low and heavy in the sky. Like an unpicked peach, the deep orange ball blotted out the horizon and threw a fuzzy halo over everything in Johanna's line of sight.

The campsite was tucked away from the road in a stand of young balsa trees. They lacked the height of those at the Santiago picnic grounds. The slightly minty smell of the leaves was the same, but it didn't disguise the stench of smoke in Johanna's hair.

They're all gone. She pinched her eyes shut as memories splashed across the canvas of her mind. *No more bony elbows in my back. No more empty bellies and belly laughs.*

"Aren't you going to tie me to a tree?" she asked as Jacaré helped her off the horse. The feeling had returned to her legs a few hours earlier, but she wished it hadn't. Every muscle, bone, and tendon ached.

She had no doubt her captors were Keepers—there was no way to explain her numbed legs and healed scrapes without magic—but they were so different from what she'd envisioned. The stories Johanna told were full of epic deeds and unerring sacrifice. Of men and women larger than life and unfailingly kind.

She should have known better than to believe in fairy tales. These people were real and scary, and much more human than anything she had ever imagined.

"I don't want to treat you like a captive, Prin—Johanna." He led her to a tree and watched as she slowly lowered herself to the ground. "I'm sorry that we couldn't save your family."

"Sorry," Johanna said with a snort. "Sorry doesn't bring my family back to life. Sorry doesn't save two little boys from being speared on the tip of a sword."

"What if . . ." Leão paused as he dismounted, moving like he was wounded. Pira hovered at his side as if expecting him to tip over at any moment. "What if they aren't all dead? There was a small boy in a tree. Your brother, I think. He was uninjured."

"Michael." She breathed his name, not daring to hope.

"He was blond and he climbed very quickly."

"He's alive?"

Leão nodded, then shot Jacaré a hesitant glance. "There was another boy, older, who was very near death. I wasn't supposed to leave any evidence behind, but I couldn't let him die. I healed him, but it nearly drained me to do it."

"Oh, Leão." Jacaré ran a hand over his tired face.

Johanna's heart pounded against her rib cage, threatening to punch through her chest. "Joshua? He was blond haired and fine boned. You were able to . . ."

She didn't need to continue. The sorrow in Leão's eyes was too plain.

"There was nothing I could do for him, but the one with dark hair, close to my age? He'll survive."

Pressing the heels of her hands to her eyes seemed to dam the tears. *Of course not Joshua, you fool, no one can bring back the dead. At least there's Dom and Michael and . . .*

"The lordling who was with me on the trail, is he all right?"

"I simply knocked him out as I did you." He offered a little lopsided grin. "I'm sorry about that, too."

"It's all right." She looked up and met the eyes of one of her captors. "Thank you."

And thank you for giving me something to go back to.

Chapter 85

Jacaré

Jacaré offered Johanna a bowl of the stew Tex had prepared. She eyed it warily before accepting the dish.

"You know the tale of Donovan's Wall?" Jacaré said as he sat down across the fire from her.

"I don't need a bedtime story. I need to get back to my family—what's left of it."

"But the story, you know it?"

"Of course," Johanna huffed. "It was built thousands of years ago to keep out an untold evil." Jacaré knew he'd offended her storytelling sensibilities. He'd seen enough at Performers' Camp to know the people took pride in their art.

Jacaré nodded. "That was its original purpose. But three hundred years ago the Keepers migrated north of the wall and added a magical barrier to protect those who remained here."

"From what?"

They had found the land beyond the wall inhospitable, rife with predators uncommon to Santarem. It was cold and the soil was poor, but they discovered the remnants of a settlement in a small valley ridden with thermal caverns. The Mages were convinced the people had been wiped out by some sort of plague, and the Keepers built Olinda over the remnants of a long-dead culture.

"We are the danger beyond the wall, Princess. At least some of us."

"You? How is that possible?" She pulled a face like she'd bitten into a sour papaya. "Most people worship them, *you*, and would look forward to a return of the Keepers' magic. Your people could stop marsh fever and bring rain to states in drought. In every story I tell, the Keepers are the heroes."

"We're not infallible or altruistic," he explained carefully. "Our magic makes us treacherous. There are some who use their power for personal gain and to exert control over non-magic-wielders."

"Exert control . . ." Her head tilted to the side, seeming to mull over his words. "Like slaves?"

"In the most extreme cases with the very strongest of our Mages," said Jacaré, looking at one Keeper who had the ability. But Leão was sound asleep. "Yes, they could completely control four or five people, and exert milder control over a larger group."

The girl laughed, but it sounded like more of a groan. "You think I can stop all of this from happening?"

"When we crossed the wall a few weeks ago, I could feel the barrier's weakness. There are places where it's thin, where someone or some*thing* from either side could push through." He touched her arm gently, trying to drive home his point. "Your family has been part of the link to that power for hundreds of years. When we return you to the wall, the power will stabilize and Santarem will be safe."

"I hate to give you the news, Jacaré, but your people are already here." She waved in the general direction of Santiago. "And already controlling mine."

Jacaré heard a quick intake of breath and caught the focused stares of both Tex and Pira.

"What are you talking about?"

"Vibora. She's just like you: tall, thin, *golden*." She talked around a mouthful of food, accenting her words with her spoon. "It wasn't just the way she looked, but her name is from the old language too. Texugo, the badger. Jacaré, the alligator. Leão, the lion."

"Vibora." Jacaré felt a wrenching pain low in his chest, where an old wound sometimes throbbed. It felt freshly torn open, and he pressed a hand across the aching space expecting it to come back bloodied.

"She must be incredibly powerful, by your standards, as she was controlling about *thirty* of Inimigo's servants."

Jacaré was hauled to his feet, and he found himself face-to-face with an angry Tex. "It's not the same Vibora." He gave Jacaré a rough shake. "She didn't have an affinity for fire and she's three-hundred-years dead."

"Of course it's not her," Jacaré heard himself say. "It's a common name."

But it wasn't. And from the glint in Tex's blue eyes, they both knew it.

"Tell us everything you know about this person," Tex prompted. "Explain how you know she's controlling people."

"I don't exactly, but she and Inimigo brought thirty servants with them who were all wearing thick, metal collars." Johanna pulled her bottom lip between her teeth. "It's hard to explain exactly, but they seemed too . . . subdued . . . even for well-trained servants."

"Tell me about the collars," Pira asked, digging around in her satchel. "Did it look like this? Silver, but dull?" She held up the dart, and Jacaré exchanged a confused glance with Tex.

What was Pira suggesting?

"I guess." Johanna shrugged.

"What if . . ." Pira seemed to be speaking to herself, clenching the dart in her fist. "I can touch it, but I can't *sense* it. Almost like it absorbs my *essência*."

Tex shook his head. "I've never heard of such a thing."

Jacaré didn't want to consider the implications. What if the collars were absorbing the wearers' *essência*? Could it be stored for later use? How many people could be controlled? He rubbed the heel of his hand against his forehead.

"Johanna, you love your brother," Jacaré said, feeling as if he'd finally found the thing that would convince her to join them. "Do you want to see him as a slave?"

"What?" she snapped. "Of course not."

"He's a Performer. A descendant of the Keepers. Performers have more *essência* than other people—it's what makes them so agile and quick."

Johanna lay down on her blanket and turned her back to the fire, as if trying to ignore him.

"If the collars absorb *essência*, Michael will be one of the first people the other Keepers will target because he'll feed them more power. And if the wall falls or if this . . . this Vibora gets her hands on other Performers to drain, then my crew doesn't stand a chance to save Santarem." He addressed the back of her head. "*Please* stop trying to escape. You could protect so many people."

She was still for a very long time, long enough that he thought she'd fallen asleep.

Frustrated, angry, he stood to prepare for bed.

"I'll do it," Johanna said, her voice quiet against the blanket. "If it means protecting my brother and the Performers, I'll do what you ask."

Chapter 86

Rafi

Rafi hated to admit it; Vibora was good at finding the trail. She even found the small campsite where the group had stopped for a few hours. Not that it mattered, the fire was long cold.

"How are they making such good time?" He dusted ash off his pants.

"I don't know, my lord," Vibora said as she walked around the campsite, studying the ground for more clues. "They must have very well-conditioned mounts."

"They have my horse. He's a good animal, but there's no way he could keep up this pace."

"There are drugs they could have given their horses. It extends the animals' ability to run without rest, but shortens their lifespans."

"During the Ten Years' War, some soldiers took drugs that inhibited their ability to feel pain and increased their energy." Rafi couldn't imagine doing something like that to his body. He'd been taught that a warrior must be able to feel pain to know his limits. "Is it something similar?"

"Yes." She put her hands on her slim hips. "It's old medicine. Easy enough to find and mix—"

"If you can make it, do." He strode back to his horse without looking to see if she followed. "I sent birds to every major town along the northern and western roads. We can pick new mounts at any stop."

"Yes, my lord. I'll find the ingredients when we rest for the night."

Rafi swung into Nudger's saddle, feeling guilty about potentially poisoning Dom's horse, but knew his brother would understand. He'd seen a different side of Dom the morning they left—a focused, controlled side he never expected from his sibling. Rafi knew it was born out of fear and anxiety, but it was good to know his brother had grit.

No matter what happened now, Santiago would be safer as soon as Inimigo rode home. The duke intended to leave Maribelle behind for an extended visit, so she could "become accustomed to country life."

More likely Inimigo wants a spy in place, searching for our weaknesses, and a reminder of what's waiting for me at home.

Not that Rafi would agree to a betrothal unless some serious changes were made. Like an agreement from Inimigo not to pursue the throne, and that would never happen.

Snout rode beside him but hadn't said much since he'd discovered a scrap of bloody linen stuck to the thorns of a *palo barracho* tree.

Rafi could feel the material rubbing against the skin at his wrist, where he'd tied it around the narrow band of silver he wore there.

"She tried to run, my lord." Snout pointed out crushed weeds and broken twigs from Johanna's attempted escape. "One of them knocked her down, and let her tumble into the tree. She was hurt, so they rode away from here double. Can you see these prints are much darker?"

Rafi couldn't tell the difference, and he didn't care. Someone had hurt Johanna, and they were going to pay for it tenfold.

He rubbed the bit of linen as he rode, a tactile reminder of his mission.

CHAPTER 87

PIRA

The horses drank like they'd been running across a desert. Their sides heaved as they gulped, their coats gleaming with sweat under the evening sunset.

Pira knelt to fill her canteen and took a few long swigs of the clear, cold water before splashing a bit on her face. Her cheeks were flushed, and the tunic she wore over her leather breeches was sweat stained. She looked awful compared to the pampered little princess.

The girl was attractive in an obvious way, petite and fair-skinned, with small hands and delicate features. Pira wanted to hate her, but she had to give Johanna credit for a toughness that belied her size. She didn't complain about the hard ground or rough food, and didn't cry when her attempted escape left her scraped and bleeding.

Leão certainly hadn't missed Johanna's beauty and gumption, consoling her and patting her on the back when she needed comfort.

It was infuriating and charming all at the same time.

Pira picked up a flat rock and skipped it across the stream, trying to distract herself from thoughts of that night, of that kiss, of the way her body fit perfectly next to his.

You're being ridiculous. She grabbed a handful of rocks and threw them all into the stream. *It was nothing. It meant nothing.*

"Hey," a voice called from over her shoulder.

Pira jumped. Leão shouldn't have been able to sneak up on her, but his natural ability to be silent and her loud thoughts had overwhelmed her senses.

"The horses are almost done drinking. I'll be back to camp in a few moments."

"Actually." He took a couple of steps closer to her, but the look on his face was anything but inviting. "There's something I wanted to talk to you about."

She busied herself gathering the nearest horse's reins, so she wouldn't have to look at him. "Sure. What do you need?"

He stopped and took the reins out of her hands. "Johanna could be the leader of Santarem someday. I think it would be good if we made an effort to befriend her."

Pira gave a half laugh and shook her head. "Too bad there isn't a hayloft or a Performer's wagon convenient."

"Wh-what are you talking about?" His green eyes were wide, his mouth open in shock.

"A perfect political match. Give her a few kisses and I'm sure she'll be amenable to whatever *diplomacy* you have planned." The words spilled out of her mouth and she had no way to dam them. "I'm surprised you haven't tried it already." *Oh Light. Stop talking.*

"You can't honestly think . . . Miriam was—"

"You even remember her name!" She forced a cold smile to her lips. "I'm impressed."

"Pira." His voice dropped to a murmur. "The night I kissed you—"

"Was one I'm sure you'd rather forget." She stepped past him, backing toward their camp. "Me too. Go ahead and finish up with the horses. I have other duties to attend to."

Chapter 88

Rafi

They'd gained ground on the kidnappers. Both Snout and Vibora agreed that the tracks were fresher, but they were still more than a day behind.

Rafi called for a short stop where both the men and animals could rest.

He settled by the small cooking fire and pulled his lumpy saddlebag toward him. He'd been too involved with last-minute details to take the case Snout had found in Marin's hands out of the bag, and the metal rectangle brushed against his calf as he rode. It was a constant reminder of why he was on the trail and the person he was looking for—not that Johanna was ever far from his mind—but he felt battered enough without the bruise the box inflicted.

If I wrap it in my cloak, it will dull the edges. When he tugged the box free, the entire lid tore off and a few coins spilled out across Rafi's lap. "Blast it."

He dropped the coins inside, where they disappeared between sheets of paper. He slid them aside, wanting to make sure that all of Johanna's money was accounted for, and saw something that made him freeze.

It couldn't be . . .

Trying not to disorder the papers, he reached for an envelope with a navy-colored blob of wax. He lifted the paper and tilted it toward the light. Sure enough, it was the hawk from his family's seal.

It's probably a request for a performance, he convinced himself, but the wax had never been broken.

There was no name on the outside of the envelope, but it was his father's seal—Rafi's seal now—so the letter had something to do with his dukedom.

With a hint of guilt he opened it. The handwriting was cramped and hurried; blots marred some of the lines, but it was completely recognizable. The message was undoubtedly from his father, but the words it contained were life altering.

> *This letter is to assert that the girl raised by the acrobat Arlo is the child of King Wilhelm and Queen Christiana. On the event of my death, these words are to stand as a testimony of my knowledge and actions concerning the Princess Adriana, who is known to herself and her family as Johanna Von Arlo.*

The letter described how Arlo, under the king's command, had smuggled the child out of the Citadel by means of a rear gate that few besides Wilhelm and his closest confidants knew of.

> *The political environment of Santarem is dangerous, and the princess's enemies are many and widespread. For her*

safety, she's being kept at Performers' Camp and hidden until there is an appropriate time to return her to the throne.

Arlo is the bearer of the king's emerald pendant—a flawed green stone, set with a golden cap. The edges of the cap are scalloped. Wilhelm used this pendant rather than a sigil ring to seal all his correspondence and political documents. Arlo will give the necklace to the princess when she comes of age. Each of the dukes will recognize it as a talisman, and its bearer as their leader.

"You brought your accounting books with you, my lord?" Vibora dropped beside him, stretching her long legs toward the fire with a sigh. "I didn't think you were the type to be so concerned over your daily finances."

"Ah . . ." Rafi slipped the letter into his shirt. "You can never be ignorant when it comes to the care of a ducal estate." He sounded like a fool, but Vibora didn't seem to notice.

"If you can't sleep, you should at least eat and lie down, my lord."

He couldn't sleep now even if someone mixed passionflower in his food.

Johanna *was* the princess. His father had always known . . . had always known his betrothed was alive and could take the throne. Yet the duke had done nothing about it.

Because it could lead to civil war. Inimigo would stop anyone who tried to rule Santarem and this time Belem might fight at his side.

Suddenly the evidence was stacked against the overweight lord. The attack on Johanna in the forest, the theft of her necklace, and the killing of her family—all of it to stop her from claiming the kingdom that was rightfully hers.

"At least your muscles will rest."

Had she said something else? Rafi grunted and rubbed his eyes, feigning exhaustion.

A quick look at the group proved he was the only one having difficulty relaxing. Snout stirred the thin stew in aimless circles. Both Rafi's guardsmen held their heads in their hands, one already dozing off. Lucas, Vibora's collared servant, had collapsed on top of his bed roll without crawling under the blankets.

The horses chomped in their feedbags, seeming more energetic than their human companions. Vibora's medicine—whatever it was—had done its job for the animals.

"You wouldn't by chance have a miraculous energy pill for humans, would you, Vibora?"

"Well . . ." She took a bite of dried fruit and chewed slowly. "There is something I could try that may refresh you, but there's no guarantee it will work."

Snout cleared his throat and tapped his spoon against the side of his bowl. His distrust for Vibora and her skills hadn't faded, no matter the miles they'd traveled together.

"Perhaps in the morning," Rafi said, pulling his blanket around his shoulders. "No need to refresh me till then."

Vibora's smile held, but her eyes seemed to dim a bit. "Yes, my lord. In the morning."

CHAPTER 89

LEÃO

Something is wrong.

Something is wrong.

Something is wrong.

Leão gasped, hauling in lungfuls of air like a swimmer who'd been under too long. The fire had burned down to flickering coals, giving him just enough light to see the two forms on his right. Jacaré and Texugo were still sleeping, both resting peacefully. On his left, the princess was curled up on her side.

He scanned the camp's perimeter, trying to find a familiar shadow.

"Go back to sleep, Leão." Pira's voice came from somewhere above and behind him.

Rolling to his feet, he moved toward the tree she'd perched in. Her legs dangled from a branch even with his head. "Did you hear or see anything? I felt . . ."

"You had a nightmare. The only thing I heard was your thrashing." Her face was turned away from the fire, protecting her ability to see by the moonlight. "Or maybe that was just an excuse to move closer to Johanna."

He wanted to reach out and touch her calf, to stop the one leg that was swinging idly, but kept his hands at his sides. Touching her would only get him into trouble. "I have no interest—"

"There's a herd of marsh deer out there," she continued, ignoring him. "I crossed their tracks when I came back from the stream."

"I could have sworn I felt something with a strong *essência*." He closed his eyes and focused, trying to sense anything besides the three other members of his crew and Johanna.

"I may not have your oh-so-superior *Mage* abilities, but if there was anything out there besides deer and a few titis, I'd know it."

"Pira, I wasn't saying—"

"Go back to sleep, Leão. You've got last watch." She readjusted her position in the tree, drawing her feet up onto the branch and away from him.

Leão returned to his bedroll without another word.

Chapter 90

Rafi

"Don't ever let her touch you."

The words were spoken in a rushed whisper over the top of Rafi's head. He looked up to find Lucas standing beside Nudger, the servant's collar the only bit of brightness in the predawn light.

"What did you say?" Rafi asked as he straightened from tightening his horse's girth.

Lucas toed the saddlebags by Nudger's side. "Would you like me to secure this for you, my lord?"

Vibora's servant never offered to help, not with setting up camp, or cooking meals, or collecting firewood. Lucas kept to himself, barely speaking to the other men and sleeping every moment he wasn't in the saddle.

"No, thank you." Rafi hefted the bag. Even though it was wrapped in his cloak, he could feel the sharp edges of the metal box inside. He wasn't sure what else it had in it, but he had no intention of letting it out of his sight. The letter was too important to put back, so he kept it tucked in his vest's inner pocket. "I can manage on my own."

Lucas stood for a moment more, studying the ground, before Vibora called him to her side.

Something about the way Lucas moved reminded Rafi of a kicked dog, or maybe it was a dog that expected to get kicked. Vibora whispered a few words to her servant, and if it was possible, the man's shoulders seemed to slump farther. She lifted his face with her fingers, forcing Lucas to make eye contact.

It was an odd interaction—actually there were a lot of odd things about Vibora, Rafi realized. Her skills as a tracker, her control over the servants, the respect Inimigo gave her, and of course Maribelle's fear.

Rafi shook his head, recalling Maribelle's words as they picked raspberries. Vibora couldn't possibly command *magic*. That was ridiculous. All the stories said magic had disappeared when the Keepers crossed Donovan's Wall, if it had ever existed in the first place. The perfect weather, abundant crops, and miraculous recoveries had all seemed a bit far-fetched.

Miraculous recoveries.

Was it possible to heal the horses to return their energy? To keep them running all day without tiring?

Vibora leaped into her saddle.

"Are you ready to ride, Lord Rafi?" she asked, eyeing him askance. "Are you feeling all right?" She reached for the pouch at her waist. "I do have some gentle restoratives. They aren't as powerful as what I give the horses—"

"No." His tone was sharp enough to draw her attention. "I'm fine and will be better once we find Johanna."

"Of course, my lord."

Rafi followed Snout out of the clearing, wishing Vibora rode at the front of the group.

Never turn your back to a viper, his father had once cautioned, as he pinned down the head of a black-and-red-banded himeralli. *That's an invitation to strike.*

Rafi would have taken a pit full of the vipers with their bright stripes and flesh-melting bites over one Vibora, whose true danger was unknown.

If she could wield magic, Rafi didn't want to present her with any opportunity to attack.

Chapter 91

Jacaré

With a village ahead and provisions to replenish, the crew had to slow their pace or risk drawing attention from any travelers who might venture down the wooded road.

The delay, and Johanna's constant prodding, irritated Jacaré to no end.

"I need to send a letter. A note. A messenger pigeon. Anything," she said as she rode the big black horse beside him. "They need to know that I'm safe and that I'll be coming back soon."

He shifted in his saddle, but it didn't ease his guilty conscience. He'd promised Johanna that she could return to Santiago as soon as possible. "Possible" was a broad term, and in this case it meant "someday." Maybe.

"My little brother thinks he's alone in the world. Michael needs to know that at least one member of his family survived."

"We *cannot* send a letter," he said, trying to keep his tone level. His eyes searched the roadside, looking through the browning leaves for any hint of danger. "No one can know where you are or where you're going, at least for now. We can't give away our position."

"Please, Jacaré—"

Her words cut off when a dozen deer burst across the road, dodging around the horses, eyes frantic as they darted into the woods.

"What was that?" Johanna asked, her head swiveling as she watched the animals disappear. "What would make an entire herd bolt?"

"A predator." Jacaré whistled, hoping it would carry to Leão, who was scouting the trail ahead. "Johanna, get behind me. Tex take point. Pira—"

The hair along Jacaré's arms stood on end, the sensation reviving long-dead memories. Reacting instinctively he reached for his *essência* an instant before Tex's horse dissolved under him in a column of flame.

"Ambush!" Jacaré created a shield of air that stretched across the trail. It shimmered and almost collapsed under the impact of another fireball. "Pira, take Johanna and ride into . . ."

Arrow points punctured his barrier, seeming to hang in a glistening curtain. *They've divided us from our most powerful crew member,* Jacaré realized as men stepped onto the trail, crossbows cocked. *Leão's either too far away or he's—*

A round of bolts smashed into the shield and the edges faded. He wouldn't be able to hold it for long.

"Ride back to Santiago!"

Johanna put her heels to her horse and wheeled south. Pira hesitated, her mount dancing.

"Go, Pira!" The strain of holding the defense made his voice break. "Protect the princess."

She looked up the trail for one breath, then turned and plunged after Johanna.

Jacaré's shield took one more blast of fire, then evaporated like dew under sunlight. With weak, trembling arms, he freed his sword from its sheath.

Five men. All carrying weapons and all wearing collars. He could ride away and be shot in the back by fire or arrows or . . .

He spurred his horse and the animal reared, its hooves providing a distraction while he slipped from its back. Rolling as he fell, Jacaré stopped on his knees in front of the closest man. One slice and the man dropped to the ground, bleeding from thigh-high wounds.

Four.

The sword's arc continued across Jacaré's body to stop a downward strike. The impact jarred his shoulder but saved his head. It was an awkward position, one he wouldn't be able to maintain for long. Using the last trickle of his *essência*, he sent a focused channel of air into his attacker's throat, crushing the man's windpipe.

Three.

The remaining men eyed each other nervously. "He's like them," one said as he raised a hatchet into a defensive position.

"Like who?" Jacaré used his sword to lever himself to his feet, expecting to be incinerated by a Keeper waiting in the trees. It had been a common tactic during the war, using humans to tire out an opposing Mage, then blasting away their remaining defenses with a magical barrage.

The men lurched into motion, as if their bodies weren't wholly under their own control, and Jacaré raised his shaky blade.

Chapter 92

Leão

Leão doubled back the instant he heard Jacaré's whistle, knowing that something was amiss. He urged his animal to gallop, and it did for ten body lengths before smashing headfirst into an invisible wall.

Its neck broke on impact, twisting far to one side and throwing Leão into the barrier. His right arm bore the brunt of the collision, crumpling under the force.

He felt the bones shatter, he heard the ominous crack, but the pain didn't register. For a moment his mind was perfectly clear; every sensation, every detail slipped into acute sharpness. Pine needles fell from a tree, spinning in the air before coming to rest on his cheek. Their smell sharp and pungent. A few poked through his shirt, jabbing him in the back.

The *essência* of another Mage, powerful and unfamiliar, was impossible to ignore now, as were the fainter sensations of other people nearby.

The deer, he realized. *All the deer around our camp last night were masking the Keeper's presence.*

Then the pain hit.

Leão groaned, keeping his teeth clenched shut to stop himself from screaming. He tried to find his *essência,* but it slipped away.

"Relax," he said aloud. "Ignore the pain."

Something shrieked in the distance. Smoke filled the air. Jacaré's voice filtered through the woods, but Leão couldn't make out the words.

With a deep breath he tried again. The power to mend his arm was there, just out of reach, but pain blocked his access to it.

"Come *on*."

There was a twang of crossbow bolts. The sky south of him flashed orange.

Fireball.

He forced himself to sit up as images of his crew, burned, bloody, and dying, raced across his mind. They'd all try to protect Johanna, with Pira as the last line of defense. Her blue eyes would narrow with concentration. She'd use every skill, all her power, and it wouldn't be enough.

"No." Leão smashed his uninjured fist against the dirt.

She'd disappear in a flash of flame, nothing but blackened bones remaining.

"No." The earth crumpled as he punched it again.

Johanna would be killed, and their mission would fail.

"No!" The next blow exploded before his fist met the ground, shaking the trees around him. The trail buckled, rolling away from the force of his raw, unfiltered *essência*. The energy forced his bones into alignment, replacing one pain with another.

Under his freshly repaired hand, the transparent wall felt as solid as granite. It shattered under Leão's touch.

He rushed past his horse's corpse, toward the screams and smoke.

I'm coming, he thought. *And someone's going to die.*

Chapter 93

Johanna

"How far have we come?" Johanna slid off Breaker's back and knelt next to the stream. The horse drank greedily as she filled her canteen.

"Not far enough." Pira cupped water and poured it over her head, letting it drip down her shirt. "You better hope your friends are actually following us. I can't stand against power like that alone."

Who could?

The stream of fire had been so bright that it marred Johanna's vision for hours. She wasn't certain anyone could survive such intense heat.

And now what?

Johanna was exhausted; the horses were heaving. They'd ridden so far, but their mounts couldn't take any more punishment, and Pira said she wasn't capable of healing more than a few scratches. They couldn't cover any ground until the animals recovered naturally.

Worse, Johanna doubted they'd make it to Santiago without something awful following her into the state.

"We *could* cross the marsh," Pira said, but her eyes were distant, focused inward.

"That will slow the horses down. We'll spend more time hauling them out than moving forward." Johanna had traveled all over Santarem and knew exactly how dangerous the marshes could be. Her troupe once spent an entire day strengthening a bridge so that the wagons could cross without sinking.

"You've never crossed a marsh with a Keeper like me." Pira's face broke into a crazed sort of smile. "With any hope, whoever is following us hasn't either."

The road had been built to circumvent the marsh completely, and Johanna couldn't see any way to cross without sinking into the murky black sludge that hugged the roots of mangrove trees. Patches of grass looked like stable territory, but most wouldn't hold Johanna's weight and would swallow Breaker in a matter of heartbeats.

And if the stagnant water wasn't bad enough, the creatures inhabiting it certainly would be. Black caimans were notoriously hazardous to people who tried to fish the marshes. The giant reptiles would wait for the perfect moment before lunging out of the water and crushing their prey with crocodilian jaws.

Johanna shuddered. "This is a very bad idea. We could be bitten or poisoned or drown in this mess—"

"We die if we get caught." Pira waded into the murk. "We might die this way too, but I'll choose 'might die' over 'will die.'"

Johanna watched as Pira carefully threaded her way through the trees and over a weed-covered landmass. She never sank deeper than her ankles, and despite her horse's rolling eyes, it didn't disappear into a sink hole.

Pira's path wasn't straight, but she moved forward with purpose. "You coming?" she shouted over her shoulder.

"Won't someone just follow our tracks?"

"There are no tracks in this mess." There was a challenge in Pira's tone, and while Johanna hated to admit it, she saw no other option.

For hours they moved forward at a steady pace. "How are you doing this?" Johanna finally asked. "Is this a special Keeper power?"

Pira snorted. "You could say that."

"So what makes this possible?" Johanna couldn't figure out how Pira chose where to put her feet. There didn't seem to be any rhyme or reason to the path she picked.

"I can sense metal, where it is, and how much there might be." Pira moved like she could see a road that was invisible to Johanna. "I only take a step where the concentration is the heaviest, because I know there is something under the water besides more water or weeds or roots."

Twice as they crossed the marsh, Pira couldn't find a spot dense enough to support their weight so they had to back up. The delays made Johanna's teeth chatter with fear, knowing every second brought an unnamed enemy closer. And yet, they eventually emerged from the marsh—filthy, bug bitten, and exhausted—but otherwise unharmed. The animals and snakes kept their distance, sticking to the banks, and absorbing the sunshine. All unfazed by two women moving through their territory.

More importantly, they'd managed to cut a day's ride in half.

"Are we far enough ahead now?" Johanna asked as she cleaned mud out of Breaker's hooves. Even with the lead they'd managed, they couldn't risk a lame horse slowing them down.

Pira grabbed a handful of weeds and did the same thing for her horse. "I doubt it."

Chapter 94

Jacaré

Jacaré knelt among the dead, leaning against his sword to stay upright. He was responsible for four of the bodies. The fifth, lying a little farther from the rest with a loaded crossbow at its side, had been Leão's doing.

The younger Keeper had saved Jacaré's life, slaying the bowman with a bolt of lightning before disappearing into the woods to hunt the Mage.

"Anything?" Jacaré asked as Leão returned to the trail. "Any sign of them?"

"No. After the fire and the wall, he may not have had enough *essência* left. But Jacaré . . ." He paused and ran a thumb over his eyebrow. It left an ash mark on his forehead. "I found Tex."

"Oh."

Dying in one blast from some unknown Mage? Jacaré shook his head, cursing the cruelty of Mother Lua. Tex had lived through so much. *I should have left him in Olinda, given him the chance to die in his bed. Not that Tex would have appreciated that.*

The sudden loss was a knife keenly edged. Tex's death cut deep, tearing a thread from the tapestry of Jacaré's life. He'd been one of the only people alive who understood Jacaré, who remembered what life had been like before.

Unless this enemy is an old one . . .

Using his sword like a crutch, Jacaré pushed himself to standing. "Lead me to Tex," he said, fighting off waves of dizziness and emotion. "We'll take care of his body."

"And then?" Leão asked, his voice soft in the failing light.

"And then we finish this."

Chapter 95
Rafi

Every night Vibora disappeared into the woods to collect the materials she needed for fresh "medicine" for the horses. Her servant, Lucas, stumbled along a few steps behind her.

What a fool I've been, Rafi thought as he listened for her step to fade away. *I didn't even ask what she was giving the horses because I was so grateful that it worked. Why was it so easy to trust her?*

Snout knelt over the fire, boiling water for their evening meal. His two guardsmen gathered wood at the camp's perimeter. Rafi waited till he was sure they were out of earshot to begin.

"Snout, I think Vibora is working some sort of magic." The words sounded insane as soon as they left his mouth. "I don't know how it's possible—"

"I think she's taking energy from Lucas and using it to fuel the horses," Snout said. "Every time she goes off into the woods with him, he comes back looking like he's one step closer to the grave. Minutes later, the horses are stomping and twitching like they've been penned up for days."

"Why didn't you say anything before?"

"I was trying to work out a plan before I mentioned my suspicions."

The tracker shrugged. "I don't know anything about witches, but I know she's not a good person."

"What is she capable of?"

"I don't know that, either, Lord Rafi." Snout scratched the side of his nose and straightened. "If we're going to stop her, it will have to be a surprise. I've been thinking that we might be able to take care of her while she sleeps."

Rafi called the guardsmen over. One stood close enough to hear, but with his back to the fires so he could see when Vibora returned. They worked together to lay out a plan. Snout would incapacitate Lucas, and the other three would knock out Vibora. While she was out, they'd drizzle a sleeping tincture into her mouth. It wasn't brave and it wasn't honorable, but it might work.

As they were finalizing the details, a dark figure stepped out of the woods, and all of Rafi's carefully laid plans evaporated.

Chapter 96

Johanna

Johanna smelled of rotten leaves and marsh sludge. Her hair hadn't been washed in days and stood all over her head at crazy angles.

And she didn't care.

"Rafi." It was said on an inhale and the sound couldn't have carried very far, but somehow he heard her voice across the clearing.

He moved slowly at first, blinking and shaking his head, like he couldn't believe who stood in front of his eyes. Then he was sprinting, hurdling saddles, startling the horses, and crushing her in his arms.

She dropped Breaker's lead rope to return the embrace, pressing him as close as physically possible.

"Johanna, Johanna." He whispered her name like a secret, his lips moving against her hair.

She pressed her cheek against his neck, dark scruff scratching her skin. It felt perfect; it felt safe.

"I should have known that if anyone could, *you* would find a way to escape."

"And I knew you'd be out here looking for me."

Before she could question propriety or decorum, Johanna did

what felt right. Rising up on her toes, she brushed her lips over Rafi's.

It was a simple kiss, the merest contact. She pulled back, face flaming, heart skipping, but Rafi didn't let go. Kissing her once, twice. Nervously, then hungrily.

If the men watching murmured, she didn't notice. If Pira, lurking in the shadows, growled her distaste, Johanna didn't care. His arms were around her waist; her fingers were in his hair.

It didn't last long enough.

Someone cried out; Johanna and Rafi jerked apart, turning as one of the guardsmen stumbled into the fire. Snout grabbed the man's shirt and rolled him to the side. The quick action saved the tracker's life as an arrow whisked over his head. The second guardsman wasn't as lucky. A bolt shot clean through his throat, exploding through the back of his neck.

"Run!" Snout shouted. The arrow that caught him in the back spun him in a tight circle before he dropped to the ground.

Rafi took one faltering step forward and froze. His shirt was pasted against his chest as if he was caught in a stiff breeze, no part of him moved except his wide-open eyes.

Johanna yanked on his arm, trying to force him into action, but even her strongest pull did no good.

"There's no use trying to move him," Vibora said as she strode into the camp. A collared slave with a loaded short bow followed a few steps behind. He aimed the arrow at the center of Rafi's chest. "I've got him wrapped in a pocket of air. It's so tight he's probably having a hard time breathing."

Instinctively Johanna reached for the dagger always in her sleeve.

But her wrist had been bare for days. Pira hadn't returned Johanna's weapons. She had nothing, no way to defend herself except feet and fists, but with any hope she had *someone.*

Pira, please be close enough to hear me. Please know I'm in trouble.

"Let him go!" Johanna shouted, using her stage voice to fill the clearing with sound.

Vibora clicked her tongue. "You are a vehement little thing."

"Please, you don't need him. You've been after me the whole time." Johanna stepped out from behind Rafi, holding her arms out wide. The slave swiveled, training his weapon on Johanna as she moved. "I'm here. Kill me, take me, whatever you want, but let him go."

Vibora stepped over Snout's body, worked her way around the fire, and stooped next to a black saddle. "What in the world do you have to offer me? I hold all the cards." Digging around for a moment, she found a collar just like the one her slave wore.

"Not quite. I have information I know you'll want." If Pira still waited outside the camp—that had been their plan till Johanna could explain why she brought one of her kidnappers with her—she'd have to be close.

"About the Keepers you've been traveling with?" Vibora opened the clasp on the collar with a small key she wore around her neck. "I knew it had to be someone with magic. They couldn't have covered so much distance without it."

"If you let Rafi go, then I'll tell you everything I know about them. Their names, their powers, where they are now." Something smacked into the back of Johanna's hand.

What was that . . .

It fell to the ground with a tiny plink, but in the firelight she saw that the pebble sparkled with metallic speckles.

"As soon as I get this around your neck, you'll tell me anyway."

A second pebble caught Johanna in the cheek, forcing her head to turn to the camp's north side. She couldn't be certain, but something Pira-size moved between the trees.

Keep talking. Keep Vibora distracted till Pira can do whatever she has planned.

"Oh, I think you'll want to know everything about these men before you turn me into a mindless slave." She tried to smile, to keep Vibora guessing. "Especially about the Keeper who has known you since before he crossed the wall."

That did get Vibora's attention. "He must be incredibly old. And probably just a weak soldier. Anyone on assignment from the Mage Council is a Keeper they could afford to lose."

Whatever Vibora had done to the collar was finished, and she straightened from beside the saddlebag. "Now let's just get this on—"

"Even if it's Jacaré?"

The woman's confident smirk melted into a soft O of surprise. She recovered quickly. "I don't know who you're talking about."

Johanna didn't either, but it didn't matter, because at that moment Pira let loose a storm of rocks that pelted Vibora. The woman took one shot to the head and fell to her knees. The bowman immediately followed, his weapon clattering to the ground beside him.

Rafi gasped; his lungs filled with air as Vibora's hold on him disappeared.

Pira materialized from between the trees, a short sword in one hand and a dagger in the other. "Get on that horse and ride," she commanded. "You know where I'll meet you."

"But—"

"If I'm not there by dawn, tell Jacaré I'm sorry and Leão—"

The rest of her words were cut off by an angry growl. A dizzy Vibora struggled to her feet, one hand pressed to the back of her head, blood streaming from every place her skin was bare.

"Go!" Pira shouted, dropping into a defensive crouch.

Rafi didn't let Johanna stay to watch. He grabbed her arm and yanked her toward Breaker.

The startled horse rushed out of the camp with the sound of a tornado on his tail.

Chapter 97

Rafi

Rafi could smell the marsh before he could see it. The stench of plants submerged too long in water tickled his nose with memories of pond scum and black mold. Still, Johanna urged him toward the swampy banks rather than to the bend in the trail.

"You're sure this is where she wanted to meet you?" he asked Johanna as he slid out of the saddle.

"I'm positive." Johanna followed him to the ground. "Pira and I walked through the entire thing. She could find her way like the trail was a paved road."

Something splashed into the water. The marsh was dangerous enough during the day, but to venture into it at night when all the predators were awake? Suicide.

"You think this is safe?"

"I think we don't have a better option."

Rafi didn't disagree. How could he? He saw a woman create a hailstorm of pebbles after another had frozen him with air.

"I don't have Pira's skills, but I have an idea." Johanna worried her bottom lip between her teeth. "We'll have to let Breaker go. He can follow the trail, and will undoubtedly run to safety. Vibora will be more likely to follow his tracks than believe we'd try to cross the swamp."

"That's because it's crazy."

Johanna shrugged. "What isn't?"

She was right. They'd become part of a Storyspinner's tale—complete with magical barriers and mind control—and Johanna was at the heart of it. The heir to Santarem's throne was alive, was his betrothed, and he'd kissed her. All subjects he meant to talk to her about when they weren't running for their lives.

"All right. Let's go."

Rafi slung one saddlebag over his shoulder, knowing he wouldn't be able to carry more than that if they were slogging through mud.

Pressing his forehead against the white star on Breaker's nose, he whispered a soft good-bye. He hated to send the horse away, especially when there was a good chance he'd never see the animal again.

Johanna found a branch, taller than she was, and waited at the edge of the swamp. "I'll lead. You keep a lookout for *things*."

Rafi didn't need a clarification.

Chapter 98

Johanna

Johanna wanted to move faster, but her process was slow. She prodded the ground with her stick before taking a step in any direction. Rafi kept his sword in his right hand and his left balled into the hem of her shirt.

The weight was comfortable and reassuring. It was nice to know that someone was at her back.

They didn't talk very much, afraid to attract predators, afraid to be distracted. Occasionally a splash sounded, and something big brushed past Johanna's boot when she led them into a knee-deep hole, but otherwise the call of the potoo was the only night sound.

She focused on the black water directly ahead of her, made blacker under the half-light of Mother Lua. It was her single-minded focus that almost killed them.

Rafi's hand tightened in her shirt, pulling her back hard enough that she smashed into his chest.

"Stop," he whispered. "There's something ahead."

She felt his heart racing against her shoulder blade and knew whatever he'd seen was deadly.

"We've got to go backward," Rafi continued. "Slowly. Make as little noise as possible."

Backing up scared her just as much as going forward. There was no guarantee that the step Rafi took wouldn't land them in a pool of mud that would instantly close over their heads.

"There's a tree ten feet behind us. We're going to climb it and . . ." He hesitated, and Johanna knew he was deciding the plan as he made it. "And stay there till it's light."

The water around her calves rippled. Something big swam toward them. She couldn't make out the animal's shape, but as it turned its head, a bit of moonlight reflected on a pair of eyes just above the water level.

Caiman, she thought. *And if there's one, there are probably many.*

She followed Rafi, step for step. His arm stayed tight around her waist, his head swiveling as they backed away from the creature.

Off to their left they heard a near-silent splash, followed by another.

"We're almost there." But almost wasn't close enough.

The first attack came as a hard bump against Johanna's shin. She stumbled, and Rafi threw her toward the tree's roots. Brackish water closed over her head and she thrashed, feeling something cold and solid against her palm.

Oh Mother Lua, help. The water filled her mouth and she surged upward. Her head broke the surface, and her flailing arm slammed against tree roots.

"Climb, Johanna!"

She couldn't see Rafi, but she hauled herself out of the water and onto the arching roots.

"Rafi!" Blindly she gripped the bark, searching for a fingerhold, a knot, anything to pull her body away from the creatures Rafi fended off with his sword.

She didn't need it. A strong arm gripped her around the waist and boosted her to the lowest branch. Johanna caught it and swung her hips over like it was a trapeze. Dangling, she reached for Rafi.

"Come on!"

He took a few more swipes at the animals crowding around the tree's roots, knocking one caiman back into the water when it tried to use the roots to propel itself toward him.

Grabbing her outstretched hands, he braced his foot against the trunk. Johanna used all of her strength, all of her body weight, to pull him into the tree.

She heard him gasp and felt something tug him back, yanking on her arms till she was certain they were going to pop out of their sockets.

Then he was free, scrabbling onto the branch beside her.

From their vantage they could see at least five caimans waiting below, snapping their empty jaws and growling at the humans invading their territory.

"Are you hurt? Did one of them bite you?" She traced his arms with frantic fingers searching for an injury. Her mind raced with the possibility of infections and of a dripping wound attracting predators of a different variety.

He surprised her by laughing. "I'm fine." He covered her hands with his own, squeezing tightly. "It got my boot heel and yanked it clean off my foot."

He held up a perfectly intact foot and wiggled his stockinged toes.

Johanna wanted to laugh, but the noise that bubbled over her lips sounded more like a sob. Tears immediately followed.

"Light, Johanna, I'm sorry." Rafi pulled her tight against his chest, which was incredibly awkward as they straddled a tree limb.

"No, I'm sorry," she cried into the middle of his chest. "I dragged you into a swamp in the middle of the night and almost fed you to giant reptiles."

"Just think. It will be an incredible story to tell our grandchildren."

Johanna raised her head slowly. "*Our* grandchildren?"

Rafi's hands stopped drawing the soothing pattern on her back. He took a deep breath. "Oh, Johanna. I have *so* much to tell you."

They found two branches farther up the tree that grew almost parallel, giving them a more stable place to spend the night. Rafi edged his back against the tree trunk, and Johanna sat between his legs.

His hands draped loosely around her waist as he told her everything. His grip tightened when she cried—the grief over the deaths of her family fresh and raw. It wasn't that Johanna had believed her mother or Thomas had survived, but an unreasonable part of her heart had hoped. Johanna would never get a chance to set things right, to apologize to her mother for the words she'd said in anger.

Please, Mother Lua, Johanna prayed silently. *Tell my mother I love her. Tell her I'm sorry. Tell her . . .*

"Michael is safe." Rafi whispered the promise against her ear. "He was brokenhearted, but between Dom, my mother, and our household staff, he'll be well cared for."

Johanna nodded, relieved at least in that.

"And then there is the matter of the lockbox from your wagon." His hands traced down her arms, and he wove his fingers between her own. "Light . . . I don't know how to say this."

She felt his Adam's apple rise and fall. He cleared his throat and described how Snout had found her mother's body curled around the box.

"I knew it was important, so I brought it with me. Inside was a letter from *my* father. I recognized the seal and opened it. I'm sorry if that was prying."

"It's fine." Johanna squeezed his hands, urging him to continue. "What did it say?"

"I have it here in my vest, and you can read it for yourself when it's light enough."

"Just tell me. Please?"

He didn't speak for a long time, and the quiet made every muscle in her body tense like a bowstring.

"You *are* Princess Adriana. Arlo rescued you from the Citadel as it fell."

She closed her eyes and pressed her head against his collarbone. It wasn't new information, but it was verification. Hearing it from Rafi made it truer. And more awful.

"I already know. The people who kidnapped me, well, they're *Keepers.* You saw them use magic. You know it's true."

Rafi gave that little cough-laugh that held no humor. "I can't deny it, but I can't believe it either. Keepers are characters in your stories."

"I wish that were all." Without any of her typical eloquence or lyricism, Johanna laid out the details of her capture and the reasons why she was taken. "They're trying to protect us from more people like Vibora—people who will try to enslave all of Santarem."

"What do we do now?"

"We could go back to Santiago and hope all of this fades away."

He took a deep breath like he was going to say something, but let it go with a sigh. "If that's what you want."

"It is what I *want* to do," she said, turning to look at him over her shoulder. In the darkness she could make out the strong shape of his jaw, and the perfectly straight line of his nose, but she didn't need to see his face to know it would show disappointment. "But what am I *supposed* to do?"

"If what the Keepers said is true . . . if there are more people like Vibora and they're in league with Inimigo and Belem . . ." He shrugged. "I won't make that decision for you. If you choose to return to Santiago to be with Michael, I'll go with you. If you choose to go to the wall, I'll go too."

"What would you do?"

He tucked her hair behind her ears, letting his fingers trail along her neck. "To save all the people of Santarem? You know what I'd do."

And with that statement Johanna knew exactly what she *had* to do.

Acknowledgments

An author writes a story, but it takes an enormous team to publish a book. I owe a huge thanks to all the folks who made this novel happen!

My publishing team—editor Dani Young, publisher Justin Chanda, copy editor Brian Luster, designer Michael McCartney, managing editor Bridget Madsen, and the rest of the crew at Margaret K. McElderry Books—made my dreams come true! Thank you for encouraging me to stretch my characters and make this story into something *more*.

Without my fantastic agent, Jennifer Laughran, *The Storyspinner* would be a measly two chapters at the bottom of my WIP folder. Jenn picked my first manuscript out of the slush and stuck with me till I started writing what I love. Thank you!

So many writerly friends helped turn this pile of words into a book-shaped thing. I'm so grateful to Nicole Castroman who read every page at least six times, and her beautiful daughter, Sophia, for being my first teen reader. Jessica Lawson loved my characters and sent emails with slightly inappropriate subject lines exactly when I needed them. Lynne Matson and Diana Wariner offered incredible insight on how to fix this plot and make it sharper and more interesting. And to my awesome readers, Trisha Leaver (my very first reader ever!), Lindsay Currie, and Mary Waibel. Thank you, thank you!

Several noncyber friends knew about my secret wish to be an author and helped me along the way. Stacy Sorensen is the world's best faux assistant and a better friend than I deserve. Jen Wegner, aka Perfect Friend, offered unflagging support from the very beginning. Lezlie Evans set me on the *right* writing path. Brynn Hansen lent me her name and enthusiasm.

My parents, Dave and Ardy Vallett, taught me to love reading and to never fear hard work. Thank you for *every single thing.* To my grandma, Edie Winkelman, for thousands of phone conversations and hundreds of sandwiches with chips on them. To my siblings, Lizzy Standiford, Joel Vallett, and MeChelle Anderson, and their spouses for cheering me on and keeping me sane. And to my inlaws and outlaws—Rick and Olivia Wallace, Brandon and Elizabeth Wallace, and Jarod and Brianne Stewart—for babysitting and for not going glassy-eyed when I start talking about books.

My little family has been so patient when I disappear into another world, and can't hear them even when we're in the same room. Thank you for loving me even when I'm not entirely present. To my husband, Jamie, for walking me through fight scenes and taking my work seriously. To my babies Gavin, Laynie, Audrey, and Adelynn for being everything I've ever wanted. Love you all!

BECKY WALLACE
THE SKYLIGHTER
THE KEEPERS' CHRONICLES

Pira

Millions of tiny feet stampeded over Pira's skin, under her shirt, through her hair, into her nose. Leather strips bound her wrists and ankles together, making it impossible for her to dislodge the nasty little creatures. She thrashed, rolling across the gravel-strewn campsite, trying to crush the *paraponeras* under her weight, but nothing deterred them from reaching her flesh.

As if responding to a silent command, the ants sank their needle-sharp pincers into her body, injecting a venom that burned and throbbed. She bit her tongue to keep from crying out, and letting the ants crawl *in.*

"You will answer my questions," a voice whispered from somewhere both near and far. Coming from both within her mind and without.

Pira couldn't see the speaker, couldn't see anything with her eyes shut tight against the agony. Sweat dripped from her forehead as her body shuddered and rocks dug into older wounds. Those injuries gave a different sort of hurt, dull and achy, the bruises from an earlier battle.

She clutched that ache like a lifeline to reality. *It's magic,* she realized. *These ants aren't eating me alive. It's all in my head.* Knowing didn't stop the phantom pain, but it gave her the strength to hold on a little longer.

"Tell me about your companions. Tell me their affinities. Tell me about Jacaré, and I will make this all go away." The voice had a sibilant quality, stretching out the words with a hiss.

Vibora. The viper.

Pira tried not to think about the events that led to her capture, afraid the collar around her neck would somehow relay the information to her captor, but the sensations flooded her mind unbidden. She saw the ambush and Tex burning in a column of flame; she felt the marsh, stagnant and thick against her ankles as she led Johanna toward Santiago; she heard the hail of pebbles thunk against Vibora's flesh and the sound of the horse galloping away with Johanna tucked close to Rafi's back; she tasted the acrid words she'd shouted at Leão the last time they spoke—words she'd never be able to recant while living as another Keeper's slave.

Rolling to her side, Pira tucked her knees tight to her stomach, as if she were protecting herself from the magical barrage. The position also hid her efforts to remove the collar. She could feel metal pressing somewhere between her chin and her collarbones, but she couldn't *feel* it.

Metal was Pira's specialized affinity, but her gift failed her.

Jacaré had warned that someday she'd have to fight against a weapon she couldn't sense. She never imagined the battlefield would be inside her own head.

"Your *essência* is draining away," Vibora said with a laugh, a sound like scales slithering over dry leaves. "The collar will suck away every drop, and when you recover, I'll drain you again. I will use your own power to torture you until you tell me Jacaré's location and his plan."

Pira's muscles began to spasm, a late reaction to the *paraponeras'* bites. Her body believed the magic, even if her mind recognized the truth.

"Tell me."

The ants bit again.

"Tell. Me."

Pira opened her mouth.

And screamed.

Johanna

Dawn, pale as fresh butter, melted through the tangle of branches above Johanna's and Rafi's heads. The light nibbled away the mist that hung over the marsh and revealed a strange sort of beauty in the twisted limbs of their temporary haven.

The light did not, however, expose a safe route for escape from the caimans that had chased them into the tree. At some point during the night the lizards had stopped hissing and snapping their teeth. Disappearing into the black water, they were content to wait for their prey under the knotted roots of the mangrove trees. She couldn't see them but knew they were out there lurking. Hidden. Hungry.

And they weren't the only cold-blooded monsters stalking her.

Keepers, the heroes of so many of Johanna's stories, were real and nothing like she'd been trained to believe. She'd sold so many lies as a Storyspinner, unwittingly building up the Keepers as magical saviors. As soon as she had the chance, she'd correct those misconceptions, recounting her own adventure as their captive.

Would people still idolize the Keepers who had kidnapped Johanna as she was weeping over her brother's dead body?

Probably, she realized with annoyance. Jacaré and his group did have a noble purpose; an audience might approve of any tactics that would save Santarem, especially given the real villains they'd been pitted against. *Vibora.* Thoughts of that magic-wielding witch and her mindless slaves made Johanna shiver. She'd spent only a few moments in that woman's clutches, but it had been a few moments too many.

If Vibora had her way, the story would conclude with all the people of Santarem serving as her slaves. It was the only fate worse than having Duke Inimigo, the failed usurper and the tyrant of the Ten Years' War, on the throne.

Unfortunately for Johanna—*and everyone else, really*—the country's future rested on her very unprepared shoulders. She'd been raised as a Performer, instead of as a princess, and was unsuited to rule anything greater than a few wagonloads of acrobats and Fireswords. But a princess she was, albeit a reluctant one. And Santarem's tale would come to a very unpleasant end if she failed to reach Donovan's Wall and secure the magical barrier that kept her country protected from the Keepers' land beyond.

Thinking about it all—the deaths of her family members, the truth of her heritage, and her duty to the people—made her lightheaded with anxiety. A dangerous thing to be, considering her precarious perch.

We have to reach Donovan's Wall.

She took a deep breath, trying to calm her racing heart, and Rafi's arms tightened around her waist in response. His touch sent her pulse sprinting for a different reason.

Even though they'd spent several hours nested together, her back to his chest and his back against the tree, the closeness between them was a new thing. It made her feel timid and green; it was a new high-wire routine she hadn't quite mastered, and there was real danger if she fell.

"Are you awake?" Rafi asked in a hoarse whisper.

"Of course I'm awake. I couldn't possibly sleep with you snoring in my ear."

"At least I don't drool."

Rafi's tone was dry, but she felt his chest bounce with a barely restrained laugh.

Johanna frowned, feigning offense she didn't feel. They had spent weeks circling each other like snarling animals, taking every opportunity to nip at the other's confidence and pounce on the other's flaws. It was easier for her to slip into the familiar role of prickly Performer than to think of the night they had spent together.

It was the wrong turn of phrase, and her whole body blushed with the implied meaning. They had kissed—*More like you threw yourself at him*—and it had been perfect and delicious, and then horrifically interrupted by Vibora, intent on Johanna's capture.

Rafi laced his fingers around Johanna's middle, as if sensing she needed comfort. During the night, when she'd mourned for her family, she'd sobbed brokenly in his arms, but now she shrugged out of his embrace. Instead of soothing away her pain, his touch made her keenly aware of every loss.

Johanna maneuvered around on the branch to face him. "I hope she defeated Vibora. I hope Pira escaped. I hope . . ."

There was so much sympathy in Rafi's eyes that she couldn't hold his gaze. Instead she studied the water below and added Pira's name to the tally of casualties. The list had gotten very long, very quickly. *Joshua, Thomas, Mama, Captain Alouette, Snout, two of Rafi's guardsmen, and now Pira.*

The loss of life made Johanna sick to her already empty stomach.

"The caimans probably moved to the banks to sun themselves when the sun rose." Rafi snapped a handful of twigs off the branch over his head and threw them into the water. Nothing rose to the bait. "This is the best time for us to make a run for it."

The safest, maybe, but there was no guarantee that either of them would make it out of the swamp alive. They had no food or water and only one weapon, and Rafi had lost a boot and his sword in their frantic flight from the caimans.

"It'll be easier to find our way out with the daylight," Johanna agreed, trying to reassure both of them that they weren't about to face death at the jaws of a hungry beast.

"I'll go first," he said, sliding his dagger free of its sheath. "If anything happens, then you can still escape and repair the barrier."

"You couldn't get into the tree without my help. And if the caimans do attack, then it will be much easier for you to pull me back up." She didn't give him the chance to argue. Johanna smacked his elbow with the top of her fist, and the knife popped out of his grasp.

"Jo—" He reached for the weapon, but she clenched the blade between her teeth and scurried away. "What are you doing?"

She smiled around the dagger and fell backward, hooking her knees around the branch.

It wasn't much different from swinging on a trapeze. She flipped, catching the lowest limb. It bowed under her weight, dislodging a spray of leaves. They floated on the water's black surface, flecks of green on an oil slick.

"Stop, Johanna." His voice broke on her name. "Please."

Nothing stirred. Nothing lunged out of the water. It didn't mean the animals were gone, but it did give her a bit of hope. She looked up once more, catching Rafi's wide eyes. Her heart gave a painful thump at the distress on his face, but sitting in the tree was certain death—from starvation or *when* the evil Keepers found them.

Praying her instinct was correct, she dropped onto the clump of roots that arched out of the murk.

CASSANDRA CLARE'S

#1 *New York Times* Bestselling Series

THE MORTAL INSTRUMENTS & THE INFERNAL DEVICES

A thousand years ago, the Angel Raziel mixed his blood with the blood of men and created the race of the Nephilim. Human-angel hybrids, they walk among us, unseen but ever present, our invisible protectors.

They call themselves Shadowhunters.

Don't miss The Mortal Instruments: *City of Bones,* now a major motion picture.

PRINT AND EBOOK EDITIONS AVAILABLE

From Margaret K. McElderry Books

TEEN.SimonandSchuster.com